I0681615

MISPLACED
Affection

By

WADE KELLY

Published by Wade Kelly Books

http://www.writerwadekelly.com

This story is a work of fiction from the author's imagination. Names, characters, and incidents either are fictionalized, and any resemblance to actual persons, living or dead, business establishments, events, or locales is entirely coincidental. Although Westminster is a real town, all family situations, interactions, and implied outcomes are not real events.

Misplaced Affection © 2014 Wade Kelly.

Cover Art© 2014 Wade Kelly.

Cover content is for illustrative purposes only and the person depicted on the cover is a model. Cover Model/Artist: veronicagomezpola/shutterstock.com

All rights reserved. This book is licensed to the original purchaser only. No part of this book may be reproduced or transmitted in any form or by any means, electronic or mechanical, including photocopying, recording, or by any information storage and retrieval system, without the written permission of Wade Kelly. Duplication or distribution via any means is illegal and a violation of international copyright law, subject to criminal prosecution and upon conviction, fines, and/or imprisonment.

Editor: Ally Editorial Services

http://allyeditorialservices.weebly.com

ISBN-13: 9780692350249

ISBN-10: 0692350241

Kindle: B00R1E8MT4

eBook ISBN: 9781501442933

First Edition January 1, 2015

Second Edition with corrections January 6, 2015

Third Edition with additional corrections January 22, 2015

Readers love: Names Can Never Hurt Me

"This is by far my favorite Wade Kelly book so far. I loved the story, and I loved the way she wrote Nick as the story's narrator. I highly recommend you get this book today. You will enjoy every page. This one is the real thing. A true M/M Romance."

~ Dan, Love Bytes Reviews

"The story here cannot be encapsulated in a few sentences. Rather, you must involved yourself in this novel, immerse yourself in the life of a young man who is conflicted, attention deficit and simply unable to see beyond his own shallow image of himself to the real person inside. …RC rocks Nick's world the real journey for both men begins, a journey of understanding, remorse, forgiveness, and healing. It is a beautiful trip that carries the reader along and shatters us with its breathtaking truth. I highly recommend this novel to you." ~ Sammy, Joyfully Jay

"What makes this book so good are these characters and how they relate to one another. Wade Kelly does an amazing job of creating realistic, flawed-yet-wonderful people that you grow to love. … Overall I loved this book, loved the topics Wade fearlessly tackled and the relationships she allowed to grow and change over the course of the story. It was sweet, sexy, sentimental and an excellent read. I highly recommend it!" ~ Morgan, The Blogger Girls

"This is a wonderful book about an important topic not only for college kids and college grads today but also for people in general. In this era where everyone is so quick to judge and apply labels to people, this novel takes a deep dive at the damage those labels can cause." ~ Jeff Adams

"This book was an emotionally charged and endearing story about a very slow building love between two unlikely men. … I devoured this book in one long setting. I was so intrigued by the dynamics of the characters, and the way they bounced off each other. Sexy, romantic, endearing and realistic are just a few words to describe this book. Definitely a must read." ~ Tams, M/M Good Book Reviews

Wade Kelly Titles

Misplaced Affection

Published by Wade Kelly Books

http://www.writerwadekelly.com

***

My Roommate's a Jock? Well, Crap!

Names Can Never Hurt Me

UNCONDITIONAL LOVE SERIES

When Love is Not Enough

The Cost of Loving

Published by DREAMSPINNER PRESS

Acknowledgments

For my readers, who continue to support me with encouragement, love, and praise; I need you, I thank you, and I could not go on without you.
For my beta readers, who keep me on my toes and push me to reinvent myself in order to deliver the best story possible.
Thank you **Beth, Taryn, Jeff & Will** for believing in me.

And for Mrs. Moore, the very best English teacher I have ever had. You made English grammar come alive for me. For the very first time, I see the tools of my trade for the amazing puzzle pieces that they are. I hope to always grow and improve my art, and create beauty with my words.

Shout Outs

Michael & Anthony: You guys are the best! Love you both so much. Your friendship means a lot to me.
Matt & Brad: You teach me so much about love and life. The poem is for you, as well as that "other" scene. ;)
Sam & Rick: Sam is an inspiration of strength and courage. Such wisdom you have. I wish you both all the happiness in the world.

And to MANY wonderful friends online (some of whom I get to hug in real life):
Gregory, Lucien, Lynn, Kade, J.P., Jordan, Sara, Leigh, Jason M., Scott & Greg, Jason F., Chris, David B., Brandilyn, Ken, Heather, Elisa, Julie, Tina, Jackie, Kage, Ben, Mary, Lena, Kazy, Bonnie, BJ, Paul W., Katie, Simon, Helén, Sheri, Carole-Ann, Mandy, Frances, Hope, Thomas, Ijeoma, Mari, Debra, Rashell, Terry, Johnny, Elaine, Stacy, Tracy, Johanna, Marc, Tammy, Juli-Anna, Karrie, and I can ALWAYS mention Jeff & Will, Taryn, and Beth over and over, and SOOOO many others. Lots of hugs! <3

Dedications
R.I.P. my dear friend Gina W. You were one of the most godly women I ever met. Thank you for your love and guidance.
R.I.P. dear, sweet Josh. You are never far from my heart.

Prologue

April 26, 2014: The Day

She loves him. I could see it in her eyes—that deep sense of longing—as she peered over her shoulder toward the ushers, family members, and friends who gathered to prepare for the day's festivities. As workers from the cottage set chairs in rows on the grass and hung strings of white lights in the trees, "Ophelia", as Zach called her on occasion because she looked like she had stepped out of a painting by that title, wandered farther away, picking flowers and occasionally wiping the tip of her nose. Why had I noticed? Why had I cared? Because I felt the same disconnect she wore in her expression. Only, my reaction wasn't to pick flowers, it was to sit on a folding chair on the edge of the bustle of activity and sulk.

It was no surprise to me that Amelia was in love with Zachary Mitchell; after all, he had the kind of smile that lights up a room and personality enough to power a city. Zach was vivacious and charismatic and able to draw people in with a glance. Everyone loved Zach, so I couldn't blame her for falling hard. The only trouble I foresaw rested with her assigned position as Maid of Honor. How would the sweet "Ophelia" handle walking down the aisle on "Prince Hamlet's" wedding day, only to step to the left, and allow room for his bride to join him at the altar? I didn't know.

I could imagine how hard this was for her. I had been there at Zach's house last July, expecting burgers and an exchange of college stories, when out of the blue our annual birthday dinner turned into an engagement party. I certainly hadn't expected it. I distinctly remembered Amelia's squeal of delight because it pierced my eardrums and caused me to promptly cup them, but her high-pitched cry and joyful enthusiasm had been immediately followed by vain attempts to hide her tears. I'd had my own issues that day, my own internal debates and misgivings, but I would never forget the look in Amelia's eyes as she caught me watching her. Her joy had been as bittersweet as mine.

Luckily, Gwendolyn mistook her sister's sadness and jealousy for happiness and hugged her until she smiled again. Poor girl. She should have said something. I should have said something. But the words got stuck in my throat as I watched the happy couple, Zach and Gwendolyn, hugging and toasting. Gwendolyn asked her sister to stand beside her at the altar two seconds before Zach turned his charm my way. Keith would have kicked me if he hadn't been standing across the room as I helplessly agreed to be Zach's best man. I had never been able to refuse Zach anything in the past, so it stood to reason that I wouldn't have been able to change the course of history. Of course I had accepted.

Acceptance—*fuck*—look where it had brought us nine months later; an outdoor wedding straight out of a Shakespearian play; complete with strolling minstrels, flutes, mandolins, Victorian gowns, puffy shirts, and poet hats. Stupid hats, they messed up my hair and covered my pink highlights. I didn't want to be here. My only solace was that all my friends seemed just as unhappy.

As I watched Amelia stroll along the opposite edge of the wooded garden, picking flowers and sampling wild raspberries, I thought to myself how beautiful she was. Her luminescent auburn locks tumbled down her back, tendrils lifting in the slight breeze; beckoning those around her, including me, to touch, caress, and become lost in the alluring tresses. She had tucked flowers in her flowing mane as a weaver might include jewels among his threads, which made her even more stunning. She looked remarkable in her billowing white gown, and I knew without asking that she longed for Zach to notice. But he wouldn't. Zach's eyes were set on the fiery redhead who waited beyond the willow tree for the minstrels to start their strumming.

Our "Ophelia" would never garner "Hamlet's" attention as she did in the Shakespearian play, which was why she chose to pick flowers instead of attending to her sister, the bride-to-be, Gwendolyn Pierce. Amelia gathered her skirts, creating a basket of fabric in her arms, and filled it as she went with red poppies, white daisies, and blue cornflowers. Oh, to be so carefree and peaceful at a time like this. She looked so serene, but on the inside I knew she was falling apart. Amelia was a casualty of war in a sense, mourning the loss of her heart with the impending phrase: "I do." So as she stepped barefoot through the grass, weeping in silence and collecting flowers like a child, I watched and shed my own tears, mirroring her sorrow, empathizing with her pain, and dying inside because the same woeful revelation suffocated me—I was in love with Zach as well.

Fuck! The revelation hit me like a truck on a highway. Keith had been right all along.

I curled forward over my legs and cradled my face in my hands. *What a mess.* Less than an hour to go before this stupid wedding and I realize I'm in love with the groom, Amelia's in love with the groom, and the poor bride is obliviously readying for possibly the world's most clichéd wedding. The worst part, if it could get any worse, was the unsettling notion I had that Zach was actually gay.

What was I supposed to do?

I sat back and scanned the scene again after rubbing the weariness from my eyes and cheeks. Most people seemed joyous. My dad was talking and laughing with Zach's aunt Krista, one good by-product of this event, but those included in our close-knit group of friends seemed to feel the tension. Kelly and Grace weren't laughing; they were texting. Keith, my ex, was sitting on the opposite side of the seating area; near them but not with them, arms folded, scowl firmly affixed to his face. I wasn't even sure why he'd come today except that maybe Grace had threatened him.

Tom and Greg were most likely with Zach, my best friend, where I should have been since I was supposed to be his best man. But how could I look Zach in the face after what had happened after the bachelor party last night?

Oh God. "I'm probably going to hell," I whispered, thinking about what we had done. As a tear forced its way from the corner of my eye, I asked aloud, "How did things get so fucked up?"

Part 1

Flynn

Chapter 1

August 31, 2010: Junior Year

The first day of junior year and what did I notice? A really cute guy looking at me. Well, not really *looking* as much as trying not to appear as though he was looking. I've had plenty of experience in the *not looking* department since I normally check out the crowd for anyone checking out the crowd same as me. Most of the time I catch sight of the shy guys surreptitiously checking out the cheerleaders. Rarely did I notice a guy checking out other guys, although it has happened, but I have yet to notice someone checking out *me*! Wow, it actually caused a zing in my gut.

I needed another art credit, so I chose Art II. I liked drawing and stuff, and I had gotten an A in Art I, so I figured it would be an easy class. We had assigned seats, but thankfully not alphabetically. (Alphabetical seating charts had gotten old around sixth-grade.) The guy checking me out sat across from me; he kept glancing in my direction and then looking away. It was seriously cute. I think he thought I wouldn't notice. I guess, if I weren't gay, I probably wouldn't have thought anything of it. He was stealthy enough.

After class, he pretty much bolted and I was hard pressed to catch up. I tried, but lost him in the crowded hallway. I sighed and headed to my next class knowing I had all semester to chat-up Keith Leppo. *Keith...* I liked that name.

Thankfully, it didn't take all semester. By the very next class the teacher, Mrs. Moore, assigned an activity pairing up the students to play her version of Pictionary. Basically, she read the questions aloud to the class and each team had a chance to draw. Two students against two students, and we kept score among ourselves. It was meant to be an icebreaker, a way to get to know the people at our table, and teachers who played games during class were pretty cool in my book.

Keith sat next to Grace and I sat next to Kelly so that meant Keith and I were on opposite sides. The teacher read the first question. "What was your first pet?" Keith drew one curved line and then another curved line underneath connected at one end, but crossing over the other.

"Fish," I said.

He smirked as his eyes caught mine. I didn't think he could get any cuter.

Next question. Mrs. Moore asked, "What is your favorite food?"

Kelly quickly drew squiggly line after squiggly line and added two circles to the mix and an oblong oval around the bottom. "Spaghetti," Keith said.

The questions went back and forth like that for about twenty minutes. We guessed them all right. It was either because the questions were easy, or because we all drew well enough to depict the answers accurately. It didn't matter, because the goal was in the exercise itself, and the four of us shared quite a few chuckles.

After class, I caught up to Keith in the hall. "Keith," I called.

He turned and smiled at me as I stepped up next to him.

"Where are you headed?" I asked.

"Honors Algebra II."

"Ah. I have that fourth mod. I have English now, which is in the same direction, do you mind if I walk with you?"

He smiled and shook his head as he pivoted on his heels and started walking down the hall. I stepped in synch and we walked together to the opposite wing of the school. "How is it the teachers don't give you crap about wearing a hat in school?" I was curious, because I thought it was school policy or part of the dress code to take hats off in school. So far he'd worn it for two classes and Mrs. Moore hadn't made him remove it.

He shrugged. "I don't know."

When he didn't add more to his statement, I thought he must be shyer than my first assessment or he didn't want to talk about it. I kind of watched him out of the corner of my eye as I walked, almost the same way he had watched me the first day of class, but I was careful not to run into anything to avoid looking like an idiot. He had dark curly hair from what I could see sticking out from under his knit beanie. He wore glasses with black plastic frames—a very *in* style. I liked it.

Keith and I were dressed oddly similarly; from his jeans and grey Converse (mine were brown), to his short-sleeved plaid button down worn over a white T-shirt. Sort of hipsterish, if that was a thing. I wasn't sure what the definition of "hipster" was, but maybe we could pass as hipsters. He was slightly taller; I would guess five-eleven, but I suspected we were both not done growing. I noticed some dark fuzz over his lip, which fascinated me, and I had this sudden urge to rub my thumb over it.

When we got to the stairs he said, "I guess I'll see ya," as he continued on up without waiting for my reply.

"Um, bye." I limply waved.

Keith hadn't looked back and I was disappointed.

We continued like this for the first week of school. Then, after Labor Day weekend, Keith lingered a couple times in the hall outside of class waiting for me to catch up so we could walk down the hall together. Although he remained quiet, I was happy about the change, and I caught him glancing at me and smirking more and more. He was into me, and knowing it made me nervous; like when I rode my very first roller coaster. It was a feeling I wanted to experience every day.

***

"I think I made a friend," I told Zach one day when we were hanging out at his house. I'd been sitting on his bedroom floor for twenty minutes, doing my homework and thinking of a way to tell him about Keith. It's not like Zach was my only friend and making another one was unheard of—I had other friends—but Keith was the first friend whom I'd ever wanted to pursue as a boyfriend and I didn't know how to broach the topic with Zach. Zach didn't know about me.

"Oh yeah?" Zach answered, sitting at his desk without bothering to look up.

"Yeah. He's in my art class."

"Oh."

"Yeah." I tapped my pencil on my notebook. How to tell him? *Hmm.*

Zach had been my closest friend for years. My family had moved in next door to his before I was born. Zach and my brother, Nathan, were the same age and we had always hung out as a group, although we never pretended to be the three musketeers. Then, after my brother had died in a car accident, it was just Zach and me. By default, and by luck, we gelled and had remained steadfast friends.

Lately though, things had gotten strained. I hoped it was because he had started college and I was still in high school, but if I was honest, the strain started two years prior. I prayed the newest changes in our lives wouldn't push us apart, as often happened with old friends, but I had no guarantees. Zach *was* two years older than me, after all. He wasn't always into the same things, but it hadn't mattered so far. We had always made time for one another in the past. I had watched him play football, he had come to some of my tennis matches, and every year we celebrated our birthdays together. Ironically, we were born on the same day, so celebrating together started back when I was five and my mom and his thought it would be fun to rent a pavilion together in Piney Run Park. Together by fate as much as by our parents' hand, I guessed.

Zach knew practically everything about me, except for the parts I feared would conflict with his religious beliefs. Zach's family had always been very religious and strict, where mine was not. Especially after the accident. My dad had only attended church for my mother and brother's funeral, but to my knowledge had never gone since. Part of him died with them. Part of me died too. I believed in God because of my mother, but I knew I didn't believe in the same God Zach's family often spoke about, so we had chosen years ago "to agree to disagree" and therefore church-talk never came up. Zach respected me that way. I only wished our fathers could come to the same intelligent understanding. So far, they hadn't.

The key thing I never talked about, second to my personal beliefs in God, was my sexuality. Zach had no idea I was gay; in fact, no one knew. I had always been afraid our relationship would change, or worse, be destroyed if he knew. We had come close to ruining everything by kissing once back when I was fourteen, but that had been a black thundercloud of hurt, which I desperately avoided repeating. I was fairly sure Zach had initiated that kiss, but it was clear from his shitty reaction that I needed to keep any and all attraction or curiosity from Zach as far as Australia was from Iceland. Our friendship was more important than any stupid kiss; therefore I'd grown accustomed to suppressing and ignoring any feelings I may have had in 2008.

Now I had to be careful how I worded my explanation of Keith's friendship to Zach. If I said too much, Zach might get the wrong impression—a "gay" impression. So far, Keith and I were just friends. Even if I thought he was adorable, and he certainly gave the flirtatious signals that he liked me back, we had only just met. Maybe one day, if he and I were seriously dating, then I could tell Zach I was gay, but now was not the time. I would rather appear as a dateless loser than face the talk about my sexuality with my best friend who might very well tell me I was headed for Hell.

Nope, not happening.

Only… nothing else was happening either. Zach wasn't getting it. He was surfing the Internet, or whatever, and he couldn't be bothered to turn his attention my way for a second. So, I added, "His name's Keith. He's really talented. He even told me he auditioned for America's Got Talent as a pig trainer so he could hug Heidi Klum and maybe squeeze her ass. She kissed a guy's pig once, so I think he stands a chance. Plus, he said pig training is a lost art."

Zach swiveled his chair around to look at me. "Wait… what?" His eyes went wide and he blinked in shock.

"You'll never change," I lamented, shaking my head. "I said I made a new friend named Keith in art class. He's pretty cool. He plays guitar and paints, and wants to be an architect. I think you'd like him." I was trying to be congenial, but truth be told I didn't think they had much in common other than knowing me.

"So… he *didn't* kiss a pig?" Zach's blank stare made me roll my eyes. He could be dense.

"No, idiot. He's my new friend, since you're in college meeting new people I figured I better do the same. We don't get to see each other that much anymore. I need someone to talk to, ya know?"

Zach sighed and slumped back in his computer chair. "Yeah, I know. I'm sorry, man. This college crap is hard. I gotta memorize Latin names of trees and stuff, but I like it. Except, I'm not sure how long I'll be able to drive home on weekends; I think I need to stay on campus and study. I want to get this two-year horticulture degree in two years, which means I need to do well and not screw around. Oh, and speaking of meeting new people, my roommate is pretty awesome. His name's Greg. His father's a police officer, so he's not too keen on underage drinking. No lame excuses necessary about not getting hammered. Talk about convenient."

"And you can also avoid the awkward explanation involving your overly religious parents and their rules against drinking, sex, drugs, swearing, and staying out past curfew," I pointed out.

"Exactly. I think he's the perfect roommate. Well, besides you." He gestured to me, which I appreciated.

"That's nice. I bet my experience will be the exact opposite. I'll probably get paired with a drug-addicted kleptomaniac who would hide all my underwear or something." We shared a chuckle.

"You do have the worst luck of anyone I know." Zach gave me a grin and swiveled back around to look at his computer.

"Born under a black cloud I guess."

Zach glanced at me. "Maybe, but here for a purpose. I stand by that."

"Maybe one day that God you believe in will explain it to me. I'm not so sure sometimes. My dad is still hard to deal with. He drinks too much."

Zach's expression grew serious, his amusement disappeared, and I knew what he was thinking. I hadn't wanted to get into a deep conversation, but as soon as I brought up my dad, or the occasions when he brought up his parents, we both knew what was coming. It was an unspoken sign to drop our walls and spill.

Zach got up from his chair and wandered over to his bed. He flopped on it face up, like he always did when we had our heart-to-hearts. His theory about sharing our souls was that it would be easier to talk about deep, troublesome topics if we didn't have to look each other in the eyes. I thoroughly agreed. I got off the floor and followed him.

Normally, I would lie on the far side of his twin bed, up against the wall, and he would lie on the nearest side along the edge. My guess was that he didn't want me accidentally falling off. This time, he was on the inside and I was on the edge. It felt odd, like changing roles or something, but I liked the closeness of being up against the side of his warm body. His arm was cocked and folded under his head; my arms were resting at my sides with my fingers laced together over my stomach. It was a tight fit, but we'd always made it work.

After a moment of silence, Zach asked, "Does he still work like fifty hours a week?"

"Yeah. Sometimes I think it's closer to sixty. All he does is work." We were on his bed, staring at his ceiling—no walls, no boundaries.

Zach wiggled and adjusted his shoulders on the bed. I felt his warm skin against my arm. "I've heard that hydrologists are in demand," he said. "I think your dad's field is overwhelmed with work and projects. In some ways, he's lucky to have so much work. My dad comments all the time about people he knows getting laid off."

His reasoning was kind, but I had lost my rose-colored glasses long ago. "Maybe, but it's been six years since Mom and Nate died. I think he's hiding," I confessed. We hadn't done this in a while, and the familiar vulnerability felt nice. "I think he's denying that he misses her and buries himself in work on purpose. I think he's scared to try again. I think he worries I'll reject his choice of female companionship, so he doesn't even try. I think he drinks because he's lonely. I think he stopped talking to me about things beyond the weather and my grades because he's worried about giving me the wrong advice. I think—"

"Have you told him?" Zach interrupted.

I knew what he meant, but I asked anyway. "Which part?"

"All the parts, Flynn."

I closed my eyes. *This* was precisely why we spoke about stuff like this while staring at his ceiling. Tears welled in the corners of my eyes. I didn't want to cry in front of Zach. I knew I *could* cry, and he would understand, but I didn't want him to see me cry. I squeezed my eyes shut until the wave of emotion subsided. "No," I replied quietly. "I don't know how."

"I think you should," Zach whispered back. "I think the two of you avoid each other because neither of you worked through your grief after the accident."

I disagreed, "Sure we have."

"No, you haven't. When's the last time you and your dad went to your mother's grave together, and laid flowers on it?"

I couldn't answer.

After my silence went on for too long, Zach asked another question. "When's the last time you and your dad talked to your brother's grave and told him about all the cool things you've been up to these last six years?"

Again, I couldn't say anything. I could only lie there and listen to him breathing. I think he knew I needed some time to think so he didn't move or comment for the longest time. "I've gone," Zach finally whispered. "Not often, but a few times. I sat in the grass and asked Nate his opinions."

"On what?"

Zach spoke so quietly; even being this close I could barely hear him. "My parents. Their beliefs. What he thought I should do that time my dad hit me."

"Oh." I wasn't sure how else to respond. I had known the argument happened because I heard raised voices across the space between our houses, but Zach had never spoken about it to me directly. "I hope you know you can talk to me about that stuff. I'll listen."

"I know."

When I was younger, Zach and I shared everything from swapping gum to "what do you want to be when you grow up?" We'd had few barriers between us and I could confidently say we told each other all the details of our lives. But as years rolled by, the intimacy changed and the level of sharing grew more and more topical. I avoided considering our kiss in 2008 as the cause, but no other explanation presented itself. We had kissed, and afterward our relationship dynamic had shifted.

I knew about the fight back in June, and I also knew Zach never wanted to talk about it. I swallowed and took a deep breath. *What should I say now?* Then the bed shifted and he rolled over onto his side. He was breaking the "unspoken" rules and looking directly at me, leaning his weight on his elbow. Helplessly, I tilted my face in his direction.

"I know losing half your family sucked big-time," he said somberly, his brown eyes doing everything to reflect his sincerity. "And I know that you know it felt like half my family disappeared too; Nate and Mrs. B meant a lot to me."

I nodded and felt a lump forming in the back of my throat. Zach had shifted the conversation back on me, rendering me powerless. Talking about my family got to me every time, and holding back the tears was not going to be easy if he kept looking at me while he spoke.

Zach explained, "But I think it's been long enough. For six years you've been hiding too, just like your dad, minus the alcohol. I think it's time you visited their graves and dealt with your loss. I hear talking to dead family members as if they can hear you is very therapeutic."

I swallowed again, licking my lips nervously. I wasn't sure I liked how close he was, it made me uncomfortably anxious. "Where'd you hear that?" I asked quietly, trying to focus on the conversation and not the way his eyes dipped down to follow my tongue when I had wet my lips.

Zach shrugged casually. "I was listening to a group of college girls chatting in the cafeteria. One was a psych major."

"Eavesdropping isn't polite."

He grinned. "They didn't know."

"And talking to ghosts helps?"

"Yeah. Some people talk to God about their dead relatives; others talk right to the relatives. Whatever helps."

"Do you think they can hear?" I asked. I hadn't attended church, but I held the belief that there was something beyond this life that I just didn't understand. If dead relatives could still hear us, I think I'd feel better about it. I wanted to know my mom could hear me.

Zach gave me a soft smile. "Yes, definitely. I think those who go before us can hear our prayers. I think God watches over our family, your family, and allows those we care about to feel our joy. I know we differ in our beliefs, but I really do think God has a great purpose for you and that's why you didn't die that day. You're a fighter, Flynn." Zach looked at me very tenderly and gently ran the backs of his fingers down my arm. His throat bobbed as he swallowed. "I think it's time you face your fears and visit your mom. If you want, I'll go with you."

"You will?" I was surprised when my voice didn't crack. The look he gave me mirrored the one from two years earlier, when we'd kissed. Not a day went by when I hadn't remembered that kiss, but I also remembered the way he had treated me for months afterward, and I would rather suck the contents from a sewage pipe than go there again. He had been such an asshole.

Then he licked his lips and my dick pulsed in response. *Shit.* I glanced away hoping he'd pick up on my discomfort before it was too late. "I guess we could," I added, speaking in the other direction. "I'll try. This year the date falls on the same day as the accident. Sunday."

I could feel my heart racing. His fingers still trailed up and down my arm and the sensation was waking up my groin. *Not good.*

"Huh? What? Um, yeah," he replied, pulling his hand away and leaning back. "I forget about that sometimes. It was the Sunday after Thanksgiving." Suddenly, he vaulted over my body and was in his computer chair before I could react. "Will you and your dad come over for Thanksgiving dinner again?"

"Yeah, I think so. I don't know. You know my dad doesn't get along with yours. Last year I thought he was going to throw his fork at him." I sat up and swung my legs over the side of the bed. I thought if I sat there quietly, he wouldn't notice my erection. I also knew he wouldn't question why I wasn't going back to doing my homework, so I could dawdle without it appearing odd.

While Zach scanned his notebook as if homework was suddenly imperative, I tried willing away my hard-on. I could've avoided moments like this if I'd simply explained I was gay, but no, I liked torturing myself. He wouldn't have looked at me that way if he'd known. He wouldn't have touched me so tenderly if he'd known. But then… maybe he wouldn't have felt comfortable lying next to me on the bed, staring at the ceiling, and talking like we'd habitually done. Losing that closeness would hurt too much. No, Zach was better off not knowing.

I slipped off the bed and sat on the floor next to my books.

Zach looked my way and commented, "I know they hate each other, but I hope you'll make it. I checked, the twenty-eighth *is* on a Sunday this year. I'll be there for you."

"Thanks, Zach."

He nodded uncomfortably and changed the subject. "So, you made a new friend?"

I grinned and nodded. "Yup." *Nice topic shift back to Keith.* I had had enough of thinking about my dad, and worrying about visiting my mom's grave.

"Good," he said. "Friends are good."

I picked up my pencil and went back to Algebra.

An hour later, his mother called us down for dinner. I actually missed these times with his family, now that he'd gone to college. I was extra glad he had come home for a visit because not only could I tell him about Keith, but I could also reconnect with my best friend. He was the only one in the world who could make me feel twenty-five emotions at once. And besides, I think he was right about me avoiding my grief.

Chapter 2

November 28, 2010: Memories

My dad and I went over the Mitchells' for Thanksgiving dinner like we had every year that I could remember, but after we left I got the distinct impression that it had been the last time. Conversations were too strained, Zach did everything *not* to look at his father the entire time, and I was running out of small talk to share with Zach's sister Amy. There was nothing left, so next year we'd have to decline or come up with an excuse not to go.

And then dreaded Sunday rolled around. "Sunday, Bloody Sunday" as the song by the band U2 says, only my Sunday wasn't about war, it was about the loss of my mother and brother on the one and only day my father had agreed to go to church. Come to think of it, maybe Alanis Morissette said it better than U2 when she sang, "Isn't it ironic… don't you think"? We'd been on our way to church when a drunk driver struck our car at 9:32 in the morning and our lives had changed forever.

Fuck! I hate this day.

I waited for Zach, but he didn't show when he said he would. It happened from time to time so I wasn't pissed. I knew he'd have an explanation, but without Zach I had to make a decision about visiting my mom's grave alone or staying home and feeling sick about avoiding it for another year. I had almost gone last year on the anniversary of their death, but halfway to the cemetery I had chickened out. I knew if Zach was by my side I could handle it. Alone, I wasn't convinced.

I paced my room several thousand times and then headed downstairs before I wore the carpet down to the padding. I texted Zach again—no reply.

My dad was in the kitchen, standing at the window, staring into the back yard. He did that a lot, especially lately. He didn't talk; he stared. Sometimes he sipped coffee as he stared, like he did now. Sipping and staring. Staring and sipping. I watched him from the doorway and wondered if he was thinking about my mom. The remnants of her garden were out there.

She had asked him to plant roses years ago. I remembered thinking they were really pretty until I went to pick one and punctured my finger. Rosebush thorns are huge! After that, I looked at the stems of each flower carefully before I broke it off and made a bouquet for my mom. Dad fussed at me for "ruining" the garden he maintained for her, but my mom had always accepted my gifts with grace, smiling and thanking me for my thoughtfulness.

"They're just flowers, Vic. They'll grow back," my mom would say.

Then the family had decided to get a pool when I was nine and my dad had to replant the roses and a couple other bushes once the work had been completed. Using a Bobcat to dig a huge hole had made a mess of the yard. Once it was finished, my mom had told him it made the yard more private, but he still fussed at the extra work. The pool ended up taking over the entire back yard and the hedge of golden euonymus and my mom's roses were about the only plants left, which made watering them easy. Plus, the only grass to mow was in the front and side yards, a bonus for me.

Our property sat between Zach's and a section of land the County had purchased for a War Memorial; so our tall, thick hedge and roses blocked prying eyes from random people visiting to read the monuments in that garden, as well as those walking down the street out front, or down the small lane running behind the back of our plot.

I'd never liked living next to it until visiting the Vietnam Veterans Memorial in DC during a school trip in eighth-grade. After reading the names of the veterans on that very long wall, I felt a sense of pride for my country as well as a deep sadness. The Korean War Veterans Memorial, which sat nearby, had "Freedom Is Not Free" written on its wall. As the guide explained the significance of the sculpted soldiers in that memorial, and hearing there were over fifty-eight thousand names on the Vietnam memorial, I truly understood that the freedom I enjoyed in my country was not free at all.

The miniature memorial next to my house was for those who'd come from Westminster. While on the field trip, we'd been given the task of finding one of those names. My group found James Byers on section 14E. I had scanned the wall for the name "Brewer" and found a Richard Brewer, and a Daniel Flynn. I'd been relieved somehow the names had not been combined.

None of this really mattered in the larger scheme of things, I supposed, except that seeing the memorial had left a strong impression on me. It mattered to *me* and had changed my opinion of the memorial next to my house.

So, with the War Memorial on the left side, and only Zach's family's property on the right, the Brewer backyard turned into a swimmer's sanctuary. After a couple years, the hedges had grown so dense you couldn't even hear traffic going down Center Street. Total paradise.

As I watched my dad standing by the sink in his boxers and white undershirt, I felt sad for him. Mom wanted that pool, but barely got time to use it before she died. He had to be thinking about her. I missed my mom, but it had to feel a hundred times worse for my dad. I'd never understood the connection two people in love could share because I'd been too young when she'd died. But now, I'd started processing emotions in a different way; love in a different way. Maybe it was because this was the year I'd met Keith and my emotions felt different. I didn't know. It was the only thing I could think of as to why, all of a sudden, I got it: my dad was still mourning for her.

"Hey, Dad," I said softly, intruding carefully into his moment of meditation.

He turned his somber expression my way. "Morning, Flynn," he greeted me with little enthusiasm, yet I was used to it.

When my dad was home, he remained solemn and taciturn, yet direct. Conversations were succinct, but not in a way that suggested I bothered him. He simply had little to contribute. We didn't hug. We didn't laugh. We didn't cry. I guess we existed in a vacuum, for lack of a better description. It was like living in a world without emotion. More than likely, my school counselor would deem it an unhealthy environment. Maybe. But for six years, since the passing of my mother and brother, this was how our life had played out.

I walked over to the coffee pot, took out a mug and filled it. I sipped my black coffee and took a spot next to my dad by the sink. After a few minutes I commented, "I'm going to see her today. Zach said he'd go with me to the cemetery."

My dad grunted.

"Maybe you could go with us," I suggested. "Safety in numbers. Zach said that talking to dead family members is therapeutic."

My dad set his cup in the sink and walked off, leaving me looking out at the pool alone.

"I guess he's not ready," I mumbled.

I checked my phone, but Zach hadn't gotten back to me. I knew I had to go alone. If I waited any longer, I feared that I'd lose my nerve and back out entirely. I drank my last bit of coffee and headed out the door.

The cemetery was only a short walk from my house. We lived smack-dab in the middle of downtown Westminster; most places were an easy walk. I *could* even walk to school if I had to. Middle school had only taken me five minutes because East Middle was one street over; but if I had to walk to the high school it would probably take me a half an hour. I'd have to cross six lanes of traffic plus turn lanes, which would be a pain during rush hour, so I was thankful for the bus.

I walked down Willis Street, continued through a side road next to the Carroll County Circuit Court, and followed the green wire fencing all the way around to the cemetery entrance on North Church Street. I went through the open iron gates and chose the paved lane to my left. Somehow, I knew the way. As if propelled by an internal homing device, I circled past headstones for Mathias, Lovell, and Zepp and kept walking, even though I hadn't been there for years. True, I'd walked around the outside of this cemetery often, but I hadn't walked among the tombstones since my dad and I had watched Mom and Nate's caskets being lowered into the ground. Perhaps I'd been afraid when I was younger, or I feared learning there was nothing after death but ashes? I couldn't answer that. The whole concept of God and heaven and hell was still only that—a concept. My faith was minimal and based solely on what I had seen modeled by my mother.

I walked past many old, worn, marble headstones and read familiar Carroll Country names such as Bixler, Koonz, Witte, Sauble, and Wisner. I contemplated how cemeteries traditionally gave people the creeps—other people, not me. It could have been due to shows like Buffy The Vampire Slayer, The Walking Dead, and The Vampire Diaries desensitizing my generation to evil, or it could have simply been from coming close to death myself. After overcoming broken ribs, broken legs, broken fingers, a collapsed lung, and kidney failure, I pretty much laughed in the face of the Grim Reaper and all his minions. I figured if he wanted me that bad, he wouldn't have muffed it up the first time. I walked confidently through life, never fearing death, but not arrogantly so. I knew I'd been given a second chance for a reason, just like Zach had always told me.

I normally joked about having a black cloud over my head that wouldn't go away, but in truth that cloud hadn't shot lightning at me for years. I'd settled nicely into a routine of school, chores, solitude, and the occasional night of bowling with my friends. Before I knew it, years had drifted by. Now I was sixteen, almost driving, two years away from college, and my black cloud felt more like a force field of never ending dreariness, holding me in a virtual loop of repetitive tedium. This was the year for change though; I could feel it. My life *had* to change.

The grass had been neatly trimmed around the base of each upright stone and I marveled how *none* were lying flat. Okay, maybe four or five lay flat, but relatively few compared to the whole cemetery. I guessed it was due to it being an older cemetery. Newer ones contained mostly flat grave markers because the grass was easier to mow. Every single gravestone I saw in this cemetery was upright. Some markers resembling marble cinderblocks—rectangular, thick, and heavy—while others looked like small houses. Were those what people referred to as mausoleums? I wasn't sure.

Some graves had flowers on them, some didn't, and it made me wonder if I should have brought roses. Would my mom know she was worthy even if I'd forgotten?

My stomach trembled from worry over seeing her name on the headstone for the first time in six years. As I spotted the one grave marker that gave me a sudden flashback like the ones in movies, I stopped cold. The family name, Thomas, was etched into the base of a marble structure from 1924, which resembled the Washington Monument. That's why it had stood out so significantly to me back in 2004 when I'd been listening to the pastor's last words and watching everyone cry. My eyes had wandered and stopped on a tall, white, needlelike memorial erected maybe twenty feet away.

I turned my head and looked up the small hill. My mother was only two rows up the slope. Her resting place wasn't hard to find even after so long. The newer graves were all made of granite and the color stood out amidst the white marble of the older ones. But up the slope, to the right of another, smaller, needlelike monument for a Wenzel buried in 1910, sat two shiny granite headstones side by side.

Oddly, the same "tan brown" granite my dad had requested for our new countertops in the kitchen. The eerie realization made me question if I'd ever view our kitchen counters the same.

I approached slowly, climbing the gradual incline and circling around to face the fronts of the stones. I stopped abruptly once I saw the name Brewer. Victoria Brewer. My mom. Next to hers stood my brother, Nathan Brewer's stone. My breath came in pants, and tears immediately carved tracks on my cheeks as I fell to my knees and wept against the cold stone, imagining it was the side of her bed or the edge of our couch. Every creative cell of my being wanted me to open my eyes and glimpse her sleeping form, or maybe take her hand, but the logical side, the cruelly realistic side, reminded me repeatedly she wasn't really there.

So my tears were bitter, my sobs fruitless.

Some time later, a shadow fell across my mom's headstone and I knew it was Zach's. "You found me," I said quietly.

"When you weren't at the house I knew you'd be here, loser." His sarcasm didn't bother me. It never bothered me. "You could have waited. I told you I'd be here for you."

I remained seated where I was, cross-legged, in the grass, and I didn't look up. I felt hollow inside and I couldn't be bothered to humor Zach. Besides, there was no need. Zach would understand. He was only trying to lighten the mood, but I knew he was aware it wouldn't work. I picked a couple blades of grass and rubbed them between my fingers as Zach sat on the ground next to me.

"I'm sorry," he said. "There was road construction and then my phone died and I couldn't find my charger. I should have been here." He spoke to me as if we were in a library. I guess a cemetery deserved the same reverence. Hushed tones showing respect to the deceased.

I accepted his apology without adding to the distraction of excuses. Feeling his presence next to me was enough. I needed the security of our friendship to relax and open up. Normally it was on his bed as we studied the cracked paint on his ceiling, but for the first time I was okay with semi-public vulnerability. I'm not saying I'd be fine sitting there if a funeral had been going on ten feet away, but the exposure to possible onlookers didn't scare me. We were there, and this was about my mom and brother, and it felt different.

My eyes remained on the headstone in front of us, but I spoke to Zach as the memories of my mother came flooding in like water on a leaking ship. "I remember this one time, when I was eight years old, two years before she died, we were at my grandmother's house and I was supposed to be taking a nap. I had gotten up and walked through the living room, but no one noticed. Nate was watching cartoons or something and my grandmother was knitting in her rocking chair. I walked out the back door and saw my mom lying in the grass." As I spoke, I knew Zach would understand even if my thoughts seemed random. I knew he'd remain silent and listen as I said everything I needed to.

I continued, my voice hushed, as I lifted my hand allowing the blades of grass to blow away. "I didn't know why she was lying on the ground so I walked down the back steps. Silent. Tiptoeing. Down the wooden stairs, across cement stepping stones, between pink peonies, over a sleeping cat, I approached my mom. Knees shaking, gut clenching, fists tightening, I stepped closer, scared something had happened because I wouldn't know how to tell my dad. I rounded the side of a forsythia bush and that's when I noticed the most beautiful sound I'd ever heard. Like an angel's voice, sweet and harmonious, my mom's voice caressed me from the inside the way hot chocolate warms your belly in the winter. Deep down, somewhere that doesn't have a definition, her singing touched my soul. I closed my eyes. No music. No audience. No expectations. No pressure. No holding back. My mom, an angel sent from heaven, sang a song to God."

"But your family never went to church." Zach jolted me out of the memory.

Other people might have been offended by his blunt observation, but not me. I knew what he meant. Plus, this was classic, no-tact Zach. Growing up living next door to him prepared me to accept his directness. He wasn't a malicious person, simply clueless. "You're right," I said. "We didn't. But I think my mom always had this sense of who God was. Something in her song reminded me of a time I'd heard her talking to your mom about the Holy Spirit and seeing God shine from people's eyes."

"Mrs. B talked to my mom about God? When?" he asked.

I turned to face him, his eyes locked with mine, attentive and engaged. "That one time in the kitchen when we made whipped cream cookies and got powdered sugar all over the floor and the counter and our clothes."

Zach chuckled. "Oh yeah, I remember that. My mom made me mop the whole kitchen floor twice." His brow furrowed. "But I don't remember her talking about God."

"She was on the phone. I tend to pay attention when people talk about God. I know I ribbed you about eavesdropping on that girl at school, but your mom was on the phone in the kitchen, so it was hard not to listen. My family might not go to church, but that doesn't mean I don't believe in God. I'm pretty sure He's real."

"I never said you didn't."

"I know." I picked a few more blades of grass and tossed them. Looking across the graveyard, picturing my grandmother's back yard, inhaling deeply, I picked up my memory where Zach had interrupted. "Anyway, I remember my mom and the day I found her lying in the grass. It was as if God filled the air as it swirled around her. Sunlight streaming, butterflies flitting, birds chirping as she sang, 'Just from Jesus simply taking, life and rest and joy and peace.' I think it was the closest I've ever felt to God. My mom's voice saturated the space around me, yet inside I felt something warm and strong and comforting holding me like a hug. I knew I was safe."

"I don't think God's ever felt like that to me," Zach replied.

I lifted the corner of my mouth slightly. "Maybe that's why your mom never agreed with mine. My mom always felt peace with God. Your mom always spoke about obligations *to* God. But I don't want to debate religion today."

I glanced at the headstone in front of us and reached out to trace the V carved in the cold and hard granite. "She was so beautiful," I whispered, my voice cracking. "I miss her so much."

I snatched my hand back and hastily wiped away my tears before Zach noticed. Except he had noticed and proceeded to side-hug me. The idiot's compassion caused me to cry harder, and I'd rarely cried over my mom's death before today. "I'm sorry."

Zach squeezed my shoulder and said, "Why?"

"For crying like a girl."

"You're not, so shut up. I miss your mom too."

I leaned my head against him and allowed my emotions to run their course. Zach remained silent and supportive as he had so many times throughout the years. He was as he always had been—my refuge.

When I got home it was dark outside. I walked in the front door and turned on the front lights. I didn't know where my dad was, everything in my house was quiet and dark as if he wasn't home. But as soon as I started up the steps to my room, I heard his voice coming from the other room. I backed down the two steps I had gone up, turned the corner of the banister, and headed out to the dining room. I turned the light on and found my dad.

"Why are you sitting in the dark?" I asked.

He was sitting at the table, leaning forward on his elbows, his head bowed. When he looked up and met my eyes, the look on his face stopped me cold. "Dad?" I asked urgently. "What happened?" His eyes were bloodshot.

"Did you talk to her?" he asked, his voice like sandpaper.

"What?" It took me a few seconds to realize that this was the same phrase I heard him say when I was heading up the steps. My dad was asking if I…. "Yeah, I did. I talked to Mom… and Nate."

He slowly nodded his head. He looked down as I approached but I saw the tears streaming down his cheeks. "Dad." I moved to his side and fell across his shoulder and upper back. I hugged him as he sobbed. I hadn't seen him like this since we'd buried them. For years, he'd been quiet, distant, and emotionless.

It took probably ten minutes for him to turn and pull me into a hug. He cried and I cried. It drained every ounce of energy I had, and I'd thought I left everything at the cemetery.

"I feel so guilty," he finally confessed. "It should have been me."

"Dad, don't say that. I wouldn't want to choose Mom over you."

"No, at the cemetery with you. I should have gone and talked to her. I should have been with you so I could ask her to forgive me for avoiding her for so many years. I've been a terrible father, a terrible husband."

"No, Dad." I pulled out of his embrace and realized I had snot running down my chin. I grabbed a tissue from the box on the table and blew my nose. I offered him one and he did the same. Then I noticed the many balled tissues littering the floor and table. *Oh wow, he'd used a ton.* "Dad, you are not a terrible father," I asserted. He needed to be told directly. "I think Mom knows how painful it's been for us without her. I haven't gone to see her in all these years, either. She gets it. She understands."

His expression opened up and his shoulders relaxed. "You think so?"

"Yeah, I do. Zach told me talking to her would help and it did. It really did. I also don't think I have to go to her grave to feel that. I think I realized today that she never really left. She's here, in my heart. In your heart. Mom's here and she wants us to live."

His shoulders bobbed as the tears burst forth again. "I don't know how."

My dad cried for over an hour. Somewhere in the middle I found the strength to stop. I'd cried a river of tears that had been held at bay for years, and for the first time in forever, I felt at peace with her death. I could only hope that one day my dad would experience the same feeling.

Chapter 3

November 29, 2010: School

Going to school Monday morning was fucking hell. I felt like I had somehow survived a plane crash, but my body hadn't been informed of the trauma, because it kept on walking. In zombie mode I trudged to class, yet my brain wasn't engaged for most of the day. Yesterday's emotional assault had nearly killed me. I thought I'd done well visiting my mother, even with the crying, but then my dad—oh man—had lost it in the dining room. I hadn't been prepared for that.

In art, I doodled on my abstract sketch while the others at my table chatted quietly. Grace's iPod was playing and "Therapy" by All Time Low was on. *Yeah, I could relate to it.* I could probably use some therapy after dealing with my dad's overwhelming guilt and sorrow because it totally wrecked me. I had been young when Mom died, so I think I'd had more distance from the grief, initially unable to grasp its full implications. *Maybe.* Plus, I'd been injured in the accident too, and it took some time to recover. I had woken up and she was already gone. But for my dad, so many reminders remained in our house of her life, their life together; that he had gotten stuck in 2004 and he wasn't moving on. My dad was a living corpse of loneliness without her.

I heard the chair shift next to me, but thought nothing of it until the teacher stopped by our group and said, "Turn the music down or I'll have to tell you to turn it off. Playing your iPod is a privilege in my class as long as the work gets done, but music shouldn't disturb anyone else. Okay?"

Grace agreed and turned it down, and that's when I noticed Kelly was sitting across from me and Keith was in the chair to my left. "Since when are you sitting there?" I asked, with more of an edge then I intended.

I know I sounded irritated, but he didn't seem bothered by my tone. He quietly shrugged, as he was prone to. I think Keith was the most laidback person I'd ever met. "The girls decided to pair up for the sketch project, so that meant it was easier if I moved. If you want, I'll move back."

Keith next to me would have sounded amazing on any other day, but I was still reeling from the weekend. I only shrugged in reply.

I looked back to my sketch and added some shading around the light bulb. The sketch was a continual flow of objects melting into one another, maybe like a Salvador Dali painting, but in pencil. I drew a rope and a light bulb and an empty picture frame; it continued in a line around the square, eleven-by-eleven paper. I heard the girls whispering, and Keith answered, "No." I didn't know what they were talking about, nor did I care.

And then Keith slid a piece of paper across my desk, and I glanced at the words he had written on it.

"Are you okay?"

Okay? Um, no, I'm not okay, but thinking about it in my head wasn't going to satisfy the group. I knew enough to surmise that the girls put Keith up to passing the note. He might smirk flirtatiously, but so far he hadn't done much else in the thirteen weeks since we'd met to suggest he liked me. Yes, I admit I was counting. I took the paper and thought about what to say, how much to say, and how not to dwell on why I felt wasted, because I didn't need a repeat of the weekend's emotions rushing out.

"Yeah. I'll be okay." I passed the paper back and continued my drawing.

He slid it back. *"Do you want to talk about whatever it is? You look like shit. (Grace's words, not mine.)"*

I grinned at glanced over at Grace. She smiled back at me. I wrote, *"Not really. It was a rough weekend. We're in school and I don't want to think about it."*

Keith added more and shoved it back. *"Talk after school?"*

"I'll miss the bus."

I read his answer. *"Kelly drives. We could all walk over to Starbucks and get coffee or something."* I looked across to Kelly. "You drive?"

She nodded. "Seems I'm the oldest here. You in or what? We need to cheer that ass of yours up."

I grinned. These were some really great people I was getting to know. "Okay. I'll go."

Starbucks was good, and I didn't have to talk about my personal pain at all. My friends goofed off and told me more about themselves than they asked about me. It was great not having any pressure on me. Kelly drove us all home; Keith and I in the back seat and Grace in the front. I wasn't sure if it was because they sensed something brewing between us, or because Grace and Kelly were practically BFFs. I didn't ask.

"I live on Willis Street, near the courthouse," I said.

"Okay, thanks. That's easy."

As she drove, I glanced down at Keith's hand on the seat. It was inches from mine, yet so far away. I wanted to touch him, but I didn't know if that would be presumptuous. I should wait until I was sure. He was looking out the window, so I carefully took note of his features. His hair curled around the bottom edge of his beanie, leaving some of his neck exposed above the collar of his T-shirt. He had a mole at the base of his neck, and one on his jaw below his ear. The hair on his cheeks was patchy, but thicker than the last time I noticed it. Not quite scruffy, but noticeably appealing to me. I liked his face, and my desire to touch it seemed stronger now that we'd spent more than ninety minutes in art together. Seeing him outside school made me physically aware of my growing crush, as flutters suddenly tickled my insides, and my groin warmed up.

When Kelly parked in front of my house, I hated getting out. "I guess I'll see ya." My lame attempt at stalling basically made me seem like an idiot. Of course I'd see him. I was in his art class. I heard the girls giggle in the front seat and I instantly glared, which did little to stifle their amusement.

Keith lifted the corner of his mouth and said, "Yeah, I'll see ya." He dipped his head shyly and wouldn't look me in the eyes.

Without knowing what else to do, I got out of the car. It wasn't like this had been a date. We'd gotten coffee and talked. I couldn't explain why I felt so self-conscious. "Bye," I waved, walking backward across my front lawn.

Keith's eyes glinted as he grinned at me through the window just before they pulled away.

***

Art class and Keith became my favorite *new* things. Zach was a part of the old me, and my life from childhood into teenagerhood. If that was indeed a word. Keith, Kelly, and Grace were all a part of the new life I was discovering now that Zach wasn't around twenty-four-seven. Without Zach, I had to redefine myself and these guys were the ticket.

As the teacher gave a demonstration for our final project, Keith shifted in his chair as if a bug was crawling up his back or he had to pee. Most of the time he sat very still and I had to look to see if he was sleeping, but today he was fidgety. We were instructed to consult with our partner—Keith was mine for this—and find a magazine photo to duplicate using mixed media. Keith scooted his chair closer and my stomach got a little squirrely. I hadn't planned it. I think my body had its own ideas when he was close to me.

I sat there casually, trying not to think about it. One hand on my thigh, the other on the desk, I sat listening to the teacher talk about colors and shading and such while Keith flipped the pages of the magazine. That's when I noticed something, someone, touch my hand.

Very subtly, Keith grazed his fingers over the back of my hand and I went still. His touch was so light it almost tickled. No one could see, I didn't think. We were at the back of the class and the desks provided easy cover. I felt two or three fingers at first, but as the minutes went by, I could tell Keith was getting braver. Soon, I felt all five of his fingertips caressing the back of my hand and it made me shiver.

I couldn't recall ever feeling like that.

With Zach, we'd always touched each other. Since as far back as I could remember Zach and I'd had very few boundaries between us. Although we'd never held hands in a romantic sense, I had held his hand. I'd held Zach's hand, twisted his nipple, poked his bare ass, and licked his eyeball. We'd shared goofy moments… mostly.

I breathed deeply and amended my assessment: we'd shared goofy moments with the exception of September 6, 2008. That was the day he took our goofiness too far and kissed me. I still couldn't get the thought of his kiss out of my head. I had felt his lips on mine, and nothing else seemed to satisfy the longing I continued to have for him, even after he treated me like dirt and ignored the fact it had happened. Zach's kiss was an accident. So why couldn't I shake it?

In September of this year, when I had visited and we'd had a heart-to-heart in his room, the air around us sparked. I swear he probably would have kissed me if he hadn't leapt out of the bed to scan his notebook. I just didn't understand him.

Keith must have detected my distraction and removed his hand as if thinking I somehow disapproved. I glanced over. His head was tipped down and his hands were in his lap. The teacher turned to write something on the board, so I took the opportunity to move my hand over to his. I caressed *his* fingers this time, much like he had done to mine, but then I squeezed them. Keith rolled his hand over and allowed me to hold it. I grinned and he blushed.

When the teacher addressed the class, I snatched my hand back and pretended nothing was going on, but we both knew that wasn't true. We glanced and smirked at one another and then followed the teacher's directions for the classwork. Walking to the next class was going to prove more interesting today, I suspected.

"So," Keith started to say as we entered the hallway. "Back there, was that…." I knew he purposely left the sentence hang.

After taking note of the kids around us in the hall, I smiled and answered quietly, "Flirting? Heck, yeah." Keith might have been shy, but I didn't consider myself to be. I was cautious, though.

He snickered and nodded, and we turned to walk down the hall together. When we got to our normal separating point at the stairs, I grabbed hold of destiny. If this was my new life without Zach by my side, I was going to make sure it was a good life, a fun life, the life I chose to live. "Keith, do you want to go someplace after school sometime? Like Starbucks or something, but without the girls?" I liked Grace and Kelly, but they didn't need to tag along for everything.

He blushed deeper when he nodded, looking more adorable than ever. "I'd like that."

"Cool." I nodded back. It made me wonder if he'd ever had a boyfriend before; I hadn't. "I have to figure out a ride and stuff. I don't have my license yet," I said.

"Neither do I. I have about forty hours of drive time in, so I should be able to get my provisional by February. I'm stoked."

"I wish I could say the same. My birthday is in July so I can't go until April, but I don't have very many hours logged on my learner's. I'm lucky to even have it."

"Why?" he asked curiously.

"Nobody to drive with. It's just me and my dad and he's never home. The only hours I have are with my neighbor's mom. She's nice, but I hate to keep bugging her about driving."

"Bummer. Maybe you could go with my mom," he offered happily.

"You think she'd take me?" I couldn't be so lucky.

"Probably. It doesn't hurt to ask."

"Cool." Suddenly my outlook on ever driving myself anywhere improved dramatically. "So, that leads me to my next question. I know we can walk to Starbucks from school, but if we did do you think your mom would give us a ride home?"

"Maybe. If not, I can ask my sister. She's nineteen and works at some hair salon in town. I'm sure she'd find it amusing to drive us places."

"How so?"

"She thinks it's funny I'm gay. She said she knew when I stole her Barbie dolls there had to be something wrong with me."

I shushed him and ducked my head as I scanned for anyone who might be watching us or listening in. Of course, no one was. "Dude, keep it down."

He leaned closer and lowered his voice. "Oh, I'm sorry. I thought you knew. I'm out. Although I don't exactly wear a sign around my neck, lots of people know I'm gay; my family, some kids in school, the school's counselor. Kelly and Grace. Is that going to be an issue for you?"

Right then the bell rang. "Shit, I'm late for class. I'll call you later."

Keith snagged my sleeve before I stepped away. "I haven't given you my number yet."

"Oh, yeah. Duh." I chuckled. I'm pretty sure I blushed as I asked, "Keith Leppo, may I have your phone number?"

He took out a pen and turned my hand over. He wrote his digits on my palm and for some reason it made me feel like a cheerleader who had scored a date with the quarterback. (Although Keith was far from that.) I grinned when he was finished and said, "I'll call you later."

I walked about ten steps away and turned around to find him watching me. I smiled and added, "No, it isn't a problem, but we'll talk later. K?"

Keith nodded and I walked to class feeling nervous and happy and maybe a tad fearful.

I dialed and the phone rang once. I'd like to think he'd been holding his cell phone since school let out, waiting with anticipation for my call. Whatever the reason, I think it was the longest and the most freeing conversation I'd ever had on the phone. I allowed my tears to fall, knowing I wouldn't get made fun of, especially since he couldn't see me.

We talked about the accident and why I'd been bummed that day after Thanksgiving break. I told Keith about my dad's drinking and how he worked all the time and that I'm alone almost every day. I told Keith I knew I was gay by seventh-grade, but that I hadn't told anyone. Keith had been the first to know, and I explained how nervous I was about coming out. Keith said he understood and that he would respect my decision and wait patiently. He said he knew it was harder for some people, although it had been easy for him. He said he was still wary at times because he lived in conservative Carroll County, even though he had never denied his sexuality to anyone.

He admitted he never had a boyfriend, although he'd had crushes on a few guys over the years. I told him I hadn't either. We were both virgins, which made things easier yet… harder. As soon as he said the word "virgin" over the phone, it was like lightning struck my dick. It pulsed and I was suddenly thinking of all these things I wanted to try. I'd never given sex so much thought before. I remembered *wanting* things with Zach, but I had been fourteen and I wasn't clear on what I wanted. With Keith, it was as if I discovered what the word "sex" meant for the first time. I had mental images of his jeans and how the fabric flexed and tightened as he moved in his seat next to mine during art. I hadn't remembered paying all that close attention to his jeans before, let alone his crotch, but apparently I had, and talking to him on the phone brought all the subconscious visuals to the surface. God, I even recalled how his ass looked as he walked up the steps every day.

For a brief moment, Keith thought I'd hung up on him due to my silence. *Oops.* "Flynn, are you still there?"

"Oh, yeah, sorry. I was thinking of something." *I was thinking about your ass.* "Anyway, I guess I should go do some homework. My dad said he's cool with whatever I do as long as my grades are good. I like the freedom. It means I can go to Starbucks whenever we decide and I can have friends over and stuff."

"Yeah, my parents are pretty much the same. Maybe you could come over and study here? Unless that sounds dumb?"

"No. Not dumb. I'm cool with that. Especially when this semester is over and I won't have art with you."

"I could see about switching teachers for Honors Trig."

"You'd do that?"

"Sure. No harm in asking. I'll go to the counselor's office in the morning."

I appreciated how casual Keith was about it, and inside I was jumping with joy that he would even consider rearranging his schedule so we'd continue having class together.

"So, tomorrow…," he broached. "We chill at school. Right? No handholding. No making out in the halls." The pitch of his voice went down. I knew he was slightly disappointed, but I wasn't coming out yet.

"Yeah. I don't want to start rumors."

"Okay. But you know that Grace knows I like you. Plus, I think Kelly saw you holding my hand under the desk. They know."

"Yeah, well, I want to keep it hushed as long as I can until I talk to my dad and tell Zach. They should know before the whole school. I've been fine with *feeling* gay for years, but this is the first time I'm *being* gay. You know? If you're my boyfriend, then it isn't simply a concept in my brain. I'm gay. I gotta think about how the reality of it is going to impact my life. Before you, it was a word and a feeling. Now, *gay* is real."

"No, I get it. It's fine. As long as I can hold your hand in the car when Kelly drives."

"Yeah. Of course you can. Keith, I'll talk to you tomorrow. Okay?"

Holding hands. Keith: my boyfriend? I thought about it a minute. *Gay is real.* This would change my life. Dad and I never talked about any of it. He didn't know I was attracted to guys. We didn't talk about political and cultural change, or voting for gay marriage. New York supported gay marriage. I wondered if Maryland would? My dad and I barely spoke about anything. How would he react to finding out he had a gay son?

Keith answered, "Okay."

"Bye." I hung up the phone and whispered, "Gay is real."

Chapter 4

February 14, 2011: Moving Forward

By the end of the conversation, we had decided we'd play it cool at school. No handholding, no making out, and we'd take everything real slow. I didn't want rumors spreading until I was ready to come out and Keith assured me he understood. His request to switch classes had been denied, so we only saw each other in the halls. I was sort of glad because it gave me time to think about how I would handle being out in school if I had a boyfriend. In fact, I wasn't really sure how people would react. Would kids say stuff? Would I get bullied? To my knowledge Keith hadn't been bullied, but he also wasn't making out with boys in the hall. I doubted anyone really knew he was gay, even if he thought they did.

For a couple months, going slow was easy, since we were basically limited to exchanging glances in the hallway, watching basketball games in the gym together over the winter, and the occasional coffee at Starbucks. I wasn't interested in basketball, but it did give me more time to talk and laugh with Keith. Besides, Kelly was a cheerleader, and she got a kick out of hearing us cheer for her and not for the basketball team.

Keith got his provisional license in February.

I looked over from where I stood at the kitchen counter and I saw the look in Keith's eyes. I think hanging out with him after school, in public, had helped us take our relationship slow, but now we were alone and I could tell he wanted more than a sandwich. I did too. It was weird to be considering the outside influences converging on me as I thought about my next move. I wanted Keith, but what would people say? No one talked about being gay as a reality. There was talk about the suicides that happened around the country in September, but I hadn't heard any students lamenting them. It was more like no one could believe it had happened, and then they quickly moved on to the next topic.

I guess I couldn't believe that people could be so uncaring. Those kids had been bullied solely because of their sexuality, and so far no one in my school gave it more than a moment's thought. Maybe people thought it was easier ignoring the problems in society rather than addressing them and facing ridicule from their friends. I hoped I wouldn't be part of either of those groups as I got older.

I laid a slice of cheese over the tuna and put the plate in the microwave for ten seconds, and then I glanced at Keith and gave him a wink, testing my bravery.

He groaned.

I chuckled and said, "Come here." I knew I could be myself around Keith, but until now it had only been harmless flirting. Acting on my physical desires meant confronting my fears surrounding coming out. I didn't want to be bullied, but I hated hiding. At what point would I have to choose?

He didn't hesitate. Keith walked over to me and came right up in my personal space. He placed his hands on my hips and looked into my eyes as he licked his lips. "I've never kissed anyone before. Have you?" I shifted my eyes away momentarily, and he picked up on my thoughts. "Oh, that's right—Zach, but you haven't kissed anybody else?"

Our many conversations over the last couple months did make it around to the topic of my best friend who lived next door, and was now in college. I also told Keith about the kiss. We'd talked about being virgins sex-wise, but I had felt wrong letting him think I'd never kissed a boy, so I spilled the gory details over trigonometry homework.

"No," I said. We gazed into one another's eyes again and my heartbeat quickened. I felt his fingers caressing me through my shirt just above my belt. He leaned closer and our stomachs touched. Then the word "boyfriend" hit me somewhere between lust and logic. "So, should this be an official thing?" I asked, curiously, throwing him off as he blinked away his hormone-induced daze.

"Official?" He wasn't getting my drift.

I explained, "Like, it's the first time we're messing around as boyfriends. If I kiss you, then are we *officially* official or are we open to dating other people?"

Keith's grip loosened and I thought he was about to pull away, but he didn't. He hung his head as if scared to answer.

"Keith?" I prompted.

He was looking away when he finally answered me. "I don't really want an open relationship. I kinda want a boyfriend. *One* boyfriend."

"Kinda?"

He looked up sharply. "Don't make fun of me."

"I'm not," I said.

"Then why are you smirking at me?"

Keith's irritation was adorable as hell. "I'm not," I repeated.

"Yes, you are!"

He tried pulling away, but I held him firmly in my grasp. "Stop. I'm sorry. I promise I'm not laughing. I think you're adorable. I'm glad you want a boyfriend, because I do too. Really."

"Then why'd you ask that as if you wanted the freedom to go out with someone else? Someone like Zach."

"Zach? It has nothing to do with Zach. I don't want anybody else. I just wanted to find out if you did."

Keith relaxed. "Promise?"

I nodded. "Promise." I was suddenly acutely aware of our groins touching and how rapidly he was breathing. "Nervous?"

Keith nodded and swallowed hard.

I licked my lips and whispered, "Then I better make it good."

After Keith closed his eyes, I leaned in and seductively licked his lips right before pressing my mouth to his. He shivered in my embrace, not expecting me to be so bold. I tilted my head and licked his lips before kissing him again. I wasn't trying to coax him into using his tongue right away; I was teasing him, hoping he'd shake with anticipation. As soon as he opened his mouth, I backed away.

He made a little whining noise and I chuckled wickedly. "Don't worry, that's just the first taste." I grabbed a hold of his hand and brought his fingers to my mouth. I kissed his knuckles before releasing his hand. "We agreed on slow, remember?"

His look of disappointment thrilled me because he had no idea what I was thinking. Yes, I wanted to go slow and I wasn't ready for sex, but Keith had no clue about the serious kissing I planned to do later. His lips were soft and sweet, and those few touches we exchanged had me burning inside. He didn't have to go home until nine; so after we ate a snack, I planned on exploring his mouth and neck for hours.

Kissing Zach years ago felt like a dying ember compared to the sensation of Keith's lips on mine. Maybe it was because I was so much younger then, and I'd had no clue what I was doing. Zach had been in charge and I had fumbled along as he moved his mouth. Zach's kiss has been breathtaking for sure, but his mother had interrupted us and the kissing had ended way too soon, leaving this fretful hunger rolling around my gut over what could have been. The memory of his kiss followed me everywhere, but I knew it was unrealistic to think he would ever feel anything for me other than friendship.

Zach Mitchell was straight.

Keith, on the other hand, was gay and standing right here. He was warm flesh, and sensitive eyes, and his kiss kindled the spark I had felt years ago with Zach into a roaring furnace. I'd had to step away when I kissed Keith, because suddenly I was feeling new, unexpected things. Kind of like when I heard the word "virgin" from his lips and I suddenly couldn't stop thinking about his ass. Keith did things to me. I could feel my dick throbbing in my jeans, but I played it off as being devilish and teasingly making him wait. No, the waiting was for *me* so I could get myself under control. I didn't want to rip his clothes off, but I knew if we had kept on kissing, that's exactly what I would have done—he revved me up that much.

After our snack, we retired to the living room sofa. Keith stopped short of sitting and looked at me. "You want to watch television?"

I cocked my head to the side. "What do you think?"

Keith blushed and looked down. I swear he was so freaking adorable when he did that. I took his hand and we sat together. "Our first kiss, and on Valentine's Day, no less. I think my sister will die laughing from the cheese factor."

"Then don't tell her," I answered. As he leaned toward me, I stopped him with a hand on his chest. "I think we need some ground rules."

"Okay."

"You've never… done it, and neither have I. I'm not ready for sex."

"Me neither," Keith admitted.

"Good. But how far do you want to go? I mean… two guys can get pretty far without actual butt sex, ya know?"

Keith nodded. "Yeah."

"So? How far?"

He shrugged. "I don't know."

"Well, maybe we could make up a safe word in order to stop the other person when it gets to be too much?"

"Isn't 'stop' a good enough word?"

"I guess."

"Flynn, can we think about this later? I just want to kiss you," he asked desperately. "I don't know how much longer I can wait."

"Damn." I grinned, and stopped thinking so intently. I wanted this too; I guess I only worried about not being able to stop. I reached up and slid my palm over his cheek before removing his glasses. Keith set them on the end table and turned back to me. I held the side of his face as I leaned in. His lips were just as soft as they had been the first time: soft, sweet, and addictive.

I felt his hand on my thigh and it sent shivers up my leg into my groin, which didn't need more stimulation. I opened my mouth and licked and this time when he parted his lips I didn't pull away. When our tongues touched I could not have stopped my gasp if I'd tried. The feeling of our slippery tongues licking and tasting one another was the most incredible feeling on the planet. Subconsciously, I knew there were other sensations which probably outshone this one, but for now I was at the pinnacle of my sexual understanding, and I was humming with energy. I pressed forward and he took the cue to lie back against the armrest.

I disengaged our mouths long enough to bring one of his legs around so I could insert my hips between his outstretched thighs and lie on top of him. We were fully clothed, which was for the best. I wanted to make out as long as possible and if I felt his naked chest against mine, we would be doing more than kissing.

Once situated, I rested my body weight on his and claimed his mouth again. His arms were around my back and my left arm was under his shoulder while the other held his jaw. I kissed him, and licked him, and explored his mouth and teeth with my flicking tongue and teasing kisses. Keith groaned, and his one hand slid down and then up the back of my shirt, caressing my skin.

My heart thudded in my chest as I moved my hand up into his hair. I rocked my hips and felt Keith nudge back just as I moved my mouth to his throat. I heard him moan my name seconds before I heard my father echoing him in a different tone of voice.

"Flynn?" my dad questioned from the doorway.

I snapped my head in his direction. "Dad!"

I struggled to untangle our limbs as my dad shook his head and headed out of the room. "Shit," he mumbled.

As I stood, I heard Keith apologize, "I'm sorry, Flynn."

I turned and sat back down. I took Keith's hand and squeezed it. "It's not your fault. I wouldn't have planned it this way, but it is what it is. I think you should go while I talk to my dad."

"Okay."

"Maybe we need a new rule that we can't be alone."

"Why?"

"Because the next time we are, I am getting at that body."

Keith probably blushed. It was too dark to see his cheeks, but I knew that grin. "I'm okay with that."

I kissed him and said, "You better go."

He grabbed his glasses and headed out the front door.

When I closed the door behind him, I went to find my dad. He was in the dining room pouring a Scotch. Dread loomed in the air. My dad drank Jack Daniels habitually, vodka socially, and Highland Park single malt Scotch whisky seriously. So when I watched him drain one glass and then pour another, I knew this was not going to be a good conversation.

Without turning he asked, "How long has this been going on?"

I swallowed nervously. "Today. We haven't kissed or anything before today."

"I mean… prancing around like a fairy."

"Dad, I've never—"

"Save it! I should've known you'd turn out this way. I'm never around. You were always a momma's boy. Look at your hair! Who dyes their hair with streaks of blue and purple, and an odd patch behind one ear? Queers!" He took another sip and staggered over to a chair.

How many has he had in the last five minutes?

I didn't know what to say. I hadn't always had colors in my hair, so it couldn't be that. For at least a year I'd had "normal" highlighted streaks and he hadn't said a thing about it. True, the blue chunk behind my left ear was unusual this year, but no one at school gave me a hard time about my hair or my pierced cartilage. One jock called me an emo freak, but no one called me queer. I had figured if the kids at school weren't harassing me, I might have hope with my dad. So far… not so much.

"Dad, can we talk about this rationally?" I begged.

"Rationally? I walked in on my son making out with another boy on my couch. How is that rational?" My dad ran his hand through his hair and paused with his hand against his forehead. Thinking, I supposed.

His quiet ate at me. My dad and I didn't have many chances to talk, but when we did, it had always been normal, simple, pleasant conversation. I hadn't ever experienced the tension that thickened the air now. I felt trapped, sick, and worried. What if my dad turned out to be like those other parents I'd heard about? What if my dad hated me now, or threw me out of the house? I'm resourceful, but I didn't think I could make it living on the streets.

Plus, I generally had terrible luck. What if this was fate laughing at me again?

After a while, my dad finally looked at me, his eyes dark and his face weary. "What are people going to say, Flynn? Have you even thought about that? What is that self-righteous Stewart Mitchell going to say when he finds out my son is a homosexual?" I hadn't ever heard my dad sound so desperate. I thought he'd yell, and he started off sounding angry; but now his voice—possibly alcohol induced—sounded hurt and seemed almost pleading. "I'll tell you what he's going to say," he continued, as I sat quietly at the dining room table. "He's going to tell me I should have paid attention more to your upbringing. He's going to remind me about all those times you went on camping trips with him and his son and I made excuses because of work. He's going to say it's my fault."

He covered his face again and groaned. "Oh, Flynn. I don't know if I can take the ridicule. I'm doing the best I can, but this is not something I needed right now."

"Dad, no one knows," I explained quickly. "No one has to know. I'm not ready to come out. I'm worried about what people will think too, ya know. Zach's my best friend. I don't know what I'd do if he suddenly hated me because I like boys. Dad, look at me, I can keep this to myself." I reached out and touched his arm and felt relieved when he didn't recoil. He looked so drained.

"You'd do that?"

"Yeah, I would. Keith and I haven't done anything at school that would draw attention, other than hanging together. We've only ever kissed tonight. I can ask him to chill."

My dad nodded. He sat quietly, gathering his thoughts, and nodded again before saying anything else. "Flynn," he said, reaching for my hand, "I appreciate your discretion." He took a deep breath and smiled weakly. "I'm not disappointed in you, just so you know. I still love you. I think seeing you on the couch like that was a bit of a shock, but I'm not mad. Not anymore. I just want to prepare myself for whatever Stewart Mitchell has to say about it. The longer you take before you flaunt it, the better."

I was hurt by the way he worded it, but I got the impression it wasn't intentional on his part. "I already told Keith I wanted to go slow. I'm sure he'll understand."

My dad nodded again, and then rose from his chair. "I'm going to bed."

"But you just got home," I pointed out. "And you haven't eaten anything."

"I don't feel like eating. Plus, I have an early morning." He turned and lumbered toward the steps.

"Good night," I called after him, and heard him mumble something back. I slumped in my seat. "That didn't go very well, but I suppose it could have gone worse."

Then Keith texted me: *Hey. How'd it go?*

Okay, I guess. He doesn't want me to "flaunt in public," but he isn't angry.

What does that mean?

My dad doesn't want me acting gay in public because he's worried about his reputation and what the neighbors will say. I didn't go into detail about the neighbor in question being the overly religious Mr. Mitchell, Zach's dad.

Oh. How long do you think he'll feel like that?

It was a text, but I could tell Keith was disappointed. *IDK. A while. We only JUST started fooling around. We can be quiet about it, right?*

I guess. I just want to hold your hand in school and stuff. It'll be hard holding back.

I texted back: *I know. I'm sorry. But I don't want my dad freaking out. I mean, what if he decides I can't see you anymore? Wouldn't that be worse than keeping our relationship a secret?* I hoped he understood. I didn't want to press the issue further, but I would. I didn't want Zach finding out by accident. I wanted to be the one to tell him when the time was right.

Okay. I'll wait. But I can drive now, so I want to drive us places. You know? Go on dates and stuff. I don't want this summer to fly by with you in the closet the entire time. Think about it. I understand working up to it, but you eventually have to come out publically.

I know. I will. Just give me some time, okay?

I already said I would.

Thank you.

Keith said good night, and the next day at school he acted fine about everything, but somehow I knew my timeframe and his were on two different scales.

Chapter 5

June 24, 2011: In The Closet... Still

By the summer, any normal person would have been excited about the prospect of hanging out for hours on end, and swimming in a private pool with several of his closest friends, but I'm not normal. Being around Keith in swim trunks was a test of my self-control. The way his back moved as he glided through the water and how the muscles of his legs flexed as he dried off had me tangled in knots practically every day. I wanted him so bad.

One time, I even excused myself from the company of my friends, disappeared into the bathroom, and jacked off while watching Keith through the little bathroom window. Keeping my promise to my dad was increasingly hard to do. While in school, things were fine. Out of school, I found it difficult keeping my hands off Keith. But if I was affectionate in public, wouldn't someone notice? What if that someone knew Zach, or worse, Mr. Mitchell, wouldn't that screw me in the end? I had grown more paranoid about it as the days passed. I wanted to be the one to tell Zach. I needed to do it soon.

I had been daydreaming about Keith's back when he suddenly hauled himself over the edge of the pool right in front of me. He walked over to Grace and shook his hair like a dog, sending a spray of pool water all over her and Kelly. I snickered at their high-pitched protests. He'd done the same thing three other times as they sunbathed, the two should expect it by now.

Keith turned his attention back my way and sauntered over. His erect nipples made my mouth water. It wasn't like Keith had the body of an athlete; he could best be described as an average guy, without any distinguishing body-type characteristics. But what he did have—smooth skin, hair below his navel, strong shoulders, and a dimple on one cheek—made me crazy.

"I suppose I shouldn't shake water all over you, although you do look a little too warm and dry on that lawn chair."

I shielded my eyes from the sun as I peered up at him. I was looking at his face as we held the conversation, but that didn't mean I wasn't aware of how close his wet body was to me. Rivulets of pool water streaming down his legs, droplets clinging to his chest, swim trunks low on his hips, oh God yes, I was fully aware of the total package. "You could, but I might not invite you back."

Keith grinned and rolled his eyes. He knew I was all bluff. He paused longer than he normally did after a swim. The past few times the gang had come over, Keith would say something similar and then go dive back into the pool. He'd swim for a while, dry off again after messing with the girls, but he hadn't eyed me so openly as he was right now. I was in swim trunks too, but I wasn't glistening with water droplets.

He ogled me again and suggested, "You should probably flip over. You've been face up for a while now. You don't want your chest to burn and your back to be white. We all know how much you *don't* tan."

I hadn't rolled over because I wanted to watch him swim. "Maybe, but if I lie on my stomach I might fall asleep."

"No you won't. I'll make sure you don't. Roll over, I'll put sunscreen on your back."

I hesitated and gave him a knowing look. He returned it and didn't deny my implication of his desire to run his hands over my body. *Oh God.* I adjusted my chair so it was flat and I lay so my head was at the foot of the chair in order to watch the pool. Keith sat on the edge of the chair, pressing his hip close to mine as he squirted cold lotion on my back.

To say I was nervous was an understatement, but it wasn't like anyone except Kelly and Grace could see us. Our house had a high hedge around it, and the only house that was close enough to see the pool was Zach's. I was fifty percent sure no one would see as only one window in Zach's room had a clear view. My dad loved the privacy and so did I. I remembered many clothing optional late night swims. I wondered if maybe Keith and I could try that this summer. I'd have to ask him.

When Keith started sliding his hands over my shoulder blades we heard catcalls from our spectators. Kelly whistled and hollered, "It's about time!"

I was slightly embarrassed, but the two of them knew we were dating. I didn't know why I felt the need to constrain myself around everyone the last several months, but I had. My dad's little talk in February had me bottling up all kinds of desires and impulses. But now? Wow. Keith's massaging fingers made me realize that I'd been stupid. I didn't have to have sex on the courthouse lawn, in front of the police station; but I also didn't need to treat my boyfriend like he'd infect me with Hepatitis A if I touched him. No, I didn't want Mr. Mitchell finding out, but yes, I needed to get over myself.

As he made circles with his fingers over my neck and shoulders, my dick took notice. As he slid his hands south, massaging my lower back, my balls ached. I opened my eyes and turned my head, stealing a glimpse as he globbed sunscreen on my thighs. He looked serene as he rubbed it in, sliding his fingers up and down the backs of my legs. How could he be so calm? Didn't he want to… I jumped and sucked in a breath as Keith snuck his fingers under the hem of my trunks.

I rolled to my side and found that he was far from calm; his eyes were blazing. I reached for him at the same time he brought his mouth down on mine. I heard the girls gasp, but I ignored it. Keith put his arm around my ribs as I held him firmly at the base of his neck. Our kiss was strong and desperate, as if we hadn't kissed in ages. I tried to sit up, and as I did, I ended up knocking our teeth together.

"Ow!" Keith pulled away, cupping his mouth. His fingers and lips had blood on them.

"I'm sorry. I got carried away. Let me see." I examined his lip and found a small gash I'd made with my teeth. "It's not bad, but it's bleeding a lot. We should get a towel or something to hold to your lip until it stops."

I got up and motioned toward the side door into the house. I didn't want to go first because the girls would notice my tented trunks, so I made him lead.

"Way to spoil the show, Flynn," Grace complained from her lawn chair.

I stuck my tongue out as we passed her by, hoping her eyes wouldn't stray from my face downward.

As I reached for the door handle, I heard raised voices coming from Zach's house. I stopped, and Keith opened the door. He paused as he entered, and started to ask me a question, but I put him off, holding up my hand. He left me by the open door as I strained to hear what was going on at my neighbors' house.

"But Mom, I'm not ready to get married," I heard Zach yell. I could tell he and his mom were in the kitchen. Their kitchen and ours were only separated by about ten feet of grass and bushes, so loud voices traveled freely. Our houses were built far too close together to miss any heated discussions.

"I didn't say it had to be tomorrow," his mom shot back. "I'm just trying to explain that your promiscuity needs to come to an end. You are not a kid anymore, Zachary. Dating cashiers and cheerleaders might have been fun for a high school quarterback, but it isn't what makes your future. Look at your brother and sister. They are both happily married. Your brother is rising in the ranks of the church and your sister married a very prestigious man. I can see him doing great things one day."

"But Chad and Amy don't even go to our church."

"That is neither here nor there. I'm sure Chad will convert once Amy talks some sense into him. She assured your father it was only temporary."

Of course, I'd known Zach's dad had been angry with Amy's husband for some reason, but I hadn't known it was about church. Church. Seemingly the subject in every conversation in that house.

Keith returned with a paper towel to his lip. "I put a piece of ice...." I shushed him with a finger to my lips, and then I pointed over at Zach's house. "Zach," I whispered. We sat together on the porch and eavesdropped.

"Amy might have gotten married when she was nineteen, but that isn't *my* plan Mom," Zach argued.

I felt bad for Zach. He couldn't tell his mom that Amy and Chad had gotten married because she'd been pregnant. Sex outside of marriage was a huge no-no in their church, and their family. Amy and Chad had hoped to cover it up by acting like teens in love and then once the baby came along, they banked on no one counting the months. Sadly, none of it mattered as Amy miscarried a month after the wedding. Zach had kept her secret, telling no one except me.

Zach continued, "And Clark *just* got married. Will you at least allow me to graduate first?"

"Fine. But I think you need to be more careful whom you date. No more playing around. Dating should be for marriage anyway; I'm not sure why your father let you go out with all those girls in the first place. He knew it was a mistake. Perhaps I'll ask some mothers at the church for any available prospects your age."

"Mom! Come on. We aren't going to argue about this again, are we? This isn't the Elizabethan era. People don't arrange marriages anymore. It's the twenty-first century. I just don't understand why our church is afraid of change, why Dad is afraid of change. He needs to let go of their archaic bylaws and embrace the future. As far as 'being proper,' that's a joke. You have to know I'm not a virgin."

That's when I heard a crack. Keith and I looked at each other. He shot his eyebrow up. I think we were both thinking the same thing: that sounded like a cheek being slapped. And now that the space between our houses was saturated in abrupt silence, the idea seemed still more plausible. I couldn't believe that Zach's mom had slapped him. Over what? A comment about his old-fashioned church? A church with more rules than good sense? Or his comment about his father? I couldn't blame him for voicing his opinion, because I would have in his situation. If my dad had decided years ago to join the Mitchells' church and the elders had forced strict obedience on our family like it had on so many others, I would have rebelled.

As it was, I never had to worry about it. My dad was not on the same page as Stewart Mitchell regarding religion, or many other topics for that matter. I was especially glad for that now.

Keith gestured toward the Mitchells' house. I knew what he asking. He wondered what we should do, go over or stay put? I wasn't sure myself, because if Zach's mom was still in the kitchen, I wouldn't know what to say, or how to hide the fact that I'd been listening in. For all I knew, Zach could have gone up to his room or out the front door.

Our indecision was short-lived, as Zach came out the side door. We saw him, but he hadn't seen us. He bent over and picked something up. He cocked his arm back and threw it; ducking suddenly, as the object, a rock, ricocheted off a tree nearby and shot back in his direction. If we hadn't been watching, the projectile would have hit us. Keith jerked to the side and I yelped as the rock grazed my arm during my haste to dodge it.

I grabbed my arm and looked back to where Zach stood, on the other side of the hedge. His eyes caught mine and he almost smiled right before his lips curved downward. He hung his head and walked over to us. "I guess you heard all that," he said.

"Yeah. Hard not to," I replied.

"Sorry about the rock. Did I hit you?"

"Yeah, but it's nothing. Is your mom really bent out of shape over you not getting married yet? You're only eighteen."

"Nineteen next week," Zach corrected. "Speaking of which, we are getting together, right?"

"Oh, yeah. Of course."

Zach shifted his gaze to Keith. "And you can bring your friend."

"Keith," Keith said, sticking his hand out to shake Zach's.

"Keith, right, Flynn told me about you. You're an artist or something?"

Keith nodded.

For a second I thought Keith was going to tell Zach that he was my boyfriend, but he didn't. He just sat there quietly, as if waiting for me to add more information. I didn't. "Yup, he's the artist, and our friends Grace and Kelly are in the pool, but don't change the subject. What's got your mom all hell-bent?"

Zach's fraction of a smile disappeared, but he should have known by now I wasn't going to let it go. We knew each other far too well for that. I noticed how pink his cheek was, but I'd avoid mentioning it for the sake of his pride. If he asked to talk later, after Keith left, I'd understand, but I wanted to press it now if he was willing.

Zach stepped over to the porch and took a seat next to me. I felt Keith's fingers on my elbow, gently stroking. It made me nervous to think he might make a bolder move by tucking his arm around my waist or something, but so far he remained surreptitious. I carried on nonchalantly, looking at my best friend, and waiting on his explanation.

Zach spoke quietly, either to keep his mom from possibly overhearing, or because what he was going to say was more serious than I thought. "How much did you hear?"

"Um, I don't know." I glanced at Keith and then back to Zach. "That part about getting married."

He huffed and rolled his eyes. "Oh, Flynn, you don't know the half of it. You only heard the last part of the argument. It started in my room when she asked if I ever surfed porn."

"What?" I questioned sharply. I thought that was a weird question for his mother to ask. What mom *ever* asked that?

"Yeah. Just what I wanted to talk about with my mom at ten in the morning."

I looked at Keith, and back to Zach again. "But isn't it noon?"

"Yes. We've been going at it for a while now. I think it's the longest argument in the history of my family. She normally doesn't keep going, but it wasn't as heated in the beginning."

"But why'd she ask about the porn?"

"She heard about a kid up the street getting busted in school for surfing porn."

Keith almost busted out laughing, but I appreciated how he contained himself. "What idiot does that?" he asked. "I thought the school's computers had filtering software and stuff."

Zach answered him. "They do. He was messing with his phone during lunch and a teacher walked past him. She saw what he was watching over his shoulder. He got suspended. He might have gotten expelled, I don't know."

"Didn't that happen in May?" asked Keith. "I thought I heard about that guy."

Zach nodded. "Yeah. My mom is a little slow. She abhors gossip, yet seems to think gathering facts about local kids is acceptable because it 'affects her family.' Whatever. She found out it was a kid up the street and suddenly he became a bad influence on the other boys in the neighborhood. She came up to my room and asked about searching porn, right before she transitioned into postulating that the whole street was full of sinners going to hell. I'm telling you Flynn, I'm glad I went away to college. I'm not sure how much more I can take."

Keith's caressing fingers poked my thigh. I shot a glance at him and narrowed my eyes. What was he suggesting? Did he want me to question Zach's beliefs about gay rights just then or something? I ignored him. "How do you mean?" I asked Zach.

"It's like..." he paused, running his hand over the top of his head, thinking. "People always joke about being an adult when you turn eighteen. It's a joke, because for the most part I don't think many of us are ready to go live on our own, independent of our parents, and be responsible twenty-four-seven. But for me it's like my mom and dad took it seriously. The day I turned eighteen last year, a switch flipped in Mom's brain that told her I should have it all figured out. She treats me like I should know everything, then gets shitty with me when I don't. I've never pretended to know it all. I've never acted as if my parents were stupid. You know I always asked questions and paid attention growing up. I didn't rebel. I didn't go against any of their wishes. I pretty much watched what my older brother and sister did and made sure I didn't make the same mistakes. It wasn't that difficult."

Zach touched my hand. "You follow what I'm saying, right? I've tried so hard to be everything they wanted, but now… I don't know anymore, Flynn. She was seconds away from asking to check my browser history when Clark texted and that's when she morphed into a lecture on marriage. My mom is seriously wacked." As soon as he said that word, his shoulders bunched and he ducked his head a fraction, glancing over toward their house, as if checking to make sure she hadn't heard.

I could see the strain in his eyes. There was something he wasn't saying. His expression bordered on one signaling his need for us to assume our positions on his bed and stare up at the ceiling. Did he require that privacy to share his deepest feelings? I hoped not. I didn't want to ditch Keith in order to help Zach sort through his problems. "I bet she wasn't too thrilled with your lack of virginity."

"You heard that, too?"

Zach sounded embarrassed. I nodded, thinking I probably shouldn't have pointed it out.

"No, she wasn't," Zach said. He didn't have to add that it was at that point at which his mother hit him. The evidence was still on his cheek.

"Why?" Keith asked, very innocently. I appreciate that he was trying to understand, but I felt bad for Zach.

"Our church has a strong stand on sexual purity. That's why Amy was worried about, well, you know." Indeed I did, but I could tell Zach didn't want to voice it in front of Keith. "They preach no drinking, no sex, no drugs, no smoking, no working on the Sabbath; pretty much anything that has an unhealthy impact on living a Godly life."

"That sounds dumb," Keith muttered.

"Keith," I chastised him. "Don't be rude." He'd *just* meet Zach.

Keith continued anyway, in a more assertive tone, much to my chagrin. "I'm not. I'm being logical. At the rate at which our culture is evolving, it stands to reason that churches whose beliefs don't acknowledge this societal change will diminish or disappear completely. Personally, I come from what could be considered a very religious, Christian family, yet they don't see change as bad, but as something to be understood and integrated. All culture changes as society grows. Our country has to evolve to embrace the diversity we have simply from all the countries that seek refuge on our shores. We're supposed to be 'one nation under God,' but there are too many opinions about who God is to make the 'one nation' part of the creed plausible.

"And as far as keeping a list of don'ts so that your congregation will learn to live a Godly life, I think it's ignorant at best. The law of God is there to point out our *inability* to meet God's standards. To say 'no sex' will insure Godly purity is naïve and small-minded. Jesus even pointed out that lusting after a woman is the same as adultery because in a lusting man's heart he's already desired sex and thus tarnished his purity. We're intelligent beings who think that by making lists of rules we can do it better than the next guy, but we miss the point by striving with our feeble human efforts. It's not that I'm against sexual purity, but I think the concept of why some keep it is foundationally wrong."

I stared at him a moment. Shocked. I think it was the longest I'd ever heard him speak at one time. Although I could tell from being around him, Keith was not shy about saying what he thought about anything. I raised my eyebrow and commented, "Okaaay."

"Yeah, well, I didn't mean to burden you or start any political or religious discussions." Zach rubbed his hand over his short brown hair, like he normally did when he was nervous or unsure of what to say. He breathed a sigh and said, "I'm sorry Flynn."

I shrugged. "It's fine. You can talk to me about anything." I hoped he knew it was true.

"I don't mean to be a pain in the ass," Keith added. "I'm just tired of people insisting that refraining from the 'evil pleasures' of life will somehow make them better than everyone else. I'll shut up now."

Zach and I eyeballed each other for a minute, silence growing, tension rising, until Zach's eyes widened as if a thought had occurred to him. He asked, "Did you hear about the guy who lives next to the funeral home on the corner?"

Squirrel moment, I laughed in my head. Zach had those often. "Mr. Blevins?" I hadn't heard anything about the man. He normally kept to himself. I thought he was my dad's friend, though.

"Yeah. My mom said he's gay," Zach said.

Okay. I didn't like talking about religion, but *this* subject was worse.

"My mom suggested we get a petition together to force him out of the neighborhood since the middle school is basically behind his house. She thinks he's going to abduct kids or something." Zach stood up and shifted his weight as if he had needles and pins in his foot.

"That's ridiculous," I said, shocked to hear he was gay, but even more that Mrs. Mitchell would want to force him to leave the neighborhood. "Do you… think he should leave?" I was scared to ask. If Zach said yes, it would confirm for me where our relationship stood, and that it would end if he knew I was gay.

Zach looked bothered by my question. He glanced away and said, "I don't know. My opinion doesn't matter anyway." He stuck out his hand to Keith. "It was nice meeting you, but I gotta jet."

Keith shook his hand and I jumped up to follow Zach as he hastily left. "Hey wait," I said, grabbing his arm before he could escape. "Your opinion always matters." He gave me a half smile, but he would not meet my eyes. I felt the need to press him. "Zach, what are you not saying? You know you can talk to me." When he remained silent, nervously shifting his eyes to his house and then back at me, I touched his arm and softly added, "Do you want me to come over? We can go to your room and talk like we always do."

Zach stiffened and pulled his arm from my grasp. "I'm not a little kid anymore." The harshness of his tone was not lost on me. In fact, it hurt.

"I never said you were."

"Look, Flynn, I hate to say this, but there are some things I just don't want share with you."

I wasn't sure what had changed in the last few months. It had only been last September when we talked about my need to visit my mom and deal with my grief. He seemed perfectly fine lying on his bed with me then. "But you'll share them with my dead brother?" I shot back with attitude.

His eyes widened for a second. I don't think he expected my quick reaction to being blown off. "As a matter of fact, yes. Sometimes it's easier to talk to Nate because he doesn't judge me. Nate doesn't talk back, and he certainly doesn't pressure me."

"What? When have I ever—"

"Go back to your friends, Flynn. I'm done here." He reached into his pocket and took out his cell phone. Before I could say anything he answered a call. "Hello? Oh hey. Yeah, I'm still on. Yup. Okay. Hold on a second."

Zach pulled the phone away from his mouth long enough to say, "It's Tom. I gotta—"

"Go. I know."

"I'll see you next week."

I watched as Zach slipped back into his house as if nothing had happened, talking on the phone to his other friend. Had college changed him? Or had he always viewed me as a "little kid?"

When I felt Keith's hand on my lower back, I was too stunned to fear Zach seeing. Besides, I doubted Zach would even notice since Tom's call was apparently more important. "Jeez. Rude much?" Keith commented.

I would have defended Zach in any other context, but I knew Keith was right. "I guess he has his reasons," I said weakly, turning to face my boyfriend. "I'm sorry. I should have told him."

Keith shrugged and settled his hands on my hips. "It's okay. Given the circumstances of the fight and what his mom said about the man down the street, I guess I can forgive you." He held a straight face for a few seconds and then smiled so I'd know he wasn't mad. "He's got to work out his own stuff. I won't hold it against you for waiting until the time is right. Besides, I saw his cheek."

"Thanks." I took Keith's hand and led him into the house and closed the door before leaning forward and kissing him gently. "You're a great boyfriend."

He grinned and shrugged in his Keith-like manner. "I try to be. So, what's next week? A backyard Polka party?"

I smirked. "No. It's my birthday." I looped my arms around his waist before I added, "And Zach's birthday."

"Ah, the shared birthday event. If he's so emphatic about not being a kid anymore, why does this tradition linger?"

"I don't know. I guess because he's been my best friend since my brother died. We've always celebrated together."

"If your brother was still here, do you think you'd be best friends?"

I pulled away. "What kind of a question is that?" I crossed my arms over my chest.

"One that makes sense. People often bond over traumatic events who may not have done so otherwise. Haven't you ever thought about it?"

I turned away. "No."

"I'm sorry. I just don't see why you're so stuck on Zach. He seems kind of condescending to me, with the whole comment about 'not being a little kid.' He blew you off rather harshly, if you ask me."

I whipped around. "I didn't ask you."

Keith stepped back. "No. You didn't. You also didn't think it important enough to tell him I was your boyfriend."

"You just said you forgave me!"

"I did. But if you're going to be an ass every time I ask a simple question, then I'm not going to pretend it didn't hurt."

"And you weren't acting like an ass by disrespecting his religion? Keith, come on! That was rude."

He shrugged. I hated when he shrugged like he wasn't bothered by anything. In fact, sometimes I hated how unaffected he was. "I was simply saying what I thought; given that he sounded as if he didn't like the way they run the church anyway."

I was going to yell, but I stopped. It didn't make any sense to have an argument right after we'd overheard Zach and his mother doing the same thing. If Keith and I disagreed, it didn't need to be advertised. "Can we just… let it go?"

He nodded, but by the way he crossed his arms loosely over his chest, I knew he was hurt. He wasn't looking at me, and this great day that started with sunscreen and kissing had gone down a path I regretted. I didn't like the tension between us.

"Keith. I'm sorry. Zach hasn't blown me off for his other friends in years. No, I've never thought about our friendship as just a result of my brother's death. I don't think about what-ifs. What if my brother and mother never died? What if my dad had remarried years ago? What if we'd moved after the accident because Dad said the house was too big for the two of us? I hate those questions."

Keith must have gotten it, because he reached for me. I settled against his chest as we held each other. Keith whispered, "I'll go with you next week. I promise not to give us away."

I squeezed him tightly. He had to be the nicest, most understanding boyfriend in the world. "Thank you."

***

July 2, 2011

For the life of me, I couldn't understand why I thought celebrating my birthday with my best friend would go well if I invited my boyfriend to come along. How the hell was I supposed to keep the two most important parts of my life separate? In hindsight, I suppose the answer was I shouldn't have. The pieces needed to be part of a whole.

Things between Keith and me were relatively new. We were past the initial flirting stage, where our relationship hadn't been too hard to conceal. Kelly and Grace came along to help defuse the attention we would garner if we had shown up just the two of us, and the plan had worked! But afterward, Kelly made a point of telling me how hurt Keith was that I hadn't said anything about our relationship to Zach or to his friends. I didn't think one more day would matter so much. Or one more week, or one more month. Boy, was I wrong.

As he drove me back to my house, the argument started.

"Tell me again why I went with you? Because I saw absolutely no reason for me to be there. It was you and Zach and his friends, while Kelly, Grace and I twiddled our thumbs."

Keith was pissed. He had said he understood why I wasn't ready to come out to Zach, but he didn't really—not when he got bent out of shape over sitting across from me. I knew he wanted to sit next to me when we had arrived, but I also knew he probably would have accidentally taken my hand or leaned over and kissed my ear while whispering to me. Since school had let out, our relationship had become way more "touchy." I liked it, don't get me wrong, but I knew he wasn't going to be able to restrain himself one hundred percent in front of Zach. I knew he'd slip up. So, I chose to sit across from him when the waitress sat us at a large booth. Tom had arrived late, so he got seated at the end.

"I thought Greg did a great job trying to engage you all in the conversation." I was trying to be positive. Greg did seem like a great guy, just as Zach had described.

"He did, but my point is that *you* didn't." Keith paced my room, which was kind of hard, since there wasn't a lot of space to walk. It was more like he took two long strides and turned around. I sat on my bed watching him. "I felt like a third wheel. Or maybe a fifth wheel considering how many people were there."

"It wasn't that bad."

Keith stopped and gawked at me. "What? Where were you sitting?" Then he slapped his leg. "Oh, yeah, that's right. You were sitting with birthday boy number one and his college buddies! You were a part of the in-crowd while the girls and I watched from a distance."

"You were at the same table."

"No, I wasn't. We were the nerdy high schoolers watching the jock table in the lunchroom. We were the artsy outsiders wondering what it would be like to be that popular kid."

"You aren't like that," I countered.

"No. It was a metaphor." His anger twisted his growl into biting sarcasm. He was also getting louder. I hoped my dad couldn't hear him. "But you were on the cool-kid side of the table, Flynn, yuckin' it up like you were in the same fraternity. Why? Because all the stories were about you and Zach. I felt like an outsider, and you just left me hanging there."

"I didn't mean to," I pleaded.

"Yes, you did. The minute we walked in the restaurant you took a step to the left and put too much space between us. You chose him over me. I'm your *boyfriend*, Flynn. I didn't like being treated as if I had the plague. Guy friends can stand next to each other without anyone assuming they're a couple. We would have been fine."

"I was afraid you'd touch me and he'd see." It *was* what I feared. I thought it was only fair to say what I'd been thinking.

"I told you I wouldn't. That just proves how little you trust me."

"I trust you."

"No you don't. You think I'm going to paw all over you every time we're out in public, and that's just not true. I have self-restraint. I am able to be near you and not touch you. We fucking did that most of the school year. I just don't *want* to not touch you. I *want* to be a couple like other couples, but you don't want that. I know this is all new for you, but we've been dating for months. You need to get over this irrational fear of your religious neighbors finding out you're gay. Your dad likes me, can't that be enough?"

Logically, Keith was right. But emotionally, I wasn't ready to have that talk with Zach. I didn't want to look Keith in the face, so I stared at his shoes. He'd worn the same gray All Stars every day since I'd met him. Maybe I should surprise him with another pair. "I need more time," I whispered, almost unwilling to hear myself say the words. I knew he didn't want to hear it.

"More time?" His voice went up. "Fine. Take all the time you need, Flynn, but I'm done."

I looked up when I heard the door slam. I called after him, "Keith?" I jumped up when he didn't answer, and raced down the steps. I grabbed his arm as he was exiting the house. "Stop. Wait a second."

Keith pulled his arm from my grasp. "Wait?" he asked shrilly. "I've been waiting. If you aren't willing to suck it up and grow a pair, then we're done."

"But…."

"Go cry to your best friend who *isn't* me."

Keith shut the door in my face before I had the chance to think of a reply. I understood Keith's point, but I didn't understand why he had to have things his way all the time. I had only ever asked him to give me time to come out to Zach. That was it. I wandered back up to my room and stood in front of my window.

Zach's room was opposite mine. His curtains were drawn. I remembered so clearly the times we'd sit in our respective windows and talk for hours. I think we'd both been in middle school then. Maybe. It didn't seem so long ago that we laughed about everything.

Tonight, though, had been strained. I flopped down on my bed as I thought about it.

I hadn't wanted things to get so out of control that Keith would break up with me. I'd only wanted a nice birthday dinner, just as it had always been when Zach and I celebrated together. But things had changed. Zach had been different. His friends were different. I wasn't sure what I had expected when we went, but I felt the tension. I liked Zach's new college friends. Greg had been great. But I could also see that the differences between Zach's friends and my friends made it difficult to carry on a conversation. To be fair, it was the first time we'd gotten together as a group. Perhaps we all simply needed more time to get to know one another. Maybe a pool party?

I took out my phone and texted Keith: *Can we talk?*

He texted back: *No. Find another boyfriend to string along.*

I set my phone on the table next to the bed, trudged over to turn off my light, and then shed my shirt and shorts before sliding under the covers.

Tomorrow would be lonely without Keith.

A few days later, I texted him and didn't receive a reply. I hadn't treated him well, but my behavior didn't deserve this type of dare I say, irrational response. I had noticed before that Keith was very moody in his interactions with his family and sometimes his friends. Maybe he just needed time to cool off. I thought the break could be a good thing, since the push and pull between us had obviously been harder on him than me. In the meantime, I could figure out what had been going on with Zach. Our dinner conversation notwithstanding, he wasn't talking to me either.

Chapter 6

July 14, 2011: Words Though Silence

I heard the rain pounding outside my open window like a bucket of marbles spilling onto a snare drum. I tried to ignore it and fall back asleep because I really liked the sound of rain, but then a light flashed in front of my closed lids and a peal of thunder shook my house. I shot to a sitting position. I wasn't afraid of storms, I rather liked them, but there was something about the incredible force of nature during a thunderstorm that can make even the bravest person shake; even if only for a moment.

I got out of bed and went to my window to see if the rain was coming in. Occasionally it did, depending on which way the wind was blowing. Because my house was so close to Zach's there wasn't much space to drive the wind my way or his, so my carpet was generally safe. I felt mist coming through the screen, but only a little. I glanced up and spied Zach across the way staring at me. I guessed he was awakened by the storm too. We both stood frozen for several minutes, staring, unable to turn away and yet reluctant to speak. Not that I could have heard him over the rain. Then he pointed at me, pointed to himself, and pointed down twice.

I gave him the thumbs-up and swallowed hard.

Zach and I hadn't spent much time together in the past year.

I'd seen him last Thanksgiving when he awkwardly came over and invited my dad and me to his house. It shouldn't have been awkward, as we had eaten with his family almost every year since forever. His family was like family to me. Amy even treated me like a little brother and asked about my grades and if I had a girlfriend yet. I liked her. I often wondered if she'd think of me differently if she knew I had a *boyfriend* instead.

I'd seen Zach at Christmas briefly, but my dad told me he was done going over to their house for dinner. He'd given Zach's mom an excuse about making our own traditions, and that was that. Dad and I had worked on making dinner together at Christmas and it had been wonderful spending time with him. Making new traditions sounded good to me.

All winter, all spring, and halfway through summer, though, I had only seen Zach a handful of times and probably texted even less. The distance between us felt strange, but it hadn't felt as painful as seeing him for that birthday dinner earlier in the month. He had joked and gone over all the "old times" we had spent goofing off, but he'd also seemed very fake. I think it was the first time I'd seen him playful without showing affection.

If Zach was implying he needed to talk now, in the middle of a rainstorm, I'd take it.

I quietly made my way downstairs and out the kitchen door. The small porch on that side of the house faced Zach's house and had enough room to sit under the overhanging roof that we wouldn't get wet. Of course, his mad dash over had him dripping already. His chest heaved, and drops of water clung to his nose. Just like the moment in our respective windows, we stood there staring at each other like strangers, or estranged lovers, or maybe just as friends who had lost each other in a flood and presumed the other was dead. We stared, breathed, and waited.

But something in my mind told me I needed to make the first move. Zach had been pulling back from me incrementally for years. Ever since the kiss we shared, things had been increasingly strange. He pulled back so far in ninth- and the first half of tenth-grade that I had been pleasantly surprised when he had started talking to me again. And even though I was glad he was still talking, it hadn't been the same. When he'd told me he "wasn't a child anymore," the thought still stung. I had never thought of him as a child. He'd always been so mature. I'd always looked up to him.

So before Zach decided he couldn't open up, I stepped out into the open and let the rain crash down on me until I was as soaking wet as Zach. When I stepped back under the porch, he was smiling and shaking his head. I motioned for us to sit and we both got comfortable sitting against the siding next to the door, legs stretched out, shoulders touching. He looked at me with such serious eyes as the drops of water fell off his hair and ran down his face before he shifted his attention to our outstretched legs and hands resting in our laps. Zach reached over and took my hand, lacing our fingers together. He tilted his head back against the house and closed his eyes, squeezing my hand reassuringly. It felt like he needed to know I was really there, that this wasn't a dream.

I didn't know what else to do, so I watched him. I wanted to talk, but the rain was so loud I would've had to yell, and by then we wouldn't be alone because my dad would probably hear and his dad would hear and we might as well have invited the whole damn neighborhood to our private moment on the porch. Time together listening to the rain was better than long silences apart pretending we were fine, but knowing our friendship was broken.

Zach's eyes remained shut so I wasn't sure if he knew I was watching him, or if he thought I had tilted my head back onto the house the same as he did. I didn't know. It was dark, but every time the lightning flashed I could see him clearly. During another flash, I noticed his lips trembling. I waited. A minute later, as a blinding flash illuminated the porch, the house, and every hidden place among the shadows, my eyes caught a glimpse of water dripping from the corner of Zach's eye. It wasn't the rain. It could only be tears that formed such a perfect river down the side of his face. A peal of thunder, like that of a metal gong, shook my house and I jumped. Zach's grip on my hand tightened, but he didn't open his eyes.

Instead, he curled into me, against my shoulder, and sobbed. I felt his free hand grab my waist as he stretched his arm across my stomach. He buried his face in my neck and cried like I had never seen him do before. His whole body quaked. I reached up and stroked his wet hair, the back of his neck, and down his shoulder.

Time stretched on and I didn't care about the pain in my back or the chill seeping into my bones, as long as Zach was in my arms; safe, protected from whatever demons haunted him. Even after he'd stopped crying, Zach didn't let go of me. I wasn't sure if he kept his face tucked against my neck out of embarrassment, or whether he really needed the solace my arms provided, but nothing mattered except being there for him. His treatment of me when I had questioned him last year didn't matter. Ignoring me every time I texted and making excuses as to why he couldn't talk didn't matter. All I could think about was how much pressure he had to be under to break down like this. I had to assume it was pressure, because if he was this torn up due to a death in the family or of a friend, I was certain he would have told me about it. No, this was something else.

When the sky lightened enough to see the house and yard beyond the torrential downpour, Zach leaned back.

He looked scared and worried, and more vulnerable than ever. I think he wondered if I would question him. Maybe he thought I would demand answers and ask for things he wasn't ready to give. But as the minutes passed and I remained silent, Zach's distress drained from his eyes and washed away like the salt off our skin. He even attempted a weak smile as he studied my face and his eyes danced over my features. He reached up and caressed my cheek and jaw, but as unexpected as his tenderness was, so was his abrupt stiffness as he pulled away and stood.

The look in his eyes reminded me of the time he had kissed me years ago—pained, resentful, fearful. Why had I thought of that now?

The rain wasn't as loud as before, but he leaned in and spoke into my ear. His breath was hot against my cold skin. "I have to go," he said, straightening and pointing his thumb over his shoulder.

I nodded and he backed away into the rain, out of the sanctuary of our stolen moment.

***

A week went by after the thunder shook my house and Zach's tears shook my heart. I couldn't understand why he hadn't texted or anything. He had to know I'd be concerned. What friend wouldn't be? I rarely saw Zach cry, and certainly nothing that rivaled an onslaught of grief. Something was wrong, and he wasn't sharing. It hurt.

I wanted Zach to need me like I needed him.

Keith wasn't around. It had been almost three weeks since he had stormed out and left me. No texts, no nothing. I missed him, but I also wanted to give him space to cool off. If he hadn't made a move by September, I'd call him. Or maybe I'd show up at his house. For now, I was okay with some distance because it gave me a chance to think about Zach and how I'd eventually tell him I was gay.

Sometimes I wished it was like sharing your major or discussing the weather in New Zealand. "Hey, yeah, I'm an anthropology major, you? Oh, cool! By the way, I'm gay. Yup. So, you live in New Zealand? I've always wanted to go there." But no, telling a friend you're gay wasn't as easy as some people assumed it was. Not for me.

For one, there are political agendas for which my support would be assumed. I don't mind if others parade down the street in a Speedo, but don't ask me to sign a petition that says men and women should be *allowed* to walk down the street half-naked and not expect criticism. I'm all for tact. I'm gay;

I'm not a nudist. I don't want to parade my junk in front of the world, or I'd be an underwear model. It's not like I'm ashamed of being gay; I'm just not a fan of ridicule.

A lesbian couple at school got belligerent about LGBT rights when a teacher asked them to stop kissing in the halls. I remembered seeing them a couple of times. It wasn't the kissing that was an issue for me, or for the teacher; it was the near-sex they were having in front of the lockers, hands down the other's pants. Why should anyone, gay, straight or otherwise, be allowed to do that? Still, that anti-gay card was thrown on the table, and suddenly the teacher was accused of being intolerant. I disagreed. Which I guess was one reason I didn't want to come out.

I didn't want to be associated with a pair like that; who used the accusation of intolerance to their advantage. I didn't want to get labeled as intolerant myself, either; I wanted to be left blissfully alone.

The word "pride" can mean many things to different people. I was proud I had a father who worked hard every day to support me. I was proud I lived in a country that didn't kill people over their sexual orientation. I was proud that a couple of states had legalized same-sex marriage, just in case I ever wanted to get married. I was glad I could live free in my decisions, once I chose them, but choosing to live openly gay was still *my* choice. I was a little peeved at Keith for pressuring me.

His coming-out process had been easy. His family was accepting and open about it.

I remembered meeting his family for the first time over spring break when we were "dating" but hadn't actually kissed more than a couple of times. I had been super paranoid about it until school had let out. His mom took our picture and immediately uploaded it to the digital picture frame she had hanging in the kitchen. I was his first boyfriend and she wanted to commemorate it. It had been sweet, yet terrifyingly surreal. I couldn't picture Zach's family exhibiting a fraction of the amount of love I felt in Keith's family's presence.

Zach's family had been like my own growing up. My dad had been a workaholic since I'd been little, so I had spent practically every day at their house. Zach and I had studied together, eaten together, even slept together in his tiny bed a bunch of times when I'd stayed over. We'd always been close. I feared the repercussions of coming out because I feared losing what little family I had in them. Aside from my dad, I had no other blood relatives to speak of. Maybe a cousin or two, but I didn't know them. Zach's family had adopted me in a sense, so was it so wrong to worry about losing them if they disagreed with my choice to live *out*?

Or worse, would they view my DNA as an abomination or perversion of "that which is Holy?" I couldn't help who I was. I was born this way. I've always liked boys as far back as I could remember. I would have loved to talk to my mom about it. I wish I had broached it while she was still alive. I'm sure she would have understood. She'd always had a light in her eyes and I'm convinced it was God shining down on me through her.

I wasn't afraid of God. I didn't think He hated me, but I wasn't going to share my opinion on that with Zach any time soon. His belief system was different from mine. I appreciated Keith's take on God, even if he was outspoken about it occasionally. It did seem logical and thoroughly articulate. I felt like God was always with me, especially after I visited my mom's grave last November. I should probably go more often, but it had been very painful to see her name etched in granite. Maybe I'd go again this year and coax my dad into joining me.

I pulled myself over the edge of the pool and found Zach standing by the gate, watching me. I felt like a fool. I knew I'd been pondering life a little too long as I swam, and that made me worry that I could also have been talking to myself without realizing. I hoped Zach wouldn't make fun of me.

I sat there with my feet still underwater, swishing them around, after Zach lifted his chin at me. He lumbered over, slowly and reluctantly, but I couldn't understand why. I hadn't pressured him to talk since that night in the rain.

"Hey," I said.

"Hey," he said, sitting next to me.

"Your butt's going to get wet." Pool water was all over the cement patio from my cannonballs off the diving board.

"I don't care."

I could sit quietly and wait, but should I? I had given him space and he hadn't texted, now he was suddenly here. "Do you want to talk?"

"Not really."

"Zach, you know that I care about you, right?"

"Yeah. Is Keith here?"

"Non sequitur much?" I almost laughed as I used a phrase Keith would have used. I liked that I had picked up some of his habits. Which may or may not have come from his unhealthy obsession with Buffy The Vampire Slayer. *I really miss him.* "No. Keith's not here."

"Kelly?"

"No."

"Or the pretty one. What's her name, Grace?"

"Yes, Grace. And they're both pretty, but she's not here either."

He grinned. "Yeah. So, no one's here?"

"Nope." Didn't I just say that? Zach was acting weird.

I loved the feel of the water on my feet. It always had a soothing effect on me. I could have been anxious, but as I swished my feet and watched a leaf swirl and float on the water, I relaxed, knowing the conversation would happen in its own time.

"Don't you have a job yet, slacker?" He nudged my arm with his shoulder.

"No. Asshole. The lead singer of All Time Low is still with the band."

He laughed out loud, mocking me. "You want to sing with All Time Low?"

"Maybe." *Either that or sleep with the rhythm guitarist.* I told him, "I could do it. I could sing like Alex Gaskarth. I'm just as hot as he is." He laughed at me more. I liked seeing him relax as I joked. It was good to break the tension. I nudged him back. "No," I said, feeling like I should at least answer his question. "I don't have a job yet. I just got my provisional license last week, but I don't have a car. Dad keeps me busy with yard work and chores, so I'm fine without one." I didn't go into details of how I got my driving hours in and I hoped he wouldn't ask. Mrs. Leppo had been kind enough to drive with me.

"So you're like a Cinderella."

"No. Cinderella didn't get paid. Dad gives me an allowance for all the work I do around here. Plus, I weed gardens and trim hedges for some neighbors. I don't really need a job."

He grinned. "And he doesn't lock you in a tower or make you wear a dress, so I guess you have it pretty good."

"Dude, you have the weirdest sense of humor."

Zach sort of chuckled, but it was strained, as though he was searching for something amusing to say. As the laughing quieted down, the tension ratcheted up my back. Why did I get the daunting impression something bad was about to happen? Tick-tock, tick-tock, the water in the pool felt cooler as my bare back sucked in the sun's heat like a basketball court blacktop. I leaned forward and scooped some water and splashed it on my face and neck.

"How come you never come by to swim anymore? It's been at least a year, maybe two."

Zach stared across to the diving board. Was he thinking about the back-flips he used to do off it? His silence worried me. Finally, he said, "I don't know. I guess I lost my desire to swim. One too many sunburns or something."

I didn't buy it. Unlike mine, Zach's skin tanned easily. I tried another subject. "Are you still seeing the cashier from Arby's?" I asked.

"Kaitlyn? No. After the fight, my mom called her mom and told her I wasn't going to be around anymore. She said I needed to grow up, and that her daughter wasn't the kind of girl she wanted as a daughter-in-law."

"Ouch! That's cold."

Zach bobbed his head, but I guessed there wasn't much to say about it after that. Zach had dated several girls in high school. Kaitlyn wasn't the one who took his virginity. Deanna Devilbliss could boast about that. She'd been the girl who Zach told me sat on Ricky Middleborough's lap in the limo ride home after prom. And when I say "sat," I mean "fucked." He'd been better off without her, but Kaitlyn didn't deserve such a harsh putdown. Zach's mom's comment was downright mean.

"Flynn," he said very seriously. "Has your dad ever hit you?"

The ice in my chest contrasted the heat on my back. *Shit*, this was serious. "No. He works a lot, and falls asleep after he drinks too much Scotch."

"Hmm."

Not a very committal "hmm" if I had ever heard one. Did that mean his dad had hit him or not? I broached carefully, "Has yours?"

I knew about a time years ago that his dad had hit him because of a broken umbrella. Another time, right before Zach's high school graduation, his father had hit him, and I saw it through the window, but I couldn't imagine what could have occurred lately. Although, Zach *did* get into that argument with his mother only weeks before crying on my shoulder in the rain.

I sat. I swished. I worried.

"Yes," he said like a whisper full of dismay and misery. Then to make the sickness in my stomach turn to acid, he lifted the hem of his shirt and revealed a dark purple line down the side of his ribs. I could not imagine what his father used to make that sort of mark. An iron rod? Where the hell would he even get one?

Zach was watching the water in the pool, but I think he knew what was going through my mind because he added, "Golf club."

The words made me sick to my stomach. Somehow, I found enough voice to offer, "You can stay here if you need to." I didn't know what else I could possibly do. For a family who preached so often about the importance of being Holy and good, I had witnessed all too often things that would shock the neighborhood if they only knew what happened behind the Mitchells' closed doors.

And that bruise… it was awful.

"Thanks." His whisper carried a little hope with it that time. "I'm glad you're my friend."

"I'll always be your friend."

"Even if I can't tell you everything?"

I hated the word "can't," but I didn't want to fuss at him for using it. I needed to suck it up and be the friend he needed, the friend who didn't pressure him to conform to my needs. I had to let Zach be Zach and trust that he'd tell me when he felt he could. At least he showed me the reason for his silence, even if it made me sick thinking about it.

His hand was resting on the curved edge of the pool, inches from mine. I reached over and clasped his fingers. "Even if you can't tell me everything."

Zach squeezed my fingers, but then let them go and stood up rapidly. "I have to go. I have an internship with a forestry board. I need to meet with someone to talk about labeling trees on the community college campus."

It was the first I'd heard of him talking about work. "Cool. Sounds neat." I stood up with him. "You get to use all the tree knowledge you're learning."

I made him grin. "Something like that." He took a step backward. "And, um, I'm sorry about the other day. The comment I made about being a little kid—I was out of line."

"It's okay."

"No. I mean it. I shouldn't have said that. We've always had our heart-to-hearts that way and I shouldn't have cut you down in front of your friend. I guess I just don't know how to talk seriously like that anymore."

"But we just did." I hoped to make him see it was okay, even though I was disappointed to know we'd probably never be in that same place again. The distance between us was growing with age and all I could hope for was that Zach would find another way to communicate before everything we had as children faded into dust.

Zach smiled warmly, and I think he got my meaning. "Thanks, Flynn."

"Anytime."

Zach walked away and disappeared beyond the bushes, leaving me to the pool and the sun and the solitude of my backyard.

Chapter 7

July 31, 2011: Break-Ups And Make-Ups

Weeks went by, too many in fact, but not enough to fast-forward summer vacation. It was still technically July. I was stacking dishes in the dishwasher when heard a knock at the front door. I opened it to find Keith standing there in his khaki shorts and gray plaid, button-down, with the sleeves rolled up, open in the front to reveal his white T-shirt underneath. He scuffed his shoe on the step and paused before looking up. I thought he'd look more excited to see me, but something in his eyes seemed sad. It worried me. I'd been dealing with enough dreariness this month; I needed a little bit more happy in my life.

"Keith," I said, holding in my excitement. I didn't want to appear as desperate as I was to hold him.

"Can we talk?"

I nodded and opened the door wider.

"Is your dad home?" he asked, scanning the living room as he entered.

"No. You just missed him. I think there are still some pancakes and bacon if you're hungry." I closed the door and turned around.

"No. Thanks." He walked in a wide circle, scanning the room and hall as if making sure I was telling the truth that no one was home.

I met him in the middle of the room. "How've you been?" I asked casually, restraining myself until I saw some positive reaction come from him first. So far, he seemed uneasy.

"Fine. I got a job at Target stocking shelves and stuff. Been doing that for a couple weeks."

"Cool." I nodded. The awkward tension between us irritated me, but I figured that if he was here to talk, I didn't want to ruin a good thing before it started. I could work up to telling him how much I'd missed him. Then minutes passed and we weren't talking and he looked more restless. I started with, "What's wrong? Why do you look so worried? Is everything okay at home?"

"I…" he stammered. "I th-think we should get back together."

I widened my eyes. "You what?" I was hoping he'd come to suggest that, but I wasn't going to be so presumptuous. I never dreamed he'd be so blunt.

"I said, I think we should—"

I kissed him. I wasn't going to waste time talking about it. If he wanted me, I already knew how much I wanted him. He moved his hands over my hips and around my back, as I held his face with both hands. I kissed him deeply and I heard his moan of approval as I pressed my hips into him.

Four weeks apart was apparently way too long for both of us. We came at each other like animals, pawing and grabbing and pulling at each other's clothes. I stepped back far enough to undo his belt. Keith was breathing hard as I pulled the belt free and unzipped his jeans. He gasped as I slipped my hand inside his pants, grabbing his cock through the fabric of his underwear. He whimpered and closed his eyes, standing there gape-mouthed before me as I rubbed up and down his growing erection.

I hadn't kept track of when we decided to officially date before the breakup. I think it had been February, but we'd sort of been together since the fall. In that time we hadn't done anything but kiss. Sure, I had felt his arousal up against me a few times when we snuggled watching a movie, and I am sure he had felt mine, but we hadn't tried anything until now. I guessed all it took to break the holding pattern was a little time apart.

I retracted my hand and tugged at his shirt. "Off."

Keith opened his eyes and removed both shirts without question. I yanked mine over my head at the same time and then the two of us looked like uncoordinated six-year-olds undressing after playing in the snow, wrestling with snow pants and boots. I hopped on one foot as I tugged at my sock, which stretched like a rubber band as it stuck to my sweaty foot and then snapped off the end of my toes, throwing me off balance so I practically knocked over an end table full of books and DVDs. At the same time, Keith's head collided with mine after he slipped off his jeans and we both stood up.

"Ow." I rubbed my head.

"Sorry."

Then we both started laughing.

"I don't think this is what I pictured happening when I came over here."

"Do you want to move to the couch?" I suggested.

"No. I remember the last time we were making out on that couch. Your dad came home."

"Upstairs, then?"

Keith agreed and bent to retrieve his clothes, and we almost clunked heads again. We finally made it up the steps after dropping his shoe, my shirt, his belt, and my jeans. The inelegance of our trip to my room to make love for the first time helped make the moment less rushed. Before opening the door to my room I stared into his eyes. We both held our clothes in a heap in our arms, so we couldn't touch without dropping something else, but the clarity in his expression said so much. The insecurities of our youth were slipping away. I wasn't scared like I'd been last year at the thought of baring my flesh in front of another person. Instead, I was thrilled.

I opened the door and gestured with my head that he should enter first. I followed and nearly ran into him as he stopped short of the bed.

"Why are you...?" My question needed no answer as I spied the huge stacks of folded laundry on the bed. "Oh shit. Sorry." I deposited my clothes and shoes on my computer chair and turned back to the bed just as Keith was about to shove them all to the side. "No! I just folded those."

Keith gave me a bemused look, but didn't question me. "Okay. If you're going to properly take care of those, then I guess I shouldn't leave mine in a heap on the carpet." He picked up his stuff and walked it over to add to my pile on the chair, which I appreciated, because I normally didn't leave anything on the floor.

"I'll only be a second," I said, balancing a stack of towels on one arm, and a pile of my dad's things on the other. I put away four piles of folded towels, underwear, and T-shirts faster than I ever had before and returned to my room. I locked the door and made my way over to where Keith lay on the bed, propped up against the headboard.

"Are you still in the mood?" I asked, glancing at his groin. It was not saluting as it had been when I had dashed from the room.

"Yeah. But I, um, don't... have any condoms. Do you?"

I climbed over Keith and got comfortable next to the wall. That way, he had the fluffier pillow and I didn't have to worry about falling off the bed. "No," I said reluctantly.

"It's okay. It's not like I planned to have sex, so you don't need to look upset about it."

He was so candid with me. I liked that about Keith, but it also embarrassed me. I'd never talked to anyone about sex. Not really. Zach and I had talked a couple times in the past, but the topic was mainly girls and the things he said he was going to do with them. I had never wanted to do things to a girl so I had mainly listened. With Keith, I knew I could talk openly, but I was still nervous.

"I know," I replied. "But if we have sex, do we have to... you know... do that stuff I see in porn movies?" I leaned against the wall as I looked at him, touching his arm lightly and running my fingers up and down.

He smirked. "It depends what kind of porn you're watching. If it has to do with tying a cord around my junk until my balls turn blue, then no we aren't doing that. I'm slightly intimidated by kinky sex. I grew up in an open family where we talk about sex, but remember we're also a rather religious family. I think me and kink need to come together slowly, over time, like an appreciation of microbrews. No one dives into an IPA on their first trip to a bar, they go for a Bud Lite. I think I view sex the same way. I want to start with what is simple and easily understood."

I laughed. I knew he'd spent a lot of time listening to his older brother and father talk about beer. It was funny. Keith had a way of talking that made me feel so at ease. "Don't worry, I'm not breaking out my flogger just yet."

His jaw dropped. "Ah, but you know what that is!"

I shrugged, embarrassed. "Sort of."

Keith turned and snuggled closer to me and rubbed his nose over mine. "So tell me, Flynn Brewer, what kinds of naughty things were you researching on the Internet?"

My cheeks got hot. "Nothing. Seriously, nothing."

As if he didn't believe me for a second, Keith pressed his body up against mine and kissed me. His kisses started out sweet and light, but the longer he kept his erection pressed into mine, the stronger and sloppier our kisses became.

Suddenly and simultaneously we both stopped and stared into each other's eyes. Inches apart, we watched, deadlocked, as if challenging the other to look away first. I stared and he stared, while we both rocked our groins together with the slightest of motions. Our chests were pressed close and I could feel our sweat making our skin slippery, while our pertinent parts remained covered by white cotton. My dick pulsed in reaction to his pulsing against it. I wanted to remove the barriers, but I didn't want to spoil the feeling our thrusting pelvises gave me deep within my gut.

I knew we both felt it. Exhilaration. Titillation. Intoxication. Culmination. Rutting and rubbing our rods together until I couldn't keep my eyes open any longer. I squealed as it happened, white lightning erupting from my cock in jets of hot liquid, spewing and spurting until I thought I'd die from the enjoyment of it. I halted my motion and opened my eyes. Keith's eyes were shut and he was breathing hard through his open lips. His face was sweaty and his hair stuck to his face.

When he opened his eyes, I thought I'd come again from the look of complete and total adoration I saw there. Keith was beautiful and I had no idea why I hadn't seen it before. I kissed him before he could say a word. Before he could move away or interrupt the perfect moment with practical suggestions for proper hygiene, I maneuvered my body on top of his and kissed him as passionately as I could. I pinned his body to the bed with my hips as I held his face still with my hands.

When I stopped, he panted, "Wow."

I grinned. "I second that."

"That was pretty amazing, considering we aren't even fully undressed."

"I know. Weird, huh?"

"Maybe a little."

I kissed him again and climbed carefully off the bed. My crotch was sticky and my underwear felt glued to my penis, but all in all I felt great. "Stay here. I'll get a wet towel for you." I dashed to the bathroom and took a washcloth from the stack I'd recently put away. I removed my underwear and cleaned myself off first before wetting another towel with warm water for Keith. When I returned from the bathroom, he was naked and I gawked.

I slowly stepped closer and licked my lips as handed him the towel.

His penis was semi-erect, curving naturally to the right. The shaft was more barrel shaped than mine with a blunt tip, where mine was tapered. His balls sagged against my bed as he wiped them with the cloth. Suddenly, I wanted to be that towel: wiping them clean with my tongue.

I think he sensed my eyes on him because he looked up with a grin. "You like watching?"

He made me blush again. "Yes, you smart ass. You have a gorgeous body."

Keith beamed at me. "You do, too." He tossed the wet towel onto the nightstand. "Can we snuggle? Or does that sound too girly? Because I want to hold you, but I don't want to make you think I'm being weird or anything."

I shook my head. "No, you aren't being weird at all." I motioned for him to get off the bed so I could shove back the blankets and sheets. Once that was accomplished, I crawled over to the far side and beckoned Keith to lie down. I got comfortable on his shoulder, against his chest, in his arms, draping my leg over one of his, and sighed. "Can we leave the blankets off?" I asked, trailing my finger across his collarbone. "The room is warm, and I really just want to look at your skin."

"Whatever you want, as long as you don't want to leave my arms for the next few hours."

I caressed his stomach and chest. "Nope. Not leaving."

Keith leaned closer. I felt his breath on my forehead. "Can I assume we are officially back together?"

"Yes. How could I say no when I've missed you so much?"

Keith pulled me closer and kissed my hair. "I missed you too. I was angry for a little while, but then I couldn't stop thinking about you. I've wanted to hold you every day for weeks."

"Me, too." I loved the trail of hair he had below his navel. I followed it south with the tips of my fingers and until I got to the darker patch of hair below. His pubic hair was coarse, like mine, but thicker. I envied his hairiness there. My hair was slow growing, but at least I had hair. I knew some seniors in school who had nothing, not even armpit hair. That was sad.

I heard Keith's breath hitch as my fingers grazed to tip of his limp penis during my exploration, so I did it again. I slowly slid the back of my fingers along one side of his dick and over the head. The skin was so soft. When I moved my fingers back the other way, I noticed his penis was fuller. I watched and in seconds it moved, rolling to the center of his pelvic area as it twitched and hardened. I felt his fingers curl into my back as I teased him again with feather-light caresses.

"Flynn," he breathed my name.

My own cock swelled and I pressed it against his thigh as I took his weighty shaft into my hand and pumped. This action felt so different with

Keith. I knew what to do, I knew what I liked, but holding another boy's penis in my fist made everything inside me come alive. It was a connection to my sexuality that couldn't have been achieved through masturbation. Touching another person in the most intimate way awakened desires I had only speculated about. I wanted him in ways I hadn't even thought of until now.

Sex in porn was so one-dimensional compared to this. It was messy and carnal and contained a lot of grunting. Keith's breathy sounds were more like surprised gasps as I touched him, and the sounds he made caused my heart to race.

"Stop," he urged, grabbing my wrist. "It kinda hurts."

I lifted my head and looked at him. "I have lube," I said, springing up and over his body. I snatched the bottle from my dresser drawer and hopped back into my spot next to him.

Keith propped himself on his elbow and watched me. "You don't have condoms, but you have lube?"

I opened the top and poured some on my palm. "Uh-huh." I closed the lid and tossed it aside. As soon as I took a hold of Keith a second time, he collapsed and moaned and I snickered at his speechlessness. I couldn't blame him. Lube heightened the sensations for me, too. I could feel every vein and groove in his erect cock. I lined my body up as I had before, only letting go of him long enough to slather my cock with lube and press it against his thigh as I jacked him with more vigor.

Keith gripped my upper arm with one hand and my back with the other. He rolled his hips and thrust into my fist as I continued pulling and twisting. "Flynn," he whispered. "Flynn," he said more urgently. "Oh, Flynn, fuck, I'm gonna—" he gasped, as he started spurting in my fist and emptied all over his stomach.

I was close, but I wasn't finished. I needed to come too. I sat up and knelt over him, taking my cock in my cum-covered hand, I milked myself, pumping several more times until I added ropes of my semen to his sticky mess. When I was empty, I turned my gaze to Keith.

"Nice," he said. "I think you've sufficiently marked me."

I chuckled. "At least the bed's still dry."

We giggled and Keith grabbed the wet towel that he had tossed onto the nightstand not long ago. "Um, come to think of it, can you get me a clean towel please? This one's cold."

I shot an eyebrow up at him and smiled. "Demanding, much?" I winked, climbing off the bed and doing his bidding without question. I tossed the warm, fresh towel at his face upon re-entering my room and watched as he cleaned his stomach of our cum.

"I've never felt so hungry in all my life. You want to go get ice cream?"

His eyes brightened. "Hoffman's?"

"Is there any place better?" I asked.

"Heck no!" he answered heartily. "I absolutely love their coconut chocolate chip. Or strawberry cheesecake. Or Dutch chocolate. Come to think of it, I don't think I've ever had a flavor I didn't like. What about you?" Keith finished wiping off and grabbed his pants off the floor.

"Um, I like vanilla."

"What?" He smirked at me. "That's it?"

I replied with a nod.

"Okay. Vanilla it is. But will you at least taste mine?" Keith crossed the floor to me.

"Yes. If you ask nicely."

He leaned in and kissed me sweetly. "Please?" he quietly asked, kissing my lips between words. "Taste... my... cream?" he smirked against my lips.

"Yes," I answered dreamily, because my brain was getting sleepy and cloudy and fogged as he kissed me. "Sounds... naughty."

He squeezed my ass. "So naughty."

"I think I'd say yes to just about anything right now," I murmured as he trailed kisses down my neck.

"Good." He released me, and then shifted his pelvis around while holding the waistband of his jeans. "I guess I'm free-ballin' the rest of the day."

I held out a pair of underwear after pulling clean boxers from my drawer. "You can wear mine."

"Nah. I think I like the feel of it. It's more airy." Keith pulled on my shirt before kissing my neck again and holding me around my waist. "Thank you. That felt incredible."

I rubbed his arms up and down. "No problem. I enjoyed it. Are we trading shirts then?"

Keith nodded. "I like having your smell all over me. Next time, I get to touch *you*."

"Sounds good to me."

"But while we're out, I promise I'll behave. No PDA. I should have respected your decision weeks ago, and not pressured you so much. I'm sorry."

"Me, too. I'm just not ready."

"I know."

Keith and I kissed again before heading to the best ice cream place in Westminster. While we were there, sitting on one of the picnic tables by the parking lot, Keith stayed true to his promise and didn't do anything to out me in public. Witnessing his patience only made me want to kiss him more.

Chapter 8

August 28, 2011: Validating My Fears

"I can't believe school starts Tuesday," Keith said. His eyes were closed where he lounged next to me by the pool.

Kelly added, "I know, right? The summer flew by!"

The girls spent as much time at my house as Keith. I had an awesome pool and it was a hot summer. Keith had been at work sometimes when Kelly was there, and Grace visited on occasion without her, but for the most part our little foursome had been tight through all of August.

"I'm glad you and Keith decided to make up," said Grace as she floated around the pool on an inflatable raft Keith had purchased for her.

Keith commented, "Me too."

I rolled my head to the side and glared at him, but he wasn't looking. Or I assumed he wasn't since I couldn't see his eyes behind his sunglasses.

"Senior year," Grace contemplated. "I can't believe it."

"Not for me," Kelly said. She had graduated in June and often thought it funny to rub it in.

She was a year older, but since art was an elective, the four of us had been lucky to sign up for it at the same time. Our friendship felt real, like maybe we wouldn't drift apart once everyone went off to college. Kelly was already enrolled in the same community college I was planning to attend, and Grace had applied to two colleges locally. We had the potential of solidifying our closeness into adulthood, and I liked the comfort of that.

Grace ignored Kelly's comment and continued, "Are you thinking of going to the prom together?"

"Are you talking to me?" I asked.

"No, Flynn, I'm asking if Keith is thinking of taking Kelly."

"No need to get sarcastic," I grumbled. "I don't know. What do you think Keith? Should we?"

Keith lifted his sunglasses and shrugged as he spoke to me, "I don't know." He knew I liked seeing his eyes and how it annoyed me when he looked at me with them on. It just felt weird looking at him and not knowing if he was looking at someone else or had his eyes closed. I liked knowing I had his full attention. "You're the one who wants to keep our relationship a secret."

I winced. We'd been back together a month, I hoped he wasn't going to start an argument over it so soon. "I know. Maybe we could take it one week at a time. Prom isn't until May, right before graduation. Maybe if we take things slow during school, I can work up to acting like myself in public."

"Or you could just get over yourself now and hold my hand in the hallway."

"Keith!" Kelly hissed. "Let him alone. Not everyone has an easy coming out process, and not everyone has parents like yours."

"True," he replied. "But I was never in the closet."

"Which is my point," she said.

"And Flynn's dad knows already and doesn't have a problem with him."

"You don't know that," I said. I shielded my eyes with my hand. I swiveled my legs around in my lawn chair and put my feet on the warm concrete. "My dad hasn't really said anything since the day he caught us fooling around in the living room. He's rarely home. Just because he hasn't told me you can't come over, doesn't automatically suggest he's fine with it. He *did* tell me to keep it cool. He wasn't keen on Mr. Mitchell finding out. So asking you to chill while we're in school doesn't seem so unreasonable to me."

Kind of like when we'd kissed by the pool the first time, and I reasoned that there was little chance anyone could see; I reminded myself our bushes were like the sound proof barriers built around highways. My backyard sanctuary was relatively secure from prying eyes, and also from listening ears. Perhaps not so much between the houses, but definitely so around the back. Keith could fuss all he wanted.

I'd had enough. I walked over to the pool and dove under Grace's raft. My dives were fluid; I knew I wouldn't make ripples and knock her off. The cold water shocked my hot skin, but I needed it. Keith could be so hard headed. He wanted me to be as comfortable being out as he was, but I didn't see it that plainly. It felt complicated to me. Maybe it was fear, but I couldn't understand why he wouldn't respect my fears, even if he thought they were ridiculous. They were *my* fears!

I swam across the bottom of the pool until I needed air. I broke the surface and shook my hair out of my face as I inhaled. Keith was at the pool's edge squatting in front of me.

"I'm sorry," he said.

I held the side of the pool with one hand as I smoothed my hair back. He sounded sincere. He always sounded sincere. What I wanted to know was when this repetitive argument would end.

"It's fine." I lied.

Keith changed positions, knelt, and leaned over. He was practically falling over the edge of the pool as he beckoned me forward for a kiss. I pulled myself up a few inches as he came down. He kissed me, several times, and touched my face tenderly when he was done. "I know I'm a pain in the ass, but I hope you can forgive me. I guess I just want to show you off, ya know? I have a hot boyfriend, and I want everyone to know it."

I smiled. His compliments never stopped making me smile. Generally, I knew I was pretty cute, but Keith had a way of exaggerating the facts regarding my looks.

"So, are we good?"

I nodded. "Yeah. I forgive you." I hoisted my body over the edge of the pool and stood up with him. "I guess you can hold my hand."

His eyes lit up. "I can?"

"When there aren't many people around," I explained. "In a month or two I'll see how I feel about it."

"Okay. That's fine. I'll do whatever you want." Then he smiled. "Thank you."

He kissed me. Such a simple thing, but there were times when I thought that maybe he did it because he knew I turned to putty when his lips were on mine. I *did* want to feel confident about being myself, but something inside me just didn't feel ready.

***

October 27, 2011

A couple months later, things between Keith and I were still good and we were back in school, taking things as slowly as I'd asked. We were in two classes together, plus lunch mod, so I saw him more than the previous year, which made me happy. Keith had been patient and hadn't grabbed my hand or touched me in any way, though occasionally he brushed his fingers over mine after we left lunch as a form of transitory handshake. He would take a left toward the art department and I turned right, so we could have been shaking hands. At least that's what I conditioned myself to say if anybody ever questioned our brief contact. Keith's "fingertip caress" was slight and fleeting, and not the least bit suggestive. This was a nice, slow transition toward holding my hand in school, and I appreciated his patience.

On one particular Thursday, I'd made the mistake of watching him walk toward art three seconds too long.

"What are you looking at, Brewer?"

I turned as I took a step and found myself nose to chest with Bruce Merryman. I'd known him since elementary school. He wasn't the dumbest of jocks, nor was he the meanest, but I think being a senior had given him bigger balls. Suddenly he found more reasons than ever to pick on people. I hadn't been on his radar for years, so I didn't understand why he was being so gruff with me now.

"What?" I asked, because I honestly didn't know.

"You. I asked what you were looking at?" He pierced me with his tightly squinted eyes as his two thug friends stood behind him.

I shrugged. "Nothing."

He wrinkled his nose and made a face that suggested he didn't believe me, but he didn't say anything else. He walked around me, slow and deliberate, keeping his eyes on me the whole time. His friends did the same. Had he seen me watching Keith? I hoped not.

Quietly, they walked away.

After school, Keith met me at my locker. "Hey. We still going to Game Stop at the mall?"

I looked up. I was on my knees switching my textbooks as Keith leaned on the locker next to mine. "Hey." I smiled at him, but kept shuffling my stuff. "Yeah. Sounds good."

"What do you want to do after? My house? Your house?"

"Um, I guess I should text my dad and see when he'll be home. I know he normally doesn't get off work until late, but I don't want to assume."

Keith nodded in the way he does when considering my thoughts. "Makes sense. I'm not sure I'd know how to handle going home to an empty house every day. My dad is always home at six. My mom told me once she could set her watch by him, and I found myself paying attention to when he came home. Sure enough, he walked through the door at six on the dot every day for two weeks in a row. After that I stopped monitoring him, but it was like having an alarm set. He'd walk through the door and I'd know Mom would have dinner on the table in fifteen minutes. He's very predictable."

I stood up. "That must be nice. I wish I had that sometimes." I shut my locker and jumped. There stood Bruce Merryman; ice-cold, like a serial killer. "What are you...," I started asking, but he didn't allow me the courtesy of finishing my question. He stepped into me.

"So, what do we have here? A couple of homos?" he sneered.

"What...?" Again, I couldn't finish because Bruce grabbed my head and shoved the side of my face into my locker door. Hard. The pain in my cheek made me cry out.

"And violence is always the answer," I heard Keith respond. I really didn't want him engaging the bully who was crushing my skull; I wanted him to yell for help. I squirmed under Bruce's fat hand.

"I didn't ask you. I was talking to Brewer here." He narrowed his eyes at me and moved his face closer. I could smell Cheetos on his breath. He held my face plastered against the metal, but I could still see him. "So, did you lie to me earlier, Brewer? Is there something going on between you and this faggot? Does he suck your dick?"

"What? No!" It wasn't a lie, but it felt like one, and I hoped Bruce couldn't see it written on my face.

I heard Keith once again, from behind me. "I'm disconcerted you'd assume I suck everyone's dick that chooses to spend time with me, Mr. Merryman. Perhaps you need to check with the assistant principal, since I stayed after school with him for service hours. Or maybe the principal herself since she keeps a list of all the people I suck off to get my A's. Do you want me to go get her?"

"Keep your mouth shut, Leppo." He put his face very close to mine and applied more pressure. "I asked you a question, Brewer. Are you a fag?"

I saw his anger and I replied out of fear. "No!"

"Is Leppo your boyfriend?"

"No!"

Keith ignored Bruce and added, "I'm just saying, you can't assume to know someone's orientation based on the company they keep. If I did that, I'd assume you were a zoophiliac."

The pressure of Bruce's palm lessened for a second, as he shifted his eyes to Keith. "What the hell is that?" His lips and cheeks contorted with confusion.

"Someone who likes having sex with animals," Keith answered smugly. Sometimes I wished he wasn't so confident in his ability to outwit people. His superior tone made me worry about what Bruce might do. He was bigger than us, and he had brought two of his friends.

"What!" He let go of my head and pulled his shoulders back, making him appear even bigger.

Keith continued in his normal, casual tone as if logically explaining the difference between poison and venom, or liquid soap versus dry. I cringed, but I couldn't fault the guy who had briefly talked my head out of a vise. "Well, technically a zoophili-*ac* is someone having an attraction to or preference for animals. Whereas, zoophili-*a* is an erotic fixation on animals that may result in sexual excitement. Wikipedia even links bestiality on the same page, as defined by the desire to form sexual relationships with animals. You hang out with animals, ergo zoophiliac, or bestialiac, but that isn't actually a word."

I found it ironic that one of his flunkies chose then to growl, further proving Keith's point. Bruce stepped past me as I plastered my body flat against my locker to avoid getting knocked over. He clenched his fist and pounded it against the palm of his opposite hand. Keith was now the object of his wrath instead of me.

Keith took a step back, but didn't run. "Maybe I'm over thinking it. You're probably just your run of the mill ruffian who's habitually cruel to those weaker than himself as a way to repress some childhood trauma, which may or may not have been a result of sexual molestation." Keith kept talking, eyes forward, focus centered, even when Bruce clamped his big fist around his neck. "In which case, I can't blame you for taking your pain out on others." Keith's voice came out distorted as Bruce squeezed, yet he kept talking. "It must have been awful if your coping mechanism is beating on guys who don't fit your narrow definition of masculinity."

Bruce's accomplice shoved my chest and my head hit the locker, adding more pain to my already aching head.

"What's going on here?" I glanced toward the sound of assistant principal's voice as he approached.

Bruce let go of Keith immediately and turned to face him. "Um, nothing."

Bruce's thugs stepped back as well. They all looked worried.

Keith coughed twice and cleared his throat, then said, "Nothing. I was drilling them on new vocabulary words and Bruce disagreed with my definition. When I corrected him, he threatened me, but it was harmless." He glanced at Bruce. "Right?"

"Um, right." Bruce was stunned.

I turned my face away so no one would see my cheek. I knew it had to be red based on the way it throbbed.

"What was the vocabulary word?" the assistant principal asked.

"Superparasitism," Keith answered. "Bruce said it's when parasitized by more than one individual of the same kind, usually insects, and I contradicted him, and if you know Bruce, he doesn't like being contradicted over entomology. He grabbed my neck and threatened to separate my head from my shoulders, but it was just a joke."

"Oh. Okay," the assistant principal said skeptically. "Well, just break it up gentlemen. This appeared to be a rougher situation from across the hall."

"Of course," Keith said confidently.

After the assistant principal walked away, Bruce got up in Keith's face. "I don't know what kind of game you're playing, but that was... unexpected." He swallowed hard and snarled the rest through a whisper. "Just don't fuck with me, Leppo. We have all year to play out this dance, and next time I might forget to stop squeezing."

Bruce shoved past Keith, knocking him hard against the shoulder. His thugs shoved me one last time and I hit my head again. The pain that shot down my neck almost caused tears to fall, but I was not going to be a wuss in school. I turned and grabbed my stuff.

"Are you okay?" Keith asked.

"I'm fine. I gotta go or I'll miss the bus." I walked away in a hurry, but Keith caught up to me by the front entrance.

"I thought I was driving you."

I didn't know what to say. I looked him in the eyes and turned away before those threatening tears forced their way out. I was not going to cry in school. I just needed to get out. I pushed through the front doors and made it to my bus by the time my bus driver was about to pull away. She seemed shocked by my presence, but allowed me to get on. I hadn't ridden the bus since last semester. After Keith had passed his probationary period and was allowed to drive non-family members, then I went everywhere with him... until now.

While on route, I got a text from Keith: *I'm sorry. I saw the bruise on your cheek. You should put ice on it when you get home.*

I will.

I didn't want to talk about it. My emotions were too jumbled and I was on a bus for goodness sakes.

At home, I went right to the hallway bathroom to inspect my face. Bruised. Red and purple with a half-inch line of split flesh down the center of my cheekbone. I looked as though someone punched me, but it had been worse than that. In a fistfight, I might have gotten in a few of my own and bruised *his* face. This was one-sided. This was a stupid-ass bully harassing me over what? My sexuality? I had no idea how he'd even known.

I grabbed a bag of frozen peas from the kitchen and lay on the couch just as someone rang the doorbell. I reluctantly answered the door. It was Keith.

"Can I come in?"

I nodded, still holding frozen peas to my cheek.

Keith followed me over to the couch and pulled my dad's hassock over so he could sit and face me where I flopped on my side, resting my head level in order to keep the bag of peas from sliding off my face. "I'm sorry about today," he said.

"Why did you have to provoke him?"

"I didn't. He was going to pound you. I had to say something."

I swallowed hard, emotions swirling in my chest. "How did he know?"

"I don't know."

"That's why I didn't want to hold your hand."

"But we haven't!" he fussed, lowering his voice after his initial protest. "Much. Only a few times. I don't know how he saw anything. We were careful."

"I just can't. I'm not ready. My dad wanted me to be careful and think about how coming out would affect my life. After today…."

"After today, I understand why you'd be scared. I do. It's not easy to stand up to assholes like Bruce who only want to belittle everyone else."

I grumbled, "Why didn't you turn him in? He bullied us. My cheek is proof." I lifted the peas.

"Ouch." Keith reached over and touched me carefully. I winced and he pulled his fingers back. "Sorry. I didn't turn him in because it's only the end of the first quarter. I didn't want to start off our senior year that way. I thought that maybe talking him out of crushing your skull might help us come to a mutual understanding."

"And the stuff about entomology?"

"I know Bruce isn't a dumb jock like he wants his friends to believe. He's in some hard classes. I think his background and economic status makes him feel an allegiance to a certain social group, but I was hoping to show him he's allowed to think for himself. He can't threaten people into submission. I wasn't going to back down just because he brought his cronies. Even if he finds me in a dark parking lot one night and kicks the shit out of me, I'm not going to cower."

"So you compared him to bestialogist?"

Keith laughed at how I butchered his word. "It would be bestialiac, if that were a word. No. I was using sarcasm to draw a comparison to how he sees me and how I could view him if I used the same thought process."

"You made him mad."

"Of course. But he let go of you and that was really my goal all along. I knew I couldn't fight him."

"And you're not mad I denied being gay?"

He shrugged, very Keith-like. "No."

"What about denying I was your boyfriend. You broke up with me the last time I did that."

"I know, but this was different. You were under duress. I can't blame you for self-preservation."

"Thanks."

Keith leaned in and kissed me before standing up. "I'm going to head home. I have homework. We'll chill, okay?" I nodded. "Maybe after Christmas you'll feel more comfortable."

"Okay."

Keith smiled and left. I fell asleep on the couch, contemplating if I would ever feel comfortable being myself in public. Sometimes it seemed impossible.

Chapter 9

November 26, 2011: Emotional Explosions

Our senior year was supposed to be a big deal, and for Keith it was. He had applied to colleges throughout the summer and had heard back from a few. He also had a few more to send application essays to, even though he planned on attending Dickinson. Whereas I already knew I was destined for the local community college. Not because my dad couldn't afford college, I knew he could, money wasn't the issue since he worked sixty to seventy hours a week and had paid the house off two years ago. I was eighty percent sure I would get into any college I applied to. What I was worried about was my dad. He was a workaholic with no hobbies, who didn't go out socially or do anything for fun, and spent his nights drinking way too much. I couldn't bring myself to leave him in an empty house just yet.

In my mind it wasn't a big deal, anyway. Most colleges had standard prerequisites and I could get those out of the way at any college, which would give me three more years at home to help my dad see his need to get over grieving for my mom and move on.

I had started the process myself last year after I had finally visited her grave with Zach and had the chance to sort out some of my feelings. I also visited her grave a couple of times over the past year and it had helped. Since I didn't have a car yet, I walked over and talked to her whenever I felt the need and it had gotten easier every time. I wasn't so sure my dad viewed my "talks" the same way. Whenever I mentioned I'd gone, he appeared more sullen. Was it guilt? Sadness? Fear? I didn't know. I also didn't know how to tell him he could talk to me about it. I guess we had gotten so good at avoidance that it seemed normal, although it wasn't. I wanted to talk. I wanted a real father, not an absent drunk. Ever since last November, it had been as if each time he'd taken one step forward, he'd immediately take twelve in reverse. By the time the dreaded anniversary date rolled around this year, I hoped I would have made enough progress in my own quest for closure that I'd be able to convince him of his need for the same thing.

At least Thanksgiving had been promising. Dinner this year was spent with Keith's family, and I could not remember a time when my dad looked so relaxed. He dressed up for the occasion, and had been super polite. He only drank one glass of wine and talked to Keith's dad like normal men do: about work, cars, and sports. Their family was so welcoming I thought maybe I'd stepped into the Twilight Zone. I loved it.

But this was two days later.

"Dad," I whispered into his darkened room.

I heard him grunt.

"Can I turn on the light?"

"No."

So he was going to play it that way. "Okay. Can I ask you a question?"

"Sure."

"Will you visit Mom's grave with me? And Nate's?"

There was a long pause. So long that I thought maybe he had nodded off in his chair. "Okay," he said finally.

"Okay?"

"Mm-hmm."

"Dad, it can just be for a few minutes. I know this is hard for you."

He raised his voice. "I said I'd go, Flynn. Can you give me some time to work myself up for this? Or does it have to be now?" I could tell he was irritated, but he wasn't yelling.

"No. Not now. It's getting dark outside. I thought we'd go tomorrow, since most people will be in church on Sunday, if we go around ten it'll be quiet."

He grunted again. I heard labored breathing. Was he okay? I couldn't tell. I wanted to walk closer, but I feared he'd change his mind about visiting Mom. Instead, I backed out of the room and shut his door.

In the morning I dressed in my Sunday best. I had never gone to church, but I did know something about dressing for the occasion. I was about to go with my dad to visit my mom and brother on a Sunday. I wanted Mom to be proud. I chose a light green, short-sleeved, button down, and my black shorts. Green was her favorite color, so I thought she'd like my shirt. It brought out the green in my eyes. Keith always approved when I wore green, or gray. He said my eye color changed depending on what I wore because my pale green eyes contained flecks of gold. I'd never noticed, but Keith seemed to study every detail about me.

I combed my fingers through my bangs and smoothed them over to the side. My hair was getting longer. It was a bit shaggy-looking even after I'd gotten it cut a while back. The hairdresser used a razor to texturize it after she'd given me some highlighted streaks across the top. Maintaining highlighted hair was a pain in the butt, though, so I'd let most of the highlights grow out. After I added color, because blond streaks were too boring, it had been easier to touch up at home with one streak across the front in my bangs and a chunk behind my left ear. Especially since the color faded quickly with me spending so much time in the pool.

I'd had blue in my hair for ten months now. Maybe I needed a different color? Purple? Keith had mentioned last year he liked combing his fingers through my hair, so I had let the length alone the last time I went in. Funny, I hadn't noticed it almost tickling my neck, and how far it had grown over my ears, until now. I imagined hearing my mom fussing at me.

I grinned at myself in the mirror. "I know it's long, Mom, but my boyfriend likes it that way." I glanced at her picture on my dresser. "You'd like Keith. He's nice, he smells really good, and he loves me a lot even if we haven't used the 'L' word yet. I can just tell by the way he looks at me. I know he loves me." I sighed. "I can hear you now, asking what I might know about love. Well, Mom, I don't. I don't know anything. Not really. I'm confused more often than ever. I don't know how I'm supposed to feel or how to act. I wish Dad would talk to me. Am I in love? I wish I knew what it felt like."

I turned away from her portrait and left my room. Dad needed some prompting and then we'd be off together to the cemetery.

On my way down the steps I got a text from Zach.

Hey. I know what today is. You okay? Do you need me to come home and go to the cemetery with you?

Zach was at college. He and Greg had found a house off campus to move into until he graduated in May with a two-year horticulture degree. Greg would still have two more years, but Zach said he'd been glad to get out of his parents' house for as long as he could.

Yeah. My Dad is going with me. I'll be okay. Thanks for asking. How are you?

Fine, I guess. I'm getting through it.

Any contact from your dad after.... I stopped texting. We hadn't talked about his admission over the summer of being beaten by his father. Zach had said it, and then he dropped the subject just as quickly. I hadn't ever wanted to think about Zach's father that way, but after seeing the evidence it had been hard letting it go. The abuse last year explained a lot about Zach's behavior. Zach had always been somewhat fearful of his dad, and I speculated if maybe there had been other times just as awful.

Flynn, you know I don't want to talk about it. I want to forget I even mentioned it. Just... can we... will you drop it?

Yeah. I agreed whether or not I wanted to. *When will you be back in town? Do you want to grab some wings or something?* I knew how much he liked wings.

I don't know. Greg and I spent Thanksgiving at Tom's house. His family went to Cancun and he didn't want to be alone.

Oh. Okay. I was wondering how your Thanksgiving was.

Probably the best one I've had in years.

Good. Just don't forget about me. I know I'm only a high school kid, but I'm still your best friend, right?

Always. Later, man.

Bye.

Always. Something about that word didn't sound true. Zach hadn't been a strong presence in my life for a couple years. He'd been there, but after ninth-grade, and our kiss, things had changed. I hated to think that one stupid mistake had ruined everything.

Kissing was stupid.

I walked into the kitchen and poured a glass of milk. I placed my glass in the dishwasher after I drained it and my phone buzzed again.

Keith: *Hey. Good luck today.*

Thanks. Dad is going with me.

Okay. But if you need me just text. I can drive right over.

Okay.

You are coming to school tomorrow, right?

Yeah. I'll make it. I miss you.

:^) I miss you too. I want to feel you up against me. I miss your lips and your hair and your hands.

I blushed. I recanted my previous thought. Kissing Keith wasn't stupid. Kissing Keith was amazing. I was glad I was standing alone in my kitchen because I could imagine how stupid I looked, smiling like a fool. Keith was always saying things like that. This was how I knew he loved me, even without saying it. I think he was waiting. We'd fought a couple of times, heatedly, and had broken up once. I think it had been good that "love" wasn't mentioned when we weren't exactly on smooth seas all the time. Waiting seemed best.

Oh. I hurriedly texted. *My dad's coming. Gotta run.*

Call me later.

I will. I pocketed my phone as my dad entered the kitchen.

"I guess I'm ready. Do I look all right?"

He was wearing a green, button down shirt like me. He had remembered. I nodded. "Yeah. You look good, Dad." He'd even shaved for the occasion. Normally he'd go three weeks between shaves. I knew he'd shaved last Thursday so this was a surprise. "Mom would be proud," I added, and he smiled softly.

All he did was nod.

We left about 9:30 and walked over to the cemetery. He mentioned driving and I told him it might be easier afterward to walk home. I said it had taken a lot out of me and I had needed Zach to help me walk straight. Driving could end up being worse. He agreed, and we made our way down the street toward the circuit court building when I noticed how slow my dad's steps were becoming. It was as if he was walking to his doom off the edge of the Grand Canyon or something. I wanted to take his hand, but I hadn't held my dad's hand for years. I wasn't sure how he'd respond. It was better to walk with uncomfortable separation than to have him pull away and make the awkwardness worse.

When we got to the metal fencing that went all the way around the cemetery, he visibly paled. I knew which grave was hers even from that distance and I wondered if he did too. I could pick it out easily now that I'd been there more than once. He didn't say a word as we rounded the corner and made our way to the entrance.

As we approached the gravestone, up the slight hill, his movements were so slow as to be almost imperceptible. He probably covered one blade of grass at a time. I walked ahead, thinking I could mark out the spot as I stood silently waiting. I knew he was behind me. He wouldn't dare run, but facing her had been hard enough on me, I imagined it was worse on him.

Her name was engraved so ornately on the smooth granite. I touched the top as I waited, closing my eyes, and picturing her sleeping in her bed at home. I had snuck into my parents' room a couple of times as a kid to wake them at Christmas or cuddle after a bad dream. My mom had always looked so peaceful as she slept. Was she at peace now? I thought she was. I had faith that she was.

I heard my dad breathing behind me so I spoke to Mom for him, just in case the words were lodged in his throat. "Hey Mom. I know it's been a couple months. I've been a little busy, but I promise I'll come by more regularly now that I feel more settled." I paused, thinking of what to say. I hadn't spoken so much to her when I had come by myself, it had been mostly a comfort thing, but having Dad with me, I wanted to show him how easy it could be to carry on a conversation with her. She didn't have to be *gone* gone, only physically separated from us.

I took a breath and thought of other topics to share. "Um, I have a boyfriend. His name's Keith. I know that's something we haven't talked about before. I'm gay. And before you get all protective of me, we've been safe." Suddenly I felt awkward and I rolled my eyes at myself as I stumbled over my own words. "Well, we haven't exactly done anything to be *unsafe* about; I'm just saying we would be, you know, if it happened. He's not the kind of guy to sleep around. We met last year in art class. It took us a little while to settle down as a couple, and although we have some issues to work through, I think it's going well. I'll bring him soon to meet you. Okay?"

I felt my dad step up beside me and my heart raced. "I told you I'd bring Dad. He's here Mom. He misses you so much. I wish you could tell him you're fine and that he'll be fine, too. I think he works too much. I think he drinks too much. Mom, if you can somehow send him a message, can you tell him you'll always love him? I think he forgets sometimes."

Right then I heard my dad choke back a sob. I caught sight of him out of the corner of my eye as he collapsed, bending at the knee, lunging forward to crouch in front of her headstone and cry. He was clinging to it, sobbing his heart out, and all I could do was watch. When Zach had been beside me, he had held me as I cried. I got the distinct impression that wasn't what I should do right now. I felt as though my dad was clinging to her soul, pleading with his tears for her to come back to him. I couldn't pity him. I couldn't fault him. And I certainly would never chastise him.

It had taken my father seven years to grieve this openly, and I would stand there until hell froze over before I disturbed him. He needed this, just as I had needed to make my peace with her last year. *For everything there is a season, and a time for every purpose under heaven.* Isn't that the saying from the Bible? I recalled my mother saying something like that. I think she said it was in the Old Testament.

This was his season for mourning, or whatever it was. Release, maybe. I'd had mine, and now my dad needed his.

I wiped my own stubborn tears away, wishing Zach had come. Or Keith. I wanted to hold someone. Hearing my dad cry was harder than crying myself. I thought about Nate. It wasn't as if I had forgotten about him, but his absence had been easier for me to let go of. I missed him, but my brother hadn't been as strong a presence in my life as my mom had been.

Watching and listening to my dad ripped my heart out like a fisherman's hook down the gullet of a trout. I felt the sharp pains of tearing flesh as the imaginary hook pulled my guts out through my mouth, emptying me of life. All that from the sound of his tears.

And then suddenly, abruptly, my dad was gone. I turned and saw him running down the lane between the headstones. He turned the corner and shot through the gate, bolting toward home. Stunned, it took me a moment to take off after him. As out of shape as I thought my dad was, he still beat me through the front door. He stood in the living room, his back to me, shoulders heaving, holding onto the corner of the wall next to the sofa.

"Dad?" I said, careful not to speak too loudly and startle him out of whatever had possessed him to run all the way home. It might be a short walk, but I was slightly winded. Me, the guy in shape from swimming and tennis. "Dad, are you—"

I stopped mid sentence as he turned and hurled a vase at the wall behind me. I ducked as shattered glass flew everywhere, and he picked up another knickknack. "Dad!" I yelled, diving to the side and taking refuge in the space between the stairs and my mother's piano. The space was so small, yet I cowered there between the side of the piano and the angled end of the banister where we used to keep umbrellas because nothing else fit in the tiny space. My legs hurt as I yanked them impossibly close to my chest, but I wasn't about to move into his view.

He picked up a picture frame and threw it at another wall screaming like a madman, "You left me, Tory! Why? How could you leave me? I needed you and Nate to complete this family, and instead you leave me with a gay son!"

His words carved a larger hole in my gut than his tears had earlier. They stole my very breath and cut me deeply, to the marrow of my bones. Was this how he felt? Why hadn't he told me? He had said he was fine with it last year. Had the past twelve months been a lie?

My dad picked up the end of the chair and flipped it, knocking the coffee table into the TV stand. Our wide-screen TV wobbled, but thankfully didn't fall. "Gay!" He lifted his face to the ceiling and hollered at the top of his lungs. "What do you think Mr. Godly is going to say about that? Huh? You know he's watching me Tory! You know he hates everything I do and say. We argue about everything! How I keep my yard, and why I work all day, and why I let my son dye his hair blue, and how come I don't drive a better car? He blames it all on my lack of faith. Fuck that, Victoria! Fuck Stewart Mitchell and his fucking church! He doesn't fucking know anything!"

The lamp crashed to the floor. My dad picked up another glass knickknack from a still upright table and hurled it at another wall. Porcelain bits showered the floor, several of which hit my shoe on their way across the hardwood. I pulled my knees tighter to my chest and listened to him screaming at my dead mother. "He's gay, Tory! What the fucking hell does that mean?"

I sobbed silently, terrified as a three-year-old child walking in on a mass murder. I had no idea what I was watching, but his rage made my whole body tremble in terror. He hated me. My dad hated me for being gay and he had hidden his feelings for a year. Just when I thought I couldn't feel any lonelier or feel any more worthless, my dad yells at my dead mother about my sexuality. If I could have run for the kitchen I would have dashed in and grabbed a knife to end his suffering. He didn't deserve this. It was my fault. Maybe my dad hadn't been grieving this whole time, but rather angry at my mother for leaving him stuck with me?

I was his life's disappointment.

I wanted to run. I wanted to get away. I wanted to rip every mirror off the walls so I would never have to look myself in the face and know I was the putrescent boy my father hated. My body shook, but I couldn't make a sound for fear he'd notice and throw *me* at the wall. Or worse, beat me like Zach's father had done.

He punched the wall and sent drywall to the floor. "How the hell am I supposed to relate to him, Tory? Fuck… Fuck… Fuck!" His cursing crescendoed.

And then, like the eye of a hurricane, when the wind suddenly ceases, my dad dropped his arms and stilled. Head bowed, shoulders slumped, he breathed a deep ragged breath and sobbed like a baby. "What does that mean?" he asked again in the tiniest of voices, weak and broken. "How do I love him, Tori?"

He turned in my direction and I instinctively shielded my face from him in case he had something left to throw. "Flynn," he said so quietly I could have missed it if I hadn't been paying so close attention. "Flynn," he repeated louder when I didn't respond. "I'm so sorry. I didn't know what to do after your mother died, so I didn't do anything."

I lowered my protective arms and peered up at him.

"She was my princess, and Nathan was my first born son. When God took them, I blamed Him for everything. I was angry. I hated Stewart Mitchell and his whole holier-than-thou attitude. He tried to tell me at the funeral that God judged those acting outside his will. I had no fucking idea what the hell he was talking about, but I grappled with it for the next six years. I blamed God for the car that smashed into ours on our way to church for the first time that morning. I blamed myself for not respecting her desire to attend church with you boys for years before that. I blamed myself for not reading the Bible and trying to follow what Stewart was saying. I blamed myself when I walked in here last year and found you making out with that boy on my couch. I blame myself now for not being the father you needed me to be."

"Dad…." I pulled myself upright by grabbing onto the side of the piano, and approached him slowly, knees shaking.

He reached out and I flinched instinctively, but my dad didn't notice. He cupped my cheek as he spoke to me. "Flynn, I never meant to hurt you. I never meant for any of this. I shut myself off from everything for years and I allowed my guilt over doing nothing to build until I thought I had no hope of climbing free of it. Until last year, I hadn't thought about visiting your mom. I mean I did, but it was more like a looming thought that further compounded the weight of my already overwhelming guilt. It scared me. But then you went, and we cried about it, and I thought that maybe I could talk to her again."

"But, why did you yell about me being gay? Are you ashamed of me? I thought you said you weren't."

He opened his arms and I fell forward, collapsing against his chest.

He held me close. "No. I'm not ashamed, Flynn. I'm scared. Did you know Stewart Mitchell tried to get me to sign a petition to force Eric Blevins out of the neighborhood because he's gay? I kept thinking, *What if that was about my son next time?* I don't know how to be a good father to a regular boy, so how am I supposed to father a gay one?"

"I'm still a regular boy, Dad. I am. I have all the same parts. I still like fishing. I like swimming and tennis. I know plenty of straight guys who like to draw, and are good at math. I'm still me. I just happen to like boys instead of girls. It's no different."

He pulled back from our embrace and looked me in the eyes. "You promise?"

I snorted slightly; almost snickering, since it was not the question I expected. "Yes." I wiped my wet cheeks and reassured him, "I promise."

He continued staring into my eyes and I saw tears forming anew in the corners of his. His hand shook where it held my face. "I hope you know I love you. I told Stewart Mitchell to bother someone else with his pointless petition. There's no way the City Council of Westminster was going to honor such hate-filled propaganda, no matter how much he lobbied for it. Governor O'Malley even said something like 'discrimination against individuals based on their sexual orientation was unjust.' It's only a matter of time before Maryland legalizes same-sex marriage. Stewart Mitchell is in for a rude awakening in this state when that finally happens."

My heart warmed with pride knowing that he paid that close attention to politics, especially as it related to me. "Thanks Dad. I love you too. I'm sorry if I made this harder for you."

"No, Flynn. It's me who should apologize. I've wasted years drinking and working too much. Years I could have spent talking to you, and then maybe it wouldn't have surprised me that you're gay. I handled my own insecurities poorly, and I'm sorry."

"It's okay. I forgive you."

He studied my face and smoothed my hair away from my forehead. "Did I hurt you?"

"No. But I can't say I've ever felt that scared in my life."

He hugged me again and heaved a sigh before letting me go. "I'm so sorry." He looked around the room at the mess. "I don't think I've ever been that scared either. I couldn't control it. The rage at losing Tori and Nate, and my own anxiety over fathering you in the way you need me to, Stewart Mitchell and his crap; it all came crashing down on me while I was standing by her grave. It's me, Flynn, not you. I love you just the way you are."

"I'm glad, since I was born like this. I don't know that I could change if I wanted to."

He nodded. Dad squeezed my shoulder and patted it. "And if you like Keith, I'm okay with that, too. I think I just need a little time to let all this settle in. He's a nice boy, isn't he? I liked his family."

I nodded. "Yeah, Keith's great." I looked away, taking in the mess all over the floor. It sent a chill through me. I'd never seen my father so enraged.

"You're shaking. Are you sure you're all right?" He sounded concerned.

I nodded. I was feeling less and less sure as the seconds ticked by. Dad said he was fine with my sexuality, but was he really? The thought of all that anger directed at me, instead of the glass objects in our house, frightened me anew. What if he took a golf club out and used it on me next time?

"I think I need to lie down. I'm a little… a little freaked out, I think."

"I'm sorry." He touched my hair. "I promise things will get better. I'm not going to drink anymore, and I'll try to work less."

"Okay. But, you don't really have to give up everything. The Scotch you buy is really smooth."

It took him a second to catch up with what I'd said. Then he smirked at me. "Flynn, do I need to lock the liquor cabinet?"

We didn't actually own a liquor cabinet. His booze was sitting on a table in the dining room. Easy to find. I knew he was messing with me. "No. I only tasted it. I'm home alone all the time, what did you expect? I clean the house, I make your dinner, I sample your alcohol, and I watch porn. I'm a normal teenager."

At that, he laughed. "I don't know that all those things are normal, but I guess they are for you. You do keep the house very clean, and I appreciate it. Just try not to get me arrested for you drinking my Scotch."

"I won't. I swear it isn't much."

"Okay." Dad took a couple steps toward the kitchen and paused. "I'm going to make some food. Go lie down and I'll text you when it's ready."

"Okay." I headed to the stairs.

"And Flynn?"

I stopped on the third step. "Yeah?"

"You know that porn isn't a healthy way to learn about sex, right?"

"Um, yeah, I guess." I wasn't sure what he was getting at. I worried suddenly we were going to have "the talk," and he was going to attempt to tell me about sex. I didn't want to have to explain how far I'd already gotten.

Dad came over to the steps and looked up at me. "Your mother was my first. She was special. I think she'd want you to know and keep it in mind as you explore things on your own. Don't rush into anything, Flynn. You have plenty of time, and a long life ahead of you. Make sure it's what you want first, and not peer pressure."

"I will. We haven't done much. Really. It's all new, and Keith and I aren't in a hurry."

"Good. Good. Well, I'll make dinner. Do you want to invite him over?"

My heart leapt at the chance. "Yeah. Can I?"

"Sure. I'd like to get to know him."

My dad left the room to take care of dinner. I went to my room, texted Keith and asked him to come over. I shed my clothes and put on a T-shirt before curling up on my pillow. I didn't realize how much emotion was bottled up until I relaxed on my bed and it all came out in a rush.

Keith found me in my bed. I wasn't crying by the time he sat next to me and started rubbing my back, but I might as well have been. My nose was stuffy and my eyes stung. They were probably red and puffy. "Hey," he said softly. "Is there anything I can do?"

"Hold me." I knew I sounded pathetic, but it wasn't like I planned to let my heart explode. He arrived after I'd spent an hour trying to process the day's events. They still had not settled in my head, and I wasn't sure I knew what to tell him if he were to ask me about them. I didn't want to talk, because I think I was still confused.

To my surprise, Keith didn't question me. He took off his shoes and lifted my blanket. As I scooted over, he stopped climbing in long enough to shed his shorts and socks. Once he was settled, Keith pulled me close and rubbed my back some more as he held me against his chest, giving me his quiet security, a safe place to cry. I wasn't expecting his silence because he rarely held back his opinions or observations, but I was glad for it.

"I spoke to your dad before I came up," he whispered. "He said he yelled and scared you. After seeing that mess on the floor and talking to your dad, I asked my mom if I could spend the night. She said I could, if that's okay with you."

I squeezed him tighter and squeaked an "Uh-huh," with as much voice as I could muster.

"Don't worry. I won't leave unless you want me to."

Chapter 10

February / March 2012: Gravitational Pull

My life had been perfect for weeks after Thanksgiving weekend. It was as if my father's volcanic eruption of rage left in its wake a new man. I hadn't seen him drink in weeks. Plus, he had gotten home before 7:00 p.m. at least four times a week. I had a father again, and I loved it.

Zach was MIA, but I had gotten the impression he needed some space. He said being away from his parents was clearing his head. I left him be.

By Christmas I was on an emotional high. Keith and I decided to move to the next level in our relationship after Keith surprised me with a red jockstrap for Christmas and asked me to model it. Things naturally progressed to nakedness in front of the Christmas tree, which was romantic as hell… until Zach showed up. My stupid fear of coming out took over and I jumped for the easiest option: I hid Keith in the closet instead of explaining to Zach he was my boyfriend.

It was my fault. I owned up to it. Zach showing up with a present and another bruise on his arm clouded my judgment, convincing me that exploration into fellatio with Keith could be postponed. Yeah, right. Keith's temper and jealousy ended our Christmas magic. Well, that and the fact I kind of shoved him out into the cold so Zach could spend the night. Not a shining moment for me, but one I felt I had to insist upon to protect my best friend's pride.

I spent New Year's alone.

I would have gone over and begged Keith to forgive me, except I needed space. True, I didn't want anyone but Keith, but I also needed to be there for Zach when he was suddenly emotionally available for the first time in over a year. He told me his father had been hitting him for years, but he'd been too scared to tell anyone. He asked me to keep his secret. He also asked if I'd be willing to help him if he left his parents house after graduating in May. Of course I said yes.

Zach needed me and I figured I would do whatever he asked.

My feelings for Keith would just have to wait.

***

Predictably, Keith showed up at my door on Valentine's Day.

Unlike the last time he came knocking, this time his eyes were red and watery. I stepped back and allowed him to enter before closing the door.

"My dad's not home," I mentioned, just in case he was worried about talking openly.

"I hate being away from you," he said with a strangled sort of rasp that suggested he'd been crying for a while. "I haven't done anything for weeks. I work. I sit at home and stare at the picture of us on my phone. I see you at school and…."

"You don't make eye contact with me!" I interjected.

"Because it's too painful!" he responded, stepping closer. "I don't want this to be so hard."

I cocked my head to the side. "Then stop breaking up with me." Probably not the nicest way to say it, but it was how it came out.

"You stop doing stupid things, like picking Zach over me," Keith countered, the angry edge taking the hurt out of his tone.

"I'm not. I'm trying to pick both of you, Keith. There are things you don't understand. Just because he needs to talk to me alone sometimes doesn't mean I'm picking him over you. He doesn't have a family like yours. Can't you just trust me?" I stepped closer, challenging him.

Keith narrowed his eyes. "Can't *you* trust *me*? Let me in on your secrets. What is so terrible that you have to throw me out in order to talk about it? Are you in love with him?" He took a step closer.

"What? No."

"Are you seeing someone?"

"What?" I shrieked. "No! Why would you ask that?"

He gave me that annoying, nonchalant shrug of his. "I don't know. My mom said she saw you with someone at Starbucks last week."

"Zach. I was there with Zach."

"Zach," he repeated, and I didn't like his tone. "If nothing's going on, then tell me why you get this look on your face whenever he's around?" He took one more step and he was only inches from my face. "I don't get why you have to be there for him all the time, and to hell with *my* feelings."

I couldn't explain why I did it, but the words stumbled out, slipping through my fingers as I futilely fought to snatch them back. "His dad hits him!"

His face flushed and he stepped back. "Oh." I didn't think he expected that response. He swallowed audibly, moved over to the couch, and sat. "I didn't know. I thought they were so upright and religious."

"They are."

"That's fucked up," he said. Keith was clearly disturbed, evidenced by the uneasiness etching a line over his eyes. Now maybe Keith understood the way I felt, maybe he even had the same feelings about it.

I sat next to him. "I know."

"Is there anyone he can tell?" Keith sounded concerned, and that made me feel really good, no longer carrying this secret alone. I hoped he would understand after all.

"He told *me*. I suggested he talk to a counselor, but he's too afraid. His dad's been doing this for years." I reached out and touched his knee, and Keith took my hand. It was as if gravity was pulling us closer. We had to touch. "He's trying to finish college," I continued. "I think he just wants to get through the next couple months, find a job, and move away. I think he wants help, but I also think he's trying to keep his life together as best he can because he fears change. I can't make the decision for him. I just want to be there when he needs me. You know?"

Keith nodded, calmly rubbing my fingers with his. "Yeah. I get it. I'm sorry. I guess I'm jealous because I see how comfortable you are with each other."

"Comfortable?" I almost laughed. "We aren't comfortable."

"Yeah, you are. Very. And I don't like it."

"When have I ever given you a reason to be jealous?" I took our clasped hands and held his hand between both of mine in my lap, scooting even closer so our thighs pressed together.

"Um, yeah, how about shoving me out your front door on Christmas ten minutes after I blew you?"

Guilt yanked on my pulmonary artery and twisted. I pleaded, "I'm sorry. I really am."

"If you had shoved me out the door because of your dad, I don't think I'd have been as hurt, but it was for Zach."

I squeezed his hand and rubbed his forearm. "I *am* sorry. I've tried to spend as much time with you as I can. I've been over your house dozens of times. I've met all your family. I've told you how much I care about you, but you still push and push. I was afraid of how Zach would react seeing us together, when he's got so much going on already. You know I've been reticent at school."

"But the whole school wasn't in your living room at Christmas. It was just me and Zach, and you chose him."

"I know. I'm sorry. I behaved really badly. All I want is for you to give me time to come out on my terms. That's it. Can you stop trying to make me do what you want? Can't loving you be enough?"

"You love me?"

His mouse-like question reminded me that we hadn't actually said the words. I nodded. "Yes, Keith, I love you. You're all I think about."

"Not true. You think about Zach too."

"Maybe, but it's not the same. Look, it's Valentine's Day, the anniversary of our first kiss; can't we stop fighting about this for a few minutes and enjoy being together? I want to have sex with my boyfriend like a normal couple."

Keith smirked, squeezing my arm with his free hand. "You do?"

"Yeah. I do." We paused, gazing at one another; but gravity, again, pulled us together like rain soaking into the parched ground. We kissed and fell back against the cushions, tangled in each other's arms.

"I love you too," Keith confessed between kisses, reaching up my shirt and pinching my nipples.

I gasped. "Wow. You're more handsy than I remember."

"We're alone. If I can't touch you in public, I want to take full advantage of everything I can get away with in private. Is this okay?" He asked, rubbing my nipple in gentle circles.

Okay? Oh God. I never knew how erotic nipples could be. "Yes. Yes," I rasped.

Keith tongued my throat and moved his hand lower.

I groaned.

"Will you fuck me?" he whispered into my ear.

I thought I misheard him. "What?"

Keith pulled back and looked me in the eyes. Very seriously he repeated, "I want you to fuck me."

Here, I thought we'd simply suck each other off. That's where we had left off last time we were together. "But we haven't really done—"

"It doesn't matter. I want this. I need this. You and me. Please? I brought condoms."

Keith's hazel eyes were normally beautiful. His deep blues and greens, intermixed with a chocolate brown, could mesmerize me for hours. Indeed, I remember times not long ago when they had. But Keith's lust laden eyes had me melting. My pulse was racing as I asked, "You did? You planned it?"

"Not exactly. I hoped something would happen. I knew it was our anniversary. I thought I'd stash them in your room if nothing else."

"Are you sure?" Because the thought of sex scared me as much as it thrilled me. Could we? Wow. Sex. I never thought it'd be this soon.

Keith nodded and pulled me off the couch. He led me to my room and closed the door before stripping me of my shirt and undoing my jeans. He moved his hands all over my skin as I shoved his pants down his legs. Once on the bed, whatever bit of apprehension we harbored disappeared as we explored each other's bodies at length. Clinging and rolling, caressing and squeezing, our bodies pressed together and entwined like an octopus wrestling match.

Of course, after the initial foreplay frenzy, fucking Keith's ass was not as easy as it sounded when he suggested it. There was squirming and panting and a lot of hesitation. I almost suggested we stop all together, but Keith's mouth and tongue proved very persuasive. He had me so damn hard, I had to keep prepping him, because if I couldn't fuck him, I thought for sure I would die.

But don't let anyone tell you it's easy the first time. It hurt him... *I* hurt him. He was so tense, the high pitch of his whimpers told me to stop, but in his stubbornness Keith pushed back all at once. I sank into him and he cried out.

"Why the fuck d'you do that?" I asked accusingly, holding his hips still.

Keith and I had settled on doggy style. I'm not sure why. I wanted to look into his eyes, but he insisted on this position because he had read somewhere it was easier for beginners. I doubted it. I think it was his way of having some control as I topped him. Whatever his reason, Keith had pressed back quickly, and I filled him whether he was ready or not. I felt bad for causing his pain, but it was his own stupid fault.

He panted even more. "I… don't… know. Shit."

I hated how he sounded. "Keith?" I rubbed his ass gently and caressed his back. "Keith, let me pull out."

"Don't you dare!" he snarled, pressing back onto me. "Just… give me a minute."

"All the time you need." I said it, but fuck if it wasn't hard remaining still. Everything in my groin urged me to pull out and thrust back in. When I felt the walls of his canal shift and clench and then loosen, holy fuck! "Keith. Stop doing that. I won't be able to stay still if you—"

"Move! Oh, fuck. Move, Flynn!" He shoved back and then slid himself forward, fucking himself on my dick.

I took that cue and pushed in all the way before pulling almost completely out. I tried to go slow, but Keith did not seem patient enough. When I hesitated too long, he shoved his ass onto me.

"Stop!" I slapped him, hard.

"Ow!" he winced. "Shit. Do that again."

I slapped his ass cheek one more time and pumped my hips at a more rapid pace. If he wanted it rougher, I'd give it to him. It didn't take long to settle into the right rhythm for both of us. Maybe lovemaking was rocky at first, but I think we were both anxious and unsure about how to best move together. Synchronicity is not achieved automatically. In fact, we could have probably won an award for mechanical failure.

But coming? Yeah, that part needed no help. I was grunting my ejaculation seconds before he was crying out his. "Oh fuck, Flynn!" I saw him reach under and jerk himself, his arm moving rapidly. "Oh yeah…."

We barely moved after that. I pulled out carefully and flopped on the bed next to him, panting. I heard him murmur. I'd never felt so wasted in all my life.

"My ass hurts," Keith mumbled.

I chuckled, but it wasn't really funny. "Hurts in a good way, or a bad way?"

"A good way. I'm okay. But I don't think I'm gonna do that again for a while. My ass fucking hurts." Keith reached his arm across my chest and kissed my arm as I chuckled at the irony.

"I told you we should take it slow."

"Shut up." He kissed my arm again and whispered, "I love you."

"I love you too."

We fell asleep that way, and I woke up to find a sticky dried condom in my fist. Yeah, that was disgusting. Keith was asleep so I carefully climbed out of bed and covered him with a blanket. I walked across the hall to the bathroom and took a piss before washing up. I turned around and found my dad standing in the doorway.

"Oh Jeez!" I jumped. "Dad. What the heck?"

"Did you use a condom?"

I blinked. "Uh, yeah." I felt like I'd been caught robbing a bank. "How'd you know we...."

"I've been home for a while. I heard you."

"Oh." I looked down in embarrassment, which only doubled when I saw how naked I was, standing there in front of my dad. *After he heard me having sex. Nice one, Flynn.* "I, um...." I didn't know what to say.

"You didn't hurt him, did you? He sounded—"

I cringed and held up my hand in hopes of stopping his words from assaulting my ears. "Oh, Dad, stop! Eww. Keith's fine. Okay. But can we *not* talk about what you heard? That's just... Eww."

He snickered, nodded, and walked toward the steps. "All long as you're being safe. Okay? Don't do anything stupid."

I knew he was trying to be a good dad. It was kind of gross thinking he had heard us, but having a conversation about it seemed even worse. "Okay." I hoped that was sufficient to end the discussion. Thankfully, it was. My dad left and I went back in to Keith.

Keith.

He was sleeping in my bed.

Oh God, I loved him.

***

About a month later, I found my dad staring out at the pool as he often did, sipping his coffee. "Hey Dad," I greeted him like I normally would.

"Good morning."

I smiled. Things had certainly changed since November. Now it was March and we shared many more smiles than I remembered from the past.

"I remember making love to your mother on Valentine's Day."

I cringed. That had been weeks ago! Couldn't my dad forget he'd heard us? Why? Why did he have to bring it up… *again*? I took the milk out and poured a glass as if I hadn't heard him.

"That's why Nate was born on November thirteenth. Your mom said it was the date with the highest birth rate because it was nine months after Valentine's Day, but I didn't have the heart to tell her the Internet said otherwise. She'd been convinced." He chuckled a low, soft laugh. "I miss her."

"I miss her, too." It was the only response I knew to give. What else could I say?

"Do you think she'd understand if I found another woman?"

I almost missed the shelf as I set the milk back in the fridge. "What? Are you dating someone?"

He turned his smiling face my way. "No. But I'm thinking about it. I don't want to be alone. Seeing you and Keith, knowing you're… you know… it makes me happy to see you happy. I think it's about time I moved on. I want to be happy, too."

"I'm glad. But if you can *never* mention again how many times you can hear us, I think I'd be even happier."

He laughed more heartily and agreed. "Okay, I won't. Is he still coming to dinner tonight? I thought I'd give him a little present." He handed me a paper bag and I took it.

Inside was a box of condoms.

I closed it and hung my head to the side. "Are you kidding me? There is no fucking way you're giving this to Keith. No way. That's sick."

He laughed harder. "Your mother isn't here. It's up to me to do all the embarrassing things I can think of."

I grinned at my dad's belly laugh. "No, it isn't." And then I was laughing too. I couldn't remember a time when we laughed so hard. Just when the laughter died down, Keith walked in and my dad started all over again.

"What did I miss?" he asked, walking over to me.

I kissed my lover between guffaws and wrapped my arms around him, tugging him close. *Lover.* Oh wow, Keith was my lover and my dad had given me condoms. There was no way I could explain it to Keith, so I laughed until I cried.

Chapter 11

April / May 2012: Overcoming Challenges

The *not* touching at school mandate was increasingly hard for me to adhere to. I knew it was my rule, but damn, sex had changed things. Before Valentine's Day, I would have definitely agreed that there was a type of gravitational pull between Keith and me. Some sort of unseen magnetism that brought us together time and time again, even if we were fighting or irritated with one another. I'd felt it from the first moment his eyes met mine in art class. An unknown force of energy bringing us face-to-face, arm-in-arm, body-to-body, flesh-to-flesh; in a whirlwind of emotion, passion, and need. He had said he couldn't stand being away from me, and the truth was; I couldn't bear the feeling of being away from him, either. It was as if my very cells needed his touch to survive.

And a kiss or two, or a hundred, couldn't hurt.

We had time off in the middle of April for spring break and ended up at a café on the corner of John and Main Streets. Starbucks had been a great place to meet up initially, but the store was always crowded. This café was intimate and relaxing compared to the high volume of metro-sexual patrons cycling through Starbucks to get their lattés before work. Keith was more of a tea guy anyway, and our new hangout had more varieties of tea than I could count. It became our favorite place that *wasn't* my house.

His house was also fun, I really liked his family, but mine was empty most of the time. We liked the privacy. Well, really, we liked the freedom to have sex. But sometimes it was nice to sit at a table, sipping coffee, or tea, and flirt with our eyes or surreptitious strokes of tongues against teeth. His gorgeous hazel eyes did everything to wake up all my hormones, and his slight grin of satisfaction from knowing it had me hard and longing for what we'd do later.

"I gotta pee," he said, standing up with a wink. He touched my fingers gently before heading to the restroom.

I watched him walk away before I felt eyes on me. That kind of feeling that made hairs on my neck tingle and stand on end. I scanned the room and instantly felt a chill when my eyes landed on Bruce Merryman, standing on the sidewalk outside the café, glaring at me through the window.

My heart pounded when he entered and made his way over to our table. My mind cried, *Where's Keith?*

He sat opposite me. "I've been watching you."

Accusatory? Yes. I couldn't form a reply.

"You and Leppo are mighty googly-eyed for straight guys."

In the silent, contained, controlled part of my brain I cackled at hearing Bruce, the thug, use the word "googly-eyed," but I would never let the amusement show on my face or escape my lips. Instead I opted for ignorance. "I don't know what you're talking about."

"Cut the bullshit." I jumped when he slapped the table. "I know there's more going on, but I don't care."

"You don't?" I asked, dubiously. "Then why the harassment?"

Bruce shrugged and for the first time in his life, appeared sheepish. "I don't know. I guess because I don't understand it."

"Understand what? Me being gay?" *And yes, I just came out. Shit.* Where the fuck was Keith?

"Yes. No. I don't know." Bruce was flustered. "My cousin's gay. I don't understand him. He likes this other dude, ya know, and I don't know what to do about it." Bruce absently touched the side of Keith's half-full mug. He looked so pathetic; I couldn't help feeling sorry for him.

"You don't have to *do* anything. Just be his cousin. Be his friend." It seemed so logical to me. I guess I should have taken my own advice and just been myself, and when someone couldn't relate, I could have told them just to be my friend. Easier said than done.

Bruce looked up. "That's it?"

"That's it. He isn't a different person. You just see him differently. Stop. If you mentally paint labels on people's foreheads, like 'homosexual,' 'dyke,' 'puffster,' or even the all-purpose insult: 'loser,' it unconsciously changes your perception of them. Without even realizing it, you no longer see them as a person, but as a definition. They are who they are. Your cousin is still your cousin, same as always."

He nodded slowly, as if considering what I had to say very carefully. "You know, you're even starting to sound like Keith."

I smiled. That was the first time I'd ever heard Bruce use a first name to refer to someone. "I guess. He's in the bathroom if you want to talk to him."

Bruce stood up but lingered by the table. "Nah, that's okay. Leppo's too egotistical. He always has to be right."

"True." It amused me at how much that trait *didn't* bother me. I rather liked Keith's self-assurance.

"Thanks, man." Bruce lifted his chin as a symbolic gesture of our moment of male bonding. It was odd, but I found myself doing the same chin-lift in return.

He left just as Keith came back to join me, watching through the window as Bruce walked away. "Bruce was here? Are you okay?" he asked as he sat.

"Yeah. I'm fine." I grinned. "Bruce just needed some advice."

"From you?"

I frowned. "Thanks," I responded dryly.

"No, what I mean is; what did he want from you? I thought he wanted to beat the crap out of you."

"No. He's just as confused as most people, I think. But he'll be fine."

"Okay." Keith sipped his tea. "So, do we have anything to work out while we're here, unencumbered by Kelly and Grace's opinions, and without fear of hormonal interference?"

"Um, prom, I guess. Do we go? We gotta buy tickets."

"I don't think they'll let us go together. I'd like to ask the administration, but it might be more of a headache than it's worth. You're not out yet, so I'd be fighting the battle on my own."

Not true, I just came out to Bruce. "We could make it easier and go in a group. Grace said her boyfriend broke up with her. She's free."

"Really? But didn't they just start dating?"

"Yeah. Turns out he was only interesting in one thing and Grace said no."

"That's dumb. Does Grace know we're sleeping together?"

"What? No. Why would I tell her? It's none of her business." I couldn't explain my defensiveness, but for some reason I didn't want everyone in the world to know who I was fucking, or who was fucking *me*. It was for Keith and me only. Grace didn't need to know.

Keith gave me a look. "Sorry I asked. So, fine, we go to prom as a group. No one will know. Although, it would be nice if I could dance with you at least once."

I agreed. "We'll find a way."

"I hope so." Keith downed the rest of his drink. "Are we ready?" We both stood and put our trash in the bin. On the way to Keith's car he said, "Do we need to stop anywhere?"

He unlocked his car and we both got in. "No," I answered.

"Good." He started the engine. "I want to try the flavored massage oil your dad gave me."

My jaw dropped. "Oh no! He did not give you flavored massage oil." I couldn't believe it.

"Yeah, he did. I think it's funny."

"It is not funny at all. It's twisted."

Keith drove down Main Street and smiled hugely at me. "Yes, it is. Your dad's a trip. It's his way of being a part of your life, of showing his support."

I cringed at the thought. "No, it's not. He's deranged."

Keith reached over and took my hand as he drove. "No, baby, it's fine."

"Baby?" I questioned his first time using a term of endearment on me.

"Would you prefer something else? Honey? Sweets?"

I shook my head. I was amused, but I smiled, even though "baby" sounded odd. I consented, "Whatever. You could probably call me 'dog shit', and I'd be fine with it."

"A high compliment considering my name isn't Zach."

I ripped my hand from his grasp. "Keith! Why do you have to ruin our moment like that?"

"Just stating the facts. Zach gets away with everything, so I guess I'm seeing how far my boundaries extend."

"Public displays of affection, that's where they stop. Okay? Not outing me. That's the limit. Although... I kinda told Bruce."

"What?" he exclaimed with widening eyes. I was glad he stopped at the red light at Center Street. "That's great! No more hiding."

"I didn't say that. I'm still tentative, but I'm not as fearful. Can't that be enough?"

"Yeah. It's a great step. I'm proud of you, sweets. Should we head over to Zach's?"

"No!"

"Okay. One step at a time."

I felt relieved when he stopped pushing, so I slipped my hand back into his. I'd tell Zach, I would, but not while he had all the other crap in his life to deal with.

Later, I almost wanted to thank my dad for the oil he'd given Keith. Holy fucking hell, was that a great gift!

***

By prom, we'd decided to go as friends. Keith had done well with not pushing me, and the girls didn't have dates anyway. Kelly wasn't seeing anyone in college, and Grace said she'd rather us go as a group than try and find a date. It worked out just fine. We took pictures as a group, as well as individually. The photographer even agreed to take one of the girls, and then of us. I think he thought we were just goofing around, but it didn't matter, because by the time he clicked the camera shutter, Keith had already wrapped his arms around me.

We were dancing in a group later that evening when I felt a tap on my shoulder. It was Bruce and his thugs, in tuxedos, and my stomach seized. "Bruce." I stopped dancing and my friends closed in around me.

"Brewer. I see you and Leppo are together. Is he your date?"

"You already know the answer to that. What's it to you?" I didn't want to ask in front of his friends, but he gave me no choice. The "lie" was on the tip of my tongue, but the "truth" was fighting for the right to be spoken.

"Nothing. Just wondering." He shrugged and motioned me over to the side, away from the group. When I complied, he leaned closer to my ear and said, "I talked to my cousin. You were right." It was a heart-warming admission, even though Bruce looked uncomfortable as he confessed it. "I was thinking, maybe, someday, we could all get together. I still don't understand it, but you and Leppo seem normal."

"That's because we are normal. But yeah, okay." I agreed before thinking about it too deeply. If he wanted to cause me trouble, he could have. But something in his face said he was simply curious. "If you want to. I still live on Willis Street. You can come by if you want."

Bruce nodded. "Thanks." We rejoined our group and Bruce's friends, and he told Keith, "I got into FMAU, Florida Agricultural and Mechanical University, for entomology. Thanks for never making fun of me over it. Too many boneheads thought it was dumb I liked bugs."

"No problem." Keith gave him a short answer and waited for him to say something else. He didn't. Bruce paused, looked at the four of us one at a time, and then walked away. "Well that was interesting," Keith commented.

"I seriously thought he was going to cause trouble, or draw attention over here. Wow."

"He kept looking at you funny though. Did something happen between the two of you? Like after the coffee shop?" Keith asked.

I gave him a look. "Um, no. What are you talking about?"

"You seem awfully chummy." Keith sounded suspicious. His tone suggested he was conjuring up images of things that only Keith would think of.

"I told you. He had some questions."

"About what?" he snapped.

"My sexuality," I explained. "I already told you that. He needed to talk to me about his cousin."

"That's it? Are you sure?" Keith questioned. "Is that why you invited him over to your house? Or did he ask you out?"

That fucking jealous streak of his had to go! I touched his chest hoping to calm him down. "No. Just stop. You're being ridiculous again. You can't get jealous every time a guy talks to me. He didn't ask me out, and I didn't invite him over for anything but friendly advice about his cousin." I slid my hand up to his cheek and Keith looked into my eyes. "You need to let go of the jealousy."

Grace agreed, "Sounds like a plan to me."

Keith nodded reluctantly. "Okay. I'll try. My dad always told me words make a bigger impact than fisticuffs."

"Who uses that word?" Kelly chuckled. She had a habit of making fun of him for being a geek. He'd use big words and she'd snicker. It was a thing with the two of them. I liked it. To me it meant she was comfortable enough to poke fun, and we were all close enough not to take offense.

"Keith," I said to regain his attention.

Kelly's comment shifted his mood. Keith was now grinning and the dimple on his cheek had me yearning to kiss it. I gazed at my boyfriend and caressed the side of his face. "You never cease to surprise me. You're simply amazing."

"I know." He grinned confidently.

Right then I knew I had to kiss him. His jealousy aside, he was simply adorable. I took his hand and led him over to a more secluded area near the wall. The low lighting and disco-ball effects over the center of the dance floor created shadows, so privacy was easier to find than when the house lights had been up. Grace and Kelly both followed, and squealed as I pressed my lips to his, but other than them, no one even noticed. We were on the fringes of a crowded dance floor, still no one noticed two boys kissing. I pulled Keith into my body and kissed him deeply before taking him into my arms to dance. This was my prom and I was going to enjoy a little dancing before it was over, even if it wasn't in attention central.

So we did. Soft, slow, synchronous, our steps swayed back and forth as we gazed into each other's eyes. Keith looked absolutely smitten.

If anyone had a problem, I wasn't aware of it.

Chapter 12

Summer, Fall, Winter, Spring: Fast Forward

We had graduated in June 2012. Halleluiah. Oddly, Zach's party for graduating with his degree in horticulture fell on the same day, and his family spent time in his back yard, while my dad and I went over to Keith's. It worked out for the best. Zach texted me his congratulations.

When July second rolled around again, I faced the same dilemma I had the previous year: taking Keith to the birthday dinner. He declined. He said he didn't want a repeat of 2011. I couldn't blame him.

When I turned eighteen, I worried that I'd feel the same pressures that Zach had felt, more specifically, the pressures his parents put on him. But no, my dad was completely different than Mr. Mitchell. My dad *finally* bought me a car, and helped me enroll into Carroll Community College. He helped me fill out the Maryland Voter Registration Application and said he was surprised I checked the Republican box. I didn't know why that surprised him. I had all kinds of opinions that were far more conservative than Keith's, my Democratic boyfriend. My dad and I'd laughed about the differences between my outspoken boyfriend and me, and then we'd gotten ice cream.

By the fall, Keith was settled in at Dickinson and I was commuting to Carroll from home. Not all that difficult, but I had to admit my bed felt cold and empty without Keith in it. I was pretty sure he'd spent every night at my house in August, before he had to leave for college. It was a challenge of sorts to see how much sex we could have before we were forced to go long periods of time without it.

I had gotten my tongue pierced in late October. Keith was driving down to vote in the elections on November sixth, so I wanted my tongue to have time to heal before putting my piercing to the test.

I had decided on a tongue piercing because I could hide it. Once it was healed, I could remove the bar, or simply watch how I spoke. I doubted anyone would know it was in there. The actual piercing itself had been easy. The piercing specialist had held my tongue out with an instrument that looked like forceps or steak tongs, marked a spot on my tongue with a purple marker, and then swiftly poked another tool through the center of my tongue. The implement had to have been hollow, like a metal straw or something, because I remember feeling the guy slip another object inside the tube before pulling it free. I didn't know for sure because I hadn't asked, but two seconds later I had a silver barbell through my tongue.

The guy had told me the first metal bar needed to be longer than I'd need to wear after the piercing healed. After the swelling went down, and I left the bar in the appropriate amount of time, I could switch it out for whatever color jewelry I wanted. Having my tongue pierced had felt odd, but it hadn't hurt until hours later when it swelled. Then it hurt like a bitch. I had trouble talking, eating, and swallowing; anything involving my mouth hurt, and had to be avoided as much as possible. I sucked ice chips constantly for a week.

Planning early paid off, as everything was healed by the time I saw Keith.

"So, we're voting first, right? Getting it out of the way before heading to your house?"

I nodded, and put my blinker on to change lanes. "If that's okay with you?" I said. "Of course we could go to your house. I haven't seen your mom for months."

"Hey, wait a minute," Keith said suspiciously, reaching across the front seat to take a hold of my chin. He didn't turn my head as I was driving, only made sure I knew what he suspected as he asked me to stick out my tongue. Then he took his hand away in surprise. "Oh my gosh! You have a tongue piercing. When did that happen? And why didn't you tell me?"

"It was supposed to be a surprise."

"Color me surprised! Wow. Did it hurt?"

I pulled the car into the parking lot of the polling place and parked. "Yes and no. It didn't hurt when he did it, only later, when it swelled up."

"You know, I've read online that they don't really make oral sex better."

I held up a finger. "Ah, but I read it can add sensation, not skill. If someone is exceptionally good at sucking cock, then a tongue piercing can add a little extra something." I winked, turning off the engine and pocketing my keys.

Keith grinned and slid closer to me. "So, I guess you want to test the theory?" He raised his eyebrow.

I nodded.

"Fuck," he rasped. "I have such a hot boyfriend." Keith kissed me and moaned into my mouth. "That definitely adds an extra something. Fuck. I think I want to strip you naked right here." He grabbed my thigh and slid his palm up to my crotch.

I shoved it away. "Not here. Come on Keith, someone could see."

"Like Zach?"

"We aren't having this argument again." I got out of the car and headed over to the building entrance. Keith followed me.

"No? Then tell me how many times you've had lunch with him?"

I shrugged. "I don't know."

"Ten? Twenty?"

"I don't know. He works close to the college sometimes. I can't help that he takes lunch breaks when I'm between classes. It just works out that way. You need to get over your jealousy, Keith. We've been friends my whole life; I'm not de-friending him just because you don't like him."

He eyed me curiously. Probably choosing his words in light of my reasoning. "What did you talk about?"

"His job. He likes it and feels like he's learning stuff, so he talks a lot about the trees and different bugs he's found."

"Did you tell him about me?" Keith's challenging stare told me exactly what he meant, even though I already knew.

He wanted to know if I mentioned our relationship during our many lunches together. Of course I hadn't. It had been refreshing to spend time with Zach without pressure from anywhere or anyone. After Zach had graduated, he'd taken a job with a nationally recognized tree company. He had steady work, steady pay, and had moved out of his parents' house. For months, Zach had told me how freeing it felt. He was on his own, and his parents had left him be for the first time in his life.

"No," I answered.

"Then you're cheating on me," he huffed, heading into the building to find the line that started with "L" for Leppo.

While in the building, we didn't speak. He took his voting card over to the machine and I did the same. It was a really cool experience for me, and I ended up reading the questions two or three times each, just to know whom I was voting for and what the addendum questions were. The most important question to me was on same-sex marriage. Of course I was voting for it!

When we were both finished, we met at my car.

"Who'd you vote for?" Keith asked bluntly.

"Isn't it supposed to be a secret? I vote privately and only I know which candidate I voted for." I started the car and pulled out of the parking spot.

"Yes. But you're my boyfriend. You should be able to tell me. You voted for Romney, didn't you? You're a republican. It only makes sense. I just don't know why you would vote for him."

"I didn't." I turned onto the next street.

"What?" I shocked him. "Why?"

"Because of his religious views."

"What? Really? Do you think religion is wrong in politics? Because I'm rather dogmatic about Christianity. So far, we haven't discussed how strongly I believe the Bible, but I do. I think religion goes hand-in-hand with who a person is. For me, I'm all about loving the Lord my God with all my heart, soul, mind, and strength. What about you? Do you think Presidential candidates should keep church and state separate? Because personally I don't think that was exactly the intent of our forefathers when they drew up the constitution."

It was slightly irritating having this discussion while I drove, but I decided I'd rather hear Keith out on the way home, than when we got to my house.

I pulled my car into the one car garage at the back of our property, off Court Lane, and parked. "No, Keith, that's not what I'm saying. I couldn't vote for Romney because he's Mormon. That's it. It's not religion in particular, as much as his *particular* religion. Why? Well… because I'm gay. I don't see Mormonism as a progressive religion that embraces gay rights. Episcopalians maybe, but not Mormons. I did actually agree on many of his policy proposals; but I don't care what Romney promises because I don't believe he'll stand for, and vote for, the laws that affect *me*. So I couldn't vote for him. I may not agree with what Obama said in all his speeches, but I believe he'll pass laws that benefit the LGBT community as a whole. That's what matters to me right now."

The licentious look in his eyes backed up his next words: "You've got me so turned on right now."

I laughed out loud and jumped out of the car.

We giggled like little kids as he chased me from the garage, around the side of the pool, through the kitchen door, into my house, and up the stairs to my bedroom.

***

Winter break was just about the same as August for Keith and me. We spent every waking moment together, and saw the girls when they were available. Grace had met someone in her English class, and Kelly said it wasn't as much fun poking fun at our snuggling while watching movies as when Grace had been single, so she only hung out with us a couple of times.

Christmas that year had been phenomenal. We'd spent it with Keith's family and I had even allowed him to touch me, hug me, and kiss me a couple of times in front of them. I caught his older brother Johnny smirking at us in the living room, and for the first time I didn't mind.

February 2013 wasn't as fun as in years past. Keith's family invited my dad and me over to watch the big game on February third. It had been fun, especially since the Baltimore Ravens won, but Keith had left right after the game because he had classes the next morning. Keith was in Pennsylvania most of the time, and I was at Carroll Community College.

Generally I enjoyed reading, but being an English major destroyed my enthusiasm for it. If I'd had any sense to begin with, I should have probably set out to be a history major as I did enjoy it. I doubted my stamina to complete my degree in English, and had talked to the department chair about it. I was unfocused and unsure about what I wanted to do. I missed Keith, and my classes were boring, dull, and long.

Spending Valentine's Day alone was depressing.

By February twenty-third, I had had enough moping around in self-pity. Keith was at school earning a degree in architecture, so I considered quitting after this semester in order to de-stress my life. Eventually, he'd be making good money, enough to support an unfocused homebody who lacked the direction necessary to finish his own degree. Did I set out to become a "kept man?" Not exactly, but I wouldn't complain if it turned out that way. The thought of taking care of Keith, becoming his "housewife," in the near future made me warm and tingly. I could do that. Not completing my degree seemed less emasculating if I focused on being Keith's arm-candy instead. Or maybe I could write a non-fiction novel about the history of my hometown? I'd always been fascinated with the historical landmarks around Westminster. I could take care of Keith, and write.

I was sure my future held promise.

I walked outside and breathed in a huge lungful of winter air. It was crisp and clean. My neighborhood was quiet today, hiding under a thin layer of snow. I decided to take down the Christmas lights before Murphy's Law laughed at me and delivered three feet of snow. This season had been a disappointment snow-wise so far, and I thought that this little bit would more than likely melt in an hour or two. In contrast, 2011 had been amazing! Keith and I'd had so much fun at his house that March, throwing snowballs at his little brother; but this year I highly doubted we'd have enough snow for a repeat of that.

I'd just started undecorating the first bush when I heard Mr. Mitchell order, "Just get in the car!"

I glanced in his direction and made eye contact with Zach. He paused next to his father's car, then hung his head, presumably in shame, before slipping into the front seat. I ducked behind the bush to the left of our front door and watched them drive away. I took out my phone and texted, but Zach didn't respond. He was wearing a white shirt and black tie under his dress coat. Why was he dressed up? Why wasn't he texting back?

The possible answers frightened me.

Later, when I turned out my light for the night, I got a reply from Zach: *Can I come over? Please?*

Sure, I texted.

I'll let myself in with my key. Don't get up. I just need to talk to you. Don't turn the light on, okay?

All right.

A couple of minutes later I heard footsteps on the other side of my door. It opened and then shut. "Zach?"

"Yeah. Don't turn the light on—they might see."

"What's going on? You're freaking me out." I saw his silhouette outlined in the moonlight streaming through my window. I heard rustling and my eyes adjusted enough to see him take off his shirt. "What are you doing?" I questioned as he lifted my sheet.

"Scoot over."

"Why? Can't you sleep on the floor?"

"Come on Flynn. We've slept together dozens of times," he grumbled as he pushed his way in next to me.

"But we were kids."

"I'm not sleeping on the floor. I can't talk to you from down there without making too much noise."

"Fine." I scooted over as far as I could.

Zach fussed around in the dark, fluffing my pillow and adjusting the blankets a couple minutes before settling down enough to tell me why he had so urgently needed to come over. "I'm sorry about all this," he whispered finally. "My dad's been… really hard on me lately."

I didn't like how close he was to me. My bed was larger than Zach's, thank God, but we were still pressed against each other, lying on our backs. I just kept speculating about how badly Keith was going to want to kill me when he found out. "Harder than before? How much harder can he be? He hit you with a golf club, Zach."

"Flynn, this time… this time he's taking me away."

"What? Why?" I asked in the quietest demanding tone I could. I turned my head and looked at him. I really couldn't see much, but I could have sworn the faint light reflected off tear-tracks by his eyes.

His voice was strangled as he explained. "My dad found stuff on my computer when I came home for Christmas."

"What?"

"Amy was using my laptop in the kitchen to look up a recipe for gingerbread men. She left it open. Later, when my brother was talking about a trip he'd like to take to the Caribbean, my dad used my computer to Google the town." Zach paused. It was a gravid pause like those in horror movies right before an unsuspecting camper got skewered through the eye.

"And?"

"And… You know how Google remembers recent searches and brings up things by letter on the toolbar?"

Something about this was not right. "Yeah."

"The search window listed things my dad didn't like, so he opened my browsing history."

I knew I'd probably be embarrassed if my dad looked at my browsing history, but I don't think I'd be frightened by it. Zach sounded terrified. Keith and I had watched gay porn together a few times, some of it too kinky for Keith to stomach, but nothing that would make my dad upset. Disturbed maybe, but not upset.

I asked carefully, "What did he see? And where is he taking you?"

"Research."

What the heck kind of research? "Zach? What was it?"

He hesitated, but he finally told me. "I was looking up the differences between fundamentalism, humanism, Catholicism, and other religions. I think he mostly got ticked when one site I bookmarked listed our branch of religion as a 'cult.' He started yelling. I thought he was going to throw my computer across the room. Then he told me I needed to reconnect with our home church. He said it had been his fault for letting me slide so long. He'd been distracted by work and the demands of leadership in the church, but he told me he'd set me back on the path soon. He said we were going to take a trip out west, just the two of us."

Then I heard his sniffles. I knew Zach was crying. I would have rather been skewered through the eye by a creepy horror movie slasher, than to hear Zach cry. "You're twenty years old. If you don't want to go, you don't have to." It was clear he didn't want to.

He turned suddenly. He was now lying on his side and looking right at me. Against my better judgment, I turned to face him.

Zach hissed at me hysterically, but through a whisper. "You don't know my dad. Not like I do. I have to go. I can't imagine what he'd do if I said no. Flynn, what if he took his anger out on Amy? I gotta go!"

"Okay. I get it." I really didn't, but he needed my support, not antagonism. I hated the strain and fear in his voice, but what could I do? Zach was completely terrified of his father. "How long?"

"A couple months."

"How can you take off work that long? Won't they fire you?"

"My dad said it should fit under 'religious observation' and if they fired me, he'd hire his lawyers to fight it. I don't know if that's true, but I don't want to find out. I don't care. If I lose my job I'll find another one. I'm scared Flynn."

It dawned on me that this whole thing was about religion. I'd spent so much time with Keith's relaxed and open-minded family that I'd forgotten just how strict Zach's family had always been. Keith's was so different. I wondered what Keith would say to Zach if he were here. "Why were you looking up those things, about fundamentalism and stuff?"

I felt Zach's fingers trail down my arm. He was doing that thing again where he touched me in all the wrong ways, which wouldn't have happened if he'd known I was gay. I wasn't telling him now, though, lying in bed together, while he was under enough distress. He needed the security our friendship offered, and hearing me say, "I'm gay" wouldn't benefit him.

"You wouldn't understand," he said.

I huffed at his assumption and rolled onto my back. Looking at him was making me uncomfortable. "Sure I would. Try me."

"I don't think I agree with my church."

"Really? What led you to that conclusion?" I asked, but I was relieved to hear it.

"Just things. About eight months ago, me and this other guy were at a church picnic. It was at Codorus State Park up in PA and while we were there, walking around the shoreline, these two girls came walking from the other direction. Carl, you wouldn't know him, said we should talk to them about our church, so we walked over to them when they stopped to skip stones. They were really nice and said they'd listen, but then they started asking questions neither one of us know how to answer."

"What kind of questions?" I asked because to my knowledge, Zach always knew how to answer a question, even if he made up an answer on the spot. "Theology questions?"

"No. Relational questions. Like, 'How did my religion make me feel?' and 'What was the most amazing thing I had ever experienced because of the teachings of my church that made me want to shout it from the rooftops?' I didn't know what to say and neither did Carl. We went back to the group and he went over to his dad. I sat on the grass and stared at the lake, speculating what those girls meant. Because really Flynn, if I'm honest, I don't have an answer my dad would like. I feel empty inside. I can't say

I've ever experienced anything that was so amazing I'd want to shout about it. I'm mostly scared and frustrated. So when I got home, I started researching other religions. I wanted to understand the differences. I wanted to see what I'd been missing."

"And then your dad found your search history."

"Yeah, among other things. Now he's taking me away on some kind of sabbatical designed to help me reconnect. Part of it has us camping in the desert with some other 'troubled kids,' but the rest he won't tell me."

I opened my mouth, but promptly shut it when Zach snuggled against my arm. He looped his arm over mine and rested his hand on the inside of my biceps. I felt his nose brush my shoulder and then I felt his breath on my cheek as he nestled his face close to me on the same pillow. His face was so close I would probably have to move just an inch or two to kiss him.

"I'm leaving tomorrow," he whispered groggily. A moment later, his breaths were soft and steady.

"Zach? Zach?" I sighed. It was apparent he'd fallen asleep. I let out a heavy breath and lamented my dilemma, "Keith is gonna kill me."

In the morning, I felt cramped and my muscles ached. I hadn't moved all night. Zach's body was comfortably pressed against mine, not to mention something suspiciously shaped like a zucchini throbbed against my hip. My morning wood was not completely stiff, thank God, and I hoped I could slip out of bed without waking Zach.

As soon as I moved my arm, his eyes opened.

"Hey," I said, thinking it was the easiest to start with. He had to know his erection was poking me. I felt it pulse against me, and I resisted the urge to touch myself. If Zach was aroused, fine, but I could not get swept up in the eroticism of my situation. Keith was already going to yell at me for sleeping in the same bed with him.

Zach's hand was still holding my arm, as it had been all night. I felt him squeeze me and I automatically turned my face toward his. He was staring at me. His dark brown eyes innocently pleading for something I wasn't sure he knew I understood. It was longing. Then he moved his hand to my chin and held it as he leaned forward.

Just as his lips were millimeters from mine, I pulled back. "What are you doing?"

His eyes went wide as if he'd just realized he was about to kiss me and he pulled back. "Nothing," he replied hastily, rolling off the bed and rushing across the hall to the bathroom.

Why would he think that was okay? I looked down. My hard dick poking through the opening in my boxers apparently agreed with him, and wanted more of his attention. I idly stroked it and tucked it back in when I stood up. The thing had a mind of its own anyway, so I wasn't bothered by having an erection after waking up next to Zach, I just wasn't looking forward to talking to Keith about it.

After he showered, Zach met me in the kitchen. "Thanks for letting me stay. I needed it. I'm going to have to slip over to my house soon, or they'll notice I'm not there."

"Can you just leave?" I asked, cracking an egg on the skillet.

"And go where? They'd find me. It's not like I can run away from home and settle in Oregon. I have my sister and my aunt Krista and you! I couldn't leave here forever and never see *you* again. I have to face this. Somehow. I need to go on this trip and make my dad understand that I want to leave their church. I can't listen to them anymore. Your friend is religious, right? That artist guy, what's his name?"

"Keith?" I stirred my eggs.

"Yeah, Keith, maybe he could talk to me about his beliefs. From the impression I got that time I met him, I think his church is radically different than mine."

"Yup. It is. But I don't know if that's such a great idea." Thinking about the two of them talking made me nervous.

"Why?"

"Let's just say, Keith is very opinionated. Sometimes his statements sound like attacks."

Zach peeled a banana he took off the table. "He's your friend, right?" He took a bite and chewed while he spoke. "He can't be all bad."

"No. I'm not saying Keith is bad. I'm saying you might feel like he's challenging your whole belief system. Or, you might think he's mean." I turned my eggs over and noticed my dad hovering in the doorway. I shrugged guiltily when he shot his eyebrow up at me.

"Oh hey, Mr. B." Zach waved his half eaten banana in my dad's direction as he walked into the kitchen and poured himself some coffee.

My dad nodded and kept looking at me funny. What was I supposed to say? I wasn't prepared for Zach's arrival last night, or the near kiss this morning. My dad laid something on the counter as I transferred the eggs from the skillet to my plate.

"Here, I found this on the floor in the laundry room."

I looked down. It was the necklace Keith had given me for Christmas.

Before I could pick it up, Zach did. "Cool silver arrowhead. I like the tribal tattoo design on the one side of it. Neat. Who gave it to you?"

"Kei—elly. Kelly," I lied. My dad shot darts at me through his disapproving eyes, but he didn't say anything. *Keith is going to kill me.*

"Oh. Is she your girlfriend?" He studied my silver arrowhead necklace another moment and then placed it back on the counter. I handed him a plate and we both sat at the table where my dad had decided to read the paper with his coffee. Probably so he could listen in to our conversation and find out why Zach was at our house so early in the morning.

"No. She's just a friend."

"You should bring her the next time we get together. I'm twenty-one this summer. Maybe we should go someplace exciting."

"You might be turning twenty-one, but I'll still only be nineteen. I can't drink."

"Well, I'm having a beer, I don't care what my dad says!" Zach finished scarfing down his eggs and took his plate to the sink.

"Are you sure you'll be back by then?" I asked.

Zach's expression changed. He glanced at my dad and then back to me. Reluctantly, as if he'd never considered being away that long, he said, "I hope so."

"Where are you headed, Zach?" my dad asked, folding the paper into a neat stack on the table.

"Away with my dad. I'm not sure where. Utah, and maybe Nevada. He said we'd camp in the desert a couple nights. I don't know." And then he turned his attention back to me. "Flynn, I have to go. I've stayed too long already. I still have to pack."

He hurried to the kitchen door and I jumped up to follow. "Zach, wait. Will you text me?"

He glanced over at my father again before shaking his head at me. "My dad said no cell phones on this trip. I have to leave it here."

His eyes got glassy all of a sudden and I saw how rapidly his chest was rising and falling. Zach was visibly upset and worried like I'd never seen him before. I had no words of wisdom of how to handle this situation. I couldn't wish him luck when it wasn't apparent to me he would make it out of this experience with the same radiance he'd had in his eyes for all the years I'd known him. I feared this trip would change him, and not in a good way.

I hugged him hard and fast before he had the chance to leave and whispered by his neck, "I'll be here when you get back. Just think about that. I'll pray for you every day, even if I've never prayed before. I'll get Keith to pray. His God will protect you, I know He will."

As if thanking me without words, Zach's arms tightened around my body like giant serpents squeezing the life out of a small goat. "You promise?"

I wasn't sure if Zach was asking if I promised I'd pray, or if indeed Keith's God would protect him. I decided either one was good. I affirmed, "Yes."

***

April 2013 came quickly, but not quick enough. I had wanted to tell Keith about Zach right after it happened, but he'd been so busy with exams and papers that time drifted past. It wasn't until Spring break that I had enough time with Keith to really bring up the conversation and tell him Zach had almost kissed me.

"What!" he erupted, right in the middle of Olivia's Restaurant on Route 97.

"Keith," I hissed. "Keep it down."

"No! You're the one who kissed another guy!" He threw his cloth napkin down dramatically.

"Almost! I said *almost* kissed. I stopped him."

"You darn well better have. I can't believe you'd do that."

"I didn't. I said 'almost' like twenty times." We'd been in the restaurant for over an hour already. I suggested a nice dinner out since we hadn't seen each other for a while. I thought we could catch up before going to my house, because then we'd end up having sex all night and not really talking. I needed the talk-time first. Sex could wait.

And I can't believe I just thought that.

"I don't understand what he was doing in your room in the first place. Didn't you say it was five in the morning?"

The waiter showed up before I could respond. "May I bring you anything else?"

Keith addressed the server politely, shifting out of angry, shocked mode, into a pleasant demeanor without difficulty. He was very good at knowing when and how to act appropriately. "No, thank you. I think we're ready for the check. The Greek Moussaka was excellent, by the way."

"Thank you very much. I will be sure to tell the chef. I will be right back with your check." The server looked at me and smiled.

"Thanks." I smiled back.

He nodded and walked away.

"Stop flirting with the waiter," Keith said sharply.

"What?" I gasped. "I'm not."

"Sure looked like it," Keith murmured as he stood up. "I'm going to the bathroom. Do you have enough to cover it?"

I took out my money and counted it. "Yeah. I've got it."

"I'll pay next time. We'll finish our talk in the car. And don't flirt with the waiter on your way out."

He made me angry, but I held my tongue. I let Keith walk away and I felt the burden of Zach's "sleepover" pressing impossibly hard into my shoulder blades. I couldn't understand why it felt even worse *after* I told Keith about it. I knew he'd be jealous. In fact, he was so insanely jealous sometimes, that I just wanted to scream at him for it. But this time I kind of deserved it.

I paid and waited for Keith. He was cold and silent as we walked out to the car in Olivia's parking lot. I knew we'd have to finish this discussion here, because I wasn't about to let him stew in his seething jealousy for forty minutes as he drove me home.

"I'm sorry." I stepped in front of Keith as he reached for the door handle. "I said, I'm sorry."

He tried looking away, but I wouldn't let him. I moved in whatever direction he moved, putting my face in his field of vision. He had to see me and look at me as we spoke. He moved his face away several times, but relented and finally met my gaze.

"You're *not* sorry, Flynn. It's always the same. It's always him."

"No, it's not," I refuted, but in all honesty, I knew he was right. There was something about Zach that kept getting in the way. I felt more protective of him, and also more forgiving. Zach could say or do anything, and I would probably find away to go along with it. He could rob a bank, and I'd be the first one to defend him in court.

"It's always him, Flynn. He's the one you think about, dream about, and fantasize about. Not me. I'm just too stupid to walk away."

"You know that's not true." I never dreamed of Zach.

"He's the reason we've broken up twice. You can't tell me *that* isn't true."

"Are you breaking up with me? I told you nothing happened."

"And you told me you woke up hard for him."

I shook my head fervently. "I told you I *woke up* hard. I'm eighteen, I'm always hard."

Keith closed his eyes and turned his face away. I could see moisture gathering in the folds of skin around his eyes as he clamped them shut. He didn't want me to see him cry.

"I love you." My fall back plan. Every time I need something good to say, those words worked best.

Keith chuckled, only I knew he wasn't laughing. He opened his eyes and the tears rolled down his cheeks. "I know. That's the stupid part. I only wish you didn't love him more."

I couldn't respond. Was it true? Did I love him *more*, or just differently? Sometimes I wished I didn't love Zach at all. My life would have been much simpler. My heart wouldn't ache, my stomach wouldn't flip, and my eyes wouldn't burn from all the tears I've shed in the late hours of the night, while conjuring images of his father beating him. If I never worried about Zach, I'd be free to give everything to Keith, without borders. But as it was, I'd held something back from the day we'd met.

Instead of talking and adding more dumb words to my colossally dumb actions, I kissed him. I tasted Keith's tears on my tongue as they seeped in where our lips joined. I held the sides of his face in both hands and slowly explored his mouth, leaning into his body. I had a thing for touching his face. I enjoyed the feel of his facial hair, and how it grew in progressively thicker every year. Not yet a beard, but way more hair than I had, his scruff turned me on, especially the way his little-bit-of-a-mustache prickled my lips as I kissed him.

I turned him, pressing him up against the car door. Things heated up, like they always did, and we ended up groping each other before fumbling to climb into the back seat of his car.

I pulled his jeans down and asked, "Condom?"

"In the glove compartment."

I stretched between the bucket seats and reached for the glove box. I found lube and a box of condoms and I grabbed them. "Do I really want to know why you have a box of condoms in your car?"

"I bought them when I went shopping for my mom. I shoved them in the glove box this morning so she wouldn't find them in the bag when I got home. Then I forgot to take them out. Lucky for us though."

I grinned. "Yeah."

I slipped my pants off and glanced at Keith. He stroked himself, propped against the armrest of the back door, his head against the window, one leg hanging off the seat, the other bent and leaning against the cushion, his balls sagging low and touching the seat. He was so fucking gorgeous, it took my breath away; hot and ready for me, his cock standing tall and proud between his thighs. I dove for his mouth and we kissed hungrily.

I grabbed his leg behind his knee and pulled him toward me. "Brace yourself by pressing your foot into the roof of the car." He listened, and because he was lying flat on the seat now, with his leg cocked back, foot pressing on the roof, his ass was right where I wanted it.

I hit my head twice, the space was cramped, but at least I managed to lube him up, roll the condom on, and push in without too much difficulty. I wedged my right knee in the seat crack, while I pushed against the front seat with my left foot for leverage as I surged forward repeatedly.

Keith moaned and cried out with each plunge. "Oh God... Flynn... Shit! Oh Fuck. Ohhh... Flynn!"

I'd always enjoyed how vocal Keith got during sex. It was definitely an ego boost, if ever I needed one, but also a sign I was doing everything he liked and then some—especially now. I kissed him deep and rough, and he moved his mouth to my neck, sucking hard—the possessive bastard!

It might have been a very cramped space to fuck, but I certainly made the best of it. Ripples and waves of gratifying, orgasmic bliss throughout my body made up for the back pain I would pay with later. Keith came seconds after I did. I hit my head one more time as I gave Keith room to sit up. "Stupid roof," I swore and punched it.

Keith laughed at me.

"It's not funny," I said. I slipped the condom off and placed it on the floor hoping I'd remember to chuck it in the trash later.

"Sure it is. You're the one who insisted we do this here."

"Hey, I'm not the only one naked."

Keith picked up his jeans and turned in the small space to slip his legs in. "No. But you're the only idiot that thinks sex will solve things. I'm still mad at you."

I ignored his comment. "Next time, I'm doing this over the hood of the car. Doesn't that sound hot?" I pulled on my own pants and zipped them up.

"It sounds like an accident waiting to happen. I think we'd slide off the side and probably land in a mud puddle. We're lucky no one called the police while we were *inside* the car. And you heard me, didn't you? I'm still mad. Just because that was exponentially fantastic, it doesn't erase what you did." Keith wiped his stomach with my shirt and tossed it to me.

"Thanks," I said dryly, glaring as he grinned at me.

"Mm-hmm."

Keith pulled his shirt on and leaned against the seat, watching me slip mine over my head, carefully keeping my face from the wet spot. He snickered and I answered, "Yeah, this is freakin' hilarious." The light from the parking lot came through the steam-covered windows and illuminated his face enough to see his mirth fade into disappointment.

After I was completely dressed, I slumped on my side of the back seat. "What can I do to fix this?" I slid my fingers back and forth over his knee.

"For one thing, you can try to trust me."

I lifted my head off the seat and whined, "When haven't I trusted you?"

"All the time! We're never out somewhere when you haven't left twenty-four inches of space between us. Walk next to me like any normal person! If you don't want me holding your hand in public, fine, but you have to trust that I won't do it. Stop safeguarding yourself."

I laid my head back on the seat again, defeated. "Okay. But you need to trust me too. Nothing happened. Nothing is going to happen."

Keith might have been angry, but he took my hand as we sat there and caressed my fingers. "Maybe, but I can't believe it when you still haven't told him about us. I think... I think maybe I don't want you alone with him. And I don't want you seeing him without telling me first."

I sat up again out of shock. "How is that even possible? He lives next door and shows up randomly."

"Then you text me first so I can decide whether or not to come over. He knows we're friends, it isn't unheard of for me to show up just as randomly."

"Fine."

"And the next time we're all together, you sit next to me. Better yet, you *tell* him!"

I hated that Keith was right. I knew I should have told Zach months ago, even years ago, but every time we were together I couldn't form the words. Maybe using Zach's stress as a reason to withhold the truth wasn't such a good idea.

A sudden tap on the window jolted me upright. Someone outside shined a flashlight in, but couldn't see us because of the steam. I wiped it away and saw a cop standing there.

"Shit!" I hurriedly fumbled for the window, but the power buttons didn't work without the engine running. I unlocked the door and cracked it slowly in case the officer grew suspicious. "I can't open the window, officer. The car isn't running."

"Then step out slowly, hands out to the side," he directed, stepping away from the car.

Keith slid across the seat so we were both on the same side of the car as we got out. All I thought was, *Thank God he showed up after we had our clothes back on.*

"Are you aware the restaurant closed an hour ago?"

I glanced at Keith, he glanced at me, and we both looked at the officer. I answered honestly, "No officer. I'm sorry."

"What are you doing here so late?"

"Um, we lost track of the time."

He eyed us both skeptically. "And what were you doing in the back seat of the car?"

I wasn't about to tell him the whole truth, that was far too risky, but I hoped he would accept partial truth. "Making out," I said. Keith's hair was a mess and his glasses were smudged. He totally looked as though I'd been grabbing all over him. Plus, I was pretty sure I had a hickey on my neck where he'd sucked on me. It stung like a bitch when he did it. Additionally, the wet spot was on the front of my shirt.

He shined his light in my face again, and then it went to my neck. He grunted as if inspecting Keith's handiwork and then shined the light on Keith. "You boys faggots?"

For some reason, that word made me angry for the first time I could remember. It wasn't like I'd never heard it, and it wasn't as if I'd never been called something worse; but hearing "faggot" from someone other than a peer at school felt so demeaning. I squeezed my fist at my side, reining in the anger, and then answered him as I looked him in the eyes. "Yes, sir." Agreeing with his insult made me ill.

"Huh," he grunted and started to sneer, but just stopped his lips from curling upward. He walked around the side of the car and opened one of the other doors. "You drinking?"

I turned my head to look at him, thinking it would be better for him to see my honesty and conviction. "No sir."

He shut the door and came back around to stand in front of us. He stared at me long and hard, and then he stared at Keith the same way, maybe as a challenge. Then his hand went to his belt. He looped his thumb over the buckle and rested it there. I swear my heart was going to break my ribs with how hard it beat. I didn't know what he was about to do next. I didn't want to think about it. He was big, like a bear or a mammoth. Taller than either of us, and Keith had topped out at six-two last summer, with me being three inches shorter. I wanted to take Keith's hand, but again, I was afraid of what the man might do. I shivered, thankful we were in a parking lot and not in the woods somewhere with Ned Beatty and a mountain man.

Finally, after his long, awkward, and foreboding silence, the officer said, "Well, then I guess you boys better be on your way. Not good to get caught doing anything stupid in a privately owned parking lot."

Had I heard him correctly? "So, we can go?" I asked, wide-eyed and glanced at Keith for support.

"Yes. Only, if you're going to mess around in the back seat of a car, next time make sure you do it in a more secluded location."

I swallowed hard. "Yes, sir."

"Go on then." He pointed to the car and we scrambled to get in. Keith jumped in the driver's side and I ran around to the passenger's side. We were out of that parking lot fast, but not so much that the officer would ticket us for speeding.

Chapter 13

June 20, 2013: Everything Changes

Summer sun made yard work just… *peachy*. Sweat poured down my back as I finished up the last of eight lawns I had mowed that day, but I had pockets full of cash for my efforts. Eventually, I would need to find a "real" job, but weeding, trimming, and mowing had been lucrative so far. After sweeping the grass off Mrs. Tillett's walkway, I gathered my equipment and made my way home. I always started at the farthest property from my house and worked my way closer as the day went on. By dinnertime, I was only four doors down. I enjoyed working for my neighbors because it made me feel like a guardian angel watching over all the elderly people I'd known all my life. Ninety percent of my neighborhood was made up of the same families that had been there since before I could remember, and they all knew me. Sometimes I doubted if they'd view me the same once they found out I was gay. I knew some wouldn't care, but what about the others? How would I handle it if people I knew disrespected me after they found out? Would I stop talking to them? Would I feel sick or angry?

I sighed. *Thoughts for another day.*

I locked up my mower in the garage before making my way through my back yard, around the pool, and along the side of the house. I stopped short when I heard Mr. Mitchell's voice.

"Grab the bags out of the trunk and meet me inside."

"Yes, sir," Zach replied.

Zach!

I hadn't heard from him in months. It was as if he'd vanished off the face of the Earth once he'd taken that trip west with his father. I rushed between our houses and saw Zach just as he was about to enter his front door.

"Zach. Zach!" I called after him, but he wouldn't turn around. I knew he heard me, he had to, but the door shut in my face as soon as I reached it.

"What the...?" I stood on the front porch of the Mitchells' house until I felt like an idiot.

I lumbered home, took a shower, made dinner for my dad, and then stared at my phone. I had sent Zach twenty text messages and he hadn't answered one. I sent him another one. No reply. I stepped over to my window, hoping his window was open so I could send him some hand signals that we needed to talk, but his curtains were drawn. I didn't know what else to do, I turned my light off and left my house.

Mrs. Mitchell answered the front door after I knocked. "Hello, Flynn. How have you been?" she said, smiling as if nothing unusual was going on. *Nothing unusual?*

I hadn't been over in ages. Zach had gone on a trip, and I hadn't had a reason to visit their house. Her voice came out sweet and sappy, but there was condescension in her eyes.

I'm not a person who talks all that much about my feelings. I have them, I let them out sometimes, but I don't talk. What I do is observe, because I've learned over time that watching people can safeguard me from feelings I don't want. Like that time with Bruce before he'd worked through his shit. I didn't like feeling helpless with my face smashed against the locker. I blamed myself, as much as Bruce, because I'd trusted him to the point of vulnerability. That's not to say I could predict the actions of strangers, but I had known Bruce for years. I should have seen it coming. Since then, I had paid more attention to the people I knew. I never wanted to be bullied like that again.

So when Mrs. Mitchell smiled and let me in, and I felt a cold trail slither down my spine in reaction to her voice, everything inside me jumped to alert. She wasn't the same woman who had tried to mother me after my own mom had died. She wasn't the same woman who made Zach and me grilled cheese and tomato soup after school. This woman had a hidden agenda behind her eyes, I could see it, so my walls came up.

"Is Zach home?" I asked politely.

"Yes. He's in his room. You can go on up." She waved her hand in the direction of the stairs.

"Thank you." I walked up cautiously. I'd never known a time when she hadn't yelled up the steps for Zach. She had always announced my arrival, or someone else's, but not this time. Why?

Zach's door was open. It was normally open. I'd never thought about it in the past, but right then it hit me how odd it was to always have the door open. He was going to be twenty-one years old. Why would a twenty-one year old keep his bedroom door open? Why would a sixteen-year-old keep his door open? The answer dawned on me: they wouldn't. Every single time I'd been at Keith's, he'd closed his door when we went into his room. So did his brother and his sister. At Zach's house, none of the doors were ever closed. No privacy.

Suddenly, I felt even worse for my best friend.

I stepped into the open doorway and glimpsed Zach's bare back as he slipped on a shirt. Red lines stood out vividly and sent a chill of horror through me. What the heck had happened?

"Zach?"

He turned and smiled, but the smile was strained and cold compared to the vibrancy I was used to. "Hey Flynn. How are you?" Even his voice sounded artificial.

I stepped closer. "Fine. It's been months, what've you been up to?"

He shrugged. "Nothing. Family bonding time, a little reeducation about our church history and my role for the future, and I got to see the Grand Canyon."

Somehow I didn't see how those things all fit in the same sentence. "Yeah?" I stepped closer and placed my hand on his shoulder as I said, "I've missed you." As soon as I touched him, he flinched. This was not the Zach I knew. I took my hand back and gave him a hard, inquisitive stare.

For a brief second, I saw *my* Zach as his eyes teared up. He minutely, almost imperceptibly, shook his head in warning before his took a deep breath and responded blandly, "I've missed you too. We'll have to schedule some time this summer to catch up. I'm going to be working with my dad for a few months. I'm not sure when I'll be free. Maybe we could go downstairs and ask him."

"Oh. Okay." I was dubious, but didn't know what else to say. "But can't we talk like we used to?" I knew he knew what I meant. His bed was right there. We could flop on our back and stare at the ceiling and speak honestly, as we had so many other times.

Zach answered blandly, "I'm not a child anymore. I think we've grown past the need to let our emotions get the best of us. Don't you think?"

Not a child anymore? He'd used the phrase before with me, but somehow this time it felt different. Last time, Zach had been very emotional, almost explosive. This time, those words came out mechanically, like he was reading from a script. He sounded like a grandmother chiding a teenager for pouting over the last cookie. He didn't sound like Zach at all. I wanted to know what had changed him, but at the same time, I was reluctant to ask, given the angry lines on his back.

"Um, yeah. I guess."

Either it was all the sci-fi Keith and I watched, or the stacks of books, boxes, and uncharacteristic clutter that littered his room, but Zach didn't seem like himself to me. *Podperson? Or has Zach's body been inhabited by a non-corporeal, parasitic alien?* My Spidey senses were tingling. "When can we talk, then? Are you living at home now? What happened to your apartment?"

"Father thought it foolish to throw away money when I can live here for free. As we are working together now, it made perfect logic."

And now he sounds like Mr. Spock. Zach was so off.

"Come on. My father will know when we can get together." Zach motioned to the door and led the way down their spiral staircase.

"We're together now. Can't we talk?"

Zach ignored my question as we walked through his house.

I always loved his parents' place. It was old. I wasn't sure exactly when it had been built, but I could give an educated guess. I knew the one down the street was built in 1893. Zach's wasn't as big or elaborate, but it was close. Perhaps it had been built in the early 1900s? I didn't know. Mine was certainly not nearly as old. I had thought about taking a class on researching county records, so maybe one day I would, while my man Keith worked to support us.

We stopped at the door to Mr. Mitchell's study, and Zach knocked.

His dad looked up from his desk. "Ah, Zach, how can I help you? Flynn, how nice of you to visit. It's been a while. How's your father?"

A streak of anger pinched the nerves behind my eyes as soon as I heard the word "father" from his mouth. I knew my father hated him. I held my cool. "He's fine."

"Dad, Flynn wants to know when we could find time to catch up. Do I have a free day soon?"

"Um, let me see." He set one book aside and picked up another one. He leafed through it and stopped on one page, scanning it from top to bottom, and then he flipped the page and did the same thing again. "No, I don't see an opening in our schedule. Maybe he'd like to go with you on some of your tasks, and the two of you could talk in the car?"

I looked at Zach as he answered, "No. I don't think his father would approve." I saw tension tightening jaw as he answered without asking my opinion.

Mr. Mitchell's voice came out sarcastic in comparison. "Well, Mr. Brewer and I have never seen eye-to-eye on many things." He flicked his eyes over to me. "Perhaps Flynn needs to make his own choice to follow the proper teachings of the church, or to throw away this opportunity for spiritual growth. What do you say Flynn? Do you want to live forever, learning what God says about family and the hope of eternal life?"

The way he asked, the tone in his voice, and the look in his eyes, I could have sworn I heard Valeria's voice from the movie Conan the Barbarian when she said, "Do you want to live forever?" Why would my brain recall quotes from an '80s movie now, of all times? A movie where the evil king worshiped snakes, even killed Valeria with an arrow made from a live snake. Snakes and Mr. Mitchell in the same thought, the same sentence. It was foreboding.

I nervously refused with a tight shake of my head. "No. Thank you. I think my mom taught me all I need to know." I looked at Zach. "I think I'm gonna go. I promised my dad I'd help him fix Mr. Blevins' heat pump in the morning."

I zipped to the front door and back to the safety of my house. Why had I lied about fixing a heat pump? And why use Mr. Blevins as my excuse? Maybe my subconscious wanted to rub it in that I was helping Mr. Blevins, when all the Mitchells wanted was to force him to leave the neighborhood. I closed my bedroom door and locked it, symbolically keeping the demons at bay. I paced my room. I yanked the curtains shut in case Zach looked over at me. My heart raced and I couldn't breathe. Why?

I snatched my keys off my dresser, hurriedly opened the door, and ran to my car. I was at Keith's house in record time.

"Hey Flynn. Come on in," his brother Jeremy said after he opened the front door.

"Is Keith home from work yet?"

"No. But my mom might know when he'll get here. Mom!" he yelled.

A second later, Keith's mom came walking out of the kitchen drying her hands on a dishrag. "Jeremy. Goodness, gracious, why are you bellowing through the house like that? Oh, Flynn, how nice to see you. Are you staying for dinner? Keith should be home soon."

"See," Jeremy said. "She knows everything." He flopped on the couch fiddling with his phone.

"Is everything okay honey? You look upset." Such a contrast in maternal concern. Mrs. Leppo was warm and genuine.

I took a couple deep breaths to try and calm myself. I'd been gasping like a marathon runner as I drove here, I knew I couldn't talk if I continued breathing so rapidly. I held up my finger to signal for her to wait as I calmed myself.

"Is Mr. Leppo home?"

"Yes. He's on the back porch doing work proposals."

"Do you think I could talk to him?"

"Of course, dear. Come with me."

I shook hands with Mr. Leppo and sat at the glass table they had on their deck. Keith's mom brought me lemonade and said dinner would be ready in another ten minutes. She also said Keith was on his way home. I sat with Keith's dad, not knowing what it was I wanted to talk about or ask him, but feeling better just being in his presence. I felt safe.

Mr. Leppo was a gentle man. He spoke softly and with deliberate consideration. Not once in over two years had I heard him raise his voice, or answer harshly. Still, Keith, his brothers, Johnny and Jeremy, and his sister Katie always listened without complaint. I hadn't heard him ask anything unreasonable and when one of Keith's siblings disagreed, he always listened to their opinion respectfully. Maybe subconsciously I wanted to feel his calming presence after feeling so alarmed around Mr. Mitchell.

"I'm sure Keith will be here soon. Is there anything in particular you wanted to talk to me about, Flynn?" Mr. Leppo asked after ten minutes of silence, and me sipping my lemonade.

"Um, kinda."

"I hope you know you can ask whatever you want and I'll try to answer you as honestly as I can."

What did I want to ask? "Do you remember when you asked me what I thought heaven would be like?"

"Yes. You said you hoped it would be peaceful."

I liked that he'd remembered what I said. "Yeah, I do, because my mom is there. She always told me she could see God in people, because certain ones exuded peace. When I think of God, I think of peace."

"That is certainly one of God's attributes. The Bible says the fruit of the Spirit is love, joy, peace, patience, kindness, goodness, gentleness, faithfulness, and self-control."

"I know. I remember my mom reading the Bible to me when I was little. The fruit of the Spirit is mentioned in Galatians."

"Very good."

"I think that's why I like talking to you, Mr. Leppo, because you have the same look in your eyes I remember my mom having. It's peace." We hadn't talked alone too many times over the couple years I'd known Keith, but something inside prompted me to tell Mr. Leppo exactly what I felt.

He smiled very wide, his kind eyes gleaming. "That's one of the nicest things anyone has ever said, Flynn. What a high compliment to compare me to your mother. I'm honored."

"I meant it. I think she would have liked talking to you about Jesus. She liked singing hymns."

"I like singing hymns too."

"You do?"

"Sure. We sing all the time at church. You're welcome to come along any time."

"Thank you. I might." *Church. I wonder if my dad would go? I'll have to ask.* The niggle in my mind reminded me of the real reason I'd come over, and it wasn't to talk about heaven. "Mr. Leppo, do you think the opposite is true? Like, if sometimes you can see God in people, do you think you can see the devil in others?"

"I think I've seen wickedness. I think a lot of it has to do with spiritual warfare, and things we don't understand."

"Do you think people can be evil?"

He lifted his eyebrows in obvious surprise. "Well, that's a good question. Do I think people can be evil? I think the Bible talks about inherent sin and I think we are all born with a propensity to fulfill selfish desires. Evil can certainly manifest itself in people who only seek selfish gain, and in those who ignore Christ's call to love your neighbor as yourself. Without love, it's easy to see why others might appear evil."

I could see where Keith got his ability to talk in ways I didn't always understand. I wasn't sure what Mr. Leppo meant. "So, people *can't* be evil?"

"I think they can do evil *things*, and evil deeds are easier to accomplish than good. Good deeds come out of selflessness, and for some people selflessness is the hardest attribute to acquire. Truly selfless acts are rare. But an evil person? I believe only Satan is truly evil."

"Can Satan influence someone to be evil?"

"Yes, I don't see why not. But often times the evil we do is born out of our own desires and isn't necessarily caused by prodding from the devil. Humans, in general, think up all sorts of evil acts on their own."

Where was I going with this? I felt icky in Mr. Mitchell's company and perhaps I hoped Satan was influencing him, or I'd find some way to explain it all away, with Mr. Leppo's help. "What about a child molester?" I asked. "Or a physically abusive parent? Are they evil inside, or influenced by the devil?"

His expression changed from mild curiosity to dark concern. "Flynn, are you being abused at home?"

I took a second to register that he asked the question about me. "What? Me? No. Not me. Someone I know. I think he's being abused."

"And you think his father is evil?"

I nodded, despising myself for even acknowledging it.

"Could he simply be a cruel man? Likening him to Satan is a harsh comparison, Flynn." Mr. Leppo rubbed his chin as if thinking. "From what I know, child abusers often do so because they crave power. Keeping a child in constant fear feeds a need in some to have complete control and utter dominance. Has your friend tried to get help?"

"No. Not that I know of. I don't think anyone else knows but me."

"How old is your friend?"

I didn't want to say because he might figure out I had been questioning him about Zach. All I said was, "Old enough to defend himself, but he doesn't."

"I think your friend needs to go to the police."

I shook my head. "He won't. He's terrified."

"Did he tell you that?"

"No. I felt it. His father scares me. In fact, I'm scared now just thinking about it."

"Has his father hit you?"

"No. He's…."

"Hey. What'd I miss?" Keith walked in with a smile on his face and came over to my chair. He reached out to touch my shoulder, but before he could, I was out of my chair and in his arms. "Oh. Hi." I heard his surprise as he hugged me back.

"Can we go to your room?" I whispered into his neck.

"Yeah. Sure. Um, Flynn, you have to let go first." He gave me a concerned look as he took my hand and ushered me upstairs. I heard his father say something as we left, but I wasn't paying attention. He closed his door and I collapsed into his arms again. "Flynn, hey, are you okay? What's wrong? What did Dad mean by 'praying for your friend?'"

Against his chest, I mumbled, "Something isn't right. It felt like he's changed. His father had a sneer I'd never seen. He wouldn't talk to me. I haven't seen him in four months, and Zach wouldn't talk to me."

I felt Keith stiffen. "Wait. This all has to do with Zach?"

I pulled back and looked him in the face. "Yeah. I think his father's Satan."

"Zach's father?"

"Yes. Why else wouldn't Zach talk to me? And I saw red marks on his back when he was putting his shirt on that looked like—"

Keith pulled out of my arms and stepped away. "Putting his shirt on? Seriously? Why would he be putting his shirt *back on*? Why was his shirt off?"

"His hair was wet. I think he'd just gotten out of the shower, but that has nothing to do with it. I think Zach's dad is—"

"Why were you are Zach's house? You promised you wouldn't see him without letting me know first." He fished his phone out of his pocket. "I don't see any texts telling me you were going to see Zach? I don't see a text asking if you can visit him after he got out of the shower?" He was getting angry, and I understood why, but he was missing the point.

"Keith, this has to do with his father hitting him. Don't you get that? His father made me feel... icky. I think he's—"

"Satan. Yeah. I heard you. How did Zach's freshly showered body make you feel? Horny? Curious? Desirous? Did you want to fuck him?" His questions grew in volume with each word.

"Keith! Calm down. Stop yelling at me. Your mom's gonna hear. I didn't feel anything, okay? I wanted to help him, but his father scared the crap out of me. He questioned if I wanted to learn about 'living the hope of eternal life' and all I thought was how much Mr. Mitchell reminded me of Thulsa Doom."

"From Conan the Barbarian?"

"Exactly. He even used the line, 'Do you want to live forever?'" On any other day, I would have chuckled at how often we thought alike. We both liked Xbox, All Time Low, and classic movies from before special effects took over the screen.

Keith glared. "Snake-worshipping, thousand-year-old-sorcerer aside, you promised not to see Zach without me. You broke your promise."

"Didn't you hear me? Zach's dad is hitting him. I think it's worse than it was that Christmas."

Keith's eyes narrowed; his jaw clenched tightly, practically seething, his anger approaching its boiling point. I swore smoke was seconds from shooting from his ears. "That Christmas?" he asked hotly. "The one where you threw me out of your house seconds after I swallowed your cum? *That Christmas?* You're seriously going to compare today to *that Christmas*? Because *that Christmas*, I was about ready to buy a machete and hack your dick off. If you bring *that Christmas* up one more time, I might do it anyway."

Now I could see what Keith's dad meant about the differences between doing evil things. Between being a cruel person, or appearing to be evil because one lacked love inside. Keith was justifiably angry, but I would never categorize him as evil. He was hurt, and therefore cruelly lashing out, but I would never think he was evil. I knew he loved me and his anger was rooted in jealousy. Maybe Zach's dad was acting out of love, but to me it looked evil. Maybe I'd been reacting over nothing.

"I'm sorry Keith. I won't do it again."

"You're darn tootin'!"

"Whatcha dooooin'?" said my text message alert tone. I checked my phone.

"And you're checking your phone in the middle of an argument." Keith threw his hands in the air, then turned his back to me as I read the message. "If that's from Zach, I'll…." He grunted angrily, but waited.

Hi. This is Greg. Zach hasn't had a phone, so he told me to tell you he's sorry, but he never got your messages. (He assumed you sent some.) His father said he could have one last birthday party before he goes on a mission trip to Uganda. His house. He says you can invite your friends if you want to. Tom and I will be there. Invite Grace for me :) Please.

"Not from Zach. It's from Greg. He said Zach's having a party July second at his parents' house."

"Well, you aren't going without me," Keith asserted.

"Okay, I won't. We go together. I just think it's weird the party is at his house. He hasn't had a party there since he turned thirteen."

"Isn't he twenty-one this year? Maybe he wants his family around, too. Or maybe, since you said his parents are strict, they decided to have it at his house so he wouldn't drink."

I sat on Keith's bed. "Oh God, I bet you're right. Jeez, he's twenty-one and he can't even have one beer. That's so lame."

"It could be worse. His boyfriend might have given him an ultimatum, or threatened to hack off his dick." He sat next to me.

"Shut up. This is serious."

"I'll say it is. We go together and you *tell* him."

"But…."

"You tell him. I'm sick of hiding. I'm sick of you dicking around about this, and that is not a pun. You're gay. We're together. I want to be a couple, not be *on guard*. Can you do that? Can you tell him this time?"

"At his house with his parents there?"

"Yes."

That same debilitating fear crept up my back, spread its icy fingers over my shoulders, and jabbed its claws into me flesh. Why did coming out have to feel so terrifying some days and no big deal on others? I came out so easily to Bruce. Naturally, even. I felt scared, but only in that first-time-on-a-roller coaster sense. With Zach in mind, it felt like my first time in an airplane with Jigsaw as the pilot. Something in my stomach was telling me I was going to be forced to kill someone, or die myself, as soon as I said the words, "I'm gay."

Shaking like a leaf, I replied, "I'll tell him."

Keith took my hand and said, "Thank you. You always refer to Zach as your best friend. I guess I want to know I'm included, sometimes, like when you're with him. Ya know?"

I nodded.

Keith squeezed my hand as he leaned in to kiss me.

Chapter 14

July 2, 2013: The Twilight Zone

Getting a tattoo was my solution to facing my fears. I thought that maybe, if I could deal with a little physical pain, then I could bite the bullet and move past my mental pain. Pain? More like emotional anguish and self-torture over what I thought *might* happen, because so far there wasn't any proof that "coming out" as gay in front of Zach and everyone else was going to hurt at all. I only imagined it might hurt based on statistics, and accounts I'd read online about other people's experiences.

The little parts of my life where being gay was real hadn't hurt. I'd come out to Bruce and things between us had been fine. I'd danced with my boyfriend at my prom, even kissed him, and no one had noticed. (Over in the shadows by the wall, but whatever.) I'd gone to dinner with Keith and gotten caught in the parking lot with him right after we'd been naked in his car—something I could have gotten arrested for, but I still hadn't experienced any sort of pain. So why was I imagining "coming out" would be so much more painful with Zach?

Maybe my fear was irrational as Keith kept telling me.

Even so, it lingered, and I didn't know how to shake it; hence the tattoo.

I hadn't actually considered the "pain" part of the whole deal when I made the appointment. I was typically resilient when it came to physical pain, so I figured I could handle anything, but getting inked, wow, it was unlike anything I'd ever experienced before, including dropping a cinderblock on my bare toe. I was glad I'd gone with the piercing last year or I may have chickened out. Getting inked was way worse.

"Ouch!" I exclaimed, controlling my involuntary flinch enough not to pull away from the needle.

"Do you need me to stop?" asked the heavily inked tattoo artist.

I glanced down at the design she was doing for me. There were four lines on my finger. Four. "Shit. That's all you've done?" I gaped.

She smirked, making me feel like a complete pansy. What guy couldn't sit through a little bit of pain? It wasn't like I was getting a sleeve done. It was a tiny little thing on the inside of my right ring finger. Small. Easy. Practically invisible if I pressed my fingers together, so what was the big deal?

"I'm fine," I insisted, taking a deep breath to calm my nerves. I looked around the room at the framed photographs on the walls to take my mind off it. The photos were of many large, intricate designs that people had gotten tattooed onto their skin, displayed proudly as the business' portfolio. It amazed me that people could sit through them if it hurt this much. *Maybe I am a pansy?*

"Okay, but there's nothing wrong with asking me to stop," the girl named Tee insisted, bringing my attention back to her. "Everyone has a different threshold for pain. So don't worry about asking for breaks, you're fine."

I appreciate her direct tone. I got the idea she was trying to make me feel better. "Do you think my finger is going to bleed a lot?" I asked innocently.

She shook her head. "No. Fingers don't bleed much. But if it bothers you and you want to take a break, you won't be judged here."

"Then why'd you snicker when I gawked at how little you'd done?"

She smiled at me. "Because the look on your face reminded me of my little brother when he got his first tattoo. I think he was about your age. He's also gay, so I guess I was amused that the two of you would react the same."

"What?" I pulled my hand back and straightened my shoulders. I was stretched out on a black, leather recliner so I couldn't exactly pull far away. "What are you talking about—*also gay?*" Suddenly I felt like any security camera, which might be in the room, had live feeds to the Internet and my lifestyle had been broadcast to the entire county and state.

She blinked in surprise and held up one hand. "Oh shit," she said in a slightly higher tone. "I'm sorry. I didn't mean to assume and blurt it out like that. I'm so sorry. People assumed that of me once, and it was awful. I'm sorry, really."

Suspiciously, I asked, "How'd you know?"

She relaxed her shoulders, then answered very innocently. "My brother's been out for a long time, and we're really close. I guess I've gotten really good at reading people. I've been to gay clubs with him, and stuff. I'm sorry. I know it's a big deal, especially if you live in a conservative area like this one."

"Yeah, tell me about it."

"Look, I hope you're not angry. There's no one else here, I swear; no one to overhear me out you."

"Are there security cameras?" *Possibly hooked up to the Internet?*

"Yes, but video only. If you murder me, or rob the place, then the security company can track you down, but what we say here isn't recorded."

I relaxed and took a deep breath. "Okay." I exhaled and looked back at the girl who was by now probably scared she might say something else inappropriately accurate. I apologized, "I'm sorry too. It's not your fault. And you're right... I'm gay. I'm out to my dad and some friends, and obviously my boyfriend knows, but... thing is... tonight, I'm coming out to my best friend, and I guess I'm worried it might not go over well."

She gestured to my hand, and when I nodded the go-ahead Tee went back to injecting my skin. *Fuck, it hurt!* It started as tiny electric shocks, like I'd stuck my finger in a wall socket and was too stupid to pull it away. Then the pain intensified to something like a vibrating jackhammer stabbing into my fragile nerve-endings. The sound from the instrument was like a dentist's drill, making me think I wouldn't be able to sit quietly at the dentist any time soon. Unlike the dentist's, this drill was carving black lines into my tender flesh. The feeling was hard to compare to anything else. A belt sander to my face? No. A drill bit through my eye? No. Not even a hot poker down my throat was an accurate comparison. This pain was different; it seemed like a combination of sensations. Electric shocks, digging needles, stabbing daggers, and grinding, metal files all combined into a tiny drill that this blameless sadist pressed to my skin. The vibrating reminded me of the electric turkey carver my dad used one year. That was it! Tee was shearing my flesh off with an electric turkey carver!

My mental analogy distracted me long enough to allow the feeling to become familiar. I took it on, absorbed it, and moved ahead. I could handle it. The girl was not really a sadist, I mentally corrected. She was doing her job splendidly.

"Is he or she homophobic?" Tee asked.

This time, I didn't feel defensive with her question. I was trying my hardest to relax, and thought conversation might be a good diversion. Plus, her query came off inquisitive, not condemning. "He," I stressed the pronoun, "is religious, and his family is sort of fanatical. At least he used to be. I'm not sure now. I remember going to church with him a few times when I was younger, but I stopped because way to many sermons included the words homosexuality and sin in the same sentence. I felt targeted even though I'm sure no one knew about me."

"How long have you known your friend?"

"All my life. My family moved in next to his when my mom was pregnant with me."

"Wow. How long have you known about yourself and not told him?"

Her question was invasive, yet conversationally asked. No ulterior motives with her. I didn't feel like she was asking to judge me based on my answer. She was asking out of interest. I rarely had someone to talk to about this sort of thing, so I figured I'd let go of some of my reservations. "Seven years, give or take," I said. "I think I knew before seventh grade, but that's when it made sense."

She whistled. "That's a long time not to tell the bestie."

She adjusted the angle of her tool and I wailed, "Oh shit!"

"Sorry. It will be over soon."

I liked this girl. She was tough looking because of her tattoos and piercings, but tender in her mannerisms, another proof that outward appearances shouldn't influence one person's opinion of another without first making an effort to engage them. Something else my mother had impressed upon me at an early age. "I know," I lamented, reverting back to the comment she made about my *bestie*. "I've tried to tell Zach numerous times over the years, but every time I work up the nerve, someone interrupts us, or someone calls, or he has to run out to meet up with some girl; it's ridiculous how many ways our conversations have gotten interrupted."

"Ah, the plot thickens… your bestie is religious *and* straight. Tough combo."

"I know. But like I said, we've been friends my whole life. I'm ninety percent sure he'll be fine with it."

"But it's the other ten percent that's kept your tongue silent for seven years."

"Exactly. I thought it would have been easy once I had a boyfriend, but it wasn't. I've tried a few times, but I just can't make myself say the words. I don't know why."

"Fear of rejection," she said simply. "Fear is normally why most people *don't* tell the whole truth. It's like we, as humans, are fine with being honest about who we are as long as the people we are talking to agree with our stand or opinion, but get around others who may not be so welcoming, and all of a sudden we clam up. Free-talkers become introverts. I'm not saying it's the same across the board, I'm saying I know it happens. Fear of rejection is a powerful deterrent, even if a person tends to be honest and forthright most of the time."

I grinned. "You're surprisingly accurate. How did you become so wise? Did you take psychology classes or something?"

"No, I listen. I've been doing this for thirteen years, and I've inked a massive number of people in that time, from all walks of life. I like to talk, and I like to get them talking. When they do, I listen and pay attention. You'd be surprised how fast the process goes if my client is distracted." Then she stopped working, pulled the needle back, and gestured to my hand.

I looked down and my design was finished. "Whoa, cool. You finished just like that."

"Just like that."

I flexed my fingers. "Ouch, it hurts. And it's seeping." There were little drops of blood forming in the center.

"Yeah, but that isn't very much. It should heal quickly. Your finger might swell, but don't rub it."

I flexed my fingers again, and felt confident that it really wasn't too painful. Like she said, my finger was swollen below his knuckle.

"I have an instruction sheet to give you and you need to keep your tattoo clean while it heals. No direct sunlight, no scratching or picking at the design, and no washing dishes for two weeks. You can wash your hands, but I don't want you soaking in a tub or swimming for a couple weeks. Also, make sure you keep it moisturized with the ointment listed on the care sheet."

"No swimming?"

"Nope."

"Oh man. I guess I should have thought this through. Swimming is my favorite pastime." She explained the after-care and I paid her. "Thanks for everything."

"No problem. If you have any questions, message me on Facebook, or call the shop."

"I will."

I got back into my car and started the engine. I sat there a second as I watched Tee get into her car and pull out of the parking lot. (She'd told me I was her only appointment that day.) I liked the design on my finger, but I almost couldn't believe I'd actually gotten it. This design had been on my mind since the previous summer, but now that it was done, it looked more like watercolors or chalk than ink. Definitely not like a traditional tattoo. It appeared as though it would rub right off if I touched it.

"It's not coming off," I reminded myself, putting the car in gear and backing out of the space. "It's permanent."

Tee said that fingers normally needed touch-ups and she couldn't guarantee how long it would take before it faded. Still, I didn't care. *This* was the design. I wouldn't settle for something else.

As I drove home, I thought about our conversation about fear. It was fear—that's all. Fear. I could beat fear. I'd been facing my fears all my life, knocking them down left and right, one after the other. I could handle this next hurdle. It was fear telling me Zach would reject me, not reality. We were best friends; we'd been through everything together. Of course he wouldn't reject me.

***

That evening, I strolled over to Zach's house wearing Keith's gray plaid shirt. I thought wearing something of his might make me feel stronger, more confident. I hoped. I knocked on the door and waited. Zach's mother answered the door.

"Hello Flynn. Welcome," she said, sweeping her hand toward the interior of the house.

I stepped through the door feeling like a stranger. *Why?* I'd been in this house hundreds, probably thousands, of times. She appeared more sterile then I remembered. "Thanks. Am I the first one here?" I asked because the house was too quiet for there to be a party going on.

"Nope," Tom said from behind me. I turned. "This is the party." He shook my hand and gestured. "Come on. I'll show you into the family room." We walked about three feet, and as soon as Mrs. Mitchell was no longer behind us, he leaned into my ear. "Something's weird in here. It's not right. Just go along with it, maybe we can get an answer out of Zach when his parents aren't around."

I nodded in response.

When we entered the family room, I saw Zach sitting in a chair laughing with his cousin who was standing a couple of feet away. It was like they'd both shared some great joke. A joke like Zach and I had often shared and laughed about, except Zach's laugh sounded fake. Was I the only one who noticed? Tom gave me a look, and I could tell he heard it too. Tom circled the room and took a spot against the far wall next to Greg. *At least I know a couple of people I can trust.*

I took out my phone and texted Keith: *When are you getting here?*

Maybe fifteen minutes. Sorry. My blue shirt wasn't ironed and I couldn't find the gray one.

Oh, sorry. I kept the gray one. :p FYI, it feels weird here. Very fake. It's like Zach is a different person.

Podperson or non-corporeal, parasitic alien? I'll be there soon. Try not to kiss him in the meantime.

Shut up! :p I chuckled with his movie references, though.

I put my phone away and felt a hand on my arm so I turned. "Kelly!" I exclaimed happily, hugging her tight.

"Thanks for inviting me."

"Sure. I'm glad you're here." I glanced around. Zach still hadn't noticed me, probably because I was standing by the door and he was engaged in conversation.

"Here's a little something to say happy birthday." She handed me a tiny gift bag. I pulled on the tissue paper and found a package of Gummy Bears. "Remember?" she asked. "We went up to Ricketts Glen State Park after graduation and Keith kept throwing them at every one, including every street sign we passed?"

I laughed. "Yeah. I remember. It was fun. Except when he hit Grace in the eye, then I had to take the bag away."

Kelly leaned closer to whisper in my ear, "Not as fun as watching the two of you making out in the backseat of my car while I drove us home." She leaned back and winked.

"You watched?" I could not believe my ears.

She tilted back in with a gleam in her eyes. "Until you reached down his pants. Then I adjusted the mirror and turned up the music."

I thought about it for a second and whispered in her ear. "Oh my gosh. I remember that. I was thinking 'why the heck is she turning it up, because it was freakin' loud to begin with?'"

She whispered again, "I turned it up so I couldn't heard Keith moaning. My God, is he always so vocal?"

"You are so bad."

Kelly grinned. "You don't know the half of it."

"Flynn!" Zach called. I turned toward him as he bounded across the room and clapped me on the back in an awkward half-hug. "Hey Buddy. I'm glad you could make it." Zach motioned to the crowed room. "Everybody, this is Flynn, my neighbor and best friend. We share the same birthday, so this party is for him too."

"Birthday party?" Zach's little cousin questioned. "I thought this was an—"

"Let's go get you a drink sweetie," Zach's sister interrupted, draping her arm over the eight-year-old's shoulders and ushering her from the room.

Kelly said what I was thinking, "Well, that was odd."

Zach continued as if the little girl hadn't said a word. "I'm sure most of you know Flynn, but for those who don't remember him from all our shared parties, he's the guy who used to climb down into caves and find snakes."

"Eww," one little girl said.

"That was you?" his cousin Martin asked.

I shrugged and felt my phone buzz. "Yeah, that was me, but they weren't caves. Zach exaggerates."

"No I don't." Zach tugged on my arm. "Come on over here and sit down and I'll tell you all about the time we went over my grandmother's house."

I allowed him to seat me on the sofa while he took the chair opposite. I took out my phone and found a text from Keith. *I'm parked. Are you coming out?*

"Zach, Keith's here. I'll be right back." I left the room after he told me he'd wait until I returned to tell his stories. I made my way through the house of wall-to-wall people, and found Grace standing next to Keith when I opened the front door. "Oh, you're both here."

"I just walked up," she said.

"So, did you tell him?" Keith asked me.

I shook my head. "I just got here. I haven't had time, plus the place is packed. A lot of family, but also tons of people I've never met. Maybe from his church? I don't know. It feels weird in there, like entering the Twilight Zone. Tom said something to me when I got here because he felt it too. He told me to play along, said he hoped we could corner Zach before the night was over. He looked worried."

Keith was upset, I could tell, but kept his mouth shut. Grace seemed to sense what he was thinking and squeezed his shoulder. "Keith, let it go for now. We're at Zach's parents' house. You can't expect Flynn to come out in front of a house full of people. That's unfair. I know what this means to you, but you have to think of Flynn too."

Keith huffed. "I always think of Flynn. Why do you think I've given him years to come to terms with this? I'll be chill, okay? I promise. No shit while we're in there." He shifted his eyes off Grace and onto me. "I promise."

Since no one was around, I kissed him before we went in. "Thank you."

He gave me a half-grin and rolled his eyes. "You're welcome."

"You love me," I whispered.

"Shut up," he replied.

Grace asked, "When did you stop wearing the beanie? I like your new hair style, if I haven't told you before."

We entered the house and walked down the hall.

"I don't know. A couple months or so," he answered. "I got tired of the curls and the way Flynn always messed up my hair kissing me."

"Yeah, but now he thinks the buzzed back is too short," I commented. "So don't be surprised if the beanie makes a reappearance once it's long enough to curl on the ends." I leaned into her ear, "His hair is *really* soft. I can't help messing it up."

"It's easier short," Keith explained.

"I like it," Grace said.

We made our way back into the family room and Zach immediately called us over, waving frantically. He stood in the middle of the room with a girl I didn't recognize, while the rest of the guests formed a circle around the perimeter of the room. "I want you to meet someone," he said, grabbing my arm as soon as I drew near enough, tugging me closer. It felt odd having all those eyes on me, or us, and I wondered what was going on.

"Now that we're all here, I can officially introduce you all to the love of my life. Everyone, this is Gwendolyn Pierce," Zach extended his hand toward the redhead next to him, "and her sister Amelia." Zach swept his hand over to the side, gesturing toward a shy looking girl with dark hair.

Love? I hadn't even heard of this girl and suddenly Zach is talking love? What the heck? I reeled, stepping back slightly.

"As many of you have guessed, this isn't just a birthday party, although I am happy to be twenty-one today. This is also our engagement party. I have asked Gwendolyn to be my wife."

Amelia gasped, quickly bringing her hand up to her mouth. I noticed tears forming in her eyes at the same moment my stomach flipped and made me feel like puking. The redhead, Gwendolyn, smiled widely and hugged her sister tight. "Oh, sis, I wanted to tell you. I know this is a surprise, but we wanted it to be a grand announcement."

"I'll say it was," Zach's mother replied, entering the room and walking directly up to Zach. "Your father informed me right before I heard you announce it," she said coldly, extending her hand to the girl. "Congratulations. I hear your family is quite prominent in the church out west. How fortunate for my son to have met you while on sabbatical with my husband."

"Yes, ma'am." Gwendolyn said, forgoing the handshake and hugging Zach's mother. She looked sincerely happy, which only made me feel that much worse.

How could Zach fall in love and not tell me?

I was jealous for the first time. It had to have been jealousy, because I felt like punching the smile off her face. Then I glanced at Amelia, the sister, and she looked as resentful as I felt. This engagement was a shock to her too. I didn't know what was going on, but if I wasn't the only one left out of the loop, then perhaps there was a logical explanation that Zach would explain to me later. I could only hope.

The sister started crying and Gwendolyn kissed her cheek. "I'm so glad you're happy for me, because I want you to be my maid of honor. Will you?"

Her sister was speechless, but I doubted it was from the thrill at being asked. She nodded anyway, and Gwendolyn squealed. "I'll get you a tissue," she said after hugging her sister one more time. The girl nodded and Gwendolyn left her for a moment. I had the distinct feeling they weren't happy tears.

"Which leaves you, buddy," I looked at Zach, who reached around my shoulders and smiled his best smile my way. "Will you?"

"Will I what?" I didn't like how everyone was watching us. And Keith? I could feel his eyes on me as if he had laser vision. I knew he'd be ticked about Zach's arm around me.

"Will you be my best man? Come on, you can't say no."

Not when you put it that way. "I guess so." With all the people watching, how could I turn him down?

Zach hugged me. "It's settled! The date is set. April twenty-sixth, so mark your calendars."

People cheered and hugged, and I took the opportunity to glance at Keith who was standing over to the side with Kelly. He glared. This night was not going well. I foresaw arguments, accusations, and heaps of jealous rants about how comfortable Zach and I were with each other. But really, were we? If we were that comfortable, then Zach would have told me about Gwendolyn first, before the multitudes of people now crammed into his house. If I were really his best friend, then he should have told me first!

Suddenly, I didn't want to be here.

Then Zach announced, "Everybody, get yourselves some punch or soda and pull up a chair. I'm going to tell you all about the time Flynn and I found some salamanders in this dark hole."

My head spun. *What?* He caught me off guard. "How can you talk about our childhood, when you just announced you're engaged to be married?" I asked, incredulously.

Zach gripped my shoulder and looked me in the eyes. I could see the old Zach somewhere in their brown depths, and I liked that. He was still there, under all the phony laughing and counterfeit cheer. "Because, oh best buddy of mine, my Gwen only just met you. I've told her that she had to meet you, but she doesn't know why you're so special. So, I'm going to tell her about all the times we've spent together. She needs to love you like I do."

He hugged me one-armed as he turned and led me to the sofa once more. I sat. Zach pulled up a chair for Gwen and Amelia. Keith dubiously moved to stand opposite me next to Grace. There were a couple high tables set up on that side of the room, like for mingling and eating appetizers or something, so he set his cup down and watched me with quiet discontent. I'd give him credit though; he didn't explode like I expected.

"So, I remember this one time," Zach said, gesturing and building up the story with lots of animated facial expressions, "when we were over my grandmother's house and my mom was inside talking so we went off exploring. My grandmother lived on a dead-end street with houses lined up next to one another, but her property backed up to an old farm. My mom told me that years ago they had had cows, but when we went, it was a huge grassy hill without any farm animals. Flynn and I went running over the hill one time, and I stumbled over a metal plate in the ground. I didn't know what it was, so I thought instead of asking my mom, I'd lift the hatch and see for myself."

Zach took a sip of his soda and then continued, "I grabbed the handle and pulled. Nothing. The plate, or whatever, was heavy and probably hadn't been opened for forever. So I got Flynn to help me and between the two of us, we wrestled it open only to find a dark hole with lots of spider webs." He looked at me and asked, "Do you remember that?"

I nodded. "Yeah. I remember you sent me back to the house for a flashlight, and your mother wanted to know why we needed one on a sunny day. I think she took pity on my floundering for a reply, figuring it was just another of your silly ideas. I remember she gave me two flashlights."

"Yeah! That was cool. You came back, and we had to figure out how to get down into the hole."

"You sent me," I glowered.

Zach laughed and slapped my knee. Keith did not miss the familiar contact and shot me a look. "Of course I did," Zach laughed. "The opening was tight and Flynn was smaller. I held his hand as he climbed down into the hole."

"Yeah," I interjected with conviction, "tell them the part where you left me there."

Again, Zach laughed and took a sip of his soda.

"You left him in there?" Kelly asked, aghast. Everyone listening to the story glanced at her, then back to Zach, the storyteller.

"Yeah," Zach admitted.

"Somehow it's funnier to Zach now that he has an audience, than it was when I slugged him after he pulled me out." My statement earned chuckles from the crowd.

Zach laughed more. "I think that was the only time you've ever punched me. But yeah, I left him because when he got down in there, he found these huge black salamanders that were covered in yellow spots. I figured we could sell them or something. So I went back to the house for a bucket."

"Did you sell them?" Amelia asked, speaking for the first time.

"No," I answered. "Once we got them home, his dad told us we needed to put them back were we found them."

"But you were my perfect little minion, before minions were popular." He winked at me and mussed my hair.

"Thanks," I responded dryly, smoothing my hair back down. I wasn't sure why he felt the need to act like a kid, when he had stressed several times that he was *not* a kid any longer, but this whole evening felt like a step into an alternate reality.

After the storytelling and dinner, the evening continued drifting by in the most bizarre fashion. Keith watched me, and Kelly watched Keith watching me. Grace moved over to Greg and Tom, they seemed to be having a delightful conversation full of giggles and hair-tosses. Grace patted Greg's arm often, and if I didn't know her, I would have thought she was flirting. On second thought, maybe she *was* flirting. Greg was a good-looking guy and he seemed nice enough.

Amelia was quiet and kept her eyes glued to Zach. The way she watched everyone, I could tell she felt out of place. Gwendolyn was very lively, and engaged with just about everyone at the party, including me. I found myself mesmerized by her joy-filled smile. She seemed truly happy, and I knew Zach hadn't felt happy for a long time, so perhaps that was what he saw in her. In only a few hours, she was getting under my skin too. I was still jealous of her stealing his attention, but it was increasingly difficult to be angry about it.

"So," Zach said, startling me out of my contemplations as he plopped onto the cushion beside me and placed his arm around my shoulders. Why he kept hugging me like that, I wasn't sure. "Do you like her?"

"Um, yeah. I guess." He acted as if nothing had been out of the ordinary between us, which in itself was out of the ordinary. He'd been gone for months, and then showed up unable to talk to me, and the next thing I hear from him is that he's in love and getting married. How was I supposed to deal? My brain didn't reroute that easily. I looked down at the floor, and I guessed he picked up on my discomfort or something because he leaned closer.

"Listen, I know you see right through me, but I can't talk. You need to trust me. Please?"

The despair in his voice made me ache to go back to the days when we could talk about anything. Where had that time gone? I agreed, "I guess." I looked down at my hands. My finger was starting to throb, and I wished I'd remembered to bring some Motrin with me.

"What's up with your hand?" Zach asked, reaching over and taking it. I glanced in Keith's direction, knowing he'd be watching Zach's every move. "Whoa, you got a tattoo. I never thought you had it in you. The tongue thing was weird enough, but a tattoo? They're permanent, you know?"

I kept my focus on Keith as he used his laser eye vision to sear a hole in Zach's head instead of mine, this time. I replied, "Yeah, I know, but it's small." I held my fingers together and it all but disappeared between them.

"What is it?" he asked, bringing my hand closer to his face. "A feather?" He chuckled and lifted his eyebrow at me. "What are you queer? Feathers are for girls, dude." His mouth curved in amusement as he shook his head. Zach didn't look angry, but he was certainly making fun of me.

"It's a quill pen, asshole. I'm an English major, remember? I'd like to become an author one day."

"And what's with the colors on the end of the feather?"

"Quill pen, jerk. Writers use quill pens."

"No. The writers I know use computers. You should have gotten an apple tattooed on your hand," Zach joked.

I snatched my hand back. "Shut up!"

"Oh, come on, I'm joking. Let me see it again." He asked with a devious twinkle in his dark brown eyes as he reached for my hand again, wiggling his fingers playfully.

God, he really knows how to get to me.

"Come on, Flynn," Zach begged.

"No." Sometimes his smart aleck tone irritated the crap out of me, but right now I was glad to see that even a small part of the old Zach was left and still comfortable enough in our friendship to tease me. I was irked and relieved at the same time.

I heard low chuckling from the side as Tom came over and sat on the other side of Zach.

"What's so funny?" I asked.

"You two. Always arguing like a married couple. I find it hilarious."

"It's not funny at all. He's being an ass."

"And you always give in," Greg answered as he walked up to us with Grace in tow. "Just show him your tattoo again. Are you okay if I take Grace home tonight? I know this is your birthday thing too."

I looked at Grace who bugged her eyes out at me as if to say, *"Yes, you idiot."*

"Um, sure. I don't mind."

"Let me see your tattoo," Grace asked.

I held out my hand. I knew Zach had to have noticed it was not just random colors, but a rainbow, I also noticed he didn't point it out. If Zach wasn't going to acknowledge the rainbow design, then I wasn't going to specifically call it my "pride-feather" to Grace in front of him. "Doesn't it look like a water color, or chalk?"

Grace studied it, but didn't question the design. "Yeah, it does look like chalk. It's very colorful. Will it look like that when it heals? Because right now it seems like I could rub it off."

"I hope so." It was my original design and stood for both my writing *and* my sexuality. I thought maybe one day I could write about gay-rights to help inform people of the issues we face. In poetry, fiction, or non-fiction—I hadn't decided yet. "I'm going to keep getting it touched up until it looks the way I want. The tattoo artist said fingers were tough. Designs fade easily."

"Then why'd you get it there?" she asked.

"Because it's a quill, and I can hold my fingers together to hide it if I want."

"Oh. Okay."

Tom asked, "Where's that other friend of yours? Kevin, was it?"

I had never understood why Tom couldn't remember Keith's name. It wasn't difficult like Archibald or Humphrey. It had one syllable, for goodness sake. "Keith. His name is Keith. How is it, over the few times we've hung out together over the years, you can remember Kelly and Grace, but you always think his name is Kevin?"

"He doesn't have Kelly's body," Tom answered, lifting his eyebrows.

"Or Grace's," Greg added.

"Greg!" Grace slapped his shoulder as if scolding him, but she was far from upset. She grinned, and he grinned back. Definite flirtage going on.

I ignored it and went back to Tom's question. "Keith," I stressed his name, "was right over there with Kelly a second ago." I pointed toward the table where they'd been standing.

Kelly must have overheard me because she waltzed over to the group we had forming on and around the sofa. "He went to get me a drink."

"Are you two dating?" Tom asked.

Kelly snorted and put her hand over her mouth, coughed, and then answered him once composed. "Um, no. Just really good friends. The four of us have been friends since art class in two-thousand ten." Kelly sat on the armrest of the sofa.

"Oh," Tom said.

I grinned up at Kelly as she patted my shoulder. Once Keith returned with two drinks in hand, our group was together again. "Thanks." Kelly took the cup Keith handed her.

"If we pretended," I offered, "this would be like old times."

"I wasn't at the birthday dinner last year," Keith said.

"No," I pointed out, "but you were at the bowling thing we did three weeks later. All of us. And we had fun."

Kelly urged, "We should do it again. That was a blast!"

"Definitely," Greg added.

"I don't know," Zach said reluctantly. His withdrawn expression and fearful eyes concerned me, because he looked like the old Zach was losing the battle to the weird, fake Zach.

"You don't want to?" I asked.

"Of course he wants to, but my son is thinking about his future." His mother materialized from nowhere and answered for him. It made me shiver.

"A frivolous night of gallivanting about with friends isn't what a man does. Those things are for boys, right Zachary?"

"Oh, I don't know Mrs. Mitchell. I think my father would encourage such a thing before a man gets married as a way of 'throwing off youth,' as he would say." Gwendolyn had also joined our group out of nowhere, but didn't bring the same frosty breeze along with her. She seemed to bring warmth to offset the frost Mrs. Mitchell carried. "I know Mr. Mitchell surely agreed with my father's proposal of joining our two families' assets. Perhaps we should inquire of him whether a night or two of fun is worthwhile?"

I didn't know what game Gwendolyn was playing, but she had a strong, confident way about her, and it seemed that Mrs. Mitchell knew it. Her expression faltered and she backed down. "No dear. That won't be necessary. I'm sure you're right."

"I think so," Gwendolyn said. "It will be nice to let loose and have a break between now before the wedding. After April, we'll have little time to think, let alone go bowling or to the movies. Mr. Mitchell is grooming Zach for church planting assessment in the spring, correct? Too much pressure without a little fun might send us back west, and no one would want that. Don't you agree?"

The look she gave Mrs. Mitchell was icy and thick with innuendo. No doubt "west" was her way of referring to whatever had gone on in Utah and Nevada during Zach's trip. West was where he'd met Gwendolyn, west was where he had secretly gotten engaged, and west was now the code word that kept Mrs. Mitchell's mouth shut. Whatever the hell happened in the west, I was afraid to find out, but at the same time glad there was some leverage Gwendolyn could use in order for us to hang out again.

I needed that. I'd missed my best friend.

"Great!" Gwendolyn cried. "It's settled then! We go bowling or something in a couple weeks and get acquainted with one another. I'm dying to get to know Zach's friends!"

"Can we go roller skating?" Amelia asked quietly. She had moved over to Gwendolyn's side while she had been giving her speech.

Kelly asked, "Can we roller skate another time? I'm still doing PT for the ligament in my knee. Next month should be good."

"Zach?" Gwendolyn asked.

Zach looked uncomfortable as he darted his eyes from his unhappy mother to his blissful fiancé. I would not want to be in a room if the two women faced off, and I think Zach was thinking the same thing. "Yeah," he finally answered. "How about doing something simple. Buffalo Wild Wings and maybe bowling afterwards."

"Great idea!" Gwendolyn said.

"Flynn?" Zach looked to me.

"Um, sure. I like bowling."

Just like that we'd all agreed to go bowling later in July. Tom, Kelly, Greg, Grace, and Gwendolyn seemed excited about it. Keith, Amelia, Zach, and I, on the other hand, all wore expressions of concern or foreboding. I wasn't sure where that feeling came from, but it was equally odd that all three of them had the same looks on their faces that I felt in my gut.

If the atmosphere of the night was any indication as to what the next few months would be like before Zach got married, I was sure I'd need therapy to get me through it.

Chapter 15

July 27, 2013: The End

"Are you going to talk to me?" I asked as Keith and I entered my bedroom after a night of "fun" on the town with our gang.

Just like Gwendolyn had suggested at the beginning of the month, the nine of us met for wings before going bowling. It sounded like a good plan at first, but ended up in the toilet after I panicked and agreed to go out with Amelia. Everything had been fine until Zach winked at me. His look was mischievous and sexy, and made my legs get rubbery. Something in that look made me wonder if he knew I was gay all along and that was why he hadn't pointed out the colors of my tattoo.

He had winked at me and then I found I'd needed a couple of deep breaths to calm down. Keith had given me a weird look, and something inside my head told me tonight was the night. I needed to tell Zach the truth...

Zach, I'm gay. Can I get a Pepsi? I mentally rehearsed my lines before metaphorically banging my head on the table. That was lame. I couldn't tell him like that.

My phone vibrated in my pocket so I fished it out. It was a text from Keith.

Tell him. I can see you are thinking about it, so just DO IT!

Great timing. *No,* I texted back, thinking it was ludicrous since he was sitting right next to me.

Why not?

Because.

Because isn't a reason.

Yes it is. Look, just give me time to think of how to say it. I'll do it. Just don't... you know. I felt so guilty for asking... again, but I had to. I needed more time and I knew Keith. He was jealous every second we spent with Zach.

Keith's anger was evident in his reply, and I didn't have to hear it in his voice to know. He texted, *What? Don't treat you like a boyfriend? Don't kiss you in front of them? Don't touch your hair, or make suggestive comments? I think I've had enough practice. I'll give you time, but we are talking about this later. You hear me!?*

I set my phone on the table and looked up. Zach was staring at me. "Disturbing news?" he asked.

I grew suspicious. "No. Why?"

"Um, maybe the look on your face. You looked irritated or upset while you were texting. Who was it?"

"My dad."

"Oh."

"I need to use the bathroom," Keith said, abruptly rising from his chair.

"I'll go with you," Kelly said.

I saw the way Tom watched them walking away, so I said, "You don't need to worry. If you like Kelly, you can tell her. Keith's not interested in her like that. They're just friends." I knew Kelly had already told him, but I didn't think reiteration was a bad.

"Oh I know," Tom said. "I heard a rumor Keith's gay, so his friendship with her doesn't bother me."

I narrowed my eyes. "Where did you hear that?" I asked suspiciously.

"Yeah, where?" Zach asked, equally concerned, but I doubted his concern was for the same reason.

"Target. I was getting shaving cream and I overheard a guy who sounded like him talking about a gay club to his friend. He said he was thinking about taking his boyfriend to one last year. The girl giggled, and then they talked about go-go dancers or something. I don't know."

"You heard him. You didn't see him?" I asked, even though I knew I was the "boyfriend" in the conversation. We had talked about going to a gay club last year, but I chickened out.

Tom answered, "No, but I was sure it was Keith. Weird. He doesn't look gay."

"What would gay look like, Tom?" asked Gwendolyn.

"Why are we talking about this?" Zach cut in. "I mean really? Can we talk about anything other than Keith's sexuality and what gay looks like?"

In that moment, between my personal horror over the conversation, and my urge to slip under the table and disappear, Keith returned.

He sat and glanced around at the suddenly quiet group. "What?" The silence was awful, since I knew he had to have heard, and now no one wanted to apologize for it. "I'm gay. I have no problem talking about it. Did someone have a question?" Nonchalance. With as many conversations we'd had where Keith was angry as hell, he really did know how to control his emotions when he wanted to.

"No. No questions here," Zach answered hastily. "In fact, that makes what I have to ask Flynn easier."

And a giant hand just grabbed my intestines and yanked. I barely found my voice. "You have a question?"

Zach, who was seated next to me, leaned over. "Yeah. You see, Amelia's single. I was wondering… if maybe… you might want to take her out."

Not the question I was expecting. "Me? Why me?"

"Well, I was waffling between you and Keith, but now that it's clear Keith's gay, you're the logical choice. She's a great girl, only she's a little shy."

It felt odd since she was sitting with the rest of us that he would speak about her as if she couldn't hear. In fact, I saw the hurt on her face. It was pathetic even. I took pity on her and before I could think about it, I agreed. "Okay. I'd love to go out with her." Immediately she lifted her eyes to meet mine and smiled. I smiled back.

Keith kicked me under the table and my brain caught up to my mouth. *Shit…*

Keith paced my bedroom and rubbed the back of his neck. He was really angry. He hadn't said a word since the restaurant. We'd all gone bowling, and Keith paired up with Tom, since Grace chose Greg, and Kelly was keeping score so she wouldn't accidentally twist her knee before she was done with PT, which left me with Amelia.

I hadn't meant to pair up with her like that. It just happened. Like agreeing to date her—it just happened. Keith had to know I didn't mean it.

Okay, part of me did. I had felt sorry for her. The look on her face when Zach said that... Gosh. I didn't like how cold he'd been.

"I'm sorry, sweets," I said.

Keith stopped and glared. "No. You don't get to turn this around and use my nickname for you to gain sympathy points. Get on the bed."

"What?" His commanding tone threw me.

"Get. On. The. Bed." Keith stressed, undoing the buckle of his belt and yanking it free of his jeans in seconds.

I removed my shirt. "I am sorry. You know I didn't do it to hurt you."

Keith slipped his jeans off on leg at a time, and then his socks. "But you told him that *I'm* gay. Why?" Keith griped, undoing my jeans for me. Even though he was irritated by my actions earlier, he still kissed down the side of my neck and palmed my groin as he undressed me.

"I don't know," I whispered back, kissing him teasingly on the corners of his mouth. I tugged on his shirt hem and he allowed me to remove it. I kissed his collarbone and up his neck. "And that wasn't exactly how it all came out. Tom overheard you at Target talking to some girl about a gay club, and Zach seemed uncomfortable because you were gay."

Keith groaned as I pawed his ass, dipping my fingers down his crack. "But you know I'm already out," Keith said between gasps for breath. I was rubbing my crotch against his and I felt his body's response. Breathily he complained, "Confirming it for your friends doesn't affect me. What it does is take the focus off of you."

I was tonguing his throat and stopped when he said that. I pulled back and looked him in the eyes. "That's why you're mad at me."

"Yes. You used me as a diversion. Just like you use sex as a diversion."

"No I don't."

Keith lifted an eyebrow. "Really? What about the car after our last fight?"

"Oh. Well. That just sort of happened."

"Yeah, right. Everything with you just sort of happens."

"So... you aren't mad I agreed to go out with her?"

He bit my chest and I winced. "Oh, I'm mad as hell."

"Really? Because you seem...." I couldn't think as well while he stroked me so aggressively. In fact, his fervor made me whimper. "Keith... oh...."

He spun me and shoved. "Get on the bed. I'm fucking the shit out of you."

"What if my dad comes home?" I crawled on and flopped on my back.

"He won't care."

"But what if—"

Keith stopped me with his mouth as he moved over me. He brought his lips down on mine and silenced me with his aggression, pressing his body down on me and rocking. In the couple years we'd been sexually active, I could probably count on one hand how many times he'd been the aggressor. Keith could be an assertive person, but not in bed. He told me he liked surrendering to me and I had no problem taking charge. He pinned my arms above my head.

He pulled back and our eyes locked. "I don't like how different you are around him," Keith said. I think he knew this was the best time to call me out on my behavior, because I was powerless in my hormone-induced haze. He reached down and stroked me up and down, as I struggled for breath, listening with anticipation as to what he'd do next. "With Zach, you're submissive. With Zach, you defer to his authority, his wishes, his suggestions and opinions. With me, you dominate as if you don't think I should have a say. I do have a say." Keith slipped down my body and situated himself between my legs and took me into his mouth.

He sucked me aggressively and I moaned. When he pulled away, I felt my body suffer in response. "Please," I begged.

"Oh, you'll get more." Keith leaned back and shoved my thigh. "On your knees," he commanded. I complied, and he rubbed my ass cheeks, down the crack, and over my hole. He paused to retrieve the lube and a condom before loosening me up. His fingers prepping, teasing, twisting, and stroking made breathing a chore as I gasped at the different sensations.

By the time he inserted a third finger and rotated his hand I lost it. "Please, stop. I need you to fuck me."

He removed his fingers and slapped my ass. "I will. Don't you worry about that."

I folded my arms over the back of my head as I buried my face in the pillow and waited. I felt him move in behind me and position himself. Keith pressed in with a groan and fucked me slow and steady.

"Shit," he breathed raggedly. He held my hips lightly and caressed my hipbones with his thumbs. Three more thrusts and he stopped in the middle. "Fuck."

"What's wrong?" I asked, lifting my arm to look at him, but I couldn't see his face from my curled position.

"Damn," he fussed, pulling out suddenly. "Roll over."

"What?"

"Now! Roll over!"

I did, but he wouldn't allow me to spread my legs for him. Instead, Keith lined up my outstretched legs and crawled on top of my body, after grabbing another condom from the box. He rolled it down my dick, lubed his ass, and sat on me. "Oh fuck, yeah!" he moaned loudly, lifting up and easing back down in a perfectly acceptable rhythm I had no problems succumbing to.

His knees were bent and he used the angle to hop effortlessly on my lap. He leaned forward, gripping each of my shoulders with one hand, and closing his eyes. I watched his cock bouncing, still covered in latex, so I reached down and slipped it off. He opened his eyes and we gazed at each other as he rode me and I stroked him. I craned my neck and claimed a kiss, messy and urgent, right before he moaned and leaned back, spewing ropes all over my chest.

"Oh fuck," he panted. "That was fucking fantastic. Did you come?"

I nodded, moving my eyes all over the curves of his beautiful body.

"Why didn't you say?"

"I enjoy watching you."

A shadow crossed Keith's face and he got off me. As he lay down on the one side of my bed, I left to get a wet towel. I cleaned up and handed a fresh one to him. I knew that look. "It's over, isn't it?" I asked, hating myself for not pretending one more day.

Keith wouldn't look at me. "Are you still going out with her?"

"You know I am. Didn't you see her face? And the way everyone talks about her as if she's not in the room. It's sad. How can I—"

"Don't. Just... don't." Keith got off the bed and picked up his jeans from the floor. "I'm not doing this anymore." He got dressed as I watched. I couldn't explain my deep need to watch over Zach and help that pathetically sad girl, so I kept my mouth shut, as he needed me to. When he was done dressing, he stepped closer and ran his fingers down my chest, finally looking into my eyes. "I'm sorry. I don't think I can do this if we aren't on the same page. I've tried, but I don't understand the weird relationship you have with Zach. His parents are freaky, I get that, I felt that, and I am really sorry if his dad is hitting him. But until you see how great we could be together, I'm done trying to work on this relationship on my own. I'll try to be your friend, but I can't be your boyfriend."

He kissed me lightly and walked out the door.

Chapter 16

August 24, 2013:

Friends, Lovers, & Ex-Lovers Turned Friends

"Why are we here?" Keith grumbled from the backseat as Kelly parked the car. Grace was meeting us here with her new boyfriend, Greg, and I hoped that the group of us would be able to make it through an evening without an emotional confrontation.

Kelly replied, "To support our friend."

"For cheating on me," Keith inserted his own explanation from the back seat, most likely to take a dig at me.

I protested, "Hey. You broke up with me."

"Ye-ah," Keith whined, "for agreeing to date a girl, thereby cheating on me."

I turned around in the seat since we were all still sitting in the car. "I apologized for it. I got cornered. I panicked."

"No. You gave in. You do whatever he asks, whenever he asks it, and to hell with the rest of us."

Kelly came to my defense, "That's not true, Keith. You're being unfair." Keith was stewing anyway. He huffed loudly and crossed his arms over is chest. "Stop it," Kelly fussed. "The two of you are going to have to figure this out, whether you want to or not. Keith, you have to be less selfish and stop pressuring Flynn. He'll come out when he's ready." Then she turned her glare my way. "And you! You need to stop catering to Zach. Keith is your boyfriend."

"Was," he quickly corrected.

"Quiet," Kelly shot to Keith. She then continued her chastisement of my behavior. "If you can't consider how hard this is for Keith, then you're being just as selfish. High school is over. No one is going to crush your head against the locker or vandalize your car. There are other gay couples in this town. If you relaxed and acted the way you do in private, then you might start noticing how many other gay and lesbian couples are out there. Instead, you hide your head in the sand and pretend that society isn't changing. It is. Target has several gay employees, and Keith's never had an issue working there. I understand your apprehension, but you can't keep living in this state of tension because you're afraid of one guy's reaction, one family's reaction. I'm with Keith; it's been years. If you have no intention of coming out publically, that's your choice, but you shouldn't string Keith along."

"I'm not. He's the one that keeps coming back to me." I shot him a look. "Every. Time. We break up for a couple weeks, then he comes back around with his puppy-dog eyes, and tells me how much he misses me. We end up having mind blowing sex and things are great for months after that."

Keith spewed his venom. "Yeah, until Zach comes around, and you shove me away like a disease."

"I do not."

"Yes, you do!"

"You can't keep having this same argument!" Kelly shouted. "I'm sick of it! The two of you are toxic. Now, let's get out of this car, go roller-skating, and pretend everything is great. I want to get to know this girl Zach's setting up with Flynn, and find out why. Who knows, she could turn out to be a serial killer and end up in jail after the police find a body in her basement. Then Flynn won't have to worry about it any longer."

Kelly was trying to make a joke, but it wasn't much comfort. I got out and shut the door. Keith kept his eyes averted, and his arms crossed over his chest. Kelly stepped in front of me. "It's been a month. You need to grow up. I don't understand why you won't admit how you feel. Suck it up and tell him once and for all, or I might hire a thug to beat the shit out of you."

Kelly turned on her heels and grabbed Keith's arm as she stormed across the parking lot. I walked slowly to the door, trying to figure out whom she'd been referring. Keith or Zach? I supposed she could mean either. I'd never thought all that deeply about my feelings. Those times Keith had broken up with me, I only noticed how much I had missed him when things happened to remind me he wasn't around. Then, when he'd show back up at my door, a deep rush of lust had always convinced me I wanted him more than I had realized while we'd been apart. But how did I feel about him now? I didn't know. I was still upset he left the way he did.

How *did* I feel about Zach? Jealous of Gwendolyn, for sure. Where the hell did she come from? I didn't like any part of this situation.

I walked in the front door of the skating rink that had looked the same for so many years, I wondered if they might never decide on renovations. The walls and floor were a tad too baby blue for me, and the short weave wall-to-wall carpet that covered benches and walls alike was so '80s. Thank God the lights went off five minutes after we arrived. The disco-ball strobe lights that hung from the ceiling were cheesy, but effective, and reminded me of Robert Hayes' version of Saturday Night Fever done in the movie Airplane. Cheesy, but amusing. I hadn't been roller-skating in years, so the idea Amelia had that we come here was sort of fun.

I exchanged my shoes for some skates and laced up the front as I sat on a padded bench over by the air hockey table. Air hockey had always been my favorite arcade game. Maybe Keith would play with me after he finished sulking. I spotted him standing by the carpeted half-wall next to the skating floor with his skates already on. He was watching the other skaters circle the blue concrete floor. When I stood up and eased my way over, my first impulse was to reach for his waist and kiss the back of his neck. I wanted to apologize. Keith, with all his impulsiveness and hotheaded reactions, really had been patient with me.

Just as I lifted my hands, I heard Zach's voice. "Hey. You made it!"

I dropped my hands and rolled up next to Keith, where Zach was shaking his hand, and patting him on the shoulder. "Hey man," I greeting Zach.

"Flynn!" Zach smiled. He pulled me into a half-hug over the dividing wall. "I'm so glad you're here." He turned and pointed to the far side of the skate floor. "Amelia's over there wearing the purple shirt."

I glanced down. I was wearing my purple *A Love Like War* T-shirt. "Great," I mused out loud. "We'll match."

"Ha ha, that's funny! Hey Kelly, I'm glad you could come. Tom said he'd be here in a little bit."

"Oh really? Fun."

Zach said, "You don't sound enthused. I thought Flynn said you liked him."

Kelly leveled her hard eyes at me and I shrank away. Sheepishly I answered, "I might have mentioned something about you not being repulsed by his muscles."

"Flynn!" She swatted my arm. "Great. Keith, remind me never to say anything to Flynn that I don't want advertised."

"Don't be too harsh," Zach said. "He only told me. Flynn's always told me everything, so please don't be offended. Right, buddy?"

Zach clapped me on the shoulder, and all I could do was grin. I hoped he would not be able to tell it was a fake grin. I also hoped he wouldn't be able to look into my eyes and read my mind as I thought about all the things I *didn't* tell him.

"Right," I said.

"Well, go on then. Amelia's been waiting for you."

I did as Zach asked before Keith had a chance to grumble about it. I glided over the smooth surface with ease, and skated in time with her strides as I settled in beside her. "Hey," I said.

Amelia jumped at the sound of my voice and lost her balance. I caught her around the waist and we ended up chest-to-chest, nose-to-nose. I held her gaze calmly, and felt her shiver in my arms. Her eyes dropped to my lips twice, but I smiled gently and released my hold on her. She rolled back and took my hand.

"Shall we?" she asked, indicating we join the rest of the crowd circling the floor. I nodded a reply and we weaved our way through together, gliding left and then right, in time with the music overhead.

It wasn't so bad. Her hand felt warm and tiny in mine, I wasn't used to that. Zach's hand was bigger than mine and Keith's was about the same. I couldn't remember ever feeling something so small and delicate in my grasp. Amelia smiled at me shyly as we circled. She wasn't a bad skater. I noticed how smooth her strides were as we made our third pass around, but making the same motions over and over got boring after a few minutes. I needed more.

I released her hand and skated out in front of her a few paces before turning around. Her eyes went wide and she laughed. I kept glancing behind me to make sure the path was clear, but I continued gliding in reverse for a half-lap. I'd been skating since I was a kid. My mom had taken me. She liked ice-skating, which I was also good at, and I hadn't wanted to lose my skills, so I'd kept coming even after she died.

Sometimes there were rules against hot-dogging on the skate floor, so I had to be careful as I spun around, skating forward right next to Amelia and then circling in front of her, crisscrossing my feet and pressing my weight to the outside of my strides. I had her laughing and rolling her eyes by the time the next song ended.

"Do you want to sit one out and talk?" I asked.

"Yeah."

I slowed to match her pace and took her hand, guiding us over to the half-wall. "So, tell me a little bit about yourself."

She looked down, then out at the skaters, and then to me. "Um, I don't know. I like hanging out with my sister."

"She seems nice. Anything else? Do you like swimming? I have a pool." I caught sight of Greg and Grace circling the floor together, holding hands, and I smiled. It made me happy at least two of our group were enjoying themselves.

Amelia smiled. "Yes. That sounds fun. I've lived most of my life in Arizona. The weather here is different, more humid. I'd love to swim in your pool sometime. We only moved to Utah about three years ago and I haven't felt comfortable there."

"Really? Why did your family move there?"

"My dad's work. He's part of an agricultural development group or something. I don't know. It has to do with water supply systems and energy. I know he's explained it to me a hundred times, but I don't understand him."

"My dad's a hydrologist. It sounds like he'd be interested to hear about it."

Amelia smoothed her hair over her left ear. "What's a hydrologist?"

"He's like a water engineer. He applies scientific knowledge and mathematical principles to solve water-related problems... and I can tell my explanation went right over your head." Her eyes glazed over and she furrowed her brow. Somehow, I knew this girl was not going to follow anything else I said. "Do you want to play air hockey?"

Her eyes popped wide. "Yes!"

After one game, I figured out I had to fake a lack of skills, because she had none. No coordination whatsoever, and when I scored, she pouted. So I let her win. I concentrated on making my shots hit where I aimed them.

Left corner, right rail, one inch to the side of the goal, I was getting really accurate.

"I thought you said you were good at this," Keith mocked while strolling by.

I tapped the puck and sent it straight into the goal as I gave him a "fuck-off" glare. Amelia made a little moping noise and I lied to her about the score. "Don't worry, sweets, you're still ahead by one."

I noticed Keith's reaction out of the corner of my eye, so I shifted my gaze to him when Amelia was watching the puck gliding over the table. Keith heard my use of his endearment. Not that he used it often because he knew I preferred my given name, but he had decided on calling me "sweets" whenever he felt exceptionally romantic. I hadn't meant to use the same endearment; it just popped out. I mouthed the words, "I'm sorry," but Keith shook his head and stormed off, rolling over to the bench near the skate return. Moments later, he was out the door.

After skating, Kelly let me to use her car to drive Amelia home. Keith had disappeared, and Kelly said she wanted to spend more time with Tom, so using her car was fine. Plus, Grace and Greg were all smoochy, so they'd never notice I left.

Zach was even okay with us bailing because I think he assumed we were hitting it off well. I felt weird about that.

I walked Amelia to her door. Her family was renting a house in The Greens so it was only about ten-or-fifteen minutes away from my house. "I had a nice time," I said, standing there awkwardly by the front door.

"Me too."

"We should do this again."

"Or go swimming at your pool. I could ask Gwen, too. I'm sure she'd love to!"

"Okay." Suddenly the thought of swimming with Zach came into mind. Keith wouldn't like it. I knew it. That would be worse than dating a girl. "Just let me know when you'd like to come over."

"Okay." More awkward silence. I looked around. Porch. Wicker chairs. Cat sitting on the wicker chair. When I brought my attention back to Amelia, I found her eyes closed and her lips puckered. Girls really did that? I leaned closer, thinking I could do it quick and leave. But just as I was about to kiss her, I chickened out and pecked her cheek instead. "Bye," I said as I bolted.

***

At home, I found my dad in the kitchen, sitting alone at the kitchen table, staring at the sugar bowl. I was so out of breath from running in, and thinking about having almost kissed a girl, that the sight of my dad virtually frozen took a moment to process.

"Dad? Dad, are you okay?"

Like a hypnotized psych patient, he slowly turned his face toward mine, unblinking, and then stopped as he stared at me.

"Dad?"

He blinked. "Oh, Flynn." He took a deep breath and let it out slowly. I walked the rest of the way over to him and sat down. "I broke the sugar bowl," he confessed.

I glanced down and sure enough, it was cracked in half. "Oh. Okay. Are we out of Super Glue? Do you need me to get some?"

Quietly and mechanically, he said, "I gave it to her when we first bought this place. She wanted a sunflower sugar bowl and I had spent months looking for one. I couldn't find what she wanted, so I went to one of those places where you paint your own pottery and I painted the flowers on it. The girl at the store said it was the nicest piece she'd seen in a long time and asked if I was an artist. I laughed. I knew she was just being nice, but your mom told me it was the best sugar bowl I could have given her. She wouldn't even use it because she'd been afraid of breaking it. It sat in the china cabinet for three years until one day Nate asked if we could put it on the table because it was so pretty. She smiled and let him fill it up."

I took my dad's hand and squeezed, tears rolling down my cheeks.

"Some days are harder than others, Flynn."

I stood up and hugged my dad. I had gotten myself into some awkward situations and I'd made some bad decisions of late, but nothing I was going through could compare to those moments when the grief of losing my mother and brother snuck up and stabbed a searing, white-hot poker through one or both of our hearts. I had felt those moments before, hearing a certain sound, or smelling a type of perfume, and my head would spin until I saw nothing but *her* eyes and heard only *her* voice. I'd curl up, text Keith, and then wait for him to come over and hold me until I recovered. But who did my dad have? Me.

I patted his back. "I'm here Dad. I love you."

Sometime later, I went up to my room. So many things in there reminded me of Keith. His shirt hanging over the back of my desk chair, his flip-flops sticking out from under the edge of the bed, the necklace he'd given me for Christmas on my nightstand next to our picture from prom. We'd been so happy, but not without difficulties. Time apart could be good. I wasn't thinking in terms of the past "time apart" where I basically carried on as usual until Keith came to his senses and came knocking on my door.

No, I knew this was different. We were older now. I had to think hard about what I wanted before I let Keith back in. I had hurt him enough. When we got back together, *if* we got back together, it was going to be for good and I was going to have to be the man he deserved.

I would give it time. Maybe by Christmas. Or maybe after the wedding.

Between now and then, I had to find out who the heck Gwendolyn was, why Zach had gotten engaged so fucking fast, and why he wanted me dating her shy younger sister. I had plenty to keep me busy. My feelings and insecurities about Keith would somehow work themselves out. In time. Everything solved itself in time.

Chapter 17

November 28, 2013: In the Devil's Den

Getting to know Gwendolyn and finding out what happened on Zach's trip out west was harder than I imagined. Gwen, as Zach called her, seemed to have lots of wedding plans to work on that whisked her away with her mother, who was in town visiting for a few months. Zach had no time, per his father, to talk with me, which made me feel like an outcast, while Amelia had all the time in the world to spend with me, yet nothing at all to contribute to a conversation. I hated saying it, but she was boring as hell.

She didn't like horror movies, or action movies, or thrillers, or science fiction, so that basically left us with chick-flicks. I didn't mind girly movies per se, Grace preferred them, so I had seen my share, but when chick-flicks were the only genre we could agree on; that irked me. I mean really? No compromise? It didn't take long before I gave up the movie option.

Mini golf was okay. We both sucked at it, which made us both laugh, but it got expensive putting round after round when I was the only one paying. She claimed she had no money.

I was also back in college, taking a couple classes, but without the spark I'd had initially. I'd thought about quitting at the end of last semester, but that was before Keith dumped me. Now I didn't know what I wanted to do. Last fall, Keith and I had been communicating all the time via text, face time, and phone calls. Not to mention all the lunches I'd had with Zach. This fall, I had lost my drive. I worked on the assignments and got everything done, but I almost didn't care when I got B's. I had nothing else worthwhile going on, so the days melded into one another. Before I knew it, three months had gone by, and it was Thanksgiving break.

I heard the doorbell ring and rushed to answer it. Part of me expected Keith to be standing on the other side when I opened it, and my heart did a little fluttery thing until I saw it was only Zach. I think it was the first time I'd ever been disappointed to see him. *I really miss Keith.*

"Hey. Haven't seen you for a while. Come on in." I stepped back and Zach entered.

He looked like a little kid visiting grandma's house who'd been told not to touch anything: or else! He looked scared and hesitant to move.

"Zach," I closed the door, "no one's here. It's just us." I stepped right up into his personal space. He was an inch taller than me, but shorter than Keith, and when I looked up I saw fear in his eyes. Why would he fear me when I'd known him all my life? I reached up and placed my hand gently on his shoulder. "Tell me what's going on."

"I can't. There's too much, you wouldn't understand." His voice quivered.

"Try me. Give me the bullet-point version. Anything. I don't like seeing you afraid."

Zach pulled away and sat on the couch, slumping forward, with his head in his hands, elbows on his knees. I sat next to him and waited until he was ready to talk. When he looked up, he had tears in his eyes. "I hate how you can see right through me. I've tried so hard to hold everything in, you have no idea how much I want to say but can't."

"Can't or won't?" I didn't want to know, but it was one of those things you pushed yourself to do anyway.

"Can't, Flynn. I shouldn't be here."

He tried to rise, but I grabbed his forearm and pulled him back down. "Stop. You can sit for two minutes."

"Two."

I nodded and reiterated, "Two."

He took a huge breath, or three, and then spoke while staring at the floor. Maybe looking at me was too much, like when we were kids and we stared at the ceiling, but I'd take anything if he would just talk to me. "My dad's always hit me," he said softly, as if fearing the sound would carry his admission over to the house next door. "For years. He started with my brother, but that didn't last long. My brother knew how to play the game, and did whatever Dad wanted, so he shifted his rage unto my sister. He even broke her finger when she was in fifth-grade and coached her how to blame it on falling off her bike. She was terrified of him, but somehow made it through."

He glanced up at me as if to make sure I was still paying attention and then looked back down. "You knew about the pregnancy and why she'd gotten married so young. She needed to cover it up, but then had the miscarriage. She told me getting married was the best thing that had ever happened, because it took her out of that house. Chad really takes care of her and she doesn't have to deal with my dad every day. They still have issues, because Chad doesn't want to join the church, but he's a strong man who isn't going to be manipulated by my father."

"Is that why you're getting married?" I asked.

"Sort of." He paused. Several seconds passed without comment, and then I saw his hands shaking. Right when I thought he wasn't going to elaborate, he said, "I met her on the retreat. My dad had several contacts out west; many of them were having the same issues with their children. Children who dared question the doctrine of the church. So I guess they thought that some time in the desert; camping and visiting national parks and historical sites, would help lay a foundation to talk about our church's history. I don't know. It all seemed fine at first. I met some really neat people." He grinned at me. "Gwen was so pretty. The first time I saw her, she was walking out of the hotel with the sun setting behind her, and with her red hair, she looked like a phoenix." Zach's eyes were so alive in those seconds. He continued, sounding so happy, "I remember thinking that maybe she was my chance to be reborn from the ashes my life was becoming. I couldn't imagine her doing anything that would land her in the same unruly group as me. We 'youth' were rarely allowed to be alone. I think it was so no one would collaborate against the parents. I guess they'd been right in their assumptions, because pretty much the first thing we did was come up with a plan. Strength in numbers, I guess. Gwen and I decided to play along and act the part, especially since our dads were talking together most of the time. We were trying to think of a way out."

"So you agreed to get married?"

"Sort of. There's more to it than that, but I really should be going." Zach stood up and headed toward the door.

"Zach wait." I grabbed his arm as he reached for the door handle. "What about the marks on your back? I saw them. What happened at that camp?"

"That was me… not the camping trip. I spoke out of turn and I guess my dad had all this frustration built up because he hadn't hit me in months, so right before we returned, he made up for lost time. It was my fault."

"Nothing warrants that kind of discipline, there's no way it could be your fault. Zach, you have to see he's abusing you. You have to. You're an adult now you don't have to take it. You could—"

"I have to go." He hurriedly opened the door, but turned on the front step to ask, "Please come for Thanksgiving dinner. You and your dad. Please?"

I really had no choice. "Yeah, sure. Of course. Text me if I can bring anything."

Zach nodded and rushed home; leaving me with more conjecture about the type of situation he was trapped in.

Hours later when my dad came home, I filled him in on the conversation and Zach's fear. "Oh, I also agreed we'd go to Thanksgiving dinner at their house this year."

My dad coughed. Then he coughed some more, and fumbled for his glass of water, choking and gasping for air, his face turning red.

"Dad?" I reached for him, but he pushed my arm away.

After several more choking, coughing sounds, he breathed deeply and exhaled. His face returned to its normal color. "I sucked in a piece of chicken," he wheezed. "Try not to tell me a thing like that while I'm eating."

"Sorry."

He cleared his throat with one final, strong cough. "Dinner at the Mitchells', eh? This should be interesting."

I couldn't disagree.

***

We'd been guests of the Mitchells for years. Most holiday dinners were, in fact, spent at their house since my mother and brother has passed. It was only recently that our fathers' silent war had escalated enough to keep us in separate corners. But today, we'd all be in the same room once again.

I can't wait.

We stood on the front porch and waited after I rang the doorbell. I could hear lots of people inside. Too many to only be Zach's immediate family, there had to be aunts and uncles or cousins included as well. There were certainly a zillion unknown cars parked all up and down my street.

I breathed in the crisp, fall air, and with it I could almost taste the roasted turkey on my tongue. Mrs. Mitchell had always been a good cook, if nothing else. I could only imagine what delights lay beyond the front door. Sausage stuffing with fresh thyme, pork roast with fig chutney, gravy, cranberry sauce, mashed potatoes, and sweet potato casserole with glazed pecans. My mouth watered at the thought of it all.

We would make it through dinner, we had to; because after dinner came Boston cream pie, pumpkin pie, blueberry pie, and seven different kinds of cookies that would send my brain into a food coma where I'd lie back on Zach's couch and moan about it for two more hours. Suddenly, I realized how much I missed being a little kid. One who didn't know anything about cruel and abusive parents, or overly strict church practices that hated gays and wouldn't allow members to question their teachings.

"Being an adult sucks," I mumbled.

"What?" my dad asked.

"Nothing."

The door opened and a lovely woman with brown hair and green eyes smiled at us. "Vic? Victor Brewer? Oh my gosh, it's so great to see you!" This woman, whom I didn't recognize, proceeded to step out onto the porch with us and hug my dad, and more surprisingly, he hugged her back.

"Krista, it's been a long time."

They hugged and then looked at each other with an intimacy I hadn't seen my dad display since my mom died. He really knew this woman.

"You look good. Really good." She smiled, trailing her eyes down my dad's frame and back up again. I might be gay, but I know that look. She was checking him out.

"Thanks. My son takes good care of me, I guess." My dad did this thing where he looked down bashfully and smoothed his hair back—not that it moved it was too short.

The woman turned her attention to me and her eyes went wide. "Flynn? Oh, wow! Look at you, all grown up." She came at me all happy and familiar, clamping her hands on my shoulders, thankfully holding back from the type of bear hug she'd given my dad. I think she saw my apprehension, because she smiled and let me go.

"Um, hi," I said.

"Flynn, this is Karen Mitchell's sister, Krista. Krista, as you figured out, this is my son Flynn. Nineteen, in college, and pretty much ready to take on the world. He's a great kid." My dad clapped me on the back and I ducked my head from embarrassment.

"Thanks Dad."

"Krista was a friend of your mother's. One of her closest friends, in fact. They met at one of the birthday parties Karen used to throw for you and Zach. It was an instant bond. Two peas in a pod."

Her voice dropped with her expression. "I'm so sorry about Tory. I was on a dig in Nepal when I heard about the accident. I would have come to see you... but...."

My dad reached out. "Krista, it's been a long time. There's no need to rehash old pain right now. I'm merely glad to see you. It'll make tonight's dinner all the more enjoyable."

"Dinner! Right. I'm so glad you're dining with us." She stepped back, opened the door and walked through, showing us in. No sooner had I stepped over the threshold than I heard my name hollered with enthusiasm.

"Flynn!" Amelia descended upon me and threw her arms around my neck.

"Hi," I choked as she squeezed the life out of me.

"Come on," she said, grabbing my hand and pulling me down the hall.

I turned to say something to my dad, but he was talking and I was out of his sight in about three seconds. She yanked me into another room where we promptly stopped. "Amelia, what the heck?"

"Mom," she said proudly, arms slipping around my body again. "This is my boyfriend, Flynn Brewer."

"What?" I questioned her, but I doubt anyone heard me over her over exuberance.

She rattled on. "He lives next door. He's Zach's best friend. He's the one who took me to the movies and mini-golfing. He bought me ice cream and we ate french-fries at the bowling alley." I'd never heard her so happy in all the time we'd spent together.

Wait. What did she call me? Boyfriend. I stood there frozen in shock. *@FlynnB #Boyfriend <3.* I could imagine her on Twitter right now. *Why would she think I was her boyfriend? We'd only gone out a couple of times since July. No... That can't be right. We'd gone mini-golfing a couple of* *times. We did go to the movies and to dinner at my house once when I made lasagna and I had way too much left over and.... Oh shit. I'm her boyfriend. When the hell did that happen?*

When I was distracted obsessing over what Zach might be doing. While I took her out over and over until Keith would return my texts and forgive me... Idiot!

The ugly truth hit me as I stood there like a fool. I wasn't considering her assumptions in this set-up. I fell into this situation because I wasn't thinking about her. I wasn't thinking at all. Zach had asked me, I'd said yes, but now Amelia was here, and somehow I became her boyfriend when I wasn't paying attention. *Shit.* I hadn't even kissed her properly.

I'd known I was a little depressed this semester, but I never thought I was capable of spacing badly enough to acquire a girlfriend.

"Amelia," I urged, tugging on her sleeve. "I think we need to talk." I whispered it in her ear, but she wasn't listening. She was boasting about all the fun things we'd done over past several months.

Crap! Where did the time go?

"Amelia, can we talk?" I whispered more urgently.

"Of course, Pookey."

Pookey? Oh God.

The house was full of people, so getting her anywhere private was a joke. I pulled her into the half-bath by the kitchen and shut the door. Before I opened my mouth, her arms coiled around my neck and her lips pressed to mine. I froze. Literally froze, as in my limbs turned into hanging mackerel displayed at an open fish market, lifeless and limp, and my lips became a chiseled ice sculptures.

She pressed and moved her mouth for several seconds before she realized I wasn't kissing back, and then slowly withdrew. "Why aren't you kissing me? Isn't that why you brought me in here? For privacy?"

I didn't like the sadness in her voice, but I couldn't lead her on. I'd already done enough of that. "Um, Amelia, there seems to be some confusion between us. I'm not your boyfriend."

She blew me off. "Of course you are, silly."

"No, I'm not. Why would you think that?"

"Because of all the cool stuff we've done together. You took me mini-golfing!"

"Yeah. We golfed. I never asked you to be my girlfriend. I took you out because Zach asked me to."

"Well what kind of a guy does all those things and doesn't want to be a boyfriend?"

A gay one, I thought. I held that automatic response perched on the tip of my tongue. If I told her, she'd tell her sister who would tell Zach. We were in his house, with his family, with his father. No. I wouldn't out myself that way. Zach's "snake-worshipping, sorcerer-type" father scared the crap out of me. I'd tell Zach when we were alone.

Plus, Keith wasn't around to pressure me, so I had time. When Keith returned to my doorstep, I figured I'd be more than ready to move forward; man-up, live *out,* and get on with the next stage of our lives—marriage; maybe, or moving in together. I wouldn't have to come out just yet if I played my cards right.

For Zach, I'd appease Amelia.

"Look, I hadn't really thought about it. I guess one could misconstrue our dates as… well… *dates,* but in truth I was just hanging with you like I would any friend. Can't that be enough? Can't we be just friends?"

Her face sagged. "You think I'm ugly, don't you? Everyone thinks I'm ugly compared to her. She's fun and I'm just the frumpy one in her shadow. I should have known you'd reject me. They all reject me."

"No. Wait. I'm not rejecting you, I'm—"

"Yes you are! I knew I couldn't have Zach, but when he suggested you, I thought you'd be perfect. We'd see them all the time, Zach and Gwen. I'd have all the time in the world to be with him, because he constantly talks about you. We'd go swimming in your pool, and I would get to see his glistening body, rippled with muscle. Yes. But you spoiled all that, you evil trickster." Suddenly her weepy tone turned to rage, and she came at me, fists in the air, about to strike.

I've got fast reflexes. I grabbed her arms at the wrists and held them securely in the air and out to each side. She pulled, but I wouldn't let go, while her eyes glowed with the fire of a psychopath. She yanked as couple more times and when it was evident that I wasn't letting go, she relaxed. I asked, "Are you going to be good?"

She pouted, "Yes."

I let go and she took a step back and turned around, curling her back and hugging herself around the middle. Then I heard her crying, and it only grew louder as the moments passed.

"Amelia. Amelia, please, don't cry." I hated when girls cried. Kelly cried in my arms one time when her ex-boyfriend had done something stupid. I hadn't liked that experience, but Kelly was one of my closet friends. Amelia was only an acquaintance. I didn't know her, and the longer it went on, the guiltier I felt for being the cause. I *had* led her on. I'd been the one to take her on all those dates, maybe six total or seven since July. That was a lot, right? "Amelia, I'm sorry I led you on. Truth is, I had a really hard break-up, and I need more time before I consider dating again. Can you please understand it has nothing to do with you? I don't think you're ugly. I think you're really pretty." Most of that was the truth.

She turned sharply, smiling so I could see every one of her white teeth. "You do?"

I shrugged. "Yeah."

"Oh, thank you!" Again she wrapped me in a huge hug and pressed so close I could feel every curve of her body. "You do care for me."

"Okay. Yeah. Can we just go back in to the party? I'm sure everyone is looking for us and I kinda want to talk to Zach." Her frantic, psycho personality aside, I needed some air.

Thank God she let go. "Sure." Amelia grabbed my hand, opened the door, and tugged me through the house to where Zach and Gwendolyn we seated near the fireplace. "Look, Gwen, my boyfriend's here."

What? My mouth dropped open and I would have said something, but Zach had gotten up right as we entered, and he hugged me before I had the chance to protest her "boyfriend" tag. *Women!*

"Hey Buddy," Zach greeted me warmly. "Glad to hear things are going well."

I answered dryly, "Yeah. Whatever. When's dinner?"

Right on cue, his mother announced, "Dinner will be served. There are tables lined up in the basement since the dining room is too small to seat all forty-five guests. There are nametags at each place setting. Please sit in your assigned place, so everyone will get to know someone new. That way we can *all* get acquainted before the wedding."

It sounded terrible initially, but I ended up sitting next to Zach's sister Amy, whom I really liked, and Amelia was across the table and three places down. Far enough away not to bug me, but close enough I could monitor any proclamations of our undying love. Thankfully, there were none.

There also weren't any evil vibes dripping off Zach's dad. I only saw him once, when he gave a blessing before dinner, and then he was seated the rest of the time, angled away from me.

And *my dad* was yucking it up with Zach's aunt and having a good ol' time. I'd not seen him so relaxed in what felt like forever, and it made me both thankful and resentful. Sure, I wanted him to have fun, and I knew it would happen eventually, but to *see* it happening made me feel weird for my mom. Was she watching?

Chapter 18

Winter 2013 / Spring 2014: My Life Sucks

I thought that by Christmas I'd be able to tell Zach the truth, but his family, including the soon-to-be in-laws, decided to take a cruise to Hawaii. They'd be gone at least a month. It must be nice to have that kind of cash, to be able take off work; but that wasn't me being bitter, no sir.

I drove past Keith's house, contemplating knocking on his door to see if he was open to talking, when a strange car pulled up in front of his house. I slowed in that stalker-like way, and stopped my car two houses down. Keith came out wearing his blue knit beanie and tweed jacket. He looked hot in that jacket. Plus, I had to admit, I'd missed the beanie. I used to like taking it off and running my fingers through his hair.

As he approached the car, a guy got out and rushed over to open the passenger door for him. I slumped in the seat. *Keith's on a date.*

I slid down so they wouldn't see me as they passed, and after the car had driven off, I sat up and drove away. Five months had passed, Keith had moved on. I felt sick. I assumed he'd come back to me. I thought he said I was the one. I thought our troubles were temporary.

I'd been an idiot.

Once the car was out of sight I called Grace. "Hey," she answered, knowing it was me from her caller ID.

"Hi. What do you know about a guy Keith's seeing?"

"Um… what do you mean?" She sounded hesitant.

"I know that voice. You know something and you aren't telling."

"Keith asked me not to. His name is Carter," she relented.

I knew him. "Carter Langley?" I fussed. "Really? I didn't know he was gay. What does Keith see in him?" Carter graduated the year before us. I thought he moved to Boston, but I guess I was wrong.

"Flynn, it's just a date."

"Yeah. A date. Sure. I went on 'just a date' and he broke up with me. I guess he's moving on. Look, I gotta go. Don't tell him I know about Carter."

"I'm sorry. I know you still love him."

"I don't want to talk about it." I hung up and drove home, eyes burning from the fucking tears that wouldn't stop carving tracks down my cheeks, a stream of clear liquid dripping from my nose like a leaky faucet. I parked and staggered in, half-dazed by the image of Carter opening the car door for Keith. What else would he being doing for Keith? Or *to* Keith?

I made myself sick considering the possibilities.

I heard laughter in the kitchen as soon as I opened the door. My dad… and a woman. A woman's laughter was in my house. I dashed up the steps to my room and collapsed on my bed, burying my head under my pillow and pretending I wasn't nineteen, in college, and ready to take on the world. My world sucked. I would give anything to go back to being a little kid.

***

After Christmas, I didn't much care about anything. My life was ruined. Keith was with Carter and I was cemented in a prison of my own design—I was dating a girl!

***

I spent Valentine's Day—Keith's day—with the one person I *didn't* consider a Valentine: Amelia. She'd called me up and asked me out. When I started explaining why we couldn't go, she made up some story about taking sleeping pills so the terrible day would pass by like a hazy hallucination. I kept thinking she was really fucked up, but I agreed anyway. It was either go out with her or think about Keith; either way my homework wasn't getting done.

At least I liked my dinner.

***

By the time April rolled around, I was so excited to spend one freaking night with Zach that I didn't even care his other friends were with us. That morning I'd gone to the hairdresser and gotten a trim for Zach's wedding the next day. I'd gotten my highlights done in fuchsia this time— one strip in my bangs across the front and the patch behind my ear. I thought Zach would say something, but no. I guess he was too distracted to comment on the color, though Amelia had said she liked it better than the blue.

Keith always liked the blue. I wonder what he'll think of the pink?

It didn't matter, he was with Carter, and I was in a limo with my best friend, who was getting married. I was sitting next to Zach as Tom and Greg poked around the mini-bar. Zach stood up through the sunroof and hooted really loud before sitting back down.

We all laughed.

"So, Zach," Tom broached. "Are you going to fill us in on the past year? What happened, man?"

Greg added, "Yeah. How'd you meet Gwen, and why get married so fast?"

Both mirrored questions I had, but they spoke them first.

Zach looked at Chad, and then pointed to Clark, his brother, who was sitting in the front seat next to the limo driver; an odd place for someone to sit if you asked me, but Clark was a weird guy.

"They can't hear us," I told him.

Zach motioned for a football huddle, so we all crouched forward. "Clark could be recording this, or have a microphone back here."

Tom gave me a look. One that said, "When did Zach become so fucking paranoid?"

I shrugged and looked at Zach. His eyes weren't shining like they used to when he was younger, and full of adventure and happiness. They were dull, as if they'd seen combat, a soldier's eyes, one who'd witnessed too many deaths to be mirthful. It was like Zach was admitting defeat and giving in to despair. Was that why he wouldn't talk? Had he simply given up?

I let it go and watched the traffic outside the window.

We ended up at a couple clubs downtown. No one drank, which was odd. The dancers we saw were (A) girls, and (B) not strippers. Tom complained in my ear because he was looking forward to seeing some flesh. Personally, I was fine without it. It was fun, but all I really wanted was to talk to the friend who used to be able to tell me everything. What I got instead, was a closed-off shell of that person.

At the end of the evening, we ended up back at his place. His parents greeted us like teenagers, urging us to hit the hay, because we had a big day ahead, and it would start early in the morning. I walked home, sat by my window, and waited until every light in the house was out. I knew this was my last chance.

I crept outside and grabbed the rose trellis next to the screened-in porch of Zach's house. On the third rung I heard it creak, but so far the wood held my weight. I hoisted myself up one rung, and then another, slowly, deliberately, until I was outside his bedroom window. I didn't dare knock, because it would make too much noise. Instead, I pushed the frame up, hoping he hadn't locked it from the inside. Nothing else in his house was locked, and to my delight, neither was his window. As soon as it was cracked an inch, I slid my fingers under it and lifted.

His window lined up with the end of his bed, so I didn't make it inside before I felt him grab my arm.

"Flynn?" he whispered.

I popped my head in the window and whispered, "Yeah."

He let go of my arm and whispered, "What are you doing?"

I held my finger to my lips and climbed the rest of the way in. Like walking on eggshells, I tiptoed to the door and eased it shut, letting out a sigh of relief when the hinges didn't squeak like they always did in movies.

I turned, and Zach was right behind me. "You can't do that. My dad'll flip," he whispered urgently.

I motioned for the bed, and thankfully he allowed me to guide him over to it. We sat, facing one another. "We're gonna talk," I whispered. "Tomorrow you get married. Tonight, we're talking about why."

I was thankful the streetlight always shined into his room, because it ensured I could see him clearly. Zach said he hated how well-lit his room was at night, but he could have easily closed the drapes. I suspected he didn't like the dark.

His eyes told me he was scared, but he agreed. I moved closer, as close as I could get, my knee folded and resting practically in his lap, and leaned in to whisper in his ear. I knew I didn't have much time to belabor the point of my visit, because if we spoke too long his parents would most likely wake up and notice the closed door. Luckily, their door was at the end of the hallway. I had to make my questions count.

"Do you love her?" I asked, and leaned away.

Zach nodded. He leaned in, "Yes. Sort of. It's complicated."

He leaned back and I leaned forward. "Try me. You used to tell me all your secrets. Remember? You can trust me."

He glanced down, thinking. He wrung his hands for a moment. He leaned back in. "Do you like her sister?"

I made a face. "I'm here to talk about you and Gwendolyn, not me and Amelia."

"But it is about me. I'm marrying Gwen tomorrow. If you marry Amelia, we would be brothers."

I didn't have an answer for that, so I ended up just staring at him. His gentle eyes glinting on one side as the light from the street reflected in them. His hair tussled, his lips glistening, Zach waited for my reaction. I could tell from the bare skin of his chest, dotted with goose bumps, that he was nervous. He'd done the only thing he could think of to keep us together. Zach set me up with his soon to be sister-in-law. I tried to smile, but it was not wholehearted. "Yeah, she's okay."

"So you didn't see her before we left?"

I didn't know what he was talking about. We were all in his front yard when the limo pulled up. Of course I'd seen her. Tom and Greg got in, then I ducked into back seat, followed by Chad and finally Zach. He hadn't gotten in right away, but I just figured it had been Gwen holding him up. "No. What are you talking about?"

"Nothing. If you didn't see, then it doesn't matter."

"Why are you acting so odd?"

"I don't want to lose you."

I gave him another look. One I hoped would convey my opinion of the sheer stupidity of his comment. How could he think that? I leaned in again. "You'll never lose me."

Zach grinned, and then he reached over and took my hand. He studied our hands, and I wondered what was going through his mind. My hand looked the same as it always had. I'd been as honest as I always was. I didn't think I'd ever given him the impression he couldn't share intimate details with me. I was, and would always be, his best friend.

"Stop worrying," I said. "Just because you're getting married doesn't mean I'll never see you again. Who knows, once you leave your parents' house, maybe I'll see you more."

He smiled and nodded. He tugged on my hand so I leaned in. Zach was extra close to my ear and his breath tickled. "Are you sure I can tell you anything?"

"Yes."

He licked his lips. The way he looked at me reminded me of the last couple times I'd been with him in his bed, or that one time in mine. He looked scared, but hungry, and I wasn't sure being this close was the best idea. Something in his eyes worried me.

"I think…," he paused. "I think I'm bisexual."

"What?" I asked, confused. *Did he just say bisexual?*

"I said… I'm bisexual," he repeated. "At least I think so. Gwen's been talking to me about it and we're pretty sure that's why I feel like I do."

I recoiled, crinkling the skin around my eyes and curving my lips in a sneer. "Why are you telling me that?" I whispered loudly. Thinking I may have overreacted, I remained seated on his bed, determined to hear him out. What I really wanted to do was scream, and run, and punch the wall for all the years I'd been afraid to tell him *my* secret, because his was way worse.

"Because I'm through hiding it," he said, resigned. He took a deep breath and continued before I had the chance to interrupt. "Because you're supposed to be my best friend and when I'm with you, I feel like I have to pick and choose everything I say or do so you won't hate me. Because all these years I've tried to get you go to church, you joined me a couple of times, and I was terrified you'd learn I'm some sort of abomination to God." His voice hitched, maybe holding back a sob.

"I'm telling you all this now because I can stand hearing hate directed at me from the pastor since he doesn't know me, doesn't care about me, isn't a part of my life; but there is no way in hell I could stand the thought of *you* believing the very same things about me, so I hid it from you. I pretended to be normal, because it was easier in front of my parents, but I'm not normal, Flynn. I'm sick."

"You're not sick," I protested automatically. "I think your parents made you think that, but I don't think God feels the same way."

"Are you sure?" he pressed closer. "You don't know the things I've done. You weren't there that night in the hot tub with Nate."

"Dad got rid of the hot tub years ago. Besides, what's Nate got to do with anything?"

"You don't know what happened. I've been afraid of trying it again."

Now I could see tears in his eyes. He squeezed my hand so hard I thought he'd cut off the circulation.

"I became whatever my parents wanted so I wouldn't lose you Flynn. You have to believe me. I didn't want them to send me away to a facility that changes people with shock therapy or gender counseling. I know who I am, and I'm sick. Gwen doesn't believe there's anything wrong with me, so she came up with a plan. We get married, and then I can explore my feelings. She said I could. I believe her."

My heart was pounding so hard I could almost hear it rebounding off the walls of his room. The air around us was deathly silent, but if I wasn't careful, the beating of my heart would wake up his parents. Zach started at me, and I stared back, afraid to move. Minutes passed and neither of us blinked. Normally, I wouldn't care what he was thinking. Any other time I would offer my opinion and move to the next topic. But not this time. This time he had revealed the biggest secret of his life, and his best friend—stupid me—had nothing to say in return.

My non-reaction pissed me off.

"Fuck this." I threw my words like darts, holding my hands up in defeat. It wasn't worth arguing. Zach was getting married in the morning. Nothing was going to change that. I reached for his door and he stopped me.

"Please don't leave like this. You asked. I told you. I knew it was wrong, but I had to be honest. I know God hates me and I'm the biggest hypocrite around, but please don't hate me too. I need you. You're my best friend. I'll get help. Counseling. Anything. But please tell me you don't hate me."

His begging got the best of me. His pleas ripped away the shame I felt from hiding my sexuality. He needed to know. I only hoped he wouldn't hate me for not trusting him sooner.

"I don't hate you, Zach. I never could. I'm gay. I'm sorry I never told you, but I'm pretty sure you just outlined all the reasons I could have come up with as to why I never said anything. So now... we're even."

Zach wasn't blinking. "Wait... You're...."

"Gay," I finished when his mouth still hung open.

Bewildered, Zach stumbled back and I took that opportunity to leave. We would be able to finish the conversation after the wedding. I knew I needed some air to sort through the thoughts in my head so I quietly raced down the steps and reached for the front door.

As soon as I turned the doorknob, I felt Zach whirl me around. He shoved me up against the door; each of his hands gripping my shoulders and his eyes burned into mine. If he was going to hit me, I was sure he would have done that by now. Something in his rapid breathing made me worry that I'd said too much. Whatever was racing through his mind had him pumped full of adrenaline, and perhaps only reining in his anger because his parents were asleep upstairs. His grip on my shoulders tightened and I winced, enduring the pain instead of trying to break free.

Just when my anxiety told me it was time to bolt, I saw the anger in his eyes transform. Confusion took over, and then seconds later he dove forward and kissed me, hard and rough. Zach's hands released their hold and I was able to wrap my arms around his waist as he kissed me passionately. Our bodies pressed together. Our tongues and lips were frantically devouring each other's mouths, tasting toothpaste and sweat.

Then he ripped himself away. Standing inches from me, his heaving chest was like an impenetrable wall, his eyes boldly daring me to move for fear of punishment, and his silence a blade at my throat. What would he do?

I swallowed hard, unable to keep myself from licking my lips, the lips he had just kissed. His eyes flicked downward momentarily as he caught the motion. He came at me again, only this time not with his lips. His hands went for my belt and he adeptly unbuckled it. I tried to help, but he grabbed my wrists with his vise-like fists and shoved my arms against the door. His glare warned me not to move again. He finished undoing my jeans and pushed them out of his way.

I was scared shitless, but also exhilarated beyond measure. What was he doing? More importantly, why was he doing it? I didn't want him using me as an experiment, or thinking I was okay with him forcing himself on me just because I was gay. I had no idea what was going on in his mind until he freed my throbbing cock and sank to his knees. When I looked down, able to see his expression because of the light coming through the front window, instead of hatred and spite, I saw innocent timidity in his eyes.

Zach extended his tongue and licked the underside of my dick so slowly I could feel his shaking breath on my sensitive skin. He licked me again more boldly before closing his lips around my cockhead. He wrapped his fingers around the base and pulled me lower to get a better angle, so he could take more of me into his mouth.

I wanted to moan, but I bit my tongue. I couldn't breathe. I couldn't move my arms because he wanted them against the door, so I curled my fingers into my palms as tightly as I could. Zach's mouth felt so good I wanted to thrust forward. I wanted to run my hand over his head and feel his short hair between my fingers. I wanted to groan encouraging words like "yes," "so good," or "faster," but if I made a sound he might pull away, and I couldn't chance it. So I rode out the frenzy with every ounce of self-control I had.

Only when I was seconds from coming did I utter a word. "Zach," I gasped.

He took that cue and let go with his lips, but continued stroking me with his hand, aiming it for his mouth. I started shooting, and Zach kept going until I was finished.

He stood up and stared at his hand, but the splatter was on his cheek too. Not to mention, I'd seen my spunk coat his tongue in the two seconds I managed to open my eyes and watch as I struggled to remain standing.

I watched his fingers sliding back and forth over each other as if testing the texture of my cum to gage whether he liked it before he brought his attention back to meet my gaze. He looked surprised initially, but then hardness returned to his eyes, and he sneered at me.

"Zach… I…." I tried to say something, but he stopped me.

He clamped his clean hand over my mouth and hissed, "Don't fucking say a word. This never happened. Okay? You and I never happened. I'm getting married tomorrow, and you aren't going to say another word about it. You hear me? Is that clear?"

He released me so I could respond, "Y-yes."

"If you say anything, I will fucking beat the shit out of you!" His harsh whisper might as well have been a scream, the way it hurt my eardrums.

I nodded rapidly, feeling the tears welling in my eyes. He had to have seen them. Even in the dark Zach always knew when I was crying. But he didn't comfort me this time, instead he whispered, "Get out."

I left as fast as I could, fumbling with my pants and stumbling over the boxwoods as I trampled the garden on my way home.

Chapter 19

April 26, 2014: The Day

I'm in love with Zach. At least, I think I am.

What the fucking hell could I do with that? I had tried denying over the years, ever since that kiss on his bed. I think it was the fear of losing his friendship that held my tongue. I couldn't remember. Years of confusion over why Zach and I had such a strong connection were finally clear. "Shit," I grumbled. "I'm in love with my best friend, but he's getting married. To a woman."

What a big fucking mess this was turning out to be. I should have said something last night. I should have told him I loved him on my way out of his bedroom before he corned me in the foyer and blew me, but it seemed too cliché in the moment. It was bad enough he kissed me when I was younger and treated it like a mistake, but why the hell did he suck me off last night? The look in his eyes, just before he licked me did not suggest he did it maliciously. I saw tenderness. I know I did. Tenderness, and anxiety, and innocence. When Zach put his mouth on me, he wasn't doing it *to* me; Zach was doing it *with* me. It looked as though he needed it.

But where did we stand now?

If I had only kept my mouth shut, I would be in the cottage helping Zach get ready for his wedding, as any good best man should, instead of twiddling my thumbs and watching Amelia meander across the garden. I was such an idiot. I told him I was gay and then he banished me like a leper. I would leave now, but then who would dance with Amelia? I couldn't make her suffer because of my mistakes.

She was in the same sinking ship, after all. Her heart was attached to the same unattainable goal as mine. She wanted me because she couldn't have him, and I wanted Zach because Keith had moved on. Gwen wanted a way to get out of her parents' house just like Zach. It was a vicious circle, really. Seeing her picking flowers an hour before the ceremony gave me the impression that Amelia had been banished from helping the bride just as I had gotten banished by the groom. Maybe somehow Gwendolyn found out she was in love with Zach?

True, she never used those words with me, but what else could it be? I remembered her saying, "I knew I couldn't have Zach." Something else like, "I'd get to see his glistening body, rippled with muscle," when we were all swimming at my pool. What else was I to assume? Plus, Amelia was sort of a psycho.

I rolled my eyes at the absurdity, and directed my attention back to Amelia just as she miss stepped and tumbled forward. I chuckled but quickly caught myself. *Oh, shit.* I leapt out of my chair and dashed over to her side, looking down at the mass of silk and taffeta that lay at my feet. I wondered what my next action should be. She lifted her chin and peered at me through her mussed hair.

"Well? Are you going to help me or stand there snickering?" she inquired, with an edge to her voice.

"I wasn't snickering," I quickly replied.

She glared.

"Okay, okay. I snickered. It was funny." I reached down, but hesitated as I assessed where to grab her. "Um, um…." If I yanked on her arm, she wouldn't be able to stand if her feet were still tangled in her gown. I had my hands at the ready, but I couldn't figure out what to do with them. "Um, I don't know how to help you."

She huffed. "Just hold my hand so I don't fall again." I did, and Amelia gingerly wiggled backward until she was squatting. Once her feet were firmly underneath her, she stood. "Thank you." Then she glanced down at her gown and gasped. "Oh no. I got mud and grass stains on the front. I can't walk down the aisle looking like this."

"Chill, I know some tricks. Let's head over to the cottage and see what supplies they have. My mom taught me how to handle laundry emergencies because I was constantly ruining my clothes."

Amelia hoisted up her layers of dress, and moved beside me. As we walked toward the cottage, she asked, "Didn't she die when you were ten?"

I had only known Amelia for a few months, so the question felt intrusive. "Yeah. So? I paid close attention when she was alive. I remember everything about her."

I think she heard the hard edge in my voice. She apologized, "I'm sorry. I didn't mean to be rude."

I held the door as she stepped inside the stone building. "No, I'm sorry," I said. "I get defensive sometimes."

The venue Gwendolyn had chosen for the wedding was a stone mansion built in the 1840s. It was gorgeous. With its Tudor-style architecture, wide brick walkways, manicured gardens, and old-world furnishings, this mansion fit Gwen's Shakespearian style wedding perfectly. I had to admit, the girl had great taste.

I led Amelia into the reception area and helped her into a chair. With all the puff her gown had, sitting wasn't an easy task, and I almost made the mistake of laughing again. But I didn't. I found some supplies and set about removing the stains as best I could. There was no need for her to worry about the dress, when so many other issues loomed over this "happy" day.

"There. Done."

Amelia inspected her skirts. "Wow, you can't even tell they were there. How did you do that?"

I shrugged. "I'm awesome."

She laughed. "Yes, I guess you are. Thank you. You're the perfect boyfriend."

I ignored her comment. "You're welcome. I'm gonna give these back." I tilted my head in the direction of the kitchen, where I'd procured the items, and left her for a minute. When I returned, she was waiting by the window, looking out toward where the ceremony was to take place. You couldn't see the particular garden from here, but I knew she was watching Zach in her imagination.

"You love him," I whispered. "Don't you?"

Her head snapped in my direction, bringing with it a look of shock and surprise. "What?" she asked, alarmed.

"You don't have to worry. I won't tell."

Her initial shock transformed into weariness. "Oh Flynn, I don't know what to do." Tears that had been kept at bay for the last few minutes tumbled down her cheeks. She grabbed both my hands and looked me in the eyes. I noticed for the first time how red hers were, indicating she had been crying most of the day.

"There's nothing to do. Gwen and Zach are getting married." It sounded so cold, so dead when I said it. It was a matter of fact, nonnegotiable. The sooner Amelia understood that, the sooner she could move on. Like me. I was powerless to stop the inevitable, and she needed to come to terms with her own powerlessness. Zach didn't love her. It was only fair to tell her, right? I wasn't being mean; I was being truthful. She'd beat herself up endlessly if she didn't come to terms with it now.

"How did you know?" she sobbed.

"I remembered your comment in the bathroom on Thanksgiving, and I tend to watch people. It clicked while you were strolling around out there picking flowers. It's why you settled for me, even though I told you I'm not interested. Correct?"

Amelia's tear filled eyes closed, and she fell against me, sobbing in my arms. I held her, if for no other reason than because I was helpless to do otherwise. "There, there," I said, repeating the comforting words all grandmothers murmur to little children. *Great, now I'm acting like a grandma.*

"I kissed him," she said between sobs.

"You what?" Her confession caught me off guard.

She pulled herself together enough to look at me. Her body still shuddered randomly, but she had stopped sobbing. "I said, I kissed him."

"When?" Because I wasn't aware of a time when they had been alone.

"Yesterday. Before the limo left. He was hugging everyone as they left the house, and just as he pulled out of our hug, I jumped forward and kissed him."

"What did he do?"

"Nothing. He stared at me. He looked confused. Then you popped your head out of the door and asked if he was getting in. What do I do now?" Amelia asked, tugging on my arm. "Do I tell Gwen?"

"No."

"Do I say something to Zach?"

"Oh, gosh no." Little wheels turned in my head. Zach had had a busy day yesterday, no wonder he seemed out of sorts. "Listen," I told her, placing my hands on either shoulder to make sure I had her complete attention. She gazed back helplessly. "You can't do anything rash. The wedding is going to start in like twenty minutes. If you start anything now, you're going to ruin it. Think about Gwendolyn, your sister, how would she handle it if you told her, on her wedding day, that you'd kissed her fiancé?"

I watched her swallow as she looked away guiltily. "She'd die."

"Exactly. What about Zach? If there was anything going on in his head, don't you think he'd say it?"

"Not if he's confused about his feelings for me."

"Amelia," I said sternly, "Zach doesn't have feelings for you." I hated being so blunt, but false hope would make the situation worse.

"You don't know that."

"Yes, I do," I stressed, while thinking to myself: *Because he kissed me!* This maze of subplots created our own little soap opera here in po-dunk Maryland, minus the pregnant cousin who everyone thought was dead, and the deranged uncle who was just released from prison. It was bad enough everyone at the wedding appeared to be vying for the groom. No wonder he was confused.

"But what if he *does* feel something and I keep my mouth shut, and then it's too late?"

"Amelia, you and I cannot interfere. If Zach decides to interrupt his own wedding, that's his decision. You can't speak up without a valid reason. One kiss is not enough."

"But, I love him."

"No. I'm sorry."

If anyone had a valid reason, it was I. Still, I'd hold my tongue until hell froze over. I would not be the one to ruin a beautiful wedding because of unrequited feelings. I loved him too, but I was not that selfish. He told me he loved Gwen, and I had to believe he wanted this wedding.

After a few minutes, Amelia's tears stopped, and we were able to walk back over to join the wedding party and perform our expected duties. Just as described in a romance novel, the music started, the guests rose, and the bride walked down the aisle without knowledge of the brewing betrayal. I never would have guessed that the Trumpet Voluntary or Prince Of Denmark's March could feel more like a funeral procession than a grand entry, but as I caught a glimpse of Amelia's ashen face, empathy washed through my veins, because I plainly saw her broken heart reflected in her eyes. I only hoped Gwendolyn hadn't noticed.

Not to mention Keith. He hadn't made eye contact with me since he'd gotten here. He looked good in his suit, even if he was stewing, arms-crossed, in his folding chair. He was either pissed he'd come with Grace, or angry that he couldn't bring Carter. I didn't want to know.

What a fucking disaster!

Nothing short of a satellite landing on the gazebo could stop this wedding. Nothing less than a hailstorm out of the blue, or an act of God. It was a done deal. It was my private hell. I wished last night hadn't happened, because only then would I be able to feel truly happy for Zach and Gwen. Except, last night *did* happen, and I would probably live with the burden of it for the rest of my life.

I heard a loud crack from above and turned toward the sound, just as a gigantic tree limb came crashing down. In that split second, an array of disjointed ruminations my grandpa told me shot through my mind. "Did you know there are about two thousand species of firefly in the world?" I remembered him saying. Or, "I always wash my hands *before* I use the toilet. Never want to touch those parts and forget you had jalapeños for lunch." His stories and silly sayings made me laugh as a child, especially after my mother died. I missed my grandpa.

But then my chest was burning, and I didn't understand why.

I could see, but all the images blurred like a watercolor painting that Keith had done a couple years ago. He had painted a garden scene, like the setting Gwen had chosen for her wedding, but Keith had allowed the colors seep together so they overlapped, blending the images. Everything looked like that now. Why did it look like that now? I could hear screaming, crying, and shouting, but the voices were distorted like chords strummed on bent guitar strings.

My chest was burning. Why was it burning?

I heard my name in the foggy rush of noise. "Flynn! Flynn! Stay with me! Don't you fucking leave me! Flynn, look at me."

It sounded like Zach, but it couldn't be. He was standing at the altar.

His face came into focus in front of my eyes, and I noticed a long bloody gash across his cheek. *I hope the blood doesn't get on his shirt.* Why was he screaming at me? He looked up and yelled some more. He looked frantic. Why? He should be happy. He was getting married. The man I loved was getting married to someone other than me.

"Flynn!" he screamed at me again. Maybe he knew my thoughts? Maybe he was yelling because I shouldn't be having these thoughts when he was getting married. But I couldn't stop them. I wanted to be the one at the altar. I wanted to look into his eyes and see him smile and hear him say, "I do." *I think. Maybe.* It was too confusing. I wanted so many things.

Except my chest was burning, and I couldn't catch my breath enough to tell him what I needed to tell him before he kissed her.

"Flynn!" he looked at me with tears in his eyes this time. I could see other shapes moving quickly past me, but I couldn't make out what they were doing or who they were. All I saw was Zach. My Zach. Not close enough to touch because something was wedged between us, something large across my chest. I tried to move it, but my arms felt weak. I floundered. My arms weren't working.

Why couldn't I lift my arms? Why did my chest still burn? Why did Zach look so afraid?

"Zach," I whispered, the effort stealing the last puff of breath from my lungs.

"Flynn? Oh my God, Flynn! Stay with me. They're getting help. Don't close your eyes. Look at me."

"I...." I tried to tell him, but the effort was so great. I felt as though I had been asked to blowout the candles on a birthday cake across a stadium, but somewhere in me I found the will to push my effort onward. Like an arctic explorer climbing a glacier, cold air burning in his lungs, everything inside me told me to press on. I had to say the words, wedding be damned.

Zach's eyes locked with mine. He was all I saw. "Don't try to talk. Save your breath. Someone help me!" He looked around in a state of panic before gazing down at me again.

Once I knew he was with me, seeing me, hearing me, I attempted to utter the words again, hoping the elephant on my chest would budge, allowing me to breathe. "I... lo... love... y-you... Zach."

"Oh Flynn. Don't say that."

"It's... true. Love... you."

"Flynn, don't close your eyes. Don't close them! Flynn!"

I heard strangled cries. I heard Zach's voice catch in a way that suggested great sorrow. I should go to him. I should comfort him. I should tell him whatever made him sad would be all right, but I felt trapped under something very heavy, and I was too tired to try and lift it. Maybe I needed sleep. Yes. Sleep. I liked sleep. Sleep is good. Maybe when I wake up this burning in my chest would have ceased. When I wake up, maybe Zach will tell me he loves me too, and this whole wedding was a dream. Maybe.

Part 2

Zach

Chapter 20

September 6, 2008: What Have I Done?

I could see Flynn's back yard from my bedroom window. Sometimes, when Flynn was supposed to be helping his dad, he'd hide up here because we could watch Mr. Brewer from my window and gauge the moment he might come looking for Flynn. It was all in the way he threw things when he was angry. Flynn wasn't bothered because he knew his dad would never take his anger out on him, not since the accident, but Flynn also knew when his dad would get upset enough to hit the booze. Flynn was perceptive that way. It was one thing to avoid work for a little fun, but it was another to push too far, which might lead to heavy drinking.

Watching from my window had also been convenient for *me* right around the start of junior year. I had begun having feelings I had never considered before and I had noticed Flynn in a completely different light.

Flynn was a freshman. He was fourteen. He was skinny and awkward and started highlighting his hair. I say "highlight", but sometimes the streaks weren't blond. Sometimes he had streaks of black, blue, purple, or green. He started dressing differently too. For the longest time he seemed to be a younger version of myself. In middle school, he often wore the exact same shirt as me, even though we never discussed it beforehand. It was odd when I was in eighth-grade because kids made fun of us, but after I moved up to high school the jeers lessened.

Now though, Flynn wore what I called grunge. Ripped jeans, flannel shirts over a graphic T, Converse shoes, Flynn even got his cartilage pierced twice on the left ear. Somehow, though he was only fourteen, he didn't look like a little kid to me anymore.

So one day, when I was peering out the one window in my room with a view of his pool, I noticed Flynn walk out the back of his house and over to the in-ground pool. He stood at the edge for a moment, looking around, and then he pulled his pink, breast cancer awareness T-shirt over his head. I watched him undo his belt and drop his jeans at poolside just before pushing his underwear down and diving in. I had never seen him do that before.

True, his backyard was secluded. He had a high fence and lots of bushes all the way around it. His mother had loved gardening and had started a mini arboretum years before she died. Mr. Brewer maintained it as best he could as a way of honoring her memory, but the pool had taken up most of the space. Flynn helped too, but sometimes gardening got on his nerves, and that was when he'd hide out in my room while I studied or played music and stuff.

I watched him swim from my concealed location, admiring his strokes, and appreciating his technique. Flynn was a beautiful swimmer. How had I not noticed that before?

After a few laps, back and forth, he hoisted himself over the lip of the pool and got out. He shook his short hair like a wet dog after a bath before picking up his T-shirt to dry his face and groin. He snagged his underwear next and pulled them on. I watched as he strolled over to a lawn chair and laid back on it, stretched out. His skin glistened in the afternoon sun. I imagined it was covered in water droplets and I suddenly had the inclination to lick them off his chest.

I turned away sharply, embarrassed. What if Flynn knew I was thinking such thoughts? I glanced out my open bedroom door. What if my dad knew I was thinking such thoughts? I couldn't be found out. I wiped my face as if the swiping motion would clear away the impure thoughts that hid inside my skull. My groin pulsed and I looked down, noticing the bulge there. *Shit!* My brain wasn't the only body part engaged in my spying. I cupped it, squeezing gently, willing away the desire welling in the pit of my stomach. I shouldn't think such thoughts.

Flynn was a fourteen-year-old kid. Flynn was my neighbor. Flynn was my best friend. Worse, Flynn was a boy. I couldn't go through it again.

My phone sounded as it received a text message so I pulled it out of my pocket. A text from Flynn: *Hey. What ya doing?*

I couldn't very well tell him I was watching out the window and fantasizing about him. I couldn't say I was disappointed when he put his underwear back on because I hadn't gotten a good enough look. I'd sound like a pervert. I texted back: *Nothing. You?*

Nothing.

I turned around and found him where I had left him—on the lawn chair. Only now his jeans were on the cement next to him since he had needed them to get his phone from the pocket. If I was down there with him, I could straddle his waist and massage sunscreen into his chest, thumb his nipples, lean down and kiss his neck.

I turned away again. *Shit!* I rubbed my groin again after realizing how cramped I felt. This couldn't happen!

Can I come up? He texted.

Come up? "Yeah you can come up," I mumbled. "And then I'll come all over you." I texted back: *Sure.* I watched as he snagged his jeans and pulled them on. He slung his T-shirt over his shoulder and left his shoes and socks where they sat by the edge of the pool. "Don't walk over here shirtless," I chided as if he could hear me through the window and across the eighty feet that separated us.

I cupped and squeezed myself again, willing away my erection. It wasn't working. Flynn would be in my room any second and I had a hard-on. I jumped over to my computer chair and sat, wheeling myself under the desk and opening my laptop. I had just opened Safari when Flynn entered my room. Still shirtless. *Shit.*

He sat on my bed and pointed to my laptop. "I thought you weren't doing anything."

I closed it. "I'm not. Just surfing porn." I joked, but he missed it. I'd never surf porn in my house for fear my dad would find out.

"Ah. Being productive. Nice."

I half-heartedly grinned. "Yeah. So what's up? You look like shit." His expression was sort of down, even if the rest of his body looked good to me.

"Today's my mom's birthday, or would have been." Flynn shrugged.

Her birthday? "Oh shit, I forgot. September sixth. I'm sorry." I moved from my chair and sat next to him. Today had traditionally been the day when Nate and Flynn would make their mother breakfast and I would help them by bringing flowers in from the garden. Years had passed since her death, but the memory of our annual surprises for her had always brought with it sadness because of her absence. I clasped Flynn's shoulder.

He glanced at me and grinned. "Thanks," he said, returning his attention to the floor. He stared a couple minutes and then turned, maneuvering his body across my bed and crawling up to plop his head on my pillow, face down.

"You're gonna get my pillow wet," I joked, referring to the fact his hair was still wet from the pool.

He shoved the pillow away and let his cheek fall flat onto the mattress. He looked pathetic.

"I was joking, buddy. It's fine." I tossed the pillow on top of his head and he readjusted, encircling it with his arms and testing its comfort with a couple nudges of his face. He closed his eyes.

I allowed my wandering eyes to move along his skin, over his bare shoulder, down his bare arm, along his bare ribs, and stop at his bare waist. I licked my lips and then moved so I could lie next to him on my side. We had done this before, for years, it was no big deal to share a bed. I used one arm for my pillow, folding it under my left ear, and reached out with my right hand to touch his back. *I've done this before,* I rationalized. I had patted his shoulder, rubbed his neck, or hugged him on many occasions when he had been feeling down about his mom and brother. Some days were worse than others, but I had been there for him as best as I could for the past four years.

Very gently I caressed his skin, still cool from his dip in the pool, hoping he wouldn't notice how much I enjoyed it this time. I could feel each bone down his spine. *He's so thin,* I thought. *I bet I could count every bone in his body.* I trailed my massaging fingers up to his neck.

"That feels nice," Flynn murmured, eyes still closed, arms still clutching my pillow.

"Yeah?"

"Mm-hmm."

I lifted up onto my elbow instead of laying flat next to his side. The position allowed for better reach. I used a circular motion as I moved my fingers from one spot on his neck, across his shoulder, over his clavicle, down his ribcage, and almost to his hip before he jerked his body sideways. "Ticklish?"

"Yeah," he said.

He hadn't opened his eyes. Flynn merely wiggled out of my reach and then settled again once I stopped touching his ribs that far down his side. He looked peaceful. He enjoyed my touch. I moved my fingers back up his spine and I scooted my body closer to his. When my fingers reached his hair I lifted my hand and fingered the wet strands. I liked the highlights. They suited him. I circled the outer rim of his ear, over both small silver hoops, and grazed his cheek with the backs of my fingers. I caressed his neck again and moved my hand back over his shoulder and down his back. His breathing had increased, his ribs rising and falling quicker than they had been moments before. I pressed closer still, my groin now against his hip and my chest inches from him.

I nudged my dick against him. I couldn't resist. I was so hard by this point I needed friction and his smooth body was right there, adding to my aggravation as well as my titillation. Why did he have to be so pretty? Just as I ran my fingers across his lower back I glanced up to find his eyes open this time. Flynn was watching me. Our eyes locked.

Then Flynn rolled onto his side, inviting me in with his hungry eyes and heaving chest.

I hesitated. This was wrong. He was so young. I felt his hand touch my arm and logic fled. I moved closer and he rolled onto his back, watching me intently. I touched his stomach and watched my fingers as if they belonged to someone else, tentatively making their way north over his ribs to stop at his nipple. I touched the flat brown area with certain fascination and then looked at Flynn's expression. He was breathing rapidly, lips parted, eyes glazed. I moved closer. Now my body was fully against his, all the way down our lengths. I curled my knee over his and rocked my hips slightly.

Flynn closed his eyes and swallowed.

I leaned down, ghosting my fingers along his jaw before stopping within an inch or two of his lips. I felt his breath coming in puffs against my face. His lips were dry. I felt his hand on my back. He opened his eyes again, probably wondering why I continued hesitating. Only, I had to hesitate. This was Flynn. If I kissed him, I would cross that line between friend and... *what?* Something other than friend. How would I handle that?

Flynn blinked lazily, making his hungry eyes appear drunk. Was I making him drunk as he lay beneath me? Why did Flynn have to look so gosh darn beautiful staring back at me? I licked my lips and Flynn shut his eyes as I closed the slight gap between us. Our noses touched, our breath mingled, and our lips brushed ever so slightly as I hovered there worrying what would happen to our friendship. When I heard him whimper, the sound shot through my ears and into my gut causing all thought to cease. I pressed my mouth to his and kissed him. One slow touch of his lips was far from enough. I moved my lips and claimed another kiss.

Several sweet kisses and I followed my urge to trail my lips down his chest. I started at his chin, over his larynx, the base of his throat just above his sternum, followed by three down the center of his chest. His skin was cool against my lips and tasted of chlorine. I felt his hand touch my arm and I looked up to see him watching me.

I had always thought his pale green eyes were stunning. I thought mine were boring because they were so normal—plain brown. I envied Flynn because his were unusual with several flecks of gold that caused the color to vary depending on what he wore. Girls would flock to me if I had eyes that color. The shade they were now, darker and heated by lust, was the color I wanted them to remain. Flynn was hot and bothered because of me.

I touched his chest with the tips of my fingers, slowly, deliberately. He closed his eyes again and sucked in a quick breath through his mouth. That mouth. That luscious mouth. He nervously licked his lips and I traced my fingers around his left pec. It wasn't defined, but I didn't care. This was Flynn and I was going to do all sorts of things to his body. I kissed his waiting lips again, and again, and again, and again. And just as I worked up the nerve to utilize my tongue, I heard my mother calling up the steps to me from the foyer.

"Zach, is Flynn up there? I found his T-shirt on the floor."

I flew backward as if Thor's hammer had connected with my chest, and hurried to my open door to call back down to her before she ascended the steps. "Um, yeah Mom. Flynn was just in the pool and came over." I glanced back at Flynn, who hadn't moved an inch. "Get out of my bed," I hissed as quietly as I could, waving frantically with my hand so he would get the point.

"I figured as much," she said, still at the bottom of the steps. "It's still damp. I found it wedged under the front door. He must have dropped it when he closed the door. I'll hang it here on the banister."

"Thanks Mom."

"Is he staying for dinner?"

I glared at Flynn. "No," I yelled down to her. "I'm pretty sure he has homework."

"Okay. Tell him to give me a hug before he leaves. I know he misses his mom."

"Okay." I paused, listening in my open doorway in case she did indeed walk up the steps. Nothing. I looked back at Flynn. "You need to leave," I said harshly. "I can't have them thinking something happened between us. One look at your face and they'll know. Plus, a pink shirt? Who the fuck wears a pink shirt?"

"Everyone. It's for breast cancer awareness."

"That's in October," I argued.

"Some of us started early."

He sounded hurt and weak, and not at all defensive, as I had expected. "Whatever. It still looks gay to me. Only faggots wear pink in September," I spat.

Right then, he really did look hurt, but I didn't care. I needed him gone. I needed his fourteen-year-old ass, and his fourteen-year-old virginity to leave before anyone saw the two of us together and deduced what I'd done. Worse yet, what I *could* have done, given more time. He was a kid. I was not going to become a pervert just because of some stupid fascination I had with him. It would pass. I was desperate and horny and my sinful desires would soon pass.

"Leave," I asserted one last time. I saw his jaw tremble and what could have been tears in his eyes as he shoved his way by me. "Don't forget your pink shirt!"

A couple seconds later I heard the front door slam and I breathed a sigh of relief. Flynn was gone. No one would ever know. I was safe. This whole incident could be written off as a mistake.

Flynn was gone.

Chapter 21

April 26, 2014: Falling Apart

What do I do? I don't know what to do? I have to do something. They won't let me do anything. There was blood. So much blood. He saw me. He spoke to me. Did he really say it? Did I hear him correctly? Flynn said he loves me. But he can't love me. Loving is wrong. He's a guy. Guys don't love other guys. It's a sin. Is it a sin? What would Jesus do? What would Jesus say? I know what my father would say. I know what my pastor would say. But that's why I want to leave that church. They're wrong. They have to be wrong. I feel so alone. Why can't I understand? Flynn loves me. I can't... I can't love him back. It's wrong. But Flynn....

I stopped pacing the hall long enough to glance down the impossibly long corridor to where he had disappeared. The paramedics or nurses, I didn't know, people, medical people, they wheeled him away. Away from me. Flynn was barely alive and it was all my fault.

"Zach, thank God, are you okay?" I heard my sister speaking, so I turned around. She looked worried. She reached out and gripped my shoulder. I stared at her. "Zach? Did something happen in the ambulance? Did they tell you something about his injuries? Zach. Say something. I saw the blood. Zach!"

I blinked. "Um, I don't... I don't know." I couldn't answer. I didn't know what to say. Flynn loved me and now he was going to die.

"I think he's in shock," my dad said.

"Honey, sit down. Let me get you some water." My mom's voice drifted to my ears.

She was there, she had to be there, but I didn't remember seeing her. I felt a hand on my arm and someone guided me to a chair. My knees hit the edge and I sat, but as soon as my ass hit the seat I jumped back up and started pacing again.

I can't sit. Only criers sit. Weepers and moaners wailing their grief like echoes in a cave. I wouldn't become them. I'm not grieving. Flynn's not dead. God wouldn't do that again. God couldn't do that again. Please God don't do this to me again. I lost Nate. Please don't take Flynn.

I fell to my knees and curled my body over my legs, hugging the back of my head and pulling my shoulders into toward my thighs. I probably looked like a ball of quivering limbs and weakness and shame, but in that moment weakness won. The tears fell no matter my insistence they stay in my head. I didn't want to cry like a baby. Not here. Not now. Not like this with everyone watching and thinking I couldn't control my emotions. But nothing worked. All my effort to remain calm, to remain in control, to remain stalwart, collapsed. Why? Because I knew it was my fault.

I sobbed. I could hear myself. I felt a hand on my back and someone was speaking but I couldn't discern who. I didn't care who. I didn't care that I was in the middle of the floor. I didn't care that people needed to get through. This was my fault.

I saw it. I could see it all. I was standing at the altar watching the bridesmaids walk down the aisle. Each of them looked so pretty. Then Gwendolyn appeared at the back with her father. Her face was veiled, yet the fabric wasn't woven thick enough to conceal her face. I could see her. The two of them walked down the grassy aisle stepping on the rose petals her little four-year-old cousin had strewn. She was so pretty. I was so lucky. I should be the happiest man on the planet.

Suddenly, my memory deceived me by flashing an image from the night before across my mind. An image of Flynn up against the door with his pants pushed down, his hands shaking by his sides, and his dick in my mouth. I was standing at the altar, yet I could almost taste his salty sweat and musk in my mouth as I concentrated on the memory. He was shaking as I captured him there. I took him off guard. I bet he was scared. I was scared. I wasn't sure what I was doing until I was doing it and even then I wasn't sure.

I remember what he'd said in the bedroom. We were talking about Amelia. I had asked if things were going well and he was noncommittal. Then he looked at me with this strained expression and told me he was gay. I wasn't sure why at first. I thought he was joking. I thought he was going to say something else, but he opened the door and fled instead. I couldn't let it go. Why couldn't I have let it go? I had had to press the issue.

I dashed down the steps three at a time, hoping my parents wouldn't wake up from the noise I made, and I stopped Flynn just before he'd left. I whirled him around to face me and challenged him with my eyes. I wanted to shout. I wanted to scream at him. I wanted to know what else was going on inside his brain after I confessed to being bisexual. I had to know if he thought I was perverted or deviant. I wanted to know if he hated me, or was making fun of me by saying he was gay.

Except, instead of asking, I kissed him. Hard. Rough. Passionate.

I had imagined how he would taste for years. I had thought about his mouth late at night as I in lay my bed pondering how different things would have been if I could have told him how I felt. I imagined what the world would be like if I could have walked over to Flynn in his front yard, in broad daylight with neighbors watching, and kissed him. How different would my life have been if I had told him I loved him that afternoon on campus when we had lunch together and he showed me his tongue piercing? Or the following year when he'd gotten that tattoo?

Instead, I had made fun of him, as I was prone to do. The seriousness felt too weighty for birthday conversation, so I suppressed it. I tossed my feelings aside, again, for the thousandth time. It wasn't right anyway. My feelings betrayed my good sense. Guys didn't love guys. Not in my church, not in my family, not in my world. It was wrong. I couldn't give in, so I denied everything.

After all, I had Gwendolyn. I had told her some things, but not everything.

Years had passed since that one stupid kiss in my room, and everything between Flynn and me had remained the same. He was my buddy, and now Gwendolyn was my girlfriend. I wasn't gay. I was a straight guy who happened to feel a very strong attachment to his best friend. That's all it was. A strong attachment. Maybe Gwen was wrong about her assessment? I couldn't be bisexual. It was wrong.

Hearing the word gay threw my perceptions askew, and I started thinking and questioning how I hadn't figured it out before. It made sense. Flynn hadn't shown much interest in girls even when Kelly and Grace were two of his closest friends. And they were hot! I had never seen him serious about girls at all. Not even Amelia. As far as I knew he'd never slept with any of them. One time I thought he had had a hickey, and he told me it was a bug bite. That didn't make sense.

Suddenly his friend Keith came to mind. Keith. Flynn had said they were close. How close? I remembered Tom had said Keith was gay. Had Keith given Flynn that hickey?

My lust had surged last night and I had dashed down the steps to confront Flynn and ask him what was going on, and tell him I had feelings for him, and I wanted to tell him it was all wrong and the Bible spoke against it. But when he looked at me that night, when those beautiful green eyes locked with mine and I saw him struggling with what I assumed was desire, I dove in. His lips tasted like Pepsi and our tongues were sticky and dry at first, but I kept licking his tongue and the inside of his mouth until saliva flowed freely between us.

He made me ravenous with that one kiss. I wanted to crawl inside his body. My groin burned for him. I remember thinking how badly I wanted to feel his hands gliding over my naked flesh. I wanted him to undress me right there in the foyer and make love to me on the floor. Flynn had stolen my breath right before I dropped to my knees and fumbled for his cock.

I'd seen it before. His male parts, my male parts, they weren't supposed to be a big deal. My mom had told me when I was young that undressing in front of boys was okay because we had the same parts. With girls I had to cover myself, but boys... *Oh man.* What my mom didn't understand was how much I wanted to see the boys naked and I couldn't give a hoot about the girls. For years, I glanced at Flynn's body when we had gotten out of the pool and changed on the sun porch. I knew it was wrong, but I still could not stop myself. Girls *did* become appealing by middle school, but boys had always been my fantasy.

I had wanted Flynn then, and I still wanted him the night before my wedding.

So I took him. I got down on my knees, uncovered his cock, and took it into my mouth. I was so scared my parents would find us, but not scared enough to stop. His skin slid over my tongue and I had to have more. I felt him trembling as I sucked and bobbed and licked. The taste was strong like sweat. He had probably showered that morning, but we'd been out all day and all that night. His musky scent filled my nostrils and pumped my adrenaline with its spicy allure. I wanted more of him in my mouth, so I opened wider and went down hard, but the head of his dick hit my throat and I choked. I pulled back so I wouldn't gag myself to the point of puking, but not enough that he would notice—I hoped. I wanted it to be good for him.

It was Flynn. He had been my closest friend since his brother had died, and the person I had loved for the last five years. Of course he had no idea, because I was a coward, and I had kept my feelings hidden, but I hoped he would understand as I sucked him and loved him on my knees and made myself vulnerable for him. I moved my hand from his hip to his balls and fondled them. I heard him whimper and knew he liked it. I knew how sensitive testicles were and how good it felt when they were stimulated. How many times had I touched myself and rubbed my own balls around in their sac as I pictured his hands upon me? I couldn't count that high.

Flynn was in my mouth. Oh God, how evil my father would tell me I was if had he found me like this, but the taste, his taste, told me this would not be the last time. I had to hold onto that thought now, as he lay dying somewhere in the hospital.

How dare I even think the thoughts I'd had as I watched Gwendolyn walk down the aisle? I saw her dress and the flowers strewn across the ground and I had thought, *How can I stop this? It's what everyone wants. This wedding is what my parents dreamed for me. They wanted me to get married and have a family, children, and maybe a dog; but I don't want that, not in the way they do.*

I remembered glancing sideways at Flynn hoping he wouldn't notice as I watched him standing next to me. His cream and tan colored Renaissance-style pantaloons and tunic made him look so sexy. Oh God, I hadn't wanted to go through with the wedding. Not when every ounce of energy I had was focused on keeping my feet still and planted where I was. If I had stopped thinking so hard about standing still, I knew I would have turned toward Flynn, grabbed him and kissed him in front of everyone. I had wanted to, but instead I prayed to God. I had asked for a miracle. I had asked for some divine intervention that would stop the wedding.

God had granted my wish.

I wept deep, sobbing tears as I curled into a ball on the hospital hallway floor.

The voices like a rush of water flooded my ears. I heard Gwendolyn and Amelia. I heard my mother and my father. I heard the phone ringing and doctors being paged over the intercom system. I heard my sobs, sounding like the cries of a tiny child who fell off his bike and scraped his knee. I was crying. Oh God, I was crying so hard.

"Zach. Zach, it's me Gwendolyn. Can you hear me? Zach you have to move. People can't get through. Come on, let me help you find a chair."

I stumbled. I couldn't feel my feet. She had my arm and Gwendolyn was pulling me. I felt something hard against my legs—a chair. I stared at the floor and noticed a candy wrapper at the base of the information desk. Nurse's desk? Emergency desk? I didn't know. It was brown laminate and there were phones and people and crying, and the candy wrapper was sitting on the floor yet no one noticed. It was clear with a yellow stripe. I think it was a hard candy. Sometimes Flynn had hard candies.

He had the habit of holding one end, taking the whole thing into his mouth—wrapper and all—and then pulling the wrapper off as his teeth kept the candy inside his mouth. I told him my mom thought it was gross to suck on the wrapper. My mom said it could be dirty. Flynn never cared about any of that. He didn't care about germs. He'd even eat things off the floor. He laughed at the five-second rule, saying something about Mythbusters busting that myth. "Germs, shmerms," he'd say. "It has to do with the wetness of the food dropped. Moist food picks up more germs and it doesn't matter if it is five seconds or twenty seconds."

Flynn liked lemon candies.

"Zach?" I heard Gwendolyn's voice again. "Here's a cup of water. Will you please take a sip?"

I felt something cold on my tongue and the sensation flowed down my throat and into my stomach. I felt it. It was like eating ice cream. Flynn liked vanilla and for some reason I remembered a time when he was ten, right before Nate died, and Mr. Brewer had taken us all out for ice cream. I had always thought vanilla was a boring flavor before Flynn gave me a bite of his. Creamy and good.

"Zach?"

I looked at Gwendolyn. "Thanks," I responded, taking the cup from her hand.

The expression in her eyes softened. She rubbed my back and smiled at me. I took another sip of water and looked down the hall. I spotted Keith crumpled in a chair holding his face, with his elbows on his knees. Grace and Kelly on either side. *Keith.* I took another swallow of water. *Shit.* Keith was probably Flynn's boyfriend. He had to be. They were together all the time. Well, mostly. Plus, the appearance he gave as he waited was not one of casual concern. He was really worried. Like me.

"Do you want more?" Gwendolyn asked.

I looked inside the cup. Empty. "Please."

She took the cup and walked away.

I had to do this. Addressing my suspicions would help distract me from the nausea I felt imagining Flynn hanging on the precipice of death. If I talked with Keith maybe I could sort out my feelings and my confusion. Anything. I got up and walked over to him, crouching down in front of him. He didn't move.

I reached up, hesitating slightly at the thought of what I was about to do. I was about to comfort Flynn's boyfriend, possibly his lover, possibly the one person I should hate more than all others, but I did it anyway. I placed my hand on his arm and squeezed. I heard him sob. Grace silently moved over one chair so I could sit in the space she left for me. Immediately, Keith turned and buried his face in my shirt. He was crying, and suddenly I was the guy who was comforting him. *Oh jeez.*

Instinct told me to hug him, so I did. I hugged him with both arms, feeling clearer and surer of myself than I had since arriving at the hospital in the ambulance with Flynn. I wasn't used to feeling helpless, and holding Keith gave me purpose. I used to be the one who watched over others, no one should be worrying over me, or consoling me. I was the rock. Only weak men cowered, according to my dad.

"It'll be okay, Keith. I've got you," I whispered, rubbing his back.

I glanced at Kelly and she lifted the corner of her mouth approvingly.

My mind cleared like a cinematography project, sucking distorted sounds and images down with a snap into a single focused point of hallways, people, and the smell of disinfectant. The hospital wasn't noisy at all. I'd imagined it. The sounds were quiet and normal. Phones rang like phones, not sirens. I heard one doctor paged, but not from a megaphone. It was quiet and I wasn't sure it was even loud enough for me to catch the name. My foggy, guilt-consumed mind had distorted everything.

Comforting Keith grounded me.

I glanced around and saw that we were all here. My mom had her arm around Amelia. Amelia looked worried, but she wasn't crying. My dad was talking with my brother. My sister was messing with her iPhone, while her husband, Chad, stood nearby. Mr. Brewer was pacing up and down the hall. And Gwendolyn, my Gwendolyn, was walking toward me with a cup in her hand still wearing her wedding dress. The skirt was torn in the front and the edges were brown. She looked tired as she approached.

"How's my boy?" I heard Mr. Brewer ask.

My attention went straight to Flynn's dad where he stood next to a doctor who had appeared in the two seconds I'd been looking at Gwen. Keith jumped up and I followed him over to Mr. Brewer's side. Kelly and Grace stood with us as we listened intently to what the doctor explained. All the others moved closer, but not enough to crowd us.

"I'm confident he'll recover fully. The bleeding was caused by a deep puncture wound to his chest, and although it seemed like he had lost a lot of blood because he was covered in it, the reason was mainly from his cotton shirt. It absorbed the seeping blood like a sponge and made his injury look worse than it really was. Six stitches and he'll heal as good as new."

"Can we see him?" Mr. Brewer asked.

"Yes, but I need to make you aware of other concerns."

"What other concerns?" Keith asked, worriedly.

The doctor's eyes went to Flynn's father. "Perhaps we should discuss this in private?"

"No. They're allowed to hear anything concerning my son. They're all the family I have."

The doctor nodded. "Very well. As far as I understand, a tree fell on Flynn, correct?"

"Part of a dead tree, yes," I answered.

"While it is miraculous that he suffered no broken bones and only acquired a small puncture to his chest, Flynn's head hit the ground very hard and he sustained a serious concussion. There is some swelling on his brain and I plan to keep him sedated while we monitor for brain bleeds. Someone said he was conscious and speaking briefly after the accident?"

I answered without thinking, "Yes. He was talking to me."

"That's good. The nurse said he was semi-conscious right before I saw him. However, he's been unresponsive for the past couple hours."

"What does that mean?" he dad pleaded.

"It means we wait. Flynn's brain has experienced trauma. He needs time to heal, which means rest. Sometimes the body shuts down. Every person is different. As patients recover from severe brain trauma, they normally pass through various stages of recovery. Some people seem to slip further away from consciousness only to bounce back with no ill effects.

Others can stop while in any of the stages of recovery and remain there for long periods of time. I can give you a pamphlet to help explain the dangers of concussions more fully."

"What are you saying?" Keith asked.

"I'm saying... that Flynn's brain was shaken and at this time he is unconscious. He's been unresponsive for about three hours. Right now that does not raise too much concern, as we are monitoring his brain activity, and it seems normal. There are no signs of seizure, and his stats are good. My plan is to allow him time to heal slowly. If he wakes up too suddenly and jars his brain, the swelling could increase. Too much swelling, and we'd need relieve the pressure by other means."

"What kind of other means?" Mr. Brewer asked.

The doctor looked to each of us in turn as if he was reluctant to answer. "You have to understand, Flynn is not at this point yet."

Mr. Brewer repeated, "If needed, what other means to reduce swelling are you talking about?"

He paused thoughtfully. "We could burr holes into his skull, or remove a small section of bone until the swelling goes down."

"Oh God," his father swore, cupping his mouth.

The doctor added, "Like I said, he's not in need of this right now. He's sleeping peacefully. Sometimes being in a coma is a good thing, Mr. Brewer. I assure you."

The word made me ill. *Coma?* My stomach quaked.

"Coma?" his father questioned.

"Yes. It's the body's natural response to trauma. Some doctors induce comas to keep the patients still and allow them time to heal."

"Can't you wake him up?" Mr. Brewer asked, his voice more frantic than before.

"We could try, but for now I'm opting to wait and see if he wakes up on his own after a day or two. Your son is resting comfortably and we are doing what we can for him."

"Can I see him?"

"Yes. Only two visitors at a time, though. No loud noise. Speak to him calmly. There is no indication that he can't hear, and from my experience patients respond well from the sound of familiar voices."

I stood helpless as Mr. Brewer motioned for Keith to follow him. My assumption was validated. Keith had to be the boyfriend, why else would Mr.

Brewer take Keith and not me? Or Grace or Kelly? I had been Flynn's neighbor and best friend forever. I wanted to protest loudly as they walked away, but thankfully something inside kept my lips shut. I didn't need to act like an ass, especially if the situation was all my fault.

Flynn. I contemplated. *In a coma.* What if he never woke up? What if he never spoke to me again? What if his last words were "I love you" and I never got the chance to say the same words back?

Waves of nausea crashed against the walls of my stomach.

This was all my fault for loving Flynn. If he died... I didn't think I could live with myself.

Chapter 22

April 26 2014: All My Fault

Stunned and zoning out, I stood there half hearing what the doctor said, and partially knowing that others were still standing near me. *Flynn.* The single all-consuming thought that raced through my mind and blocked out everything else. *I did this.*

"Well, I'm going to check on Aunt Bernice." My mom's random comment startled me.

I turned to her and questioned, "What? Why?"

She raised an eyebrow at me. "Because she's in the hospital. Uncle Fred texted me twenty minutes ago explaining that the falling tree branch knocked her off her chair and she twisted her knee. She tore her ACL and needs surgery."

"Oh." I was preoccupied with Flynn and I hadn't considered any other injuries because of the tree. "Were other people hurt besides her?"

She nodded. "Our neighbor, Mel, had a laceration that went all the way down his arm. Sort of like the one you have on your cheek. You should really have that checked. It might need stitches."

For the first time I noticed a burning sensation on my cheek. I touched it and felt a crusty line of what was probably dried blood that ran from my ear, across my cheek, and down my jaw. "Oh. Huh. I guess I should."

My mother continued her account of all injured parties. The way she talked with her hands gesturing and her fingers pointing was very typical of her. At times, I remembered feeling embarrassed at how animated my mother could be, but right now it was comforting. When she was extremely worried, like when Dad had gotten triple by-pass surgery five years ago, she always got really quiet and motionless. I didn't want my mom to have the serious, worried face right now; I liked and needed the animation. "Your dad's boss's wife got knocked off her chair like Aunt Bernice," she said, "but she's fine.

Only bruised. Cousin Robert lost a tooth when another guest jumped out of the way, knocked him over, and he hit his mouth on the metal chair in front of him. And your little cousin Jeanie—"

"Tammy's baby?" I inquired.

"Yes," Mom confirmed. "Jeanie practically got trampled when people leapt out of the way of the sprawling branches. Luckily she's fine, but I think she was traumatized by the stampede."

Stampede? I think my mom's embellishment was also reassurance that Flynn would be fine. Right? He had to be fine.

My mom sighed. "Oh Zachary, this wedding has turned out to be a total disaster. I just don't understand it. I only prayed that God would be present and give you the happiness you deserve." She covered her face with her hand and started crying. "I'm so sorry. I know you were nervous about marriage. Now this? I blame your father for taking you on that stupid trip."

She started crying and I instinctively consoled her by wrapping my arms around her shoulders and patting her back. I had to; she was my mom. It was the easiest thing to do under the circumstances because it didn't require thought. I couldn't very well tell her that God had answered her prayer to a T, that this was possibly her fault for asking it. I had gotten precisely what I deserved. Strike that, I deserved way worse than a ruined wedding. I'd been thinking about the taste of Flynn's cock at the very moment my bride was walking down the aisle. I deserved to be the one in a coma, not Flynn.

Marriage was supposed to be a holy union and the marriage bed kept pure and I had defiled it. I felt horrible.

My mom cried in my arms and Gwendolyn walked up to us. "She okay?" she asked.

"Yeah." I nodded. "It's just been kind of crazy. You know?" I kept my inner angst hidden out of my shame. Poor Gwen. I knew I'd have to tell her.

"Yeah," she answered quietly. "I heard what the doctor said about Flynn. He sounds hopeful. Flynn needs time to heal and wake up on his own, right?"

That was basically what the doctor said, I guess, but it was also very vague. I didn't know much about head trauma or concussions so all I had to go on was what the doctor said. "His brain activity was normal" is what the doctor said. "He most likely could hear us talking" is what the doctor said.

Did that really mean Flynn was fine? Did it really mean all he had to do was rest and wake up? I didn't know. Although, I couldn't very well share my personal worries with Gwendolyn when I believed everything was my fault. I was a detestable person for what I had done, and now was suffering the consequences of it. God was punishing me. I had cheated on her and God was exacting his judgment.

I fake grinned, because I knew I couldn't confess my sins yet, and said, "Yeah. I guess. The doctor said his stats were good. I guess we have to wait."

"Are you going to be okay?" Gwendolyn reached out and stroked my arm.

As I opened my mouth to answer, my mom pulled out of my arms. "Honey, I think I'll leave you two alone. I'm going to check on everyone in the hospital and take you father home. I think he's on the phone with the insurance company now. He was talking to our lawyer earlier. I'll text you when I get home."

"Okay Mom. I love you."

"I love you too, dear." She kissed my cheek and walked away.

Unlike earlier, the hall was almost vacant now. I didn't see my brother or my sister. Amelia was gone. Gwendolyn's parents were gone. "Where're your folks?"

"They left. As soon as everyone checked in and the injured family members were taken care of, my mom left. My dad took Amelia home to the rental and is coming back for me in about twenty minutes so we can figure out what we're going to do. My dad said that tree should have been checked for safety if an outdoor wedding was going to take place in that garden. He thinks the venue is liable. I don't know."

"I heard my dad say the same thing. He was on the phone with our lawyer earlier." Another reason to feel guilty. I'm supposed to be a tree guy and I hadn't even noticed the dead branch because I'd been consumed with thoughts of Flynn. *I'm a horrible, horrible person.* "The venue switched gardens that morning. It was supposed to happen in the Tranquility Garden, but the ground was too soft from the rain two days ago. They switched it and I guess no one thought to look up."

"A terrible mistake," Gwen said. "I think Flynn and your Aunt Bernice got the worst of it. Everyone else was either scratched or bruised or something equally minor."

I didn't know what to say to that, so I nodded. I mean, what was I supposed to say? *Oh cool! I'm glad it was only my aunt and Flynn who got hurt. I'm glad it was only my bestest friend in the whole, wide world.* Nope, couldn't say that. I'd gladly change places in a heartbeat.

I hadn't said a word, but still her facial expression changed. She tilted her head slightly and her eyes narrowed briefly. "Are you sure you're all right?"

"Yeah. Fine."

"Okay." She didn't say so, but I doubt she believed me. She had this distant look in her eyes and she wasn't as warm as she had been in the past. Something in her restraint told me she was trying to figure out what was going on in my mind. It was freaky how she stared at me and remained at arm's length, as if she could see. *Oh God I hope she couldn't see.* She hadn't hugged me, not since she assisted me to a chair when I'd broken down in the middle of the hall. She seemed to be holding back out of... confusion, maybe? She obviously felt something going on with me even if I hadn't voiced it.

"I think I'm going to go. Amelia wasn't acting right either. I'm going to make sure she knows that Flynn is going to be fine once he wakes up."

Again, I nodded. "Okay. I'll call you later."

"Okay. If you get to go in to see Flynn, please tell him we're all praying for him."

"I will."

Gwendolyn hugged me, but only briefly, before she pecked my cheek and walked off. I felt the chill in her touch and in our embrace. Did she feel it too? Something was going on between us and it happened the moment that tree fell. Maybe Gwendolyn saw the accident as an omen?

I turned around right when Mr. Brewer reappeared through the doorway that led to Flynn. My Aunt Krista went right to him, kissed his cheek, said something, nodded, and walked away. He had tears in his eyes as he walked up to me. He wasn't blubbering like my mom had been, but his sadness was just as evident.

"What's going on? Is Flynn alright?"

Grace and Kelly appeared at my side.

Mr. Brewer swallowed so hard I heard it. He nodded. "Yes," he strained to report. "Yes and no. The nurse told me his vitals are good, but it's seeing him lying there like that...." His breath hitched and Mr. Brewer didn't finish his thought. He had no need to finish because it was obvious to me what he meant. "She handed me these."

Mr. Brewer held out his hand and opened it, palm up. Flynn's jewelry: his two hoops from his ear, and the bar from his tongue. I'd thought he'd been wearing his arrowhead necklace, but perhaps I'd been wrong.

I felt horrible for Mr. Brewer. Seeing Flynn now had to feel the same as watching his son Nathan die nine years ago. The accident that had killed Mrs. Brewer instantly, but had left Nathan in a coma for hours before he finally went. I had been at the hospital and I remembered the look Mr. Brewer had worn when he walked out of the hospital room. Losing his wife and son had taken part of his life and light; he had never gained it back. He and Flynn tried, but there was always a sense of emptiness in their house.

I reached up and touched his shoulder and the man fell against me. "I don't know if I can take this again," he confessed and he quietly cried against my shoulder.

I told him, "Flynn will be alright. You'll see. It's only a concussion. He'll wake up in no time." I had to be positive, even though the fear and dread of losing Flynn hung over my thoughts like a black cloud of doom waiting to let loose a hailstorm of pain and anguish. "He'll be okay."

He squeezed me and pulled out of my embrace. Mr. Brewer nodded again and dried his eyes on his shirtsleeve. "You're right. You're right. I'm going to go home and change and get some clothes for Flynn so when he wakes up he can wear something other than those pantaloons for the ride home."

I snickered and smiled. "Good."

The levity helped. Mr. Brewer smiled briefly and patted my shoulder. "You can head in there if you want. I left Keith with him." He patted my shoulder a second time and then continued on his way.

"Me?" I asked, glancing at the girls who also wanted to see their friend.

"You heard him. Go. We'll wait," Grace explained.

I nodded and glanced back at the door that led to Flynn... and Keith. I had to go in and make small talk with Keith. I had to go in there and act like everything was normal between us, only it wasn't. Not now. I had given his boyfriend a blowjob just last night. Flynn had basically cheated on him by allowing it to happen. And worse, Keith was Flynn's fucking boyfriend! How had I not known? I felt like an idiot. Thinking back on the times I had seen them together, nothing specific stood out. They'd never spoken too closely or ever touched. I'd noticed maybe a couple furtive glances that could have been flirtatious, but that didn't mean anything. If they were boyfriends, why wouldn't they act like it? Most of the time, Flynn sat on the opposite side of the table or walked next to one of the girls. It didn't add up. I was so confused. Was Flynn in love with Keith? Did I have any right at all to intrude on his life and say *anything*?

Heavyhearted, I made my trek to his room. The nurse told me he was in room three, but it was more like a cubicle with a curtain for a door. I ducked inside and found Keith leaning into his side, with his face tucked by Flynn's neck. He was holding his hand and whispering something. I shifted my eyes over Flynn's sleeping form and a massive metaphorical thud collided with my chest. *Nate.* I blinked, and it was Flynn lying in the bed hooked up to monitors and a blood-pressure cuff. *Flynn. Not Nate.*

I must have gasped audibly because Keith jolted upright guiltily. His eyes were red. "Oh, I didn't hear you come in."

I sheepishly nodded. "Yeah. I met Mr. Brewer as he was walking out. He said I could come in."

Keith nodded. He let go of Flynn's hand and backed away. "Do you want to come over here and talk to him?"

I shot my hand out and quickly replied, "No. Stay where you are. I'm sure holding your hand is more comforting than mine. I can talk from here."

He gave me an odd look, but stepped back to Flynn's side and retook his hand.

I studied Flynn. He looked ghastly. His face was paler than it usually was and his expression was blank. I couldn't remember Flynn looking so blank. Even when he slept I remembered pointing a flashlight in his face and seeing some sort of emotion there. Irritation, mainly, since I think he protested the light in his eyes even when they were shut, but sometimes I saw peace and joy on his face as if he was dreaming of happy things. He often dreamt of his mother, so I always assumed in those moments when I watched him sleeping over the years and he had had a smile on his face, that he was reliving the memories of his mother.

He didn't have that expression now. His face was flat, empty, and cold.

My instinct said to scream at him to wake up because I didn't care for his vacant, unresponsive appearance. It was creepy and reminiscent of his brother's. Nate had died. I didn't want to think about it, but how could I not? The memory was powerful and haunting. As much as I wanted to talk to Flynn, and tell him he needed to wake up, and that I needed him to wake up, I couldn't because Keith was there. Keith was like a barrier between us. Keith with his bloodshot eyes, sniffles, and handholding; Keith with his title of "boyfriend"; Keith with his companionship and whispering in Flynn's ear when they were at my house. Keith was the enemy I hadn't seen coming.

I opened my mouth to say something, but the words wouldn't form. I couldn't be in here with him. I backed away, moving the curtain aside I slipped back into the hall and sat in a chair against the wall.

Keith.

Now what should I do?

I leaned forward, elbows on knees, gripping my hair to the point of hurting, until I noticed a pair of shoes stop in front of me. I looked up. The shoes belonged to Keith. He was peering down at me all red-eyed and wasted. This day had been just as hard on him as it had been on me, probably worse.

When he didn't move to walk past me, and he hadn't said anything either, I stood up in front of him and waited. Somehow I knew Keith had something to say, but he was searching for the way to say it. The silence lingered. He couldn't bring himself to look me in the eyes, but I couldn't fault him for it since I wasn't exactly looking at him either. I think we both wanted to avoid talking as long as possible. It was as if we both *knew* that I knew, but wouldn't admit it.

Plus, he was wearing Flynn's missing necklace.

"How is he?" I finally asked.

"Fine, but not fine. You saw him. He's not awake. They have him drugged or something. I don't know. It's hard watching him lie there."

I heard Keith's voice crack and that prompted my compassionate reaction. I was the youngest child in a family of huggers, it wasn't difficult for me to reach out and pull Keith into a hug. My emotions lay in a disheveled heap; I knew what he was experiencing. Keith hugged me back and I felt his body quake. A minute or two later, he pulled back.

He wiped his nose on his sleeve. "If you love him, then go for it."

"W-what?" I stammered, not expecting those words I wasn't sure I had heard him correctly. "Come again?"

He sniffled, pulled his shoulders back and repeated, "If you love him, then go for it. But don't you dare make a move out of pity. He deserves better than that."

Shocked, I had to say, "I don't know what you're talking about. Aren't *you* his boyfriend?"

"Yes, and no." He looked away and rubbed his face. I could tell it was not a conversation he wanted to have with me. "Flynn and I have been on and off for years. When he started seeing Amelia, we sort of called it quits because I was not about to watch him date a girl when he was supposed to be my boyfriend."

"Oh." I felt guilty knowing I was the reason they had started dating in the first place. "I'm sorry. I don't know why he did that."

"Are you kidding? Flynn did everything for you. And because I'm just as stupid, I went along with him every time he asked. I acted straight so you wouldn't know we were together. When did he tell you? Or did you just assume because you saw me in there?"

I felt awful. All this time, all my deception, all my hiding was for nothing because Flynn would have understood all along. "Flynn told me last night. I had no idea he was gay. I didn't know about you or I wouldn't have asked him to date Amelia. I swear. I don't understand why he'd go along with it like that. Amelia kept calling him her boyfriend. I don't understand what's been going on."

"That makes two of us. Flynn's had a weird fixation on you because of your... situation."

"He told you?" I asked, bordering on panic and mortification.

"Yes, but only me. Don't worry. He's protective of you and it got in the way of our relationship. I'm glad he finally came out, but I still hate you for everything that's happened in the last couple years."

"I didn't know," I defended weakly.

"And don't think I didn't see the way he was looking at you before the accident. It made me sick," he sneered. Keith kept his voice tight and low, but I knew if we weren't in a hospital he'd have probably slugged me. He was seething, and I deserved it so I took his verbal punches. "I don't know why I went except Grace wanted someone to sit with while Greg was playing groomsman." He turned away, clenching his fists low at his sides. I'd never seen Keith like this. True, I'd never spent much time with the guy, but

I had the impression he was passive and unassuming despite his outspoken bluntness.

The fire in his red-rimmed eyes as he turned back toward me made me jump. "It was always you, and I was too stupidly in love to walk away." Tears rolled down his face as he quietly growled at me. "Even in that last moment, he said it to you. You!"

"You heard that?"

"Yes, I heard him. When the dead branch came crashing down, I was at Flynn's side about a half-second after you. I heard him say 'I love you.' I watched him struggle to breathe and I also heard your response when he closed his eyes. It was more than likely inaudible to everyone else, since most people were frantically trying to get out of the tangle of braches, but I heard what you said. You told him you couldn't live without him and that he couldn't leave you. You said he couldn't say those words and not wait for your reply. You said, and I quote, 'You have to hear them from me. I need to look into your eyes when I say it.'"

"Keith, I—"

"You share everything except your heart, Zach. Flynn wanted you to love him back. That's all he's ever wanted. But until today I thought it was an impossibility."

"Nothing's changed. I'm still engaged. Flynn and I... We... It's complicated."

"Maybe so. All I know is that today, after the tree fell, I've never seen someone so protective and authoritative." Keith stared at me and it made me nervous. "You treated him the same way he's protected you."

Of course I felt defensive. Keith was implying that I loved Flynn and that I practically confessed it as Flynn passed out. I didn't remember that part. I knew it was my fault for asking God to stop the wedding, but I hadn't wanted anything else. "That doesn't mean anything," I insisted. "I was panicking. The tree was crushing him. I don't remember half of it."

"It means something when your bride-to-be nearly toppled over when she rushed to your side and you pushed her back with a stiff-armed shove. You didn't see the look on her face, but I did. She was trying to help you, she was trying to make sure her fiancé wasn't hurt, and all you had on your mind was Flynn." His fury had diminished, but Keith was still angry. I was glad this was a hospital because maybe he kept his feelings contained so no one would come over and stop his rant. "You barked orders at everyone, even Gwendolyn. You screamed for help to get the weight of the branch off his chest. You yelled at people to get back as you repositioned his chin and blew air into his lungs. No hesitation. No apprehension of placing your lips on his."

"Again, that doesn't mean anything. I've taken CPR classes, it's required for my job in case someone gets injured. Guys get trapped by falling limbs and some get sliced open by chainsaws or prune the tips of their fingers off, and others on the job need to know what to do. I was only reacting to the situation and using the emergency training I've had." I had no need to mention I hadn't worked in the tree business since last year because of my father. This wasn't the time for it.

"No. Not like that."

"Yes, just like that."

"Have you ever had to administer CPR to a living person, a living *male* person?"

I had to think about it and paused. "Well, no. Not that I remember. We trained on dummies."

"Exactly. From the stories my brother tells, it's hilarious."

"What are you talking about? Who's your brother and what does he have to do with anything?"

"My brother's a firefighter and has been for over ten years. He's seen everything—mostly. He has had some great stories when we have family reunions and stuff, but the stories I always remembered were the ones he told about newbies administering CPR for the first time. He said there's a look that crosses a guy's face when he's about to put his mouth on another guy's mouth. It's brief, because normally the instinct to rescue someone is very strong, but it's there. Since I'm gay, I found it interesting to hear stories like that. He said he's seen that look about a half-a-dozen times, and I'm pretty sure what he was alluding to wasn't on your mind at all. As soon as you could get close enough, you went right down. You checked his pulse, you tilted his chin, you checked the inside of his mouth, you listened for his breath, and when you didn't hear anything you pressed your lips to his and blew. I've never seen anyone so determined to save a life."

"He's my best friend," I declared logically.

"You did, you know? I heard the EMT say something to your mother. He said you probably saved his life by acting so fast. Had he lain there until the paramedics came, he might not have survived, since he'd stopped breathing. You saved Flynn's life."

I couldn't form words. I couldn't remember any of that. I remembered Flynn passing out, but that was where my memory of earlier ended. "I did that?"

"Yeah. I felt useless and so did everyone else. As you hopped into the ambulance to ride with him, I put my arm around Gwendolyn. She was crying, but she was also hard and cold. She didn't want comfort or consolation, so I backed away and found Amelia standing with your brother-in-law. She was in a heap in one of the chairs and he was talking to her and rubbing her arm. I'm not sure who she was crying for, you or Flynn. I couldn't tell. She was babbling something about kissing you and dooming the wedding."

My mind snapped out of its funk and I brought my gaze up to meet his. "I... um... she...," I sputtered. "Amelia kissed me before I got into the limo last night. I kind of forgot about that with everything that's happened in the past twenty-four hours, but I guess I should talk to her."

"Yeah, probably. You also need to talk to Flynn."

"I know."

Keith took a deep breath and his eyes grew serious. He wasn't angry, or jealous. This was a guy who cared about Flynn more than anyone else did; who simply wanted what was best for him. "Look, I know it's hard because he looks so awful, but I really think he's going to be fine. It's a concussion. Mr. Brewer said they scanned his brain for clots and bleeding, and it looked clear. There *is* swelling, but it's expected since he hit the ground hard. Time and rest is what he needs. Flynn'll be okay."

I nodded. I didn't know what else to do.

"You need to consider whether you can give Flynn what he wants."

"What about you?"

"Me?" he chuckled, but the sound turned into a strangled sob. "I want Flynn to be happy. If that's with you, then I'll step back. I love Flynn, but... you were his first crush and I don't think he's ever gotten over that kiss."

"Wait... what? He told you... about the kiss?" I asked, needing clarification.

I remembered kissing him when he was fourteen. I remembered how perverted I felt when I almost took advantage of a little kid in my bedroom that day. Then, last night, when he told me he was gay, I had worried that somehow my kiss had turned him. Like, even though I believed people were born either straight or gay, I worried that somehow my kiss had flipped the switch for him.

Keith confirmed, "Yeah. Of course he did. We dated for two years, if you don't count the break-ups. We've talk about everything from first dates, to first kisses, and first inappropriate erections. Flynn loves to talk. He definitely remembers that kiss as if it happened yesterday. The thing is, Zach, Flynn's been hooked on you and that kiss so tightly there isn't any room for me. That's why I have to back down and let you in. We've been apart for nine months. If he wanted me, he could have said something in that time. If you can give him the happiness he deserves, then I'll step away because I know *you're* the guy he's always been close to. You're the one he's always wanted. Even if he grumbled at me for suggesting he loved you, it made sense to me. I know people say kids are too young to understand love at that age, but he's been in love with you a long time. I'm sure of it."

"I didn't know."

He chuckled maniacally. "Of course not." The humor fizzled fast and he clenched his jaw and narrowed his eyes as he stepped into me. It was the most intimidating stare I had ever seen on him. "But if you can't give him the life he deserves, whether it is for religious reasons or because you really are straight, then cut him loose. Tell Flynn flat out, once and for good, that you don't feel the same way. Let him hurt, but let him go."

I swallowed hard. Those were blunt terms and hard conditions. I wanted to answer, but I froze. I nodded and looked away. I couldn't even move my jaw from its slack position for a few minutes. I think Keith's ultimatum stunned me. When I looked back, Keith was gone.

I stood there staring at the floor until a nurse touched my arm and I jumped. "Sir," she said. "Can I help you?"

I shook the fog from my mind. "Um, no. I'm headed in to see Flynn Brewer."

She looked over to his room and then back to me. "Flynn's not in room three any longer. I'll check the computer for his room number."

"What? When did that happen?" I was confused because I had been standing like ten feet away talking to Keith. How did Flynn get moved and neither of us notice?

She grinned softly. "We tend to do things quietly in the ICU." She winked. "We're like medical ninjas."

She made me chuckle. "Funny," I commented, following her over to the nurse's station.

"I try to be. This place is full of sadness. It's needs a smile or two."

I grinned again. She was probably the nicest nurse I'd ever met—based on first impressions, that is.

"If you go down that hallway," she explained as she pointed, "you'll see an arrow pointing to the elevators. Go past it. Follow the next hall to the left and take the elevator on the right to the sixth floor. His room number is six eighty-seven."

"Thanks."

"Remember to show them your visitor badge. Okay? Keep your words positive. He needs to rest, but he can still hear you. Talk about happy memories and try to avoid anything about the accident. Stress causes tension, even when you're sleeping. Flynn needs to relax."

"Okay. I'll try."

She smiled. "May God bless you."

I nodded and walked away.

I made my way and found his room easily. The hospital halls were clearly marked and the nurses were helpful. When I saw the marker indicating room 687, I think the floor transformed into a tar-covered pile of goo because my feet had difficulty traversing the last seven feet. My shoes were suck to the tile and Flynn seemed miles away. The door was propped open and the room was dimly lit from a light behind his bed. It threw the light onto the ceiling, subtly, as compared to shining down on him from above. It was kinder to the eyes.

As I drew near, I heard the beeping monitors and my heart started racing. It was that sound. That beeping. It scared the fuck out of me because I had only one memory of that sound, and it was not one I wanted to relive. The nurse told me to keep the conversation light and happy. How could I do that if the beeping sound crashed in and destroyed my happy thoughts?

I swept the room with my eyes as I tried ignoring the sound. I could forget the sound if I thought about everything *but*. Window, monitor, chair, sofa, tacky painting on the wall, and last… a hospital bed. A bed with Flynn lying motionless in it. He was so still. He had an IV in one arm and a blood pressure cuff around the other. I stepped closer, running my fingers along the thin gray blanket covering his body. I rubbed it between my fingers. It was rough and not warm at all. Flynn liked being super warm when he slept. I could deal with a blanket this thin, but not Flynn.

I touched his hand and it was cold.

I cringed. "I'm sorry buddy. You shouldn't be in here. You shouldn't be this cold. Your hands are never this cold unless you've been in the pool." I took his hand in mine. It was limp, and his fingers felt like icy, dry sticks. "Oh Flynn," I gasped, my breath catching in my throat. "I'm so sorry. This is all my fault."

I looked around, but there wasn't a chair that was easily moved over to his bedside. If I wanted to be next to him, I would have to stand. I could do that, but I hated the proximity of the monitors. The beeping grated and made my skin crawl. It reminded me of... of....

I looked at Flynn. He was silent, still, sleeping. It reminded me of his brother and the details came flooding back in like a tidal wave. Before I went under, I whispered, "You look like Nathan. He was here. This is where he died, Flynn. This is the same hospital."

I knew the nurse told me to keep it positive, but I wasn't feeling positive. I was reliving the past in all its haunting glory, a past I had never shared with Flynn, and a love I had never shared with anyone... until now.

I knew I was reliving my past and speaking every word of it into the ears of my unconscious friend, but I couldn't stop myself. I couldn't feel my lips moving, nor did I hear my words, but still they tumbled from my mouth with unstoppable force as an avalanche thunders down a mountainside. Flynn would hear the story. I couldn't keep it to myself any longer.

Chapter 23

November 28, 2004: Reliving Past Horror

Strangers yelling. Long halls. Flickering lights. Beeps. Bleach. Bandages. Crying children. Nurses rushing in different directions. Lost. Alone. Wondering. Waiting. A flash of someone familiar and I'm pulled down a hallway by my flaccid fingers.

No words spoken. No tears in my eyes. No explanation. No warning. No preparation. Suddenly I'm there in the room and my best friend is hooked up to monitors and wires and bags of goop hanging on metal poles. He's lying still, and all the oxygen in the room gets sucked through air-ducts by a gigantic vacuum cleaner, and I'm left gasping for breath. An invisible hand seizes my chest and closes around my ribs until I'm crushed by its force. My heart can't beat because I have no breath, no air.

The woman, my mother, face ashen and eyes gaunt, leads me closer to the place I don't want to be. It's that twelve-by-twelve tile next to his bed that rattles my knees and tests my bladder. Quaking like an aspen leaf, shivering like my old dog in the snow, I drag my feet, rubbery and resistant, in the direction my mother pulls my hand.

I can't see his eyes. I want to see his eyes.

The bandages and bruises cover half his face, and white medical tape obscures the rest as it holds what looks like a plastic tube in his mouth.

"Nathan," my mother says as though he can hear her. "Zach is here." She looks at me and squeezes my shoulders as if transferring all her strength to me, only it drains down my arms and through a colander, pooling at my feet. I have no strength without Nathan. He has been my best friend my entire life. *Twelve years isn't enough,* I scream, but the yelling that echoes is contained in the spaces of my mind. My mother doesn't hear it. My mother urges me forward.

"Talk to him, Zach."

I muster up the jellyfish in my gut and whisper, "Nate." When he doesn't move, I try again. "Nate. Wake up, Nate. You can't leave me. We were going to build a fort, remember? Your dad bought that nail gun and showed you how to use it. Flynn is too young to hold the nail gun. Nate. Wake up."

My face is wet and my vision blurs. Then those sadistic monitors start beeping really loud and really long. One piercing, monotonous beep to wipe out every other sound in the room.

Doctors rush in. People shoving. Nurses ordering. I can't hear the words because the loud, constant beep punctures my eardrums. No words. No tears. No heartbeat. No me. I died in that room with my best friend.

By the time I was done reliving the past and wiping away my tears, I heard the monitor beeping again. The sound was different than when I had started talking about Nathan. It was higher pitched and each sound came closer together. I look up across the bed hoping to figure out what made it change and I found Flynn staring at me.

My breath caught in my throat as I tried to say his name.

He blinked at me three times and then his eyes closed again. Frantically, I grabbed for the call button and pressed it. "Flynn. Flynn. Can you hear me? Flynn?"

The nurse's voice sounded over the intercom. "Can I help you?"

"He opened his eyes," I said. "Flynn opened his eyes, but now they're shut again."

"I'll send the nurse in to check on him."

"Thanks. Flynn, can you hear me? Flynn?"

"You say he opened his eyes?" I heard the nurse ask behind me, so I turned.

"Yes. I was talking to him about his brother and I heard the monitor sounds change. I looked up and he was staring at me. He blinked and then shut his eyes again. What does that mean?"

"Coma patients normally wake up in stages," she explained as she checked the monitors. "In the movies, they wake up and talk as if nothing happened. In reality, the brain goes through steps or phases. Sometimes each stage comes close behind the other, and sometimes it takes longer. For Flynn to open his eyes means he is making progress, but I wouldn't expect him to hold a conversation with you tonight."

"Tomorrow?" I asked, hopeful.

She gave me a smile that could have been mistaken as patronizing if I chose to take it that way. I didn't like this nurse. I liked the one who called nurses "medical ninjas." This one was cold, and definitely not positive in the least. "We'll see. It's actually best if he sleeps a while longer. If he opens his eyes again, press the button. They doctor might want to give him something to keep him quiet."

"Like what?"

"I'm not at liberty to guess."

"Oh. Okay. I'll call if he wakes up."

"You do that." Again with the belittling tone.

I looked back at Flynn. "I don't like that nurse," I confessed.

Even though he was sleeping, as he had been moments ago, the feeling in the air was different. I couldn't explain it, but I could feel his presence in a way I hadn't before. I leaned closer to him and smoothed his hair across his forehead and he took a deep breath and let it out. I could have sworn he sighed. I reached for the call button, but reconsidered. If I pushed it for every little thing, maybe they would ignore me when something big happened.

"Flynn, can you hear me?" I said softly, fingering his hair and caressing his face. He'd re-dyed the patch of hair behind his ear for the wedding. Fuchsia. God, I'd thought nothing of it other than maybe Amelia had asked him to since she liked pink. He had always favored cobalt blue, but he *had* dyed it purple or green before. Fuchsia was new.

"I like your hair Flynn." I sighed. "Oh Flynn. You have to come back to me. I know how it feels when you sit by your mother's grave. I know how empty your life feels sometimes. They weren't my mom and brother, but sometimes, Flynn, I feel the sharp pain of loss just like you do. I blame myself, you know? I think it was my fault."

I placed my arm across his chest, carefully avoiding his bandages, and snuggled my face close to his neck, almost like Keith had done. My back would hurt later from being in this position, but that didn't matter. I spoke out loud, hoping he really could hear me. "I blame myself for the accident because I kissed Nate the night before. I've never told anyone. We were in the hot tub and we started talking about kissing girls and wondering what it would feel like. It was dark and your mom and dad were sleeping. The hot tub lights were on, but everything else around us was shadowy and quiet. After a while, we just stared at each other. The water was very warm; I remember that. I also remember his hand touching my stomach, and the look in his eyes. I couldn't breathe as I leaned forward and kissed him. I remember the taste of chlorine on my lips. I remember touching his face and feeling his hands sliding around my hips as I continued kissing him. When I leaned back, he looked scared so I took a deep breath and ducked under the water. When I came up for air, he was gone."

The feeling of disappointment still had its claws in my gut even after all this time. I hated it. I could never shake the memories and that's how I knew what Flynn felt like when he would visit Mrs. Brewer's grave. Some memories never left.

I kissed Flynn's neck and rubbed my nose against his skin.

"I'm sorry Flynn," I whispered. "I feel like I did this to you. I kissed Nathan and the next day he was in that accident. Then, last night we… I… Oh, Flynn. You can't leave me. I don't know why I feel like this, but I need you to come back. We need to talk about it. I can't marry Gwendolyn while I feel like this. You need to help me sort it out. You said you're gay. What does that feel like?"

I kissed his jaw again, and tried to let my brain rest. Too much thinking was giving me a headache.

Chapter 24

April 27, 2014: Baby Steps

I remained in the room all night. Either the nurse was being extra kind, or she hadn't noticed I was sleeping on the cramped, cement-like sofa in the corner of the room. I stretched and felt a stabbing pain in my lower back, same as if I had slept out in the yard and hadn't noticed a rock under my sleeping bag. Been there, done that.

I glanced over at Flynn where he slept. Still. Silent.

I took my phone out and noticed six texts—two from my mom, four from Gwendolyn.

Where are you? My mom's text asked. Then she asked, *Text me when you get this. If I don't hear from you, I will be at the hospital tomorrow.*

I rubbed my sore neck.

My mom was coming to the hospital? I groaned. *Terrific.* I wasn't in the mood to deal with her. Kelly and Grace had been in last night for a few minutes and said they'd be by again today. Maybe if I texted my mom that I was coming home, she'd reconsider.

Mom, I'll be home soon. Mr. Brewer is coming later. They want the visitors to take turns. I didn't know how accurate that was, but I didn't think Flynn needed my mom here more than his own father.

She texted back: *Fine, I had some errands to run anyway.*

Slightly insensitive, but that was my fickle mother.

Then I thought of Gwendolyn. She was the one I was most worried about. I clicked her texts.

Where are you? Are you at the hospital? How is Flynn? That text was at least easy to understand. She probably assumed I was here and was politely concerned. Her next text was more urgent. *Zach? The least you could do is respond. Please let me know you are okay.* I glanced again at Flynn.

"Am I okay?" I asked out loud. "Not really." I felt like shit, physically and emotionally.

Next text: *Zach, I'm probably going to visit Flynn with your mom.*

Last text: *I think we need to talk. I don't know what is going on with you, but I don't like the fact that you are ignoring my texts. What is going on with Flynn? We'll be there at 10 if I don't hear from you.*

I felt bad. I didn't have an explanation even though I knew I owed her one. I texted: *Hey. I fell asleep here. Sorry I didn't text before. My mind isn't very clear. I'll head to your house now. K?*

Two minutes later she replied: *Okay.* I thought she was done and then I got another one. *Amelia is acting weird. Did something happen with Flynn the night before the wedding?*

I stood up and walked over to Flynn. I rubbed my face and spoke to him. I tried to act like he was listening just as the nurse had urged. "Oh Flynn, what do I do? Gwendolyn is asking about the night before the wedding. She's asking about Amelia. Should I mention Amelia kissed me?" I asked my sleeping buddy. I sighed. This was difficult. "She asked me if anything happened with you the night before the wedding. I know she doesn't know about... you know... but how do I reply without lying?"

Shit. I lamented. I couldn't tell her the truth though a text. *No, Gwendolyn, nothing happened with Flynn and Amelia that I know of. Mr. Brewer should be here soon. I'll talk to you later.*

Okay.

I thought she'd text more, but she didn't. It was unsettling.

The nurse came in and checked on Flynn without saying much of anything. I guess maybe they're used to family standing guard over loved ones and the less friendly nurses don't engage without being prompted. Sad, if you asked me.

I took his hand in mine and watched him sleeping. "Flynn, you need to wake up."

"How's your friend?" a pleasant voice asked.

I turned and saw the nurse from the ICU who referred to nurses as ninjas. "Hey," I said with a thin smile. I looked back to Flynn. "He's fine, I guess, but still unconscious."

"Did you talk about pleasant things as I suggested?" She walked up to my side and looked at Flynn.

"No," I answered honestly. "I tried, but all I could think of was his brother. He died in this hospital nine years ago. I ended up recalling the events for Flynn. It was probably stupid, but I couldn't stop talking about it."

"Well, at least you were talking. Coma patients respond well to familiar voices."

I nodded. "Yeah. He opened his eyes briefly, but then closed them."

"That's good. Keep talking. I'm sure he'll come around soon. Intracranial pressure often causes lower levels of responsiveness. Once his pressure is down, I'm sure he'll wake up. Just keep talking and telling him how much you miss him."

"I will."

"In all likelihood, he'll be out for a couple of days. You should probably go home and get some rest, maybe a shower."

"I don't want to leave him."

She touched my arm. "I know. But after he wakes up, you won't want to leave then, either. Go home now and change out of those clothes. You look like you were at a wedding or a Renaissance Faire."

I glanced at my attire as if I'd forgotten what I was wearing. "Yeah. A wedding."

"Were you the best man?"

"No. The groom."

"Oh? How is your bride?"

I felt bad answering because it was the truth. "I don't really know. I think she's fine, but I've been here. Flynn's my best friend."

"Oh. I can see that he means a lot to you." She smiled briefly and turned toward the door. Before she left, she added, "A word of advice. A woman is very forgiving when she knows where she stands in your heart, but the reverse is also true. 'Hell hath no fury like a woman scorned' is a well know phrase for a reason." With a wink, the ninja nurse left the room.

A woman scorned. Was I scorning Gwendolyn by ignoring her? "I guess I should go take care of my fiancé." I touched Flynn's fingers. He seemed so far away. The oxygen tube for his nose, the cuff on his arm, the wires and cords connected to the machines, everything in the room reminded me of Nathan. "Promise you won't leave," I urged Flynn. "I'm scared to walk out because I'm afraid you'll leave."

I turned sharply and hurried out the door before I lost my nerve. I had to believe he'd be okay. I had to.

***

I headed over to Gwendolyn's first. I owed her an explanation and whatever grief my mother could give me wasn't as important as taking care of Gwen. She glanced my way when I walked through the door, but turned away and continued doing whatever it was she was doing. The place was empty and I wondered where her parents and Amelia were. I could tell Gwen was upset, and I also knew I needed to take care of this situation now, before her family returned.

"We need to talk," I stated plainly, tossing my keys on the coffee table.

"I know," she replied with her back to me.

"Where is every one?"

"Urgent Care. Amelia flipped out and my mom thought she needed Valium or something. Dad drove them to see a doctor. We were all talking about visiting Flynn, but Amelia wouldn't calm down."

I hesitantly walked over to her as if on my way to disarm a time bomb. I had no idea where to start or what she'd say. "That doesn't sound good," I said plainly.

"No."

"Um, I don't know what to say."

Gwendolyn whipped around and blasted me. "Try. After all the time I've given you to pull yourself together, I think I deserve your best *try*."

"I...." The words were harder than I thought to say. "I have feelings for Flynn."

"Duh. And?"

"And... I don't know! Everything is so messed up and I don't remember half of what happened. Keith said he heard me pleading with Flynn and...."

"I heard it too. I heard Flynn, and I heard *you*. I heard you Zach!" Her eyes burned into me.

"I'm sorry."

"Sorry!" she yelled. "That's it? You practically told Flynn you're in love with him and all you've got to say is you're sorry? Did you lie to me before?"

"No," I replied.

"No? You told me in Nevada you were questioning your sexuality. Questioning! You never said you had feelings for a *particular* boy, let alone your best friend. I told you I didn't mind and we could explore the possibilities together as soon as we were free from our parents. Was all that a lie?"

"No!"

"Then tell me what changed." She challenged me to tell her the truth.

I blurted, "The night before the wedding, I... I cheated on you." Gwendolyn didn't move, didn't blink, so I continued. "After the bachelor party, when everyone else was gone or asleep, I pushed Flynn up against the door and sank to my knees."

She covered her mouth and turned away so I stopped explaining. I could add more details if she wanted them, but I didn't want to make her throw up. I waited, and after a few minutes I heard her sob. I reached for her shoulders and she jumped away before I had the chance to comfort her.

"Don't touch me!" she yelled.

"I'm sorry. I'm so sorry Gwendolyn. I never meant for it to happen."

"How many have there been?" Her eyes were cold and hard as she the question snarled at me.

"How many what? Blowjobs?"

She covered her mouth again and ran to the bathroom. Wise or not, I followed. I handed her a wet towel when she was finished vomiting bile and flushed the toilet. "Men," she asked, holding her head as she sat on the closed toilet seat. "How many men?"

"Oh. One. Only Flynn. I haven't done anything with anyone but you since we met. I swear." I hoped she believed me because I had nothing else. I was finally telling her the whole truth.

Gwendolyn wiped her face with the towel again and stood. She stepped to the sink and I backed out of the way. I followed her into the kitchen where she poured herself some water and drank. I was relieved she set the empty glass in the sink instead of hurling it at my head. I followed her back into the living room as if I was a lost puppy waiting for my next meal. I didn't know what else to do. I told her the truth and now I had to follow her around until she said something, anything, to make the conversation continue or end.

"You know what's so fucking crazy about this whole situation?" she asked, rubbing the back of her neck. She paced the small living room, between the sofa and the table and back around. "I knew. I knew!" she spat, her piercing eyes jabbing at me, proving she wasn't as calm as I had hoped she was after throwing up. "It started at the engagement party when I watched how you looked at him as if he was the only one in the room. So yesterday when that tree fell and you jumped to his side without even the slightest glance in my direction, I *knew* there was way more than friendship going on between you."

I pleaded, "But there wasn't, not really. Not before two nights ago. Flynn had no idea I had feelings for him, nor did I know anything about him. It all just… happened. When he told me he was gay, it's like something flipped inside me, and I was finally allowed to think about it."

"But it was there," she said sternly. "Something has always been there between you that was strong enough to overshadow me, and any feeling you might have had for me, that led up to this point. Flynn was your priority when that tree fell, not me. That actually makes more sense considering the fact that you cheated. I don't know about you, but from where I come from the person you marry needs to be number one. You can't offer me that position, can you?"

Gwendolyn challenged me with her words and her eyes. I was helpless. I hung my head and answered, "No. I can't. Flynn's always been number one."

I could continue staring at the floor like a gloomy Gus, or I could face her fury like a man. I chose to take it. Gwendolyn was fuming as I met her eyes, but she also seemed to be mulling over something else. It wasn't simply anger I saw blazing his her eyes. "Are you gay?" she finally asked. The way she said it made me think that even after I told her what I'd done, she hadn't wanted believed it.

I took my time answering. I didn't want to say the wrong thing, and I didn't want to lie. "Gwendolyn, I honestly don't know what I am."

"What about us?" she asked in a voice calmer and more contained than it had been for most of our conversation. "We had this discussion. I remember it. We agreed to give in to what our parents wanted, get married, and figure out your sexuality later. You said you were questioning. You said you might be bisexual, you never said you had feelings for Flynn."

"I know. I never allowed myself to think about him like that until he told me… I always thought he was straight. If I'm honest—"

"Oh, please, be honest," she snapped. Yes, the snarkiness was still on the table.

"To be honest, I need to talk to Flynn."

"Fair enough."

"I've been carrying around this bag of 'What-ifs' and I think I need to sort them out with him before anything else in my life will make sense."

Gwendolyn sat, and then promptly rose again as if sitting just wasn't an option. She shifted her weight from one foot to the other and rubbed the side of her face. "Are we over?" she asked finally. Her voice awash with emotion, but not as much anger in the mix as the question she'd just asked dictated.

I was scared to ask. "Do you want us to be?"

She threw her arm down and gawked. "No."

"I don't either," I said, stepping forward. This time, she didn't pull away, but allowed me to touch her shoulders. "I love you. I swear I do. I'm just confused. For too many years I've been denying how I felt about Flynn because I thought God would hate me."

"God doesn't hate you."

"Couple my disagreement with most of the doctrine at my church with all the pressures my dad throws at me and you have a ball of tightly woven knots crammed inside a brain that's wired to love people. I want to please my parents. You know I do. We discussed it when I asked you to marry me."

"I know." Tears streaked her cheeks, and she placed her hands on my hips. "I told you I was fine not getting married right away. We could have run away and moved in together."

"I wish we'd done that, but I knew I couldn't leave Flynn." My heart sank. She was right; Flynn had always stood between us.

"Flynn."

"I'm sorry. I wish the last two days hadn't happened." I touched her face and wiped away the tears before I leaned in and kissed her forehead. I pulled her close and she let me hold her. "I wish I could take it all back."

Gwendolyn hugged me tight for a moment and then pulled back far enough to look at me in the face. "No you don't. It had to happen this way for a reason. Now is the time to face it. Running from your fears solves nothing. I'd rather you break my heart now, than five years from now, or ten. I'd rather it be with Flynn, than some guy you meet in a bar because you were too desperate to deal with your feelings logically. I'd rather it be with your best friend, than a guy who doesn't care about you and who might use you to get off and then leave you with AIDS or some other STD. If you need to figure yourself out, then do it. Go. Talk to Flynn. But don't you dare forget me, or blow me off again." Gwendolyn gritted her teeth as she gave me her ultimatum. "You tell me what's going on and you keep me informed or so help me, I'll hunt you down and rip your balls off." I knew she meant it too.

"I will."

She nodded and then sank into my arms again. Her hair smelled like grapefruits and I breathed in extra deeply because I enjoyed that scent so much.

"Do you think anyone else heard me? Or heard Flynn?" I needed to know.

"I don't think so," she whispered. Gwen let me go and sat on the sofa. "Something is up with Amelia, though. If Flynn's gay, then why date my sister?"

I sat next to her. "Because I asked him to. The situation is all my fault."

"No. Part of it falls on Flynn." As if realizing her pun, she held up her hand, eyes wide from the shock of her own words. "You know I didn't mean it like that. I really like Flynn."

"I know."

She sighed. "My mom looked really disturbed earlier, and my dad wasn't happy with the whole situation. As soon as they sort out what's wrong with Amelia, I think he wants to go back home."

I caressed her knee. "Will you go with them?"

"Not if you give me a reason to stay."

Chapter 25

April 27, 2014: Insecurities

The idea that God was somehow punishing me chased me home tenaciously. Perhaps it was because when I was home, God loomed closer than everywhere else. Or more precisely, the judgments and wrath of God felt more real and imminent. I parked in our three-car garage out back and was relieved to find that our other two cars were gone.

My sister greeted me as soon as I walked in. "Zach!" Amy rushed to my arms and squeezed the life out of me. "I'm so glad you're home." She and Chad lived fifteen minutes away in a small apartment, but Amy often spent as much time as she could at our parents' house when she knew I'd be there. We were really close.

"Amy. I can't breathe." After she released me, and I caught my breath, I said, "You knew where I was. You could have texted."

"I wanted to give you space. You were really messed up at the hospital."

"I know." She didn't know the half of it.

"You want to tell me what's going on?" She looked so concerned. I loved that about my sister.

I glanced toward the kitchen, imagining somehow my mom could hear me even if she wasn't home, "Um...."

My sister addressed my hesitance. "No one's home, Zach, really. Mom went to get flowers or something, Dad had a golf thing, and Chad's buying real coffee. Seems Mom only buys the cheap, instant crap."

"Yeah, I never drink coffee here."

"So? How's Flynn?"

I moved over to the sofa and sat down. From here, at least we'd know when someone parked in the garage because they'd have to walk through the yard. My mother never parked on the street out front. I didn't want to talk about anything, but I knew it was inevitable. Plus, I needed to find out if Amy would remain on my side once she knew the whole truth.

"He's in a coma. I'm not clear on whether it was induced or he's unconscious from the brain injury. I don't know."

"But he'll recover, right?"

"Yeah. Most likely."

"Well, that's good."

I nodded. None of it felt real, though. Even sitting on the couch with my sister felt like a dream sequence from a movie. Any minute I'd wake up in my bed and it would be the day before my wedding and none of this would have occurred.

"Will you tell me what's going on? Mom seems pissed, more pissed than usual. Dad's obsessing about suing the venue. Gwendolyn isn't picking up her phone. What happened?"

"You mean you didn't hear everything?" I was shocked someone hadn't filled her in.

"No. I heard the crack and dove forward, but when you went for Flynn, I grabbed Amelia and pulled her away from potential danger. Chad found me and we helped the guests move out of the area. So many people were panicking that we decided to try and control the mass exodus. Luckily, only a couple people got injured."

I spilled. "Well... Apparently, I ignored my bride, saved my best friend's life, and practically told the world I'm in love with him." I boiled Keith's rendition of events down enough to fit into a nutshell. She'd get the point.

"What?" she gasped, moments before regaining her composure. Then she asked quietly, "Are you?"

I looked up. "I don't know, Amy. I don't know anything. You're the only person in the family I'd tell if I knew how I felt." I took her hand. I needed the security her closeness provided. "I cheated on Gwendolyn the night before last."

"What? How? Weren't you in the limo with Flynn, Chad, Tom, Greg, and Clark?"

I nodded. "It was after we returned and everyone had gone home or fallen asleep. Flynn snuck into my room to talk. I confessed some issues I'm having and he got upset and told me he's gay."

"Wait? Flynn's gay? When did that happen?"

"Yeah. I don't know. I think since he was young."

"Then why was he dating Amelia?"

"Because I asked him to."

"That's messed up."

"I know."

"How's Gwendolyn handling it?"

I wasn't sure if Amy was referring to Amelia's situation, Flynn's situation, or the fact that our wedding day had been destroyed. I figured I'd go with straight honesty. "She's okay for now. She's giving me time to sort things out with Flynn when he wakes up."

"So... she knows... about you?"

I nodded. "We talked about it when we were camping in the desert. We thought alike about so many things it felt magical, and the marriage arrangement our dads came up with didn't matter after that. We talked in between scripture lessons and stuff, and agreed to get married and sort things out later. Only... later ended up being the night before the wedding instead. Flynn told me he was gay and—bam!—I reacted."

"What did you do?"

"You don't want to know."

"Try me. Of anyone in the family you have to trust someone, so trust me. Please. I won't judge."

I took a deep breath and then told her. "I sucked him off the night before the wedding." Blunt and to the point, that was me. "Gwen and I had discussed my confusion. I told her I might be gay, or bi, I didn't know. She said she was fine with exploring it after the wedding." I grinned at Amy. "I think she's kind of kinky. I was relieved not to have to define myself, to have the freedom to explore it. I really do love Gwen; I just have feelings for Flynn, too. Everything's so messed up." I flopped my head back on the cushion and closed my eyes.

"I won't say anything," she said quietly. "And you shouldn't either. Not yet."

I brought my head back up and agreed, "Oh, I don't plan on it, but something will have to happen because I am through living in fear of Dad."

She squeezed my hand again. "I know. I'm here for you. You know I love you."

"I've been afraid to tell Mom and Dad about my feelings about our church. You know how volatile Dad gets, and Mom's temper is almost as unpredictable. They're both so kind and calm in public, but behind closed doors...."

She finished my thought, saying, "Behind closed doors Dad breaks your finger and blames it on your bike. I get it. Be careful."

I turned on the sofa and took both her hands in mine. "You know this all started because I googled different faiths, right?"

"No."

"It's what prompted the trip out west. Dad found out I was researching fundamentalism, humanism, Buddhism, all kinds of '-isms,' and he flipped. I even visited a different church, like a year and a half ago, and it got me thinking about God. I'd never understood the meaning of the word 'grace' before that visit. God was always vengeful in my mind, not compassionate. I wanted to go again, but I was afraid of what Dad might do if he found out."

"Oh my gosh, Zach! Chad and I thought the same thing last month. We visited this church and it was like everything I'd ever learned growing up was suddenly torn to pieces. Works, obligations, striving, doing, achieving, placating, being good, correcting error, confronting sin—everything; the pastor shattered everything I knew. After his sermon, instead of frightening me, it made me feel freer than I had ever felt in my entire life. Zach, Mom and Dad's church is like a prison, you need to get out. Tell them."

"They'll think I'm going to hell."

"So? We can't let their beliefs choke us to death. Chad said God gave us thinking minds for a reason. God doesn't mind our questions."

"Don't let Mom hear you say that."

"I need to. I should have confronted her years ago. They are so blind to their legalistic regimen of servitude that it's sickening. Maybe you and I together can show them. I was afraid before, but now...."

"I wouldn't count on me being your ace in the hole. I'm still on the fence about being gay. I don't think a homosexual brother is going to win you any points for logic. My very nature goes against God's Holy Law."

"Stop it. God loves you. I believe that."

"Thanks."

"So... gay?"

"Maybe. Or bi. I don't know. I've never had a problem getting it up for Gwendolyn. We've managed to sneak in time together a couple of times when our parents weren't around and it was awesome. Except, I've also never wanted another guy like I do Flynn, which is why I'm thinking bi."

"Chances are, if you feel something for Flynn, it will probably only grow from there. If it doesn't, then... I don't know."

"I guess I need to figure it out on my own. I need to talk to Flynn." Every time I thought about him, my skin turned cold. He was in the hospital because of me. I did it. I had to confess to someone about what I'd done. I only hoped Amy would understand and not hate me.

"Amy," I broached. "Are you sure God loves me? Because I don't feel it. I feel scared." My body ran cold and then hot. I felt the rush of emotion surfacing. "Amy, do you think God punishes people?"

"Punishes how?"

"Like...." I paused because it was hard to say. "Do you think the tree falling was because of what I did the night before?"

Her eyes widened. "No. Oh gosh no! Is that what this is about? You think God got angry and caused the tree to fall on Flynn?"

I refused to cry, but it was a struggle. "Yes."

"Oh, honey," she sighed, encircling me with her arms. My sister often mothered me, even though she was only two years older than me. I guess some guys wouldn't like it, but I found it soothing because my own mother had been harsh in recent years. She continued, "I don't think God works like that."

"Are you sure?" I asked into her hair and she held me tight.

Amy pulled back and took my face in both hands. She looked me in the eyes, which made it increasingly difficult to hold in my tears. "Zach. God doesn't smite people. He doesn't. Awful things happen because it is a part of life. Sometimes life sucks, but I refuse to think God's sitting up in heaven waiting for us to mess up and then He smacks us in the head, or hits us with a tree."

"But...." I squeezed my eyes shut, but the damn tears forced their way free. I felt them roll down my cheeks. "This wasn't the first time."

"What wasn't?" she asked.

Amy had no clue about my guilt, and the things I blamed myself for. "Nathan," I said.

Amy took both my hands and tried following me. "Nathan... what? He died because of a car accident, Zach. You were twelve, so I'm pretty sure you had nothing to do with the drunk driver hitting their car."

"I kissed him the night before," I confessed.

"You... what?" I saw the realization hit her, as her eyes grew brighter.

I wiped my eyes and took a few breaths before continuing. "I kissed him. We were soaking in the hot tub and talking about girls and kissing and stuff. Before I knew it, we were nose to nose, staring sat each other, and it just happened. I liked it... I liked it a lot. I wanted to keep kissing him, but he looked freaked, so I took a breath and went under the water. When I did, Nathan jumped out. I wanted to talk about it the next day and that's when Mr. Brewer called Mom. It was my fault, Amy. I kissed Nate and God judged me."

Sobs racked my body and Amy held me until I calmed down.

She lovingly wiped my tears and said, "You are not the cause of Nathan Brewer's death. His mom died too. She was a good person—sweet and kind—you can't possibly think that God would kill Nathan because of one kiss and allow her to die too. It was a senseless accident caused by a drunk driver. It wasn't God striking Nate dead. It wasn't you influencing God's design. Life happens, and so does death. Sometimes we can't explain it and it hurts and it sucks, but if you blame yourself for every bad thing that happens, you'll miss out on all the good things too."

"Like what?" I asked faintly.

"Like... how close you are to Flynn. I remember when Nathan was around Flynn was always the third wheel. You and Nate did everything together, and Flynn was the little brother who tagged along. Without Nate, Flynn was able to become your best friend. Isn't that a good thing?"

"Yeah, but...."

"Going out west with Dad. It was under terrible circumstances, yet you met Gwendolyn. You love her, right?"

I nodded.

"Then it's a good thing. Do you know how I met Chad?"

I shrugged. I couldn't remember. "No."

"Dad had pushed me down the stairs in one of his fits. When I hit the floor, I bolted through the front door. My ribs hurt and I had a gash on my arm, but I ran as far and fast as I could. I ended up in the coffee shop at the corner of John Street. I cleaned up in the bathroom and waited at the counter to place my order. Chad was behind me in line. He said hello," she smiled, "and that was all it took. If I hadn't run away, maybe I wouldn't have met him."

"But that's not the same."

"Isn't it? True, no one died, but I came to see that dark time in my life as a positive catalyst for change. I love Chad. I've never been happier than I have since meeting him. I believe the same things can be true for you if you allow yourself to let go of the guilt and find the good."

"I don't know how."

"Try." She patted my knee and got off the couch. "Right now, I'm going to make a sandwich and you are going to take a shower before Mom and Dad get home. Then, you need to talk to them. I'll call Chad so we can be here if Dad gets violent. Don't worry, we support you."

"I don't want to stay here tonight. Can I go home with you and Chad? I can sleep on the sofa."

"Sure."

**

April 28, 2014

Nothing happened when my parents came home. They were silent, as if tension was mounting under the surface, and the volcanic eruption needed time to brew. I'd decided to sleep in my own bed and told Amy I'd call if Mom and Dad got weird... *weirder.* The next morning I was out the door after eating a yogurt, so I could walk and think without the worry of someone verbally attacking me. Visiting hours didn't start until 8:00 a.m., so I had a couple hours until I could see Flynn anyway.

Flynn had always liked walking around town. He hadn't had a car for the longest time, but it never mattered to him. He enjoyed walking and watching people because it made him feel closer to the community. I remembered how many times he said he'd seen the same people and smiled at them. I pondered how many times he'd walked down the same pavement I was walking on now. Did he see the graffiti scrawled on the bricks, or had it only been painted recently? Had Mrs. Gentry always had daisies planted in the back of her yard, or had Flynn planted those? I knew he worked for her.

I crossed over Center Street and headed for the park where we used to play as kids. It was a Monday morning, and school was in session so the park was empty. I sat on the brick wall that lined the one side of the park and glanced across at all the playground equipment: slides, monkey bars, benches, and swings. Nate and I used to run in circles around the slides while Flynn cried about not being included in our game. A couple of minutes' walk to the right was the baseball field we used to play rec-ball on. Flynn had never liked baseball, so it was me and Nate taking batting practice and tossing balls while Flynn watched.

I chuckled, but the humor of it dampened quickly. Even if the tennis courts in between the playground and the baseball field reminded me of times when Flynn and I played tennis together, the other memories told me Amy was right. Flynn *had* been the third wheel until Nate was gone.

I stood up and walked away, not liking the memories that lingered in that park.

I recrossed Center Street and headed toward the cemetery. I often talked to Nate when I was confused, sad, or lonely. He never answered, but the thought of talking to myself made me feel psychotic. I wasn't crazy; I only needed to hear my thoughts out loud to understand myself sometimes. Nate's metaphorical presence helped me work through stuff.

As I walked down Court Lane, which turned into Court Place, I stopped in front of the old Episcopal Church on the corner. Flynn loved this church. He told me the curve-topped red doors reminded him of Lord Of The Rings. Only these doors didn't have riddles inscribed above them. Instead, the words "Church of the Ascension" were carved in the gray stone, with a date of 1844 at the very top. It was an old, beautiful church, and I rather enjoyed the thought of elves or hobbits being a part of the congregation if it were indeed set in Rivendell or another realm of Middle-earth.

Flynn has such a great imagination. I had no doubt he'd make a fine author one day. I smiled, but it faded all too quickly as heat surged up my neck bringing with it enough emotion to form tears in the corners of my eyes. *Flynn.* He'd sketched this church a number of times from the front, where I was standing now, and from the back. He could see it from his spot by his mother's grave. I followed a path next to the church and headed toward that spot on the hill where Nate and Mrs. Brewer's gravestones sat.

I watched my feet as I shuffled over the pavement and through the grass. I didn't need to look up to know where I was. I'd been there so many times. It was like walking to my bedroom in the middle of the night without a flashlight—my feet knew where to go. What I hadn't counted on was another person by their graves when I looked up. Especially when that other person was Keith Leppo.

He turned his head as I approached. "Oh jeez," he grumbled. "What are you; stalking me?"

Keith moved to get up from his cross-legged position, but I quickly said, "Don't get up."

He gave me an annoyed look, but sat back down. "Why are you here?" he asked suspiciously.

I shrugged and stepped closer. It wasn't like this was Keith's property, but I felt like I was intruding just the same. "Can I sit with you?"

He scooted over, away from me, but replied, "Whatever."

Keith was in front of Mrs. Brewer's gravestone, which left plenty of room for me next to Nathan. Keith wasn't looking at me, which made me rethink my intrusion. "If you really want me to go, I will. I just thought… well… I needed to think and I talk to Nate a lot, but he never answers back. If you're here—"

"I don't want to talk to you!" he growled. "I said all I had to say in the hospital. I still hate you, that hasn't changed. Seeing you just makes everything worse."

I felt so weak. Tom and Greg would never understand what I was going through, but I hoped Keith might. He knew Flynn. He said he loved Flynn. I didn't want to be alone, but I also didn't know how to talk to him and make him see I never wanted any of this. "Keith, I'm sorry. I wish it would all go away. I don't know what to do. Flynn always grounded me, and now he's in a coma. I need… someone…."

He covered his face with his hand and said, "It's not going to be me." His voice was strangled, which led me to believe that he wasn't as angry as he let on. Maybe he needed someone too.

"I wish things could be different. I wish Nate and Mrs. B never died. I wish I never kissed Flynn when we were kids. I wish that my parents weren't so difficult. I wish I could just work as a horticulturalist and identify tree diseases instead of preparing to go on a mission trip to Africa because my dad thinks it will help my spiritual growth. I wish I moved far away as soon as I graduated college. I wish Amy had never lost her baby. I wish I'd had the nerve to tell Flynn I liked boys years ago so that the tension between us wouldn't have culminated the way it did the night before my wedding."

"Wait… what?"

I had been staring at the carved letters in Nathan's name when Keith's sudden question pulled me out of my thoughts. I glanced at him and he was glaring at me.

"You said he told you he's gay. What else happened the night before the wedding?"

His suspicion warned me to keep silent, yet I didn't heed the signs. I spilled, bluntly, before I had to chance to reconsider what might happen. "I... went down on him." I confessed as if this were a trial. I looked down at my feet, and the blades of grass that reached up like little fingers, and before I knew it Keith was on top of me, shoving me to the ground, and punching me in the face.

Pain ricocheted from a single point on my cheek to the back of my skull and down my neck. Instinctively, I pulled my extremities inward, like a ball. I felt the throbbing pain of another punch on my jaw, and another close to my temple. He was punishing me again. I was never good enough. My actions never measured up. My grades were always just shy of expectation. My passes were one completion short of *his* all time record. My job aspirations were mediocre compared to the prospect of following one of the orders of the priesthood. I was a failure.

"I'm sorry," I cried. "I'm sorry, Dad. Please stop. Please."

The throbbing threatened to shatter my cranium from the inside out, yet his pounding ended. Perhaps those lashes in my personal, living purgatory were good enough for the day. I unfurled my body and waited for more degradation, but it never came. I opened my eyes, slowly, but my dad wasn't there.

It was Keith.

He was kneeling in the grass next to me with tears streaming down his face. He reached out and I flinched, but he took hold of my arm and assisted me upright. He took a napkin out of his pocket and wiped under my nose. "It's got a piece of old gum in it, but it's all I have to wipe the blood."

I took it and held it to my nose. It was saturated with blood in a few minutes, but did the job. "Thanks."

We sat in silence. My head hurt, but not as bad as I've felt in the past. I knew I'd be okay and that Keith hadn't broken any bones.

"I finally get it," he said quietly, after some time.

I studied his contemplative stare, but made no reply.

"After all this time," Keith confessed, "I finally understand that it was never about coming out to you. It was about protecting you. Flynn's mission in life has always been about giving you moments of joy, because somehow, he always knew what you needed. He sacrificed his needs in order to bring you hope."

"I don't follow you," I said. Thinking was more difficult with the throbbing I felt behind my eyes.

"Flynn told me your family was his family for many years. He did everything with you. If you know Flynn, you'll understand how insightful he is, how intuitive. I bet he saw your family changing over the years, and he probably knew you were being abused even before you told him. He waited for you to be comfortable enough to say something, and I bet he hoped he could figure out how to help you, if he just waited long enough.

"But then he met me and I got in the way of his plan. I demanded all of his attention. I wanted all of his love and devotion, because that's what I saw in my parents. I desired Flynn to look at me like my dad looks at my mom, but I never understood that Flynn wanted more than that. Flynn wanted to 'save your world' like a superhero. He could be Clark Kent, but he wasn't about to stop saving the world just because he was in love with Lois Lane."

His humor niggled my neck, just under my chin, and it tickled. I grinned. "Did you just refer to yourself as Lois Lane?" I chuckled, and then I chuckled harder and snorted.

"Yes, make fun of me, whatever, but the analogy makes sense to me. He was all about saving you, while he was in love with me. Until I pushed him away."

Keith's seriousness quelled my laughter. This wasn't the time for it. "I'm sorry," I said.

"It's not you, it's me. I'm controlling. I know it. It's hard not to think of what-ifs and consider the outcome if I'd just done something different that first Christmas."

"What Christmas? I don't follow you."

"It's a philosophical premise I've thought about, where changing one event could rewrite the events that follow. Some people speculate that fate can't really be altered; even choosing a different road would still bend you back around to the same result. Others think that choosing door number one instead of door number two will produce different endings. For example, if Neo had chosen the blue pill instead of the red when Morpheus gave him a choice, would he really have woken up in bed, knowing nothing, or would he still have learned the truth of the Matrix, but through a different path?"

"The Matrix? That was a cool film."

Keith ignored my interruption. "And then there's the whole God factor to consider. Are we subject to God's pre-ordained design, or do we have free will? I think about these things all the time."

"What does that have to do with Christmas?"

"Christmas two-thousand-eleven was one of those 'what-if' moments that I think could have changed our future, but it doesn't matter now. I can't change the past."

"What happened that you think it would have been different?" I wanted to understand, but Keith was being vague.

"I hid in the closet when you came over to visit. You gave him an army man, or something and I was jealous because Flynn seemed to really like that gift."

"Why were you in the closet?" Even if my head hurt quite a bit from Keith's previous rage, I still wanted to know and try to understand.

"Because Flynn asked me to hide, and don't think the irony is lost on me. I always acquiesced to him, the same way he did to you." Keith paused, taking a deep breath before continuing. "We'd just made love and then you showed up. I was pissed, but I hid in the closet anyway, while the two of you got all snuggly on the couch."

"I thought you said you were controlling. That sounds sacrificial to me."

"Yeah, well, if I'd have protested it would have meant outing Flynn before he was ready. My mom recommended I wait, so I did. She told me loving someone meant putting their needs first and relationships meant compromise. Flynn had relaxed around certain people, and even kissed me in front of his dad, Kelly, and Grace. Little by little he was overcoming his fears and I thought if I were more patient, he'd choose me over you. I hoped he would ask me to help save you, instead of donning the superhero suit by himself. I could have been Robin to his Batman."

Keith's superhero analogies were amusing, but I couldn't chuckle this time. He'd been hurt so many times because of me. So many things were my fault. If I had only said something sooner and trusted Flynn. I felt awful.

"Anyway, the day after *that* Christmas, I yelled at Flynn over the phone and gave him an earful about learning how he should put me first over his friends. Flynn wouldn't agree, so I ended our relationship for the second time that year. I've thought about how I ended it, but I also thought how I'd change it if given a do-over."

Keith loved Flynn, but I didn't think I could honor Keith's needs above my own, as he was attempting to do for me. I guess I was more selfish that way. I wasn't really Keith's friend; in fact, right now I kind of hated him as much as he'd said he hated me because he'd been so close to Flynn. If I'd told Flynn how I felt when he was fourteen, how would things be different now?

"I gotta go," I said, rising to my feet. "Visiting hours start soon and I want to be there."

Keith stood too. "Right."

"Are you going?"

"I don't know. It's basically an exercise in self-torture. He doesn't want me there. He wants you. I said good-bye months ago."

"But you still love him."

Keith face hardened. "And you're the one who saved his life. You win. Just go before I punch you again."

I stepped back. "Okay."

"Hey, I didn't mean that," Keith amended, grabbing my forearm before I moved any further. "I'm angry, and I really don't like you, but no one should have to put up with the shit you have. I'm sorry. My parents aren't like that, so I can't imagine—"

I pulled free of his grasp. "It's okay. Just forget it." I started walking away before my emotions got the best of me. Something about Keith fueled my anger, while also speaking to my compassion. I refused to like him. I couldn't. Not yet. He'd been the guy whom Flynn fell for because I'd been too stupid to open my mouth. Hating Keith made everything easier.

"Tell Flynn I...." Keith called after me.

I turned around when he paused. "What?"

He shook his head. "Nothing. Don't tell him anything."

I turned back around and walked home thinking about everything he'd said. Keith deferred to Flynn's happiness. If placed in the same position, would I have been so selfless? I wasn't sure.

Chapter 26

April 30, 2014: The Changing Tide

A couple days went by and everything remained the same. Flynn was still in a coma, I was still wrestling with my guilt and shame, my parents were unsettled yet quiet, and Gwendolyn was supportive yet distant. I wasn't sure how much longer I could go on like this. It felt like the weight of the world was pressing down on me. I knew I had to say something, but what? Did I tell my parents now, before talking to Flynn? The notion terrified me.

I was standing in my room, looking at my corkboard covered with old photographs, when my dad showed up unexpectedly, his voice behind me like a gong sounding in the middle of a silent forest at night. "So I got off the phone with my lawyer. It seems the venue has agreed to settle out of court," he said.

I turned, hoping he hadn't noticed my body shaking, because when I was scared, and he knew it, he got that much more enjoyment when he hit me. I cleared my throat. "Cool. I'm glad Mr. Diggs took care of that."

"Yes, well, if we'd done this in the sanctuary like I suggested, none of this would have happened. Gwendolyn's parents are very influential, but I doubt they will want to repeat this weekend. I'll call the church and see if we can reserve another date."

Just as he turned to go, I found my voice lurking under the bed and reclaimed it. "Um, Dad, about that," I said, holding on tightly while my voice struggled to hide again.

"What?" he asked sternly when I paused for more than five seconds. "I don't have all day, Zachary. Spit it out."

"Well, I was wondering if it was really necessary?"

"What was?"

"Another date. I mean, why do I have to get married right now? Can't we get to know one another first? I could get my own apartment and—"

"And what? Fornicate all day long? You know that sexual sin is prevalent in young men under the age of twenty-five. Getting married before lust takes over is best. You know this. My mistake was thinking you could keep it in your pants in high school. You will not embarrass me further by getting some girl pregnant outside of wedlock, and you will not pursue your carnal lusts with someone outside the church. Do you hear me?" When I didn't answer, he stepped closer and snarled, "Do you hear me?"

"Yes, sir!"

"Stewart," my mother called from down stairs.

"Yes," my dad answered back, stepping toward the open door so he could hear her.

"Mr. Pierce is on the phone. He wants to speak to you."

My dad left and I sat on my bed in relief. How was I supposed to tell him I wanted to live with Gwendolyn instead of marrying her? Or worse, how would I tell him I was attracted to Flynn? He nearly exploded before I said much of anything.

I didn't have any time to think about it, because my father returned a few minutes later. He reached for his belt, and I knew what that meant even before he yelled, "Take off your shirt and turn around."

"What? Why? I haven't done anything."

He grabbed my arm and spun me toward the bed and I stumbled forward. I fell onto the mattress, but grabbed at the back of my T-shirt instinctively. I yanked it over my head and bared my back before he took a swing. His punishment was always more severe if I hesitated. As soon as my shirt popped over my head, his first lash connected with my skin like a burning smack. *One.* I winced, but held still.

I'd been stupid enough to move in the past, which only got me lashed across the face with his belt when his swing came down. *Two.* If I held still, he'd count to six and stop. If I moved, then he'd start over at one.

"Three," he yelled, thwacking me again.

"Stewart!" my mother yelled, entering my room. "Stop! It wasn't his fault this time."

"Yes, it was!"

Four. The familiar icy-hot pain burned across my back. I buried my face in my blankets and hoped my mother wouldn't interrupt his counting. *Six. I only want six.* I prayed, *Please, let him end with six. Please, God.*

"Stewart!" she yelled.

His rhythm was interrupted and I heard shuffling behind me, but didn't dare look. I heard a crack of his hand on her cheek. It was the same sound she'd produced when slapping me. I knew it intimately. "Silence, woman!"

His belt came down on my back again. *Five. Six.* I froze, hoping he was finished. I turned my face slightly to peek at my parents, who were both still in my room.

"Pierce is backing out, Karen. All that planning down the toilet. His company's assets would have tripled my earnings. Not to mention his influence within the church. Due to one stupid accident of nature, I've lost everything!"

"Zachary had no control over the tree, over nature, over God."

"No. God saw fit to punish *me* for *your* son's insubordination. I failed to keep him in line, and this is what I get! I'm calling the mission board. A few months in Africa tending to Ebola victims should be penance enough."

Fear made me rise despite my pain. Going to Uganda was one thing, but an Ebola camp was completely different. I pleaded, "Dad, no! Please. I don't know how to help sick people."

He glared. "You need something to straighten you out! Our church has three mission groups over there. I'm sure one of them is in need of laborers."

"But, Dad...." I begged.

He left me hanging as he took off down the steps.

"Don't worry, Zach. He won't send you to Africa right away. He's angry. I'll talk to him."

My mom could be harsh, but she sometimes tried defending me from my father.

After she left my room, I inspected my back in the mirror. At least the skin wasn't broken. I had red lines and a few purple marks blooming, but nothing permanent. I grabbed my shirt, gingerly pulling it over my head, and crept out of the house before hell struck again.

Maybe Kelly would understand and let me stay with Flynn during her turn at his bedside.

***

May 2, 2014

I visited Flynn all week, but somehow Keith and I had missed each other, which was fine by me. I only knew he'd been there because ninja nurse Taryn told me so. She was about the nicest person I'd ever met. Always smiling, always accommodating, Taryn kept me informed, and brought me a drink or crackers when she thought I could use them.

Kelly, Grace and I coordinated by texts to make sure Flynn had company whenever his dad had to work. Mr. Brewer and I had overlapped a number of times. He even brought work into the hospital room. He had huge rolls of schematics that looked like blueprints, except they weren't of buildings; they were of bridges, water flow, and stream depth. It was very complicated, if you asked me. One afternoon he had them scattered across the floor as he did whatever it was he did to them.

I didn't care. What meant the most to me was how much he loved Flynn and stayed with him whenever humanly possible. I doubted my father would have worried about me so much. Mr. Brewer loved Flynn with every ounce of energy he had, and I envied them both.

Because I was *not* on my honeymoon, my father still expected me to keep up with the paperwork he left me. Most of it was pointless. I shuffled his e-mail accounts and sent work orders out to different people, but for the life of me, I had no idea what he did. None of it made sense, but that might have been because I didn't care to know. I would do anything for him to keep him from mentioning Africa again.

I was still hoping to return to my job with the tree company one day. If they'd take me back.

My sister visited Flynn and told him he'd better wake up and set me straight. She explained to him as he lay there that I was simply a mess without him. I chuckled and hugged her. I loved Amy so much.

Gwendolyn told me Amelia was feeling better. Her sister had had some sort of anxiety attack and ended up in a hospital for observation. I felt bad for Amelia, but I felt better knowing that she'd been detained; instead of imagining that she suddenly hated Flynn for what he'd said to me. Although, I didn't think she could have heard him since Amy told me she'd been cleared of the accident scene pretty quickly.

I remembered hearing Amelia from outside Flynn's room Thursday evening when her mom brought her by to see him. Gwen said the family planned on leaving the next day since the rental agreement was up on the first, but the landlord had given them until Saturday since he didn't have another tenant lined up.

Amelia was in a rare mood: cranky and obstinate. I clearly heard her say, "Why won't you wake up? Don't you love me?" That made me angry, yet I was relieved Flynn hadn't woken up for her. I wanted it to be me in the room when he came back to consciousness, and Keith had told Grace he hoped he wasn't there. Part of me felt sad for Keith; I could empathize with his feelings. He'd given up any claim to Flynn, but kept visiting for short periods because it was hard letting go.

"Zach?" Taryn called me from the doorway Friday night.

I looked up and smiled. "Yeah?"

"It's getting late," she said, walking over to where I sat by Flynn's bed and standing at my side. She kindly patted my shoulder and said, "You might want to spend the night at home tonight. I can have the night nurse call you."

"I know, but I don't want to leave. What if he wakes up? He shouldn't be alone. I told his dad I'd stay until he got here."

"Okay. As long as you get a shower every now and then." She winked.

I chuckled. "I'll get one. No worries. When Mr. Brewer comes in, I'm heading home. Promise."

Taryn smiled and left. As I watched her go I heard, "She's pretty."

I shot my attention back to Flynn and found him watching me.

"Flynn," I said, jumping up from my chair and over to his side. I grabbed for his hand. "You're awake. How do you feel?"

"Tired." His eyes blinked in slow motion. "What happened?"

"A tree fell on you, buddy."

"That sucks."

I smiled, relieved, as tears rolled down my cheeks. "You don't know the half of it."

"You look as though…" he yawned, "you haven't slept."

"I haven't. That sofa is hard as a rock, and way too short. After one night, I felt like I'd been hit by a bulldozer and then manipulated into a pretzel."

Flynn grinned and I squeezed his hand tighter.

As much as I didn't want others intruding on our moment, I knew calling the nurses' station was for the best. Taryn came in and I introduced her to Flynn. "Flynn, this is Taryn." I held his hand while she checked his vitals on the other side of the bed. "She's like a ninja," I told him with a wink and he smiled.

"I like your hair, by the way." Tayrn smiled at Flynn. "I can't say that I've seen too many guys with fuchsia highlights."

"Thanks. It's kind of a pain because the color fades too fast, especially when I swim so much."

Taryn giggled, and continued to fiddle with her instruments.

"I texted your dad. He said he's on his way."

"Okay."

When Mr. Brewer arrived, the doctor came in and explained the need for Flynn to remain as still as possible, but that his vitals looked good and if he remained quiet, then he wouldn't need to be sedated. He looked helpless and small, but I knew how brave Flynn really was. Through all of the doctor's discussion and explanation, Flynn only blinked. He didn't panic at the mention of burr holes in his skull or bleeding in his brain. Flynn held still and followed every instruction. He was a trouper.

Everything the doctor insisted upon was to keep Flynn from jarring his brain, and he understood that. He even joked about going to a rave party in the most deadpan voice I'd ever heard from him. The ninja nurse giggled and thanked him for restraining himself.

After the nurses had come and gone, and Kelly stopped by and left; his father went out in the hall to talk to the doctor, so it was just the two of us for a few minutes. I could see the city lights dotting the dark landscape as I closed his curtains for the night.

"Are you staying?" he asked very quietly.

I shook my head. "I want to, but I should probably go home. I haven't showered since yesterday morning."

Flynn smiled.

I walked over and stood by his bed. I glanced down where is hand rested and considered taking it. Before, when he'd first awoke, I could discount my handholding as a result of overabundant joy. Now, things might get awkward. Then he lifted two fingers as if he'd read my mind. I slipped my hand into his and sighed. I knew we needed to talk, but I didn't know where to start.

"Did you still get married?" he asked. "Or did the tree thing mess everything up?"

"Um, no. You really don't remember anything?" He'd told the doctor he couldn't remember the wedding or the tree, but I wasn't sure if that meant every detail or only some of them.

Flynn blinked and paused before answering, "Not really."

A cold dread sank to the pit of my stomach. He couldn't remember what he'd told me. Maybe it wasn't true. "And the last thing you remember was the limo ride?" Because that is what he told the doctor.

"No. I lied. I remember… you kissed me."

Hearing those words made me tingle all over. "Yeah, I did."

"Did you mean it?"

I nodded. "Of course I did. Don't you remember what happened after the kiss?"

"I think so. Did you really…" he let the pause linger, "because I thought I dreamed it."

"No. I did, and I meant that part too."

Flynn's gentle smile urged me to continue. I knew we were almost out of time because his father would be back any minute. I had to take a chance. If he couldn't remember saying what he'd said, then I had to say it for him. I stepped closer and fingered through his hair, smoothing it across his forehead, the way he liked to wear it. "Flynn, I have to say something before your dad comes back in."

He waited, and I felt his fingers squeezing mine for silent support. I was pretty sure he could see right through my nervousness to read my mind. Flynn's beautiful eyes beckoned the words from my lips. "I love you."

He sighed as if relieved of a huge weight or burden. He smiled, but it wasn't a happy smile. He was on the verge of crying, his hand trembled in mine, and then a tear escaped the corner of his eye.

"Flynn, don't cry. You're supposed to stay relaxed. What if the monitors go off?"

"You don't know how long I've waited to hear you say those words."

I lifted the corner of my mouth and turned his wording back around. "*You* have no idea how long I've been holding them in." He chuckled and cried at the same time. "Look, you gotta stop, or something's gonna start beeping loudly and beckon hordes of hospital staff. Okay?" I wiped his tears away and caressed his cheek.

"Okay. I will if you kiss me."

I raised an eyebrow and smirked. "Since when did you become so demanding?"

"Since the doctor mentioned burr holes."

"Good point."

Flynn and I stared at one another for a couple moments, and the incessant beeping of his monitors faded into the background. The lights in his already darkened room seemed to dim, as the light in his eyes brightened. I licked my lips. My heart quickened. This was real. No more barriers, no more excuses, no more lies, no more self-deception; I leaned over the bedrail and kissed my best friend.

***

May 3, 2014

By the time I got home, it was well after midnight. I didn't even bother getting undressed; I simply crawled into bed fully clothed. I curled onto my side, clutched my spare pillow, and closed my eyes. I had kissed Flynn.

The warmth that spread through me in those few minutes had been worth the wait. His lips were dry but enticing, and I knew that I'd get the chance to kiss him again in the morning.

I was rinsing my plate at the sink when my mother entered the kitchen Saturday morning. Originally, I hadn't planned on being home long enough to see anyone. I wanted to sleep and be on my merry way before my parents arose. Flynn had woken up and we'd kissed and giggled every time his dad had left the room, as if he knew something was up between us. But because it had been so late when I got home the night before, I was simply too tired to get up and leave before six. It was nine o'clock now, and everyone in my house was awake.

"Good morning. I didn't hear you come in last night. I thought maybe you'd spent the night at the hospital again."

"Morning. No. I came home around one. Flynn woke up." I stuck my plate in the dishwasher.

"Oh Zach, that's wonderful news."

"They are going to assess him today to figure out when he can go home, but last night the doctor on-call said he looked good."

"I'm so glad. Do you think he'd like it if I dropped by?"

My initial reaction was to scream No! But, thankfully, the realist in me replied, "Sure. You know he loves you."

Flynn had mentioned several times in the past that my mom was the only mother he had left since his real mom was gone. I knew he loved her. I also knew that his opinion of her would change if he ever found out the kinds of things my parents did behind closed doors. Hopefully, he'd never find out the specifics.

Although, in reality, her opinion of Flynn would surely change once she knew he was gay, that I was bisexual, and then my life would get exponentially worse. I knew I needed to break free of my controlling parents and the fear of my father, but I was still terrified of what they might do. Additionally, what if my dad hurt Flynn?

My mom wiped the crumbs off the counter meticulously. "Okay. I'll see if I can squeeze in a long lunch. Is Vic going today?"

"I think so. Mr. Brewer's been there every day. He said he does whatever work he needs Wi-Fi for at the office, and then he brings his schematics to Flynn's room. When I walked in on Monday, he had one sheet unrolled across Flynn's bed."

"Well that doesn't sound very safe. What of a doctor needed to draw blood or there was an emergency? He would have been in the way."

"Mom, chill. He told me he was pretending to consult Flynn on the planning. The nurse said he was talking out loud about all the measurements and details of the water management area he was working on. Mr. Brewer said it was fun. I think Flynn would have liked it. I bet he was listening the whole time wishing his dad did that with every project."

"I still think it was foolish." Negative, always negative.

I knew there was no correcting her, no pleasing her. She'd believe what she wanted, but I was glad Mr. Brewer had thought of ways to spend time with Flynn while working.

I slowly made my way out of the kitchen. I didn't want my mom to realize how uncomfortable I was around her, so I didn't rush. I stood in the archway and leaned casually on the wood frame. "I'm going to see Flynn soon. I'll probably be there whenever you show up. Text me and I'll meet you in the entrance."

"I can find my way around a hospital, Zach. I'm not helpless."

I held up my hands and surrendered any thought of responding to that rebuff. *Whatever.*

I headed to the café on the corner for a quick latté to go. I texted Mr. Brewer and he said he'd be there when visiting hours started. He said I didn't have to come, but I texted back that I would anyway. They were going to assess Flynn, and maybe let him go home. It seemed too soon to me, but apparently insurance companies dictate who stays and who goes home.

Keith and Kelly were sitting by the window in the café, but I couldn't duck out fast enough before Kelly called me over, "Zach." She waved and I plodded over. Keith slumped in his seat and Kelly held his hand. It would have been nice if they were a couple, but that was unrealistic.

"Are you sure this is wise?" I asked.

Kelly spoke frankly. "No, but we used to be friends before all this. I think we can be again, once everything settles down."

"Is that how Keith feels?" I settled my eyes on him and I saw his shoulders move a fraction. He was wearing that stupid beanie he always wore and I felt the sudden urge to snatch it from his head. "Are you going to visit him?"

Keith stabbed me with a glare and then looked away. Kelly answered, "No. I texted Mr. Brewer and he suggested we wait. He said Flynn might come home today, so we could come to their house later for a short visit."

"I told you, I'm not going," Keith hissed.

"He might like to see you," I said, hoping to sound positive.

"Oh yeah?" he said with a sarcastic edge to his voice. "Did he say that between giggles last night?"

"What?" His comment came out of left field.

"I was there, Zach. I showed up late in hopes that you'd left already. I peeked in the room and saw the two of you nose to nose, laughing and giggling, like little girls at a sleepover. I know when I'm not wanted."

I felt guilty for stealing Flynn away from him, but not enough to stop spending time with him. "I'm sorry."

"No, you're not! This whole damn thing is my fault. I should have never broken up with him. I should have waited until the right moment and punched you in the face for making him date a girl. But nooo, I'm the idiot who hoped he'd figure it out and come crawling back to me. Well, guess what? He never once came crawling back. Every single time we broke up it was me—the jackass—who slinked back to *him*. I'm not doing that ever again. He's with you, the pathetic excuse of a wounded soul, and I'm over it!" A sarcastic jibe from a scorned lover was pretty much the reaction I expected. Keith crossed his arms over his chest and sulked.

"Well then...." Kelly mused. "I guess it'll just be me stopping by later until Grace can get off work."

"I hate you," Keith spat at me under his breath. I couldn't fix the situation, so I stood there, uncomfortably waiting until he was done spitting venom at me. If Kelly thought we might all be friends again, I'd give it a try. I knew Flynn would want it.

Technically, I'd already won this fight since Flynn told me he loved me and I had said it back. Plus, I kissed him last night. I didn't need to be a dick and rub Keith's face in it. "I'm sorry." I reached out and touched his shoulder, but he jerked it away. I tried apologizing again. "Keith, I never meant for any of this to happen. I didn't know. I wish I knew years ago; things could have been different."

Keith met my gaze, but his eyes were not full of the anger and hatred I expected. He had tears welling in the corners. "I don't. If the two of you had hooked up in high school, before I'd met him, then—yeah—none of this would have happened, but he and I would never have happened either. I would never want to give up what we shared to avoid what I feel now. I loved him. I still love him. I only want him to be as happy as he made me."

"That's really big of you," I commented, attempting to be positive.

"I just don't want to be phased out," Keith mumbled.

"Phased out?"

"Of everyone's lives," he explained, looking at me without malice for the first time in a while. "Flynn is still my friend, even if we aren't together. I don't want to lose him completely. If he's with you, I'll deal, but I don't want to be excluded because things are uncomfortable for a while. Okay?"

Kelly leaned closer to Keith and asked, "Does breaking up with Carter have anything to do with this?"

Keith shushed her. He didn't want me knowing his business, yet he was way more mature about Flynn than I gave him credit for. I set my coffee cup down, and held out my hand. "No hard feelings?"

"Oh, there are hard feelings, I assure you," he asserted as he took my hand. "But I'm also smart enough not to alienate the one guy who could: one, beat the living daylights out of me if he put his mind to it, and two, keep me from seeing one of the best friends I've ever had. If you're willing to allow me to hate you forever, then we can be friends."

I chuckled and shook his hand. "You're really funny." I sat back, my chest still quaking with laughter. I also noted how he referred to me as being stronger than him without mentioning how I cowered in the cemetery. Keith was a good guy.

"Thank you, but I still hate you."

The juxtaposition of our status as frenemies amused me. I couldn't contain myself. I guess I saw the irony in it, or something and I let out a hearty chuckle. Kelly joined me. Whatever the reason, it felt good to laugh after so many days of sheer hell. Keith even cracked a smile. Flynn was going to be okay. Plus now, I kind of got the impression that Keith and I were going to be okay too, and I was glad.

We said our good-byes and I was en route to the hospital.

I got my badge from the visitor's desk and headed up to Flynn's room. Nurse Taryn was just leaving his room and greeted me with a smile. "You're in for a surprise." She winked as she passed me.

I wondered what she meant, and found out when I walked into his room and Flynn was standing next to another nurse and a doctor. "Hey buddy. Look at you!"

"I know, right?"

I grinned, but didn't want to get in their way. I walked around to the far side of the room and sat down. I listened as the doctor gave him some instructions about being careful not to hit his head or jar it in any way. After they left, I joined Flynn by his bed. He was allowed to sit up, but he still looked uncomfortable.

"Do you want another pillow for your back? I can ask the nurse."

"No. It's the mattress. I bet it's no better than the couch you slept on."

"No way. That bad?"

"Yeah. I can't wait to sleep in my own bed."

"Wait." I helped him adjust the blanket around his waist when I saw the edge had gotten caught in the bedrail.

"Thanks. It's freakin' cold in here."

"No problem. I can ask for another blanket it you want one."

"No. It's fine."

I stood there, awkwardly, speculating where our relationship sat in the grander scheme of things. Were we a couple? Should I kiss him? Should I worry about it? It's not like we'd discussed anything, and I wasn't sure when would be appropriate to bring it up. I felt like I should twiddle my thumbs or something as the silence between us dragged on. In reality it was probably only a minute or two, but those beeping sounds from the monitor made the lack of conversation even more noticeable.

"You okay?" he asked.

"Yup."

"Liar. Liar. Pants on fire."

I widened my eyes. "Shut. Up... Wow." I chuckled. Flynn totally took me back to elementary school with that one. He'd been hiding something of my mom's that he'd broken and I started singing "Liar, liar, pants on fire," while Nate ran inside to tell Mrs. Brewer. "Oh my God, Flynn, I can't believe you remember that."

"My brain's doing weird things. I can remember times from my childhood, but I can't remember everything I did the day you were supposed to get married."

My mirth died instantly. "Does the doctor know that?"

"Yeah. He said traumatic brain injuries manifest in different ways. I should be fine in a few days, although I may never remember the tree falling.

The pressure inside my skull is good, and that's the main thing. He also said that injuring my brain could affect me... sexually."

"He what?"

"Yeah." He rolled his eyes. "Imagine having that conversation with my dad in the room." Flynn chuckled. "Dad grunted, but didn't say anything. Apparently some men have trouble getting it up, while others make sexual innuendos at inappropriate times because their sex drive is altered; something to do with a part of the brain that regulates sexual activity. I don't know. What I got out of it was that brain injuries do weird things to your entire body."

"No shit." Most of that seemed obvious, but the sex thing boggled my mind.

"Scout's honor." He lifted three fingers, although he was never a Boy Scout.

When I couldn't take it anymore, I took a stab at conversation. "I saw Kelly at the coffee place you guys like."

"Oh yeah?"

"She was with Keith."

"Oh. How'd that go?"

"There was a moment when I thought he'd hit me, but he calmed down. I think we have an understanding."

"Is it the one where Keith understands you could kick the shit out of him, and where you understand that hitting my ex-boyfriend would make me want to tie you down and pull out your pubic hairs one by one?"

I stepped back in surprise, protectively covering my groin with one hand. "Ouch. I don't remember you being so vindictive."

"You've been doing college stuff, and I've changed."

"I'll say you have. You're assertive, and creatively sadistic." I had to admit the pubic-hair thing was funny in a sick and painful kind of way.

"I try. So, Keith was okay?"

"Yeah. He's fine. He said he wants you to be happy, and he doesn't want to lose you as a friend just because you two aren't together."

"He said that?"

"Yup."

He nodded and looked at his lap, adjusting and readjusting his blanket. "I'm glad."

"Are you? You're fidgeting."

"No I'm not."

I grabbed his hand. "Then stop messing with the blanket."

"I feel bad knowing I hurt him."

"I feel bad, too." I wrapped my fingers around his and slid my thumb back and forth over his hand. "Gwendolyn and I argued about it. I know I hurt her."

"Fuck. I forgot about her. What did you say to her? What did she do? Did she throw things at you?"

"No projectiles. Lots of crying. She's pretty much on the same page as Keith, she wants me to be happy."

"Do you think we can be?"

"I hope so. Although I have a feeling there's a lot about you I need to discover. I want to get to know the bossy side of Flynn." I loved having his hand in mine.

He chuckled. "I'm not bossy."

"Okay. Do you want to take orders?"

"No."

"Not even if I tell you to kiss me?" It had worked when Flynn said it to me. I figured I could try the same tactic and see where it led.

"Nope." He smirked a challenge at me. I could tell he was waiting for me to make the first move. He wasn't going to budge.

I saw through it, but I still gave in. "You jerk." I leaned closer and kissed him. I felt his lips vibrate as he chuckled. I kissed him through his amusement, and then pulled back. "You're an asshole."

I caressed his cheek, but the nurse came in again. I winked and made faces at him while she did her thing.

After she left, I asked, "So your dad was here when the doctor checked on you?"

"Yeah. You only just missed him. He had to leave for work. He said he's going to try to get tomorrow off so he can take me home."

"You're going home tomorrow? Kelly mentioned maybe tonight."

"Yeah, I know. Dad said he'd call her later and tell her to come here instead of my house. The doctor wanted to monitor me one more day for vomiting and blurred vision. As long as things look good, I go home in the morning. I was told to continue resting. Still no TV, no texting, no video games, and no reading, but it is better than being here. I don't sleep very well here."

"Hey, you were asleep for days. I like having you a awake for a change."

He squeezed my hand.

We stared into each other's eyes for a few moments, and I could feel the sexual tension brewing as his eyes darkened with lust. It wasn't as if we were going to get it on at the hospital, but at the same time, I think we both knew the wait to act on our feelings had been long enough. His eyes dropped to my lips and that's all it took.

I dove in and kissed him soundly, pressing my lips firmly to his and swiping my tongue out to taste him. "Mmm, minty," I whispered between kisses.

Flynn grinned. "I brushed my teeth while I was allowed out of bed." He kept kissing me and teasing me with his tongue as he spoke. "I was hoping we'd get a chance to do this." He reached up and held the side of my neck. "All I keep thinking about is that kiss before your wedding." He leaned back on the pillows and I followed him down. The bedrail was pressing against my groin and it pinched, but not enough to make me stop kissing. Until I leaned over that last inch.

"Ouch!" I jumped back, readjusting myself.

"You okay?"

"Damn bed. It pinched my balls."

Flynn started laughing.

"Shut up. Let me pinch your balls and see how you like it," I joked, but his eyes darkened and he raised an eyebrow.

Flynn moved the blanket aside. "Okay."

I looked down. He was in a typical hospital gown, which was tied in the back and only reached halfway down his thighs. I couldn't see his dick, but the tented gown made his situation clear. "Is this that 'sexually inappropriate' thing the doctor warned you about?" I hoped he wasn't serious.

"Maybe. But you're the one who blew me."

Those words did funny things to my stomach. It quivered and flipped, and I felt a rush of heat flood my groin. He was right. I had made the first move. Something in Flynn's eyes now, though, was unlike anything I'd ever seen before. He was so… licentious. I secretly hoped it wasn't from the concussion, because it would be fun to explore this side of him.

"You know we shouldn't, this is a hospital."

"So? Examine me." He began slowly pulling his gown up and my eyes followed the hem every inch of the way. He had beautiful thighs, sleek and muscular, and I wanted nothing more than to touch and kiss my way up from his knees.

My mouth watered. "Flynn."

"I want you to suck me," Flynn whispered.

He got his wish.

Minutes later, my worst nightmare became reality as a gasp came from the doorway. It wasn't Taryn, or Flynn's father; it was Gwendolyn... and my mom.

I jumped back as Flynn hastily covered himself, but it was too late. Gwendolyn's gaping mouth and my mother's green complexion as she covered her mouth told me they had seen plenty. The only saving grace was Amelia poking her head around the corner *after* Flynn had already adjusted the blanket.

I swallowed hard. "Mom."

"Oh, God," she gagged as she left the room in a hurry.

"What's wrong?" Amelia asked. She looked at me, at Flynn, at Gwendolyn, and finally at me again. She stepped closer. "What's on your... face?" Her eyes went wide and she fled the room almost as quickly as my mother had.

I heard Flynn quietly explain, "You have cum on your chin."

"Oh shit!" I wiped my cheek and chin with my hand and found copious amounts of Flynn's juice smeared there. I hadn't realized how much dribbled out as I swallowed, but my first try hadn't been as easy as porn made it look.

"Wow," Gwendolyn commented, still standing there—stunned. "I can't believe I just saw that. I mean, I knew you were going to explore things with Flynn, but that...." She rubbed her forehead and leaned against the wall. "Holy shit, Zach. I can't believe you would do that... here!"

I went over to her and reached for her shoulder, but she pulled away.

"Don't. Don't touch me." Gwendolyn turned away and walked from the room.

I looked over at Flynn. "I want to stay, but I gotta go take care of this. Kelly will be by later, right? Tell her to keep me informed."

"Yeah. Go."

I took a step toward the door, hesitated, and then jumped back over to his side. I had to kiss him again before I left. "Thanks for understanding."

Flynn smiled and touched my face. "Hey, it'll be all right. Trust me." We kissed again, and again, before I pulled away to head for the door. "And you may want to chew some gum," Flynn added with a devious wink. "You taste like cum."

I laughed weakly and grumbled, "Gee, thanks. Asshole."

I only made it into the hall before, to my utter embarrassment, I heard him call after me with an even more audacious comment. "I'll be an asshole any day, if you promise to lave me all over with that wicked tongue."

I dashed back in and gawked at him. Flynn merely shrugged and asked, "What?"

"You! I'm not sure I want your brain back to normal. Damn." I rubbed my bulging crotch. I had to admit I liked this side of Flynn.

He laughed. "Get out!"

I swear he looked as though he would have jumped out of bed to shove *me* up against the wall if he hadn't had a concussion.

I wasn't sure where Gwendolyn had run off to, but I figured my mother would be in the parking lot if she hadn't already left. I ran as far as I could down one hall and then took the stairs, because I could leap down the last six on each floor. My mom and Amelia would have to wait for the elevator. I scanned the parking lot and saw them at the far end, so I sprinted.

"Mom!" I yelled, attempting to catch her attention. "Mom, let me explain," I pleaded as soon as I was near enough to hold a conversation.

"I am not talking about this here." She opened the car door without looking at me.

"But Mom—"

She snapped, "Not here, Zachary." She held her hand up like a stop sign, either to halt my words or to symbolically separate the two of us. Either way, it worked. I stopped.

Amelia stood by the other door, half-in and half-out as though unsure of what to do. She wasn't looking at me, either. What was I going to do about her?

"Please let me explain."

"Explain what?" she asked, leveling her hard gaze on me. In all my years of fearing her wrath, this was probably the darkest I had ever seen her expression, and suddenly I wasn't so sure I could bring myself to tell her.

"Explain... that... I...."

"That you defiled yourself with that filthy whore in there?" she growled.

I might have cowered if she was saying that solely about me, but for her to speak so harshly toward Flynn wasn't fair. I pulled my shoulders back and replied confidently. "Flynn's gay, Mom, he's not filthy and he certainly isn't a whore. I can't believe you would say that about him. I thought you loved him."

"After what I saw, I think you're both disgusting, and you deserve whatever God has in store for you."

She tried closing the door once she got into her seat, but I grabbed it and held it open. "Mom! Just listen to me. I'm sorry. Okay? What happened to tolerance? I thought you told me our church was embracing tolerance after the Prop 8 thing in California." She'd told me in 2008, but I remembered what I heard.

"Tolerance?" she shrieked. "Tolerance is living my life and allowing others to live theirs, despite their sin, until we can convince them of their wicked indiscretions. Tolerance does not, however, include watching my son commit indecent and shameful acts before God, and pretending I'm not sickened to my very core. I will not sit idly by and watch you throw away your salvation for nothing. Now let go of the door!"

I ignored her and held it firmly. "Mom, I'm not!" I glanced over at Amelia who had slid into her seat and had said nothing so far. "Tell her Amelia." When she looked out the opposite window, I turned my attention back to my mother, who had turned the engine over. "God isn't like that, Mom! All I ever heard growing up was how much I had to do to please God, but He's not like that." I had to tell her in one, short, theological elucidation that my family's beliefs were wrong. "It's not about *our* works, but about what Jesus already did."

"Blasphemy!"

"Haven't you ever heard of the word 'grace' before? Or mercy for that matter?"

"I won't sit here and be lectured. Now let go of that door, or I'll back out of the space with it open. I can't wait to hear what your father has to say about this!"

My father. The thought sent chills through me. I stepped back and released the door. My mom sped away and left me in the parking lot shaking at the thought of what my father might do.

Chapter 27

May 6, 2014: Tectonic Plate Movements

The past few days were a blur, and really, I could probably say the same about every moment since Flynn had woken up. It was all a blur. Fuzzy lines and washed out colors, running together and blocking out the vivid images that any kid between two and twenty-two should never have to face. The blur kept me moving forward to find light, and the light I found was in his eyes. At least I told myself that.

Flynn. He was mine.

"Hey buddy. Look at you!" I said.

"I know, right?"

After the doctors and nurses left, I joined Flynn by his bed. We touched. We kissed. We explored the possibilities until my mother walked into the room and Amelia spotted cum on my face.

Amelia. I felt sick about the whole situation. Gwendolyn called me on Sunday while Flynn and I were in the car. Her family had caught a flight back west Saturday night, but as soon as they'd gotten home, Amelia had taken a bottle of sleeping pills. After she'd regained consciousness in the hospital, she'd blamed Flynn for cheating on her. He'd been asleep in the back of the car and I hadn't had the balls to tell him.

It wasn't his fault. It was mine. I deserved punishment.

I glanced at him where he slept, next to me. He was supposed to sleep. Rest and quiet were what the doctor ordered. No one recommended a random seven-hour drive to New York. No. That was all me. I panicked when Mr. Brewer helped me off the front lawn. He told Flynn to... He told Flynn.... Suddenly the blurry lines became sharply focused.

My father swung a baseball bat at me and I ducked. He stood on the porch, where Clark had taken the bat from his hands, yelling, "No son of mine is going to commit wicked, indecent acts and get away with it!" He flipped out as soon as I'd gotten home from the hospital. I'd avoided my parents Saturday night, but Amy told me to take a stand. She said she'd back me.

"Stop, Dad!" Amy screamed when Dad chased me through the house taking swings, denting walls, smashing furniture, and breaking picture frames.

Her screams didn't help. Dad was hell-bent on setting me straight and beating the sins right out of me. Bisexuality was a perversion and I needed cleansing. With a baseball bat. I grabbed the front door handle and pulled, but Clark was on the other side. My mother had phoned him.

"If it isn't the walking abomination himself," my brother said snidely.

I shoved him out of the way before my father caught up. Clark tripped me and I stumbled down the front steps.

Flynn had comforted me when I finally let myself cry. We had made it into the hotel room, shut the door, and I released the biggest sob ever. He held me as my shoulders quaked. He rubbed my back and moved me over to the bed when my legs wobbled. I swear we sat there for hours, clutching each other, before I laid back on the mattress and fell asleep. When I woke up the next morning, he was gazing out the window. He grinned, but I could tell he didn't want to be here. He wanted to be home with his dad.

Mr. Brewer—my hero.

"What's going on over here?" Mr. Brewer asked as he raced to my side.

I heard Clark talking to my dad, as Mr. Brewer helped me to my feet. "Give it to me, father. Let me teach him a lesson. You don't need to dirty your hands for the likes of him. He's not your son, I am."

"Not my son," my father echoed.

"He's got a bat," I warned Mr. Brewer.

I looked into the eyes of a man who'd been as close to a second father to me as my dad had been to Flynn. Only this time, his eyes weren't weary from over-work or hazy from excessive alcohol, they were hard and focused, full of fire and rage. He'd never been the recipient of my father's wrath, so I feared that his good intentions would be for nothing.

"I don't care if he's got a chainsaw, he'll never take a swing at you again."

Clark took the bat from my dad and strutted toward us. "Nothing but family business, Mr. Brewer. You might as well go home to your faggot son and leave this loser to me," he instructed.

"No. I think he's going home with me," Mr. Brewer said, grabbing my arm.

Clark ripped me free from his grasp and hurled me to the side where I fell face down on the sidewalk, right by the curb. The baseball bat hit my hip with the force of a Mack truck, thundering an undulating torrent of pain down my leg as I curled and tried to shield myself from another swing.

Mr. Brewer hoisted me to my feet in seconds and shoved me toward Flynn's car, inserting his own body between my brother and me. Mr. Brewer yelled, "Get him out of here!"

I stumbled, but I took the keys from Flynn's hand as he furrowed his brow. "You aren't allowed to drive," I explained in the front seat as we sped down Willis Street, just as a cop car pulled up to my house with its lights flashing.

"The cop took the bat from Clark's hand," Flynn said, describing what he could see as he glanced behind us.

Flynn had been in the hospital a week. In that time, I'd engaged in more meaningful conversations with Mr. Brewer than I'd ever had with my own father. Mr. Brewer listened. He also noticed the bruise on my arm from when my father had grabbed me and asked how I'd gotten it. I wanted to lie because I'd lied about every injury I'd gotten my whole life, but after everything with Flynn, I realized I couldn't hide anymore. The time for hiding was over, so I told him. He'd suggested I talk to a counselor.

Flynn had said the same thing.

Maybe when we went back to Maryland I'd stay with my sister and see about a counselor or a therapist; anyone who could help me sort out the tumultuous mess I had squirming around in my head. Maybe they'd be able to explain what I kept doing wrong to make him act like that.

In the meantime, I had Flynn to soothe my pain.

I reached over and ran my hand along Flynn's bare skin: his shoulder, his back, the curve of his ass as I nudged the sheet down with my roving fingers. He sighed. I'd never seen a more lovely form than Flynn's. He was perfect. Strike that, nearly perfect as I could see my version of perfection being him on one side and Gwendolyn on my other. Flynn was the perfect *male* form. If I was completely honest with myself, I wanted both of them in my bed, although I wasn't sure how Flynn would view a threesome which included a woman. I'd have to ask when he woke up fully. Gwendolyn, well, she hadn't been too happy the last time I'd seen her, but our talks in the desert suggested she may be open to it.

"Are you sure you want to?" I asked Flynn after removing his shirt.

"What do you think?" he replied, groping my crotch. "I was so horny at the hospital, I asked you to suck me off. We aren't coming all the way to New York, staying in a swanky hotel your father is unwittingly paying for, and not sleeping together. If you're attracted to me like you think you are, I say drop your pants and show me that cock."

I knew this wasn't the real Flynn talking. He was off. Concussion-messing-with-my-digression type of off. "Are you sure you're up for it?" I asked, worried he'd over-do something and end up in the hospital again.

He removed his pants and crawled under the covers. "Doc said no texting, no TV, no roller coasters, no driving; but sex I can do as long as you don't throw me around, or fuck me so hard my head collides with the headboard." He winked at me and ran his tongue over his teeth.

I dove onto the bed.

I never imagined it would feel this good. Finally being with him after so many years of suppressed attraction was like a trip to Candy Land or Fantasy Island. Flynn. My closest friend and confidant now turned lover. He'd been so careful with me, prepping me and caressing me, I nearly exploded right away when he pressed inside. Later, when I had sunk into him, gazing into his eyes and kissing his sweet lips, my entire body hummed like an idling jet engine three seconds from takeoff.

I kissed his arm and covered him back up. My beautiful man needed some rest before I woke him up for more loving. I heard a knock on the door and pulled my jeans on quickly before I answered it. I'd ordered room service because fucking Flynn made me ravenous. No, wait… I shouldn't say that. We'd made love. I smiled. Yeah, that was more romantic.

I almost jumped out of my skin when I opened the door and the seriously hot bellhop was holding my tray.

"I saw that look," Flynn told me as we meandered through Central Park.

We'd just passed a little footbridge lined with yellow flowers. I thought it would be a nice spot to revisit with a picnic lunch sometime in the future. "What are you talking about?" I asked. Surely he hadn't seen me cruising that guy.

"His name's Carlos."

I snapped a look of surprise in his direction. "How the heck do you know that?"

Flynn did this thing he does where he blushes and looks down like he's shy or something, only he's not shy. I've known him all my life and "shy" is not part of his description. Coy and playful, but not shy. I thought he was adorable. "He's the bellhop in the hotel who showed us where the elevator was to the west tower. He checked you out as you pressed the up button."

"He did?"

"Try not to sound too excited. I thought you were here with me."

"Oh, I am, but this is the first time I've ever known about a guy looking at me like that."

"I've looked at you like that."

"When?"

"Two thousand six, after you got out of my pool and put your pants back on."

"Flynn, I was fourteen. I'm sure I look nothing like that now."

"No. You're about three inches longer and two inches thicker." He waggled his eyebrows and we kept walking.

I had to be blushing!

I stepped into the hallway and held the door cracked as we spoke. "Hi."

"Hello. We have to stop meeting like this. People will talk," he joked. His nametag read Carlos, so Flynn's memory of Monday afternoon was correct.

I grinned. "Yeah, I guess. Had I known it'd be you bringing up my bowl of tomato soup, I'd have ordered something like fifty hot wings or the habanera quesadillas."

His eyes twinkled. "Trying to impress me?"

"Maybe."

"Does your boyfriend know you are this flirtatious? Or do you typically ask others to join in? I might be persuaded."

Shocked? Um, yes, that was me. My balls even shifted. I was into threesomes for sure, or rather, the idea of threesomes. Flynn? He seemed jealous when I'd seen Carlos earlier this evening in the lobby. I told Carlos, "He's not exactly my boyfriend. He's my best friend, but we're still figuring out the rest."

He nodded. "Mm-hmm. Seemed to me it was all figured out from the way you looked at one another. His hunger was like a lion circling a baby antelope."

He made me chuckle. "He's got a concussion. The doctor said some patients temporarily lose the ability to control sexual impulses. His 'regulatory center' was damaged, or something. I don't know. Flynn's been extra rambunctious, but I don't expect it to last. "

"Too bad."

"Yeah." I took the tray and handed him the money. "Anyway, thank you for my soup."

He smirked and nodded. "Have a good night."

I slowly backed into the room and quietly shut the door.

Flynn remained asleep, curled on his side, hugging a pillow.

"Hey, Dad," Flynn answered the phone as we waited in traffic by the Lincoln Tunnel. "Yeah, we're fine. Zach said his hip throbs, but he can move it. Yes, he can feel his toes."

I grinned and nodded. Flynn didn't need to ask me simple questions to know all the correct answers.

A car honked somewhere off to my left. Traffic was insane. What possessed me to drive to New York when we hopped in the car, I did not know. Mr. Brewer yelled to get out, so I did. New York was only a three to

four hour ride by bus, so how come it was taking us seven hours? Traffic!
Freaking traffic. Eight thousand cars and busses trying to go from six lanes
of traffic into two in order to go through the tunnel. Who designed this?

"Dad, I'm fine. I slept most of the way here. No, no vomiting. No
blurred vision. Yes, I'll call again once we get to the hotel. I love you too."
Flynn set the phone down. "My dad said the police took Clark into custody.
Apparently the cop that pulled up as we were leaving saw what happened.
He was on his way to the jail, one block over, and saw you tumble down the
steps. He saw the bat in Clark's hand and circled his squad car back
around."

"Oh wow." I wasn't in the least bit sorry for my brother.

"Dad said you might want to stop by the station this week and make
a formal statement. The police have your cell number."

"Okay."

"He wants to know how long we'll be gone?"

"I don't know. What do you think's good? My mom walked in on me
sucking you off. Gwen saw it. Amelia... I think she only figured it out by
context. I don't want to go back today."

"How about we stay until Wednesday? That will give them a couple
days to cool down and me time out of this car."

"Sounds good."

Wednesday morning came all too fast. Check out wasn't until
eleven. I had time to gaze at Flynn. We'd made it out of bed enough to see
Central Park and walk around the museum and the zoo, but mostly we slept.
Sex was good, but after an entire day of exploration and penetration, it
seemed to me his sex drive was declining, as was mine.

Something in his eyes....

Flynn was watching me when I woke up. Silently. His eyes danced
over my face, but they didn't contain the hunger I had seen every day since
Saturday. I didn't care to name the emotion I thought I saw.

"Come here," I urged, sliding my arm under his neck.

Flynn snuggled against my side and rested his head on my chest.

"I love you," I said, needing to hear myself say it once more.

"I love you too."

His hushed response settled over me like hearing "I'm fine," when
the person was really dying of some dreadful disease, but couldn't admit it. I

knew he wasn't lying, I always seemed to know, but I also knew he wasn't telling the whole truth.

"Flynn?"

"Yeah?"

I hugged him closer and tighter to me and kissed his hair. "Your brain is back to normal, isn't it?"

"Yeah. What gave it away?"

I rubbed his arm. "Well, you haven't groped me in about six hours, so I figured…." I let the sentence work itself out. Flynn would know what I meant.

Flynn rolled me over and kissed down my spine. The sensation of tenderness thrilled me almost as much as when he sucked my balls for so long I thought I'd die waiting for him to take my dick into his mouth. He seemed insatiable the last couple days. When he wasn't sleeping, Flynn sucked me, fucked me, and begged me to do all the same things to him.

His tongue in my crack shocked me. His lips on my anus made me shudder.

Flynn could not get enough and I matched his pace with gusto.

I flipped him... gently because of his head... and pressed in easily. Our bodies were lubed-up like pigs at a hog catching contest, so slipping inside him came effortlessly.

"Dude, are you coming already?" I asked. His erection was dripping huge globs of cum with my every thrust.

"I... oh, God... you're…" Flynn struggled to explain, panting between words. "You're hitting... my... prostate... oh, Zach... Fuck... So good. Ohhhh. Fuck!"

I watched and sure enough, with every thrust forward, semen dribbled out of the end of his cock. I'd never seen anything like it. It was as if I squeezed his prostate gland in my hand like a teat on a cow or something. I held that same angle and jutted harder. Flynn cried out and arched his back. He shoved the pillow off the bed and grabbed at the headboard.

"More!" he begged. "Zach!" He slapped the mattress.

But somewhere between screaming my name and actually coming, Flynn had opened his eyes and looked into my face. He was panting and shuddering, but also drifting away.

Flynn looped his knee over my leg and kissed my chest. "Yeah. I think I'm back to normal. Is that all right?"

Disappointing? Maybe. Nonetheless, I knew there was more to it. "It's fine. Do you regret anything?" I asked.

"No," he said right away. "Not at all. I found my best friend again."

"Yeah," I agreed.

Flynn stroked my collarbone and caressed my neck and chin. He was exploring, but not as a salacious lover. More like one who had to say good-bye and needed to memorize me before his train left.

"This isn't going to work, is it?" My words pained my heart, but I knew the answer before he said it.

"No," he whispered. "Too many years. I've changed, only I didn't realize it until now."

"Is it Keith?"

"Yes."

Flynn rolled off my side and pulled the sheet up with both hands.

I rolled, too, and rested on my elbow, gazing down at him. We'd gotten to that place where honesty was paramount and I wasn't going to trade that even to save my own heart. "Can we still be friends? Because I don't know how I'd—"

He silenced me with a kiss pressed firmly over my intended words. "Don't even think it," he said. Flynn rested his head back down and touched my face tenderly. "I will always love you. The bond between us doesn't make sense, but it's stronger than anything I've ever felt for another person. You feel like a part of my own body, and my own mind. I lost that connection for so long and now that it's back I'm not pushing you away because I don't love you. I do. With all my heart."

"But?" There was always a "but."

"But I'm not *in love* with you," Flynn sighed. "Had we continued after that first kiss, then maybe things would be different. You were my first crush. You were this beautiful fantasy that visited my dreams for years, but then I changed."

"You mean you met Keith."

He nodded. "He fills a different need in me. You're more like a symbolic twin. We share the same thoughts, we need each other to survive, you've got my back without prompt, but we lead separate lives. Does that make sense?"

I leaned in and kissed him. I needed to taste his lips and feel his breath on my mouth. I flicked my tongue out and Flynn licked it, eyes wide open, boldly assuring me this hadn't been a mistake. This was our good-bye to a brief respite of ravenous bliss I would never forget, nor would I ever regret. I rubbed my nose over his and tasted his lips one more time.

"I needed to find you, and I have," he mused, smiling into my heart.

Flynn pointed to the sea otters and we headed over. The New York Zoo sounded like a fun distraction after lunch. I remembered seeing the sea otters many times at the Baltimore Zoo.

"Do you remember when your mom took us to the zoo and that otter had a bottle cap?" he asked, leaning on the rail outside the viewing area.

I thought a minute. "Oh yeah! And he ran around with it in his teeth when another one wanted it?"

"Yeah," he laughed. "Then another one showed up and it seemed like they were playing 'keep away' from the little one."

We both shared a hearty chuckle.

Flynn stepped closer after the laughing died down and kissed me right there in the park. No hesitation, not furtive glances to see if anyone noticed. He kissed me and wrapped his arms around my neck and we showed our affection for one another unabashedly publicly.

I felt free for the first time in my life.

"Are you going back to him then?" I asked, fighting against my heart's desire to run away from the answer he was bound to give.

"I don't know. I miss him so much, but I'm also hurt. He's seeing this other guy because I was too stupid to realize how much I loved him until it was too late. He didn't visit me in the hospital, which shows just how much—"

"He visited you," I interjected. Keith and I might have a mutual hatred going on, but I wasn't going to disrespect the guy who had the balls to step aside for me.

"When?" Flynn was very obviously shocked. His expression and voice told me that.

"A bunch of times."

Flynn sat up, and I followed so we could talk face-to-face.

"*When*, when?" he asked again, urgently. "Because I didn't know."

"All of us watched over you. Me, Kelly, Grace, and Keith. Whenever your dad couldn't be there, we took turns."

His chest was heaving, and his voice hitched. "Keith did?"

"Yeah, Keith was there."

"Then how come he didn't come after I'd woken up? He didn't want me to know, did he? I bet his boyfriend was jealous." Flynn knotted the sheets in his fists and one tear ran down his cheek.

I wiped it away. "No. He stepped aside for me."

He gave me an odd look. "For you? Why you? What are you talking about?"

"We talked. Several times, actually. Keith had it in his head that you were in love with me, so he said he'd step aside if I was willing to give you want you always wanted."

"Why the hell would he do that?" Flynn raised his voice.

"Because he loves you, and wants you to be happy."

Flynn snorted, but it sounded more like disgust than humor. "He's got a stupid way of showing it. If he loved me, then why the hell would he date Carter Langley?"

Yup. Disgust and cynicism. I felt the need to set his mind at ease because I remembered that name from when I'd seen Keith and Kelly at the café. "I remember Kelly mentioning Carter, and Keith didn't want her to say anything in front of me. I'm pretty sure she questioned why they broke up."

"They did? Why didn't she tell me? When were you talking to Keith? He hates you."

I rubbed my jaw when the haunting memory of his fist made it ache. "I know, but I think we came to a mutual understanding. Keith hates me, and I promised to make you happy. Only, I think happiness is me walking away."

Flynn's tears burst forth as he fell against my chest. I held him tight, because that was all I knew how to do.

"I want to go home," he sobbed. "I miss my dad. I want to hold Keith. I need to sleep in *my* bed."

I chuckled. "I love you, Flynn. Oh, God." I chuckled as I squeezed him. "I'll take ya home."

We were in the lobby when my phone rang. "Hello?"

It was Mr. Brewer. "How long until you leave?"

"Um, we're checking out now. Flynn's fine. Do you want to talk to him? I think his phone died."

"No. Have him call once you are in the car heading back. I just wanted to let you know there are some things going on here you need to be prepared for."

We stepped up to the counter and Flynn pointed to the line I needed to sign on, while I continued my conversation with his dad. "Like what?"

"Thank you for staying with us. This was left at the desk for you," the woman behind the checkout desk said, handing Flynn an envelope.

He opened it and grinned, handing me a piece of paper with the name Carlos Rodriguez written on it with his phone number listed beneath.

"Shut up," I told Flynn, winking.

"Yeah," Mr. Brewer continued. "I'm not sure how much to tell you because I don't want you to panic."

"My sister told me they took Clark into custody. I called the police station last night and told them I'd be in later today to talk to someone. It's fine."

"No. That's not it." I heard him take a deep breath over the phone. "Zach, I don't know how to say this, but your parents moved."

I stopped short at the revolving door leading out of the hotel. "What? How can they be moving? No one asked me. No one said anything. It can't be because I made one mistake."

"Zach... *moved*." He emphasized the D. "This morning around four o'clock, two moving trucks pulled up to your house. In a matter of hours they loaded up everything. I saw probably twelve men out my window shuffling in and out of the house, carrying boxes and furniture; loading the trucks. By ten o'clock, they pulled away. Then a lady walked out front with a 'For Sale' sign. I walked over and looked through the window. It's empty. Completely vacant."

"Holy shit." I lowered the phone and gaped at Flynn who waited patiently for me to tell him what was going on. "My family up and moved out without me. They're gone."

Flynn's jaw dropped. "What?"

The valet could not get the car to us fast enough.

Chapter 28

May 7, 2014: Home Sweet Home

Dread loomed before me like a black thundercloud of imminent pain; only this was unlike anything I'd endured in the past. Physical pain, I understood. My father had beaten me in various ways since childhood, but the emotional distress I felt as I drove home filled me with anxiety and fear, swirling around my thoughts like taunting judges sending a convicted murderer to the electric chair.

I could hardly breathe in my distress.

I gripped the steering wheel tightly, and prayed I wouldn't miss my exit. I'd already backtracked after getting gas and taking the wrong ramp, but thankfully Flynn was sleeping in the back seat and hadn't noticed.

I glanced in the rearview mirror. He was still out cold.

I felt bad for Flynn, and guilty over dragging him into this situation. He didn't need more stress. He'd *just* gotten home from the hospital and here I'd dragged him all the way to New York in order to escape my life. *What was I thinking?* I hadn't been, of course. I'd sped off in a blur that day, and I was in the same sort of haze driving back.

Poor Flynn. He didn't deserve this. He didn't deserve *me*. I was a horrible friend; perhaps that's why he'd chosen Keith? I paused and put my blinker on to change lanes. No, that wasn't it. He wasn't the only one in that bed who'd felt it. He and I had desire by the bushel, but our chemistry lacked the substance to ignite our souls. *But God, were we passionate those few days.*

The taste of Flynn's body and the feel of his hands on my skin were exquisitely delicious. Our lovemaking was not lacking fervor, that's for sure. Flynn told me he hadn't regretted a thing and I needed to believe him. Even after we'd decided not to commit as a couple, he still kissed me several times and hadn't pulled away whenever I touched him. The closeness we'd always enjoyed as children and younger teens was rekindled into a familiar and relaxed affection I could only hope would remain after he and Keith got back together. *If* they got back together.

I wasn't a huge fan of Keith Leppo, but he had been kind that day in the cemetery. I knew he wanted to keep pounding me into oblivion, but I saw tears in his eyes when he stopped suddenly, and offered me a tissue for my bloody nose. Keith was a good guy. I guess I couldn't blame Flynn for falling for him. I'd taken so long confessing my own feelings I knew there was a strong possibility when I finally was able to, that Flynn wouldn't feel the same way. The end result, however, was better than I expected when I saw that look in his eyes that said, "this isn't real." I knew it as soon as we landed on the bed that our time together wouldn't last. Something in our desperation, I guess, which seeped into my subconscious, warned me of the forthcoming result. Flynn made love as if heading off to war, but when the sun arose, he still lay in my arms kissing me tenderly and whispering silly memories of our childhood.

I was foolish to think he'd change and push me away. Flynn would always be mine.

As I sat at a red light, finally off the highway and closer to home, I picked up the notepad Flynn had been scribbling on before he felt dizzy and needed to lie down. He'd written a poem—a love poem, but not for me. His words were eloquent and heartfelt, and jealousy rose quickly in my already emotional state. Logic, of course, stepped onto its soapbox and preached truth to my foggy idealism. Flynn loved me with all the love he could, and I would be an idiot to toss it aside because it wasn't epic "Gone with the Wind" style romantic love.

The book of Proverbs says, "A man of many companions may come to ruin, but there is a friend who sticks closer than a brother."

My own brother came at me with a baseball bat. Lucky for me he swings like a twelve-year-old girl and, because I'd had way worse from my father, the hit I took to my hip wasn't debilitating. I was bruised, and the ache was deep enough that I still felt it three days later, but I was confident I wouldn't need to see a doctor. I knew I'd live.

But Flynn… Flynn was certainly closer to me than my brother ever would be. He knew me inside and out. My thoughts, my joys, my hurt, my texture, my taste, my sounds, my longings, my fears, my weakness, and my secrets; everything was his. I emptied myself into Flynn in more ways than one these last couple days, and as we drove home, I had to trust I'd find someone out there who would fill my heart as completely as Keith filled Flynn's. I couldn't say "soul" because I believed we shared a part of each other's soul. It was more than that; we were two sides of one complete person.

Maybe that's why I originally desired a threesome with Gwen. Gwendolyn filled a different need in me, so when Flynn explained his feelings toward Keith, I understood them.

"Are we almost there?" Flynn asked shakily from the back seat.

I glimpsed his reflection in the mirror. "Yeah, maybe twenty minutes."

Flynn lifted his head and then lay back down. "I don't feel so good."

Guilt was always ready with a knife to gut me. "I'm sorry, buddy. I really am. The good news is that it's taking less time on our way back. About five hours."

Flynn murmured, but didn't talk.

I whispered, "Please Lord, just let me get him home."

As I pulled up to the curb in front of Flynn's house, my memories flashed back like buzzing flies I wanted to swat away, but they were too persistent. My dad—raising the wooden bat and swinging it at me because my mom had told him what I did with Flynn. Him swinging it—except I ducked, and he'd hit the drywall instead, knocking a chunk to the floor. Me running—ducking another swing and bolting through the front door in a desperate need to flee the same way Amy had when he'd pushed her down the steps.

I turned the engine off.

I got out of the car, left Flynn sleeping in the backseat, and walked slowly over to my front lawn.

I could hear Clark, as if he stood here now, hissing his disgust when he told my father I wasn't his son. He called Flynn a faggot and came after me right before....

I turned, feeling a presence behind me. It was Mr. Brewer.

"I'm sorry, son," he offered, holding out his arms.

I fell into his embrace and sobbed. My pain and grief and hurt couldn't be kept inside any longer. I'd been strong for Flynn's sake while we were away, but being here, the place that should be home sweet home, brought the painful memories of everything I'd been through out in a rush. He pulled me into a tight bear hug, patting my back and whispering, "It's okay. I've got you. You're not alone."

After a few minutes, when I'd cried out all there was to release, Mr. Brewer loosened his grip on my body. I looked into his kind eyes and gave a weak smile of gratitude. "Thank you."

He nodded and patted my shoulder. "They may have left you, but I haven't. I've always felt like you were family. You and Flynn spent plenty of time running through my back yard, destroying the rose bushes, and jumping off the porch roof onto the trampoline before you broke it."

I grinned and so did he.

"Once we get Flynn inside, we'll see if there's anything left of yours in that house. Okay?"

I swallowed hard. I knew he'd take care of me, but it hurt so much that he had to. My parents were the ones who were supposed to love me unconditionally.

Mr. Brewer clapped my on the shoulder and walked me over to the car where Flynn slept. My aunt Krista stood waiting next to the car. I hugged her. "I'm glad you haven't left me."

"Aw, sweetie," she said. "If I hadn't been out of the country these past ten years, I would have been over here every weekend, visiting my favorite nephew."

I pulled out of the hug, but she still held my hands. "Are you going on another dig?" I asked. She was an archeologist. In my mind, ever since I'd been little, she was the female version of Indiana Jones.

She made eye contact with Mr. Brewer before answering. "Nope. I'm here to stay."

"I hope you find a place to live that's close. Amy and Chad live fifteen minutes away."

Again, another glance at Mr. Brewer accompanied by a grin. "I have a feeling I'll be real close."

Flynn got out of the back seat with Mr. Brewer's help, and my aunt Krista took his other arm to walk him inside.

"I'm just going to go over to my house a minute, okay?"

"Sure. I'll join you in a few," Mr. Brewer said.

I went straight for where my key was hidden outside. Sometimes my parents locked me out when I'd come home after curfew. We all had keys to the doorknob, but my father thought only he and my mother had a key to the deadbolt. I lifted the rock, snatched the key, and walked up the creaky wooden steps to the door.

Part of me suspected the locks had been changed, so when it opened, I was surprised. The door creaked and the emptiness inside echoed the sound off the hardwood floors until it hit the kitchen door out back. My house was hollow, like a tomb. "Hello?" I called, expecting some ghost to answer back, but no one did. I headed straight for my room and found everything as it had been. They hadn't touched my stuff. Strike that—my brother, most likely, had felt the need to smash my TV. (Though I thought he'd been in jail.) It didn't matter. My clothes where here and I could come back later and pack them in trash bags to take to Flynn's.

I went back to the Brewers' house in time to see Flynn vomit on the floor.

"Flynn!" I shouted, diving to my knees next to him. Mr. Brewer handed me a cold towel so I used it to wipe his face. "What's happening?"

"I'm on hold," he said, motioning to the phone he held to his ear. "The doctor said to call if Flynn experienced any of the known side effects of concussions. Vomiting is one of them. I thought I'd call and see if he wanted me to take Flynn to the emergency room, or give him a few minutes. He *was* in the car a long time, it could be nausea."

"Not... nausea," Flynn said. He leaned into me as we sat on the living room floor. "I've felt awful for the last couple days. This is the first time I threw up though."

I turned the washcloth inside out and wiped his forehead. "Really? You seemed fine. Energetic, even."

He grinned through his exhaustion. "Yeah, well, I was distracted." He grabbed my knee and squeezed.

Mr. Brewer had walked out of the room and come back in a few minutes later. "Okay. Doc says I need to take you in. Since you were supposed to rest and didn't, he's concerned the swelling may have increased. Krista's going with us."

"Krista? As in my aunt Krista?" I asked, because I didn't know why she'd been here when I returned, and now needed to go the hospital with them. She was my mom's sister. Did my mom tell her about what I'd done? "Why is she coming?"

Flynn answered, "My dad's dating her."

"When did that happen? Where was I?"

Flynn took my hand and I helped him to his feet. "After Thanksgiving. She's spent at least three nights at my house since then."

We headed out the door and Mr. Brewer chuckled. "Here I thought I was discreet. You don't miss a thing, do you boy?"

"Nope," Flynn said. But then he turned sharply and hacked up bile onto the grass.

"We need to get you to the hospital now." I stated the obvious.

***

It felt like déjà vu, sitting in the hospital, staring at the floor, but this time I wasn't feeling the swirl of panic that overtook me before. The sounds in the halls were ordinary hospital sounds and the feeling that Flynn was on his deathbed was far from my mind. He would be okay. I knew he would. God didn't smite people. My sister told me life happens, but God wasn't crouched and waiting to strike down those who sin.

Flynn wasn't in God's crosshairs. Flynn's problems were a result of normal living, mishaps, and accidents. Flynn would pull through. Flynn told me Keith's God would protect me, so I had to believe that he was right and that same God would protect Flynn too.

I tapped my feet repeatedly and bounced my knee. Time was a creeping by and I was half tempted to chuck something at the wall clock. A woman's voice to my left was a welcome distraction.

"I'd say it's nice to see you again, but I generally don't like repeat customers."

It was ninja nurse Taryn. I smiled and stood up to shake her hand, but she hugged me instead. When she let go, I said, "Thanks. Yeah, I don't really want to be here."

"Is it your friend Flynn?"

I nodded. "Yeah. We kinda did a dumb thing and drove to New York the day he got out of the hospital and then we drove home this morning and he started throwing up. The doctor said there is some swelling and they want to observe him over night."

She touched my arm. "I'm so sorry."

I appreciated her sincere concern. "No, it's fine. Flynn's dad said they aren't as concerned as the last time. He told me my aunt noticed how relaxed the doctor's voice was, and she assured him Flynn would be okay."

"Is your aunt a doctor?"

"No, but she reads people well. Plus, she told Mr. Brewer she's known that doctor since their college days, and said he stutters when he's really worried. Kind of like a tell. A steady voice equals good recovery."

She giggled. "Sounds like your aunt *does* know him. I thought only a few insiders knew his secret. I'm glad."

"He might stay tomorrow night too depending on the tests. Right now he's talking with his dad, and recording something for his boyfriend."

A strange look crossed her face. Disappointment? Confusion? My stomach couldn't take much more if she blasted Flynn and called him a faggot. I really liked this nurse.

"I thought *you* were his boyfriend?" Taryn said sweetly, no judgment in her eyes at all.

"Oh, no. Wait? When we met, I told you I was the groom in a wedding. Why would you...."

"Because of the way you looked at him and stayed by his side. So... are you sure he's not yours?"

"Nah. But I'm okay. We worked it out. He's in love with Keith, and even though he and I haven't gotten along in the past, I'm willing to try for Flynn."

"Keith? The one with the beanie surgically attached to his head?"

I laughed. "That would be the one!"

Taryn laughed too. "I'm glad. His devotion to Flynn rivaled yours. I was beginning to wonder if a fight would break out if the two of you crossed paths, but he adamantly avoided you."

"Yeah, I know. We're okay."

Mr. Brewer emerged from Flynn's room and joined me in the hall. "Okay, we can go."

"What about Flynn? I need to tell him I'll be by tomorrow and—"

"Zach, he's asleep. If you want to say goodnight you can, but we should get back home and get your stuff moved to our house. Okay?"

My damn emotions swelled again. "Are you sure?" I nearly choked, and was thankful my voice came out sounding steady.

"Zach, yes I'm sure. You're a part of our family now. If you want to visit the courthouse and officially change your name to Brewer, that's up to you, but as far as I'm concerned you're my son now. I couldn't be more proud of you. Fucking Stewart Mitchell can go to Hell."

"Thanks Mr. Brewer," I said, voice cracking, and his damnation of my father didn't bother me at all.

This time, when I walked into my parents' house with Mr. Brewer by my side, I didn't shake and I didn't fear the echoing emptiness. My parents had left me for dead, but instead I'd found a life with a new family, Flynn's family, and I couldn't have been happier.

Part 3

Keith

Chapter 29

May 3, 2014: Hit Rewind Please,

And Remember To Take Pictures This Time

I hated this feeling like a sonofabitch, but it was so familiar that I couldn't push it away. I tried, but it returned like a boomerang fueled by liquid nitrogen. Flynn. Flynn was gone. Not *gone,* gone, because he'd woken up and been released from the hospital after the tree fell, but Flynn was no longer in my life. In our nearly four-year friendship, three of those had been spent in an on-again, off-again, dating relationship that meant more to me than Flynn knew. I loved him. God, I loved him. Ever since that first day in Mrs. Moore's art class, I knew… he was the one.

Whenever he was around, my skin heated up like I'd been lying on a beach for hours as I used to when my family vacationed in the Outer Banks. Only it never took hours to set my skin on fire when I was near Flynn, it took seconds. It had probably been lust in the initial stages of our friendship. He had the best smile and prettiest eyes I'd ever seen, and that ass screamed to be squeezed. But over time, the heated sensation all over my skin had remained the same, even when I wasn't ogling his ass or aching to kiss his lips. After a while, I knew it was merely being around him that made me burn all over.

I loved Flynn.

That's why I couldn't make it work with Carter, and why no other guy out there could ever fill Flynn's place in my heart.

Carter kissed me and backed me toward the bed. My parents were downstairs and my brother was in his room, but still I allowed Carter's advances, because I needed them. I needed to feel. I wanted so much to get over my obsession with Flynn, that even Carter Langley's attention would do. Not that he was ugly, not that he was bad, not that he was anything to scoff at, but mainly because he wasn't Flynn, and I needed to prove to myself

I could move on. It was October. I should be able to have sex with someone else.

He pushed me onto the bed and crawled over me. We got situated, and Carter worked his way under the hem of my shirt. He touched my stomach, and soon grazed his fingertips over my nipples. I flinched.

"Hey, everything okay?" he asked seductively.

"Yeah," I answered. Only, it wasn't. As soon as his fingers touched me there I thought about Flynn. Flynn would pinch me. Not enough to hurt, but he'd roll my nipple between his fingers enough to send shocks to my groin.

Carter didn't. He kissed me again and moved his hand down to my dick. I felt him rub me there before he pulled back. "Are you sure? I thought you'd be a bit more into it than this."

I knew what he meant. My dick was soft. It had stirred from slumber after we'd eaten dinner with my folks, but shortly after, had drifted back to sleep when it discovered Flynn wasn't around. Carter, apparently, wasn't interesting enough for Keith junior.

We gave up and Carter went home with a frown on his face.

I picked up Flynn's picture by my bed. Prom. It was my favorite picture of the two of us. I'd wanted to dance in the middle of the dance floor, but dancing over by the wall had been just fine. At least he tried loosening up. My mother had told me to give him space, but I had pushed. Too hard, too fast, and now he was Zach's boyfriend instead of mine. Why did I have to be so stupid?

"So, is there a reason Flynn's picture is sitting by your bed, instead of mine?" Carter asked as we snuck into my room after Christmas dinner with my family. My relatives all liked him, and I was glad no one asked where Flynn was.

I took the frame from his grasp. "I don't know. I guess I need a new one." I flipped the frame over and removed our prom picture. "There. Gone." I tossed it into the trash and set the empty frame back down. "I have an empty spot for you."

Carter pulled me close, kissed my lips, and then said, "In the frame, but not in your heart." He walked over to my door. "Tell your parents thanks. I'm heading home. I'll call you tomorrow, Keith. There isn't enough room in here for me, and Flynn."

My mom knocked on my bedroom door. "Keith? Can I come in?" My lack of reply prompted her own response. I heard the door creak on its hinges as she opened it. I felt her soft touch on my arm as she sighed. "Oh honey, not again."

I turned my tear-tracked face into my pillow and didn't bother making excuses. She'd witnessed this too many times to count. She rubbed my back for a few minutes before she stood up. I thought she'd gone, but then the bed dipped on the opposite side and my mom made herself comfortable next to me. She rubbed my back again, and touched my hair.

"Have you tried calling him?" she asked quietly.

I shook my head.

"Vic told me he's awake. Why won't you visit him?"

"I can't," I whined. "Not while he's with Zach."

"And how long since your last break-up?"

Her question made my stomach flip. I didn't understand why she had to bring up the amount of time we'd been apart. I was hyperaware of how long it had been. My heart knew, my fingers knew, my lips knew; all of the molecules in my body were shriveling up like prunes because they couldn't survive without Flynn. Why did my mother have to point that out?

"Forty weeks, Mom, that's almost a year, but I don't want to talk about it."

"At least I know you aren't pregnant. You'd have given birth by now."

I sat up and turned to face her. "Mom! What the heck? How can you make jokes when you know this has been the hardest—"

"Because Grace is downstairs. She asked to see you."

"Oh."

I rubbed my face and wiped away my tears. Something about her poking my anger buttons made my sad feelings diminish. Kind of the same effect a sobering, cold shower had on you after a night of throwing back shots. Of course that was a guess on my part; I hadn't ever done a night of shots because I was underage. Not even after Flynn and I had broken up.

"What does she want?"

"I didn't ask. You can't turn away from all your friends because you regret your actions."

"I never said...."

I didn't bother continuing to refute her statement after her eyebrow went up. I got out of bed and my mom walked over to the door.

She paused and asked, "Did you break up with Carter because he has blue eyes, or because he liked peas?"

"What?" I questioned. Her logic eluded me.

"I'm only asking. I figured there had to be a reason, since he seemed like a sweet boy. Dad liked him. Even Johnny—"

I blurted, "He wasn't Flynn, Mom. That's what you want to hear. I couldn't date Carter because I'm still in love with Flynn."

She looked way too pleased with herself when she closed the door, as if she'd pushed me to an answer I hadn't willingly considered. No, I'd considered it. It hadn't ever left my mind. I'd never broken up with him because I didn't love him. It had been any number of other reasons. My mom needed to stop analyzing me. She was far too intuitive for my liking.

After the first night Flynn came to dinner with my family, we dropped him at his house and watched him walking up his front lawn. My mom felt the need to continue the little chat we'd started in the kitchen earlier that night. I switched seats from the back to the front before she pulled away from the curb.

"Flynn's not out, is he?" she blurted as soon as we stopped at the first stop sign, one second from his house.

"Gee, Mom, way to ease into the conversation."

"I'm serious, Keith. He's not out, is he?"

"No." I hated how right she was all the time. Very perceptive and sometimes psychic, my mom could always gauge a situation, and never seemed to keep her opinions to herself.

"Hmm."

I looked over. "What? That's all you have to say? I know you have to be thinking more than 'hmm.' You aren't a 'hmm' thinker."

"I think you're in for a challenge."

I furrowed my brow at her. Of course, she wasn't looking, since she was driving, and I doubted even the third eye in the back of her head could see my face. "What do you mean?"

"I mean," she paused as she pulled onto Route 140 from the traffic light. "You've been used to getting your way. Even as a child you had an uncanny ability to debate a situation and sway people's opinions. You're strong-willed and intelligent."

I failed to see a problem in that. "Yeah. So why is Flynn suddenly a challenge for me?"

"Not him, his sexuality."

"It's his sexuality that's got me interested. If he'd been straight, we might have been friends, but I doubt I'd feel like this around him."

"And how do you feel?"

"Mom, I already told you. After one day of art class I said 'I'd met a guy.' Do you need it spelled out? I like him."

"Yes, I understand that."

"Then why're you asking how I feel? I don't know. I like him."

"But do you respect him?"

I felt a sudden chill. What the hell did she mean by that? Was she asking if we'd had sex? Good God, I wasn't exactly ready to talk about sex with my mom. Eww. That was just... eww. Instead, I played dumb. "What do you mean?"

"I mean, are you willing to give him the space and time he needs to come out publicly?"

Now she confused me. "What does that have to do with anything?"

"Keith, you've never been one to exercise patience. You get what you want, when you want it, or you find a way to argue a point until everyone around you agrees with why you should get it."

It bothered me that she'd figured me out so completely. I had *always* been a good debater. "What does that have to do with Flynn?"

"If he's in the closet about his sexuality, then you need to be willing to give him time to come out. Are you willing to do that?"

I wasn't even sure why she was bringing it up. "Of course! Why wouldn't I? And how'd you even know?"

She pulled the car into our driveway and put the car in park. After turning of the engine, she looked at me. "I notice a lot of things, son. Like I can tell you are head over heels about this boy, even if you haven't said it plainly."

I gawked, but remained silent.

"It's all in the way you look at him. The tenderness in your eyes, and the curve of your smile."

"Okay, this is getting too weird. Can we just go inside?" I opened the car door and she touched my arm.

"In a minute. Unless you want Jeremy hearing what I have to say?"

I closed the car door. "No. Finish."

"I could tell by the way he pulled his hands tighter to his body whenever you were standing too close."

"That doesn't prove anything. He could be xenophobic."

"You aren't a stranger to him, Keith. It was a concerted effort on his part not to touch you, or to be touched by you. He's very self-conscious about it. I could see it plainly. My worry is that you'll push him too hard to come out before he's ready."

"He's sixteen, Mom. He should be old enough to suck it up and deal with shit. I don't know why he's acting like that. He likes me; I know he does. I don't know why...." I let my words trail off when my mom touched the back of my head. She smiled softly and played with my hair. She'd always liked my curls even if I hated the way they misbehaved when I tried styling my hair. Hence, the beanie I loved wearing 24-7.

"Stop trying to control him. This is your first real boyfriend."

"We haven't actually decided on that, but I'm pretty sure it's on the table."

"Then let it progress naturally. Don't push. Don't pressure him. If I know you, and I think I do, you'll have to curb your tendency to steamroll people, and let him control his own life. Don't do it for him."

She'd known for years, before I even pushed, my mother knew I'd end up ruining it. I should have listened to her the first or fifth time she warned me about pressuring Flynn. She'd told me everyone was different. She'd told me not every family could adjust to include a gay member so easily. She'd told me personal situations and outside influences all converge on a person with contradictory messages. What was easy for me to handle, would not necessarily affect Flynn the same. In fact, it hadn't. Nothing about him seemed the same as the years passed. His thinking was different. His fears were different. His opinion of and stand on gay rights even seemed different.

I wanted him to be proud about who he was, but now I had lost him and our struggles meant nothing; our arguments meant nothing, because he wasn't mine anymore.

Another knock.

"Come in, Grace."

She smiled hesitantly at me like she expected me to disapprove of her visit. She closed the door and sat on my bed. Everyone was sitting on my bed except the one person I wanted in it.

"What do you want?"

"No need to get hostile. I wanted to see how you are."

"You could have called for that. Or texted."

"No. You can disguise your voice to sound all perky and I wouldn't get to see the bags under your eyes, or the anger in your glare when you know I can tell you've been crying."

I jumped up, pacing my room, up and back, before confronting her. "Stop assuming you know everything, because you don't. Okay. Flynn and I are done. He's with Zach!"

"I know. I thought we were all going to remain friends, though. Isn't that what you, Zach and Kelly agreed earlier?"

"Yeah, but it's only been a few hours."

"Are you going to see him? Kelly said he's spending one more night in the hospital."

"No. Why would I? He's with Zach."

"Because you're his friend."

"Then tell him to call me."

Grace got off the bed abruptly and headed to my door. "You're an asshole, Keith. Kelly's right. The two of you are the stupidest boys I've ever met. I don't care if you're with Carter, you're still in love with Flynn, and everybody knows it."

As upsetting as it was that she could see right through me, I couldn't lie. "I'm not with Carter."

"No? Then why not tell Zach to back off? You were there first."

I was glad she lingered by the door and waited to hear my answer instead of assuming she knew what it would be. People always did that. It seemed no one ever took the time anymore to ask the details. One rumor and the rest of the populous murmured its assumptions to the point of cruelty.

Guilt before trial was the new norm. Grace's inquiry reaffirmed my hope in humanity in some small measure.

"I want Flynn to be happy. I've told you that for months now. He never came back, in all those months, so…."

"He saw you with Carter, Keith."

My heart sank. "He did? When?"

"Around Christmas. I think it broke his heart. After that, he spent all his time with Amelia, trying to forget you."

"Why didn't you tell me?"

"I thought you didn't care. The two of you have always been one spark away from incinerating this town like a nuclear bomb. Kelly and I decided last fall to leave you to it; that's why we haven't interfered. But I have to say, I didn't think your stupidity would go as far as to leave Flynn in Zach's hands. That's pretty noble."

"I'm not noble. I'm… tired. Our relationship has never been easy. I guess I'm tired of trying when he's not meeting me halfway."

Grace sighed. "I'm sorry. I'll keep you posted, but I won't push. Greg and I are going to visit him in the hospital, and then we're driving down to New Orleans for a week."

"Yeah? You two are getting along well, then."

"Yup." She kissed my cheek. She paused before leaving, looking deep into my eyes. "Promise me… Promise you won't go looking for love any time soon."

"Why?"

"Because. You aren't over Flynn. I knew Carter was a distraction, but I didn't have the heart to stop you. Now I'm saying wait. Please. Give it a couple weeks and then go…." she poked me on the forehead with her finger. "Visit." Grace poked me again. "Flynn." She poked me one last time for emphasis.

"I got it! Now get out before I decide hitting a girl who pokes me in the head isn't a bad idea."

Grace rolled her eyes and left.

I walked back over to my bed and flopped back down with my prom picture.

"I can't take you to the wedding on Saturday," I told Carter *after our date.*

He continued kissing my ear, and down my neck, before my non-responsiveness prompted him to stop. He gave me a look. "You're serious? I rented a suit."

"I know. I'm sorry. I can't do this anymore."

His hands went limp at his sides. "It's Brewer, isn't it? All this time, I thought if I was patient enough, you'd get over him, but you aren't. You still love him. That's why you won't sleep with me."

I nodded, looking away. I felt guilty for stringing him along. My actions reminded me of Flynn's, and I resented our similarities.

Carter stepped back. "Fine." He held his hands in the air. "We're done. But don't think you can come crawling back and apologize this time. I called it at Christmas. You and Flynn aren't finished."

He walked away and left me on the front porch of my house.

I studied Flynn's face in the photograph. I'd thrown it away once for Carter, but had retrieved it from the trash as soon as he'd left. "It's been a week Flynn. Carter's been out of my life a week, and I don't even care. He wasn't you."

Chapter 30

May 17, 2014: When My Brother Speaks

Our stupid family reunion was at my house this year. Normally, Memorial Day weekend celebrations were held on Memorial Day weekend, but several of my dad's brothers were going hunting in Montana, so our family agreed to host the picnic early.

Joy.

I knew I had a great family, and I could honestly say I loved most of them. A couple cousins, especially my great aunt's grandson, seemed a tad beyond my ability to tolerate, so I avoided them. My issue this weekend was "family" in general, because I wasn't in the mood. My world had fallen apart. My parents tried to be cheery, but there was no use. Time had dragged on and my mood had gotten darker with each passing day. My mom hadn't exactly given up on me, but I think she'd given me over to my depression, and quietly observed from a distance just in case I started cutting or shooting up, or whatever the heck suicidal people did. I wasn't suicidal, I was depressed, and she knew nothing was going to stir me out of my funk; it just had to run its course.

I hadn't physically seen Flynn in seventeen days, but I wasn't counting. We hadn't spoken since July, ten months ago. It had been the longest I'd ever gone without his touch, and I yearned for it just as strongly as I had after that very first time in art class when he held my hand under the table.

"Do you want a hamburger? I know you're not keen on hotdogs."

Flynn had meant everything to me. I just didn't understand why he didn't love me back. Or, more precisely, why he loved Zach more than me and was willing to throw everything we had away because of....

"I said, 'do you want a hamburger?'" It took me a moment to realize my brother was speaking to me.

I looked up and noticed I was sitting at the patio table surrounded by uncles and cousins, my sister and her boyfriend, my parents, and....

"Keith!"

"W-what?"

"Snap out of it," my older brother insisted. "You've been dragging your limp ass all over the house ever since ever since Carter broke up with you."

I shook my head. "It's not about Carter, and I broke up with him, not the other way around."

"Ah! I get it," his voice lilted as epiphany struck. "You're still pining over Flynn. Dude, it's been months, get over it."

Internally, I groaned. I didn't need the entire family to know Flynn and I weren't together. I hadn't seen most of these people since the Thanksgiving before last, so most wouldn't know we'd broken up.

"Oh Keith," my aunt Sarah said, "I'm so sorry. I was wondering why Flynn wasn't here. I liked that boy. He was good for you. He always had a way of making people smile."

The flood of emotions I'd been trying to suppress throughout the cookout surged, and I covered my face with my hands to hide my sudden tears. *Why did she have to say that?* I knew why everyone liked Flynn. Of course my family members would miss him. He'd been so kind-hearted and thoughtful to everyone he'd met. *Fuck!* Why'd she have to say that?

"Is that why the other boy was here at Christmas? What was his name...? Carter?" another aunt asked. "I assumed he was a neighbor. I thought Keith was in love with that Brewer boy."

The murmuring started traveling around the picnic table as I tried hiding my face. I wanted to bolt. I felt as though I needed to hide, or scream, or punch a wall, but as soon as I caught a part of a whispered conversation about "Flynn making a mistake," I'd had it.

"Enough!" I yelled, silencing everyone at once, because I was not the kind of guy who yelled at anyone, except maybe my mom when we argued about politics, but even that was never malicious. Flynn was the only one who could stir me up about anything and everything. "Enough," I repeated, more quietly. "It wasn't Flynn's decision. It never has been. Every single time it's been my fault. Mine. I broke up with Flynn last July, and it was because he wouldn't come out to his best friend and I was tired of pretending to be straight whenever we were around Zach. It was my decision all three times we broke up, and it was me who went running back because I couldn't live without him. I am not going back this time. I'm done. He obviously doesn't love me. He's with Zach now."

All eyes were on me; staring like those of wax dummies. I guessed no one could believe that I'd yelled, or the reasons I gave for Flynn's and my break-ups. They sat, burgers in hand and red Solo cups to their lips, as if I'd cast a spell to freeze time. The motionlessness of my entire family caused a heaving in my chest, and suddenly I bolted from the table in a great whirlwind of arms and legs, escaping the laugher I was sure would follow. I'd been an idiot, and now everyone in my family knew it. I ran from their ridicule.

"Who's Zach?" one uncle asked upon my exit.

My brother Johnny followed me to where I hid behind the tree in our back yard. I'd been sitting there I don't know how long, with my knees drawn up and my eyes shut, leaning against that tree, hoping no one would bother me. Though I thought my mom would have sought me out first, about two minutes after I'd disappeared.

"Hey," he said, kicking my shoe.

I glared. "Leave me alone, Johnny."

"I will. As long as you promise me one thing."

"What?"

"Stop beating yourself up over it."

"I'm not."

"Yes, you are. You ran out off the porch as if expecting us to judge you or laugh in your face. We're not gonna. No one at the house blames you for anything. Relationships come and go. People change. Sometimes it's just life that gets in the way. Whatever the reason, we all still love you. So you don't have to hide out here."

"But I've made such a mess of things," I whined. The whining, in and of itself, just about had me thumping the back of my head against the tree trunk. I wasn't a whiner by nature. I was the most logical of all my family, besides my dad. I was the one who could see through the bullshit of life and breakdown the statistics. Me. What had happened?

"I think you need to get some perspective. Step back, and come at it logically. As I see it, you need to think about a couple things. One, do you love him? Two, are you willing to fight for him? And three, are you willing to set aside your massive pride and apologize for your actions?"

"My actions?" I scoffed. "I haven't done anything."

I looked down at the grass while Johnny lingered. I waited for him to add more to the discussion or walk away, but he did neither. He stood there challenging me with silence. He knew I knew I'd been wrong. He knew I knew this was all my fault, but I wouldn't admit it.

An ant crawled over the top of my shoe on its way to doing whatever ants do, and suddenly I saw this whole situation differently. All because of an ant. Ants. Ants didn't get bent out of shape because a big shoe blocked their path. Nothing deterred them. Ants simply saw the obstacle and either went around it, or went over it. Done! Life was simple. If I applied that to my life what would it mean?

My obstacle wasn't a Brobdingnagian-sized shoe blocking the way of my Lilliputian-sized existence. No. My entire problem boiled down to Flynn's closeted lifestyle. My reality wasn't blocked by an obstacle of mammoth proportions; it was Flynn's decision to be out to some, while hiding his sexuality from others; which didn't interrupt my whole pattern of living, it only made me have to work around it. I'd been selfish this whole time, as prideful as Johnny suggested, thinking that Flynn needed to conform to my needs when I hadn't thought about his. Zach aside, the only arguments we'd ever had revolved around my wanting one thing, and Flynn asking me to wait. Not once had he said he'd never come out. He in no way told me I couldn't be affectionate in public; he asked me for time. It wasn't as if he wanted something different than I did. He *wanted* to be comfortable kissing me in public; he simply hadn't gotten to that place yet.

I glanced back up at Johnny, who remained silent, still watching me. He demonstrated patience with me, why couldn't I have done that with Flynn?

"Do you think he'll ever forgive me?"

"For what?"

"Acting like a pushy asshole and trying to control his life?"

Johnny grinned and shook his head. "I don't know, man. I have a hard enough time trying to figure out women, I can't tell you how your ex-boyfriend will handle things. But one thing I've heard is that time heals all wounds. Give him time. If it's true that you're always the one crawling back to him, then my advice is, *don't*. Break the cycle. There is that old saying, 'If you love someone let them go. If they return to you then it's true love; if not, they weren't yours to begin with.'"

"That line's been quoted and misquoted so many times, but yeah, I get what you're saying. I'm not going back this time."

"Whatever you decide, I'm behind you one hundred percent." Johnny began backing away, one step at a time. When he was ten feet away, he winked and said, "I love you, little brother."

"Thanks." I gave him half a smile. I couldn't help it. He had always teased me about being shorter than him, as well as being younger, so the term "little" held a double meaning that only the two of us would know. Even in twelfth grade when I'd shot up four inches virtually overnight, I had still stopped shy of Johnny's height of six-four. It irked me and he reveled in it. "I love you too, John."

He nodded and turned for the house, leaving me to contemplate the real reason I hid in the yard: pride. My pride had been hurt and I hated admitting it.

I got my prideful ass up off the grass and headed back to the party. If there was anything I needed to learn from this situation, it was the importance of owning my faults. I was a proud person. In some ways, pride was good.

I could stand tall and show my pride in parades, or show my pride in rallying for same-sex marriage, or bills in congress. I could start online groups for anti-bullying and visit high schools or youth groups to give talks about being gay and not giving in to fear. I could be proud to be who I was everyday and everywhere.

What I shouldn't be prideful of was how much of a fool I'd been. I needed to own up to being a jerk all these years. So I sucked in a deep breath and headed back in to face my family. What I found around the grill and picnic table was forgiveness.

My aunt passed a bowl of potato salad, and I rejoined their conversation and fellowship as if nothing had happened to disrupt the flow. Somehow, I knew they would always accept me, no matter what.

Chapter 31

May 25, 2014: The Guy I Love To Hate

My conversation with Johnny last week notwithstanding, I still had difficulty dealing with the emptiness Flynn's absence left me with. I wanted to be strong, but I also wanted Flynn back. I wanted to beg his forgiveness and tell him I would change, but I also knew that if I did that, I'd appear to be the same person I'd been every time I went back to him. Grace had said to give it time. She said she'd be gone a week, but I hadn't heard from her.

I called Kelly only to find out that Zach and Flynn had disappeared to New York, which didn't ease my jealousy. A few days after that, she called me back to say they'd come home and Flynn was in the hospital again. She asked if I'd visit, and I told her no.

I'd asked not to be phased out, but I felt like the more I stayed away, the more I was alienating myself. If Flynn wanted my friendship, why hadn't he called?

I had to hope Flynn would change his mind. I had to hope that Flynn would figure out he wasn't in love with Zach and that I was his soul mate. But man, the more time that went by, the harder, and more depressing my life seemed.

Some days, I just wanted to throw things at a wall.

"Like today!" I grumbled, storming out my bedroom door and barreling down the steps to find out why someone felt the need to ring the doorbell three times, and why, in God's name, no one in my house saw fit to answer it. We'd gotten home from church two hours ago, and as always, everyone had dispersed to their different corners of the house to relax. Sundays were always a day to chill before the work—or school—week started on Mondays.

I jumped the last three steps and gaped at my brother, who was seated on the couch not ten feet away from the front door. "Are you kidding me?" I asked. When he didn't answer, I crossed the room and stared down at him.

He looked up, and assessing my livid expression, pulled one ear bud out of his ear and asked, "What?"

"Couldn't you get that?" I asked, widening my eyes and pointing to the door.

"Get what?"

My brother could be so dense. The doorbell rang again and I furrowed my brow at him. "That!"

He shrugged, put his ear bud back in and continued messing with his DS.

I fumed, but it did no good. I stormed over to the door and opened it without looking through the peephole. Whoever was ringing the doorbell, *again*, was about to get an earful of my annoyance.

I yanked open the door, but no one was on the other side.

"What?" Maybe I had imagined it. As I closed the door, I saw a piece of paper taped to the outside of the storm door. I opened it and pulled the note off. I stood on the front porch searching the yard for the culprit who had left it. No one.

I opened the note.

The Air I Breathe

How would I describe my love
In sentences or pictures;
When nothing tangible can denote
My heart's span of tinctures?

It flourishes of its own accord
And surpasses every theme;
And when I feel I know its depths,
Love redefines my dream.

Not found in smiles or softest touch,
Nor eye, nor lips, nor laughter;
It plays about in sunlit beams
And winks as I chase after.

No, love is not a solid thing
I choose to have or leave;
It's in that space around his soul,
His breath—the air I breathe.

It was a poem. A beautiful poem. One that only Flynn could have written. I had butterflies in my stomach. Suddenly I was trying to remember if I'd had a shower that morning and how my hair looked.

"Flynn!" I yelled, hoping he hadn't left, but remained within earshot. "Flynn!" I looked all around. "Flynn, where are you?"

Zach's presence to my left was like a pesticide, spraying the lovely cloud of butterflies until they dropped in a flutterless heap. "What are you doing here?" I barked at him. Apparently my pride was still standing firm, while my forgiveness was on vacation.

"I wanted to bring you that. Flynn wrote it." He looked down, and tentatively stepped closer.

Then Kelly materialized from behind another bush, and Grace from behind the car parked at the curb. "Hi," Kelly said tentatively.

"What's going on here?"

They looked at each other, one to the next, and then all eyes were back on me. Grace spoke first, "We're all feeling guilty."

"About what?" I was suspicious, even in the face of the guilt they exuded. The girls, especially, gave off some odd vibes, while Zach was awkward and not acting at all as if he'd won the lottery. Having Flynn in his life was worth zillions of dollars in gold, so why was Zach so meek all of a sudden? I'd never seek Zach timid except the time I'd hit him. Had they broken up? And if they had, why wasn't Flynn here instead?

"Why didn't Flynn bring the poem himself, if that's really how he feels?"

Grace answered, "He's been paranoid about cars lately, after he overdid it going to New York and ended up in the hospital. He's only gone places he can walk to."

"He could walk here." Not the nicest thing to say, I admit, but I was angry Flynn had sent Zach of all people to deliver this message.

Zach pulled his shoulders back gawked at me. "Keith! Don't be a jerk about it. Your house has to be a thirty-minute walk, at best. Flynn's been healing from his concussion, or don't you remember the tree falling on him?"

I pulled my shoulders back, too, and stepped right in his space. He was an inch shorter, and not so tough. I could take him. "Oh, I remember it. Has he professed his undying love for you a hundred more times, or was it just the once?"

Kelly challenged me angrily. "Keith, why do you have to be an asshole? Flynn loves you. Didn't you read the poem?"

I felt the icy chill of guilt crash against the fiery rage fueling my pride. Only one would win, and my pride had certainly been challenged more than once in the past few weeks. I glanced down at the paper in my hand. "Yes, I read it, but I don't understand why you're all here."

Zach explained, "He wrote that in the car on the way back from New York. He meant to give it to you and ask you to forgive him, but he started throwing up as soon as we got home, so his dad took him to the hospital. After that, things got hectic with my parents moving."

"And Zach moving in with Flynn," Kelly added.

Grace took a turn by saying, "And Flynn's dad getting engaged to Zach's aunt Krista."

"And me seeing a therapist," Zach said.

Kelly took another turn in the round-table explanation, "And that whole weird situation were Zach and Flynn had to figure out who was sleeping where, when there's only one bed in their house; it just—"

"Wait!" I interjected. "Slow down. Who the hell did what, now?"

Zach reiterated it all from the beginning, one detail at a time, but it was a lot to take in. Especially when we were still standing on the porch for all the world to see and hear. Suddenly, I felt self-conscious. My life didn't need to be on display. I might hate Zach, but I didn't need my neighbors hearing about it.

"Do you want to come in?" I offered.

"I think I'd like that," he said.

"I think that's a good idea," Grace added.

I held the door for them, and offered up to the trio, "I thought Zach hated me?"

"I've been forced to reassess my feelings." He entered the house and stood in the foyer, glancing around nervously. Zach had never been here, but both the girls had.

"By whom? Flynn?" I motioned toward the kitchen. The group followed me.

"No. My therapist. I started seeing her two weeks ago. I wish I'd done this a long time ago, but better late than never, I guess."

Zach was all apologetic looking, while I was growing increasingly belligerent with every additional second he stood in front of me. "Wow, a few weeks of therapy and you're a new man. That therapist must be a miracle worker if she's got you facing your enemy so easily."

"Keith!" Kelly protested, but Zach silenced her with a hand on her shoulder.

Zach pulled his shoulders back and took a breath. "You've never been my enemy Keith. I was never afraid of you."

"No, of course not. You've always had the upper hand in our implied competition. I'm no rival when you've obviously won."

"I understand your defensiveness, but I think I have something else to convince you." Zach reached into his pocket and took out a voice recorder.

"What's that?"

"When we took Flynn to the hospital that night, after coming back from New York, he recorded something for you. His dad always carries around a voice recorder in case he thinks of specs for a client. Flynn wanted to tell you in person, but he wasn't feeling very well. After he came home, he slept for three days straight."

"But that was three weeks ago, where's he been since then?"

They all glanced guiltily at one another.

"I thought Grace visited you after she got back from her trip," Kelly said.

Grace added, "And I thought Kelly brought you the recorder when it wasn't on the kitchen table anymore. I'm sorry."

Zach offered, "We've all spent a couple weeks assuming each of us had filled you in, while Flynn's been moping around and waiting. I think most of it's my fault since I went to see the therapist that Monday after New York. So much went on in those two weeks, I haven't thought of anything else."

"He couldn't call me?" The acid in my tone even made *me* sick. I wasn't sure why I was acting so bitter, but I couldn't stop.

"Stop. This is all because of me." Zach's calm was like heaping coals on my head, showing me how insensitive I was.

Kelly put her arms around him. "It wasn't just you, Zach, it was all of us." She looked at me apologetically. "Keith, we're all sorry. I would have brought it over sooner, but with everything going on the last couple weeks, the recorder kind of got misplaced. Krista found the poem in the car while she was vacuuming it out for Flynn. Zach remembered the message Flynn recorded for you as soon as I showed him the poem. Flynn probably assumed you'd heard it, and was too hurt to call you when you didn't respond. He doesn't know it got lost. I'm sorry."

"We're all sorry," Grace said.

"Keith, just listen to the recording," Zach begged.

I took the recorder and thought about pressing play. "Did you listen to it?"

Zach shook his head. "No. It was for you."

"Aren't the two of you…?" I let it hang because I couldn't finish the question.

"No. We tried, but he's in love with you."

I had so much more to ask, but felt sick at the thought forming in my mind. "Did you and he…?"

"You already know the answer to that Keith. Details won't make it *un*happen."

I turned sharply and nearly punched the wall, but my mom materialized next to us and I pulled my fist back one second before it connected with the wall.

"Hello," my mom said, entering the room, thereby interrupting my rapidly heating temper. I guess my mom realized I was talking to someone other than myself. She held out her hand and introduced herself. "I'm Kayla." Zach shook it.

"Mom, this is Zach. Zach, my mom." I didn't growl, but I wasn't polite either. I was simmering: on the verge of exploding all over him. "You already know Kelly and Grace."

"Hello, girls."

"Hello, Mrs. Leppo," they said in unison.

"Nice to meet you Mrs. Leppo," Zach said politely. I didn't want a polite Zach Mitchell. It was easier to hate him if he was an impolite jerk.

"Oh really? It is wonderful to meet you," my mom said cheerfully. "I wasn't aware that you were friends with my son. I'm glad he's getting over his pride." With that, she leveled her gaze at me, knowing I would gawk in protest.

"Ahhh!" I thought her comment was uncalled for.

"What?" she challenged. "You can't take being called out on it?"

"I can't believe you're going there! All this time I thought you were allowing me to work it out for myself."

"Aren't you?"

"I… Ahhh!" I threw my arms up. "I hate when you do that!" I fussed. She certainly knew how to push my buttons. I was surprised the girls didn't laugh about it.

Then, to make matter worse, she winked at him. Winked! I had no chance of winning the argument. My mom had just gutted me in front of him. I dropped our discussion in order to avoid more of her subtle chastisement. "Come on," I grumbled, waving them to follow me out onto the back porch. The back yard was more secluded than the front, but we stumbled in upon my dad out there. I couldn't win.

"Oh, hi. I thought you were going fishing today, Dad."

My dad had his permanent smile affixed to his face. Always warm, always pleasant. It made me wonder sometimes whether I'd been adopted, because my hot streak was definitely *not* from my dad. "Well, Keith, I planned on going, but my friend is sick and had to reschedule."

"Oh."

"Does that bother you, son? You sound more disappointed than I was. And who is your friend?" He asked, standing up from his chair and extending his hand toward Zach. "Hello. I'm Joel. What's your name?"

Always welcoming. Why couldn't he act suspicious sometimes? It made me sick how easily he accepted everyone who walked into my house. I sulked while they made introductions.

"Hi. I'm Zach Mitchell, a friend of Keith's."

"We're not friends," I corrected hotly.

Dad glanced at me, and welcomed Zach anyway. No one ever cared about my feelings. You'd think Dad would ask why we weren't friends, but no, he asks Zach to sit with him.

"So, Zach, tell me a little about yourself. Girls, always nice to see the two of you. Please have a seat." He swept his hand toward the extra chairs. "Zach, how do you know Keith?"

"Um," he hesitated, glancing at me.

I explained for him. "He's the Zach who stole Flynn and ruined my life, Dad."

Kelly made a strange sound, but I ignored her.

"I see. I guess there must be an important reason for you to drop by, knowing my son despises you with the heat of a thousand burning suns," he mocked.

"Shut up, Dad. Don't make fun of me," I said, hotly.

When my dad leveled his eyes on me, I backed down and slumped in one of the chairs. "Keith, I'll not have you speak disrespectfully to me. I apologize for poking fun at you, but you must see my confusion over the situation. If you hate him like you say you do, then why welcome him in?"

I shrugged. I had no logical answer and my dad obviously knew it.

"So, while Keith chews on his reasons, why don't you tell me why you're here?"

Zach looked at me as if for permission. Why was I suddenly his keeper? "Go on," I said.

"Thank you, Mr. Leppo. Flynn told me about you. Part of the reason I came here was to see if I could talk to you sometime. I wasn't thinking it would be now." He glanced nervously at me again. For a guy who had just said he wasn't afraid of me, he sure seemed afraid of something.

As much as I hated Zach, I knew my dad counseled lots of people and could probably help him sort through his past. I told Zach, "My dad likes to ask questions. But if there's anyone you can trust, it's him."

Zach was relieved and the softness in his expression made me feel even sicker about helping him. Aiding and abetting the enemy—good thing this wasn't a real war. I'd be court-marshaled for treason.

My dad said, "If there is something you'd like to talk about, I wouldn't mind having a conversation. My fishing plans changed, so maybe that was God's way of making sure I was here for you."

Zach sat up and his eyes widened. "That's what I want to talk about—God. Flynn said your family views God very differently than mine."

"Oh? What denomination are you?" he asked inquisitively. I'd always wondered that myself because Flynn never said. He told me they were strict, but that was it.

"I'd rather not say. I've lived my life believing one thing because my parents told me it was the only way. I did everything I could to live up to what they wanted, but it was never good enough. My dad..." he lowered his head, "He started beating me when I was six."

Zach's quiet admission made me shudder. Kelly reached out and took his hand.

"I remember dropping the communion plate as it was passed. He yelled at me when we got home and told me how embarrassing I was. After that, I never quite met his expectations, so he'd beat me."

Grace whispered, "You can stop any time, Zach. You don't have to explain it all at once."

He glanced at her. "I know. It helps, though, just like my therapist said it would." He shifted his attention back to my dad and continued, "When I started questioning our religion, it got worse. He said my taking lashes would atone for my sins."

This time, *I* wanted to tell him to stop, but I knew he needed to get it out. I always got furious over Christians using the Bible to justify their own horrific actions, like with that fanatical Baptist Church down South. No one should use the Bible like that. Child abuse was child abuse, and there wasn't any justification I would buy. I made eye contact with my dad and saw worry pouring from his deeply caring eyes. I knew where my dad stood on child abuse, and he wasn't going to let the conversation end until he personally deemed Zach safe from further harm.

"When you say 'lashes'…," Dad broached sensitively.

"He whipped me across my back with his belt."

"Zach, have you told anyone about this?"

Zach nodded. "Flynn knows."

"You're Flynn's friend… right?" I saw my dad had made the connection to the conversation Flynn had with him a couple years ago. Now my dad knew this was the same friend Flynn spoke about.

Zach continued without recognizing my dad's implication he knew more about the situation than Zach was aware of. "Kelly and Grace know. My therapist knows. We've spoken every other day for two weeks. She's gotten me to open up and told me it's important to know I did nothing wrong."

"She's right," my dad affirmed. "There is nothing a child could do to justify that type of discipline. If you told me you stole a football from the store and your father made you write two hundred times, 'Thou shalt not steal,' I would agree with him, but for a grown man to whip a boy across the back? I find that inexcusable. How long did that go on, Zach? When was the last time he hit you?" My dad leaned forward and spoke softer.

Zach hesitated. I think he was embarrassed to say it in front of me and the girls, but I already knew some of it from Flynn.

"Three weeks ago he whipped me, and the next day he came at me with a baseball bat, but that was the last time."

My dad narrowed his eyes. "Son, how old are you? You can't possibly be younger than Keith."

"I'm twenty-one, but I'll turn twenty-two in July."

My dad whistled and sat back in his chair. He looked dumbfounded. He gaped, and Zach breathed harder, mistaking my dad's shock for ridicule. Zach had been so calm, but now panic caught up to him as my dad sat speechless.

I jumped in to defend him, right as the words were perched on Kelly's tongue. "But he's not living with them any longer, right Zach? Mr. Brewer took you in. That's what Grace told me."

"Yup. He's living with the Brewers."

"Zach's parents split and put the house up for sale, and he went to live with Flynn's family."

Zach looked at me guiltily, eyes wide, mouth trembling. "It's not what you think, Keith. Flynn and I aren't together. I told you, he loves you. I live there, and I sleep in his bed, but nothing's going on. Not since New York. We tried to be more than best friends, but... he loves *you*."

I wasn't expecting him to twist the conversation back around to me. "That has nothing to do with... anything." I stammered, faltering under the attention. "This is about you and... Wait, you sleep in his bed?" My voice hit a pitch higher than my sister's voice when she screamed at Jeremy.

"Excuse me for a minute, Mr. Leppo." Zach turned toward me and stood, taking my arm. Why I let him, I don't know, but he led me over to the little gazebo thing my dad built next to the koi pond for my mom. With my dad on the back porch, this was more private.

Zach sat me down and I glared. "What!"

"Keith, I came here because Flynn couldn't. He originally asked Kelly to bring you the recorder, but things got screwed up, and we all decided it was best to come together. We all messed this one up; I knew I couldn't let them come here alone. I knew I had to face you."

"You? Why? I thought you hated me," I shot back.

"Keith, I never really hated you. We're not enemies. I came here because Flynn got sick and didn't want to get in the car again, and I blamed myself for forgetting about the poem. He's been moping around, thinking you didn't want to see him, and it's my fault. As soon as I figured out my mistake I came over here. I didn't even tell Flynn, none of us did. We left him at his house, swimming in the pool, figuring you showing up would be the best apology we could give."

He took the wind out of my sails with that one. "Oh."

"You told me before that you're controlling, and I can see that, but you also defer to Flynn whenever given the chance. Well now, I'm deferring to you. Flynn loves you. Maybe this time it will be different. Maybe this time Christmas will be magical for the two of you. I promise not to mess it up."

He had to mention Christmas. *Fuck!* Every single time I thought about that Christmas I got so angry, but also very emotional. My eyes started tearing up. I looked away, but Zach noticed.

"Keith? What happened that day? You don't have to go into detail, but it seems that it was a significant date."

"Fine!" I huffed, but really, there wasn't much steam behind it. Zach was kind and seemed genuinely inquisitive.

If Zach was willing to listen, then I was going to spill. I saw that Christmas as a defining moment in our relationship, and I blamed Zach as much as myself for everything that followed.

"You want to know what happened? Then sit back, close your eyes, and picture this. It was Christmas night, two-thousand-eleven, and I'd asked my parents for permission to surprise Flynn, since I had to be home by midnight because I wasn't eighteen and I still had my provisional license. You," I sneered, "Zach Mitchell, were the last person on the planet I would have thought about that night.

"I arrived at his house around nine o'clock. Nervous to give him his actual present, I stalled while we sat on his couch kissing. Kissing Flynn is like heaven, but I'm sure you know all about that. The Christmas tree added this magical feeling to the room and I hadn't wanted to do or say anything to mess it up. I wasn't fully sure if Flynn was ready for more than kissing and hand-jobs, but I was determined to ask before my time was up. I'm a stereotypical guy. I wanted his body and I admit it." I glanced at the house, but my parents, Kelly and Grace, were too far away to hear. Relieved, I continued. "Around ten-thirty I handed him a box."

Chapter 32

December 25, 2011: Past Regrets

"I hope you like it," I said, slightly worried.

"I'm sure I'll love it," he told me.

Flynn opened the box and found the red fabric. "What's this?" he asked, picking it up by the waistband. "Is this?"

"It's a jockstrap. I thought you'd look hot in it."

He eyed it curiously. "Really?"

"Oh yeah. Model it for me?"

Flynn set the box down and fiddled with the leg straps. He held it up in front of him and eyed the crotch. "There's not much material there."

"There's enough. It's like a little pouch to hold your junk."

"The key word is little."

"Come on. It's not that bad."

Flynn stood up. "Okay." He kissed me and agreed. "I'll go put it on. But I hope I'm not the only one who'll be wearing something so seductive."

While Flynn was in the hall bathroom, I dashed up the steps and grabbed the blanket off his bed. Right before going back downstairs I peeked into his dad's room. Mr. Brewer was snoring. I knew Flynn said his father had fallen asleep early, but I had to make sure.

I got back down the steps in time to situate the blanket on the floor in front of the tree just as Flynn came out of the bathroom in nothing but the jockstrap. I could literally feel all the blood in my entire body flow south. He. Was. Gorgeous.

Flynn sauntered forward and dropped his pile of clothes on the sofa. He turned around like a fashion model and asked, "You like?"

I swallowed the lump in my throat. "Um, yeah." I don't know how I managed any words at all, let alone not stuttering, because I was feeling more turned-on by the sight of him in a jock, than when I'd seen him completely naked. Especially when he turned and I got a glimpse of the back where the straps fit around his legs and left his ass showing in all its glory. Oh yes, jockstraps were the way to go from now on!

Flynn had an amazingly squeezable ass; and I pictured doing all kinds of things to it. I literally salivated thinking about licking him straight up the crack while he modeled that jock.

"That's it?"

Flynn sounded a bit disappointed that I had nothing more to say, but I swear my brain was oxygen deprived as other areas of my anatomy enjoyed the benefit of full circulation. I only nodded.

Flynn snickered and knelt down next to me on the blanket I'd laid out for us. "Nice touch. I've always liked lying under the Christmas tree. My mom used to do it with me and Nate." Flynn grabbed the pillows off the couch and arranged them for us. "Keith?" He snapped his fingers in front of my eyes.

"What? Oh. Sorry. You're just... wow. I really like your present."

"It's so much more exciting than the Xbox game I gave you."

"That's okay. We can play Xbox while you wear that and it will be plenty exciting."

"I don't think I could play in this."

"Why not?"

"I think I'd get distracted. Besides, you'd probably have difficulty watching the TV screen and your guy would die too quickly. So, yeah, I don't see me playing Xbox wearing this thing. At least not by itself. Unless it was after we already had sex."

My stomach warmed. "So... you think sex might be on the horizon?"

Flynn scooted up real close to me and ran his palm over my stomach. I knew how much he appreciated the hair below my navel. "What do you think?" He got this devilish look in his eyes right before he kissed me.

I rolled onto my back as he climbed up over my body, kissing me passionately and rubbing my torso from neck to waist. He slipped his hand up my shirt and caressed my nipple with gentle circles, and then pinched it.

"Take off your shirt," he whispered.

I did, and he reached for my groin, massaging me through my pants. I laid back and folded my arms behind my head as I watched Flynn reach his hand inside the gap caused by my flattened stomach. When he touched my naked flesh, he gave me a look. "Freeballing?"

I grinned and nodded.

"Wait. What's...?" he asked half a question as he felt my little surprise. Flynn unzipped my jeans and smiled satisfactorily at the red ribbon I tied to my dick. "Niiice." He slipped my pants off the rest of the way and stroked me. "I hope the ribbon doesn't cut off your circulation as you get thicker."

"Then un-tie it. I only made a loose bow."

He did and leaned over my crotch. "I like your idea of a present." That's when Flynn held my cock to his lips and licked me from base to tip. Every muscle in my body went limp and I struggled to breathe as he took me inside his hot mouth. I had only dreamed of this moment and it was far better than anything I imagined. I closed my eyes and let the sensations of his sucking and licking take me away; some place otherworldly. It was like floating on a storm cloud charged with electricity. Everything in me tingled.

I felt Flynn shift beside me and I opened my eyes to find his lovely red jockstrap in front of my eyes, straining to keep its package hidden. Unsuccessfully, of course. He had stretched out beside me as he sucked my cock, which meant his was within inches of my hungry throat. Flynn moaned as I freed him and licked. The taste was exquisite. He was musky and sweaty, with a hint of soap from the shower he told me he'd gotten around eight.

I took him to the back of my throat, just to the point of gagging myself, when Flynn released me and flopped bonelessly to the floor. "Oh God," he groaned. "I can't concentrate if you're gonna do that at the same time."

I laughed. "I'm not sure how guys manage this. I admit it was distracting when you had your mouth on me; but when I opened my eyes and saw your dick within grabbing distance, I had to suck it." I licked him from base to tip, and then worked the ridge with my tongue and lips as I sucked just the crown in and out, quickly and aggressively.

"Oh shit. Oh fuck. Keith. Oh!" Flynn slapped the floor with his palm and lifted his hips.

I worried he'd wake his dad, but not enough to stop.

I had a feeling it was coming before he shot his load into my mouth. I eased back and did my best not to choke. I was determined to handle it, whether or not my throat protested. Flynn needed this. I needed this. The intimacy between us could not have felt more magical than if I'd read it in a fairytale, or a romance novel. Christmas lights bathing our bodies in a rainbow of colors, Flynn's beautiful body stretching out before me like

Adonis posing for a painting, and me swallowing Flynn's ejaculate as some rare, life giving fluid straight from the chronicles of Herodotus about the land of the Macrobians. He was perfection personified.

I caught my breath as I stared at his chest, rising and falling.

I wanted to tell him how I felt right then; I wanted to say the words, but his phone chimed, "Whatcha dooooin'?" It was a sound byte from Phineas and Ferb, a cartoon my brother watched incessantly. Flynn thought it was funny and had downloaded an app to his phone. All his sounds were from that silly cartoon. I wondered who would text him this late on Christmas night. I could only guess.

"Whatcha dooooin'?" It chimed again.

Flynn grunted as he rolled to the side and grabbed his pants leg from the sofa. He pulled it across the floor and fished out his phone.

"Do you have to answer it?" I asked, suppressing my irritation. There was only one person I could think of who would interrupt our perfectly magical moment.

"Whatcha dooooin'?" It chimed a third time.

"It's probably Zach," he answered, rolling again to his back while holding his phone above his face. His limp penis was contorted out the side of the jockstrap fabric, so I carefully tucked him inside. He looked at me and grinned. "I really like my present, by the way. I might have to get you one."

"We'll see." I stretched out, hoping his text response would be a short one. "So what does Zachary, King of the Universe, have to say this late at night?"

"Um, he says, 'Hi. Are you awake?' Then he texted, 'I have a present for you that I bought in Gettysburg. I want to bring it over.' And the third text says... Oh shit!"

Flynn sat straight up and I questioned, "What? What's wrong?"

"He's on his way over."

We heard a light knock at the front door and Flynn jumped to his feet in a panic. He grabbed his jeans and pulled them on in a hurry. "Quick, get out of sight," he hissed at me.

"What?" I got off the floor slowly, while Flynn frantically grabbed all my bits of clothing and shoved them into my arms.

"Get into the closet!"

"What?" I kept asking the same question, because surely I heard him wrong. Flynn was not going to shove me into the closet. But he did. And shut the door in my face.

There I stood, in the dark; holding my bundle of clothes, naked and silent. Part of me felt humiliated, like I was some awful secret that he had to hide from the Holy Church of England or something. I remember thinking, "Zach is religious, maybe, but surely he's seen gays before?" Flynn would have to come clean about his orientation at some point. Now was as good a time as any. But that tiny whispering sound in the back of my mind kept me hidden. It was the one where my mother told me I should respect his decision and wait for him to come out on his own.

Maybe I could wait, but hiding in the closet was definitely pushing my patience to its limits. I'd never been in the closet about my sexuality, and starting now was maddening.

I heard you come in and say, "Hey. I hope it's not too late. That's why I knocked quietly. I thought I'd try knocking one more time and text again, and if you didn't answer, I was going to leave."

Why couldn't Flynn have ignored you? We'd still have been alone.

"No worries. Come on in," he said.

What? I put my eye right up to the crack between the two folding wooden doors and watched you walk into the living room.

"Is your dad up?" you said.

"No. He fell asleep a while ago." Flynn sat on the couch and you sat next to him. A little too close for my taste.

"Are things going well for you two?"

Flynn nodded. "Yeah. Real good. He's like a different person. We don't talk a whole lot yet, but he's home more and we eat together a couple of times a week."

"That's great," you replied.

And then there was silence. You were rubbing your thighs as if nervous because the room was full of unknown relatives, as you searched your brain for something to say. I couldn't understand why when Flynn had always referred to you as his best friend. A title I was completely jealous of. Surely you couldn't be uncomfortable talking to Flynn.

I bent down slowly, trying to not knock anything over in my attempt to get dressed. Standing in the closet naked suddenly felt too bizarre. I'd become a parody of the adulterous wife and you my ill-timed jealous husband. The notion made me very uncomfortable.

So why am I still standing in the closet? I thought.

I had no idea. I guess I just couldn't bring myself to make Flynn angry by confronting his fear of coming out, on Christmas of all days. I couldn't. Instead, I crouched down and deposited my clothes on the floor and felt my way, one article at a time, until I figured out which piece of clothing was which. I pulled on my shirt, a sock, my pants, and both shoes. I could only find one of my socks.

I peeked back through the crack, and you were holding out a box to Flynn.

"You didn't have to give me anything. I thought we'd stopped years ago, after discussing how spontaneous gifts were better than the expected holiday ones."

"I know, but I bought it spontaneously. Does that count?" you said, grinning.

The happiness on Flynn's face made me sick. He replied, "I guess."

I watched Flynn open the box and take out something small. It looked like an army man. The light from the Christmas tree glinted against its grey color.

You explained, "It's a confederate foot soldier. I remember you saying your great, great, great grandfather, or something..."

"Or something," Flynn added.

You grinned and continued, "...was in the eleventh Mississippi infantry and was killed in Gettysburg. My new girlfriend and I were up in Gettysburg a few weeks ago shopping for Christmas presents. I had to get it for you."

Flynn sat back on the couch and holding the little soldier in his lap. He stared at it silently. The silence stretching between the two of you was disconcerting. Why weren't you talking? I thought. What was it about that stupid little figurine that made Flynn so tongue-tied? If he was indeed tongue-tied. Maybe he thought the gift was dumb and didn't know how to tell you, the best friend, he hated it?

Flynn's final "Thank you," was whispered softly and caringly as he turned his head to look at you. It made me think the gift wasn't stupid at all. It was sentimental, and Flynn was deeply touched. My heartbeat quickened and I felt hot all of a sudden. You had given him a sentimental gift, and there I was hidden in his closet after I'd just blown him for the first time. I narrowed my eyes through the space between the doors, but my wrath was uselessly hidden in the darkness.

You pointed to the blankets next to the tree. "Were you sleeping under the tree like we used to do when we were kids?"

I strained to hear every word, hoping now was the time he'd tell you no, he'd been lying there with his boyfriend—me! "Please Flynn," I whispered.

"Not exactly." Flynn put the little soldier back in the box and set it aside and then changed the subject. "So, you have another girlfriend?" It irritated me how he'd avoid the subject like that.

"Yeah," you sighed. I'd gotten the impression you weren't happy about it. I couldn't blame you since girls had never appealed to me either, unless it was for friendship and good conversation.

"How does your mom like this one?"

"She hasn't met her. I'm afraid to even tell her. And my dad, he..." You paused with a huff. "He told me I needed to think about the future. He said it like an ultimatum. He said I needed to figure out my degree and my job situation. I got the impression he wasn't going to let it slide for long. I don't know what their problem is, but I'm not sure how much more I can take. My church has always been about family, and I guess it still is, but I'm not sure anyone has really seen my family as intimately as I have. Amy's worried about me."

"Really?" Flynn glanced at the closet. I guess he knew I'd be listening in. Was there something he didn't want me to hear? He asked you, "Is your dad still... you know?"

He asked vaguely, and at that point in time I hadn't been filled in on the details.

I wasn't sure what he meant, but I knew it couldn't have been good because you didn't answer in words. You nodded and then Flynn touched your knee, which made that little flame in my stomach that flickered before suddenly turn into a raging inferno. I wanted to beat the shit out of you. Why the hell was Flynn touching your knee?

You asked pathetically, "I don't want to go home tonight. Can I please stay here?"

"I, um...." While Flynn stuttered to answer and glanced my way, I yelled at him in my head. Say no, say no! "I guess you could stay. My dad would be okay with you sleeping on the couch."

I continued yelling inside my head, What? No! Flynn, how could you?

"Or we could sleep right there on the blanket you have out. Like old times."

"Um, yeah, I guess." Flynn glanced my way again and I wondered if he could see my eyes throwing fiery darts at him through the door crack. "Maybe you could go grab more pillows off my bed and another blanket from my closet."

"Yeah, okay." You dashed form the room and Flynn zipped over to me.

He opened the doors and I glared.

"I'm so sorry."

My half-shut eyes obviously didn't convey enough of a scowl for him to understand the depth of my disapproval.

He continued, "Zach's not in a good place right now and I think he just needs to get away from his family tonight. You understand, right?"

"No," I rumbled.

"I'm really sorry." Flynn grabbed my arm and tugged me across the room to the front door. I almost couldn't believe it was happening until he thrust me out the front door and apologized again on the porch. "I'm sorry. This isn't how I planned to spend Christmas."

I didn't believe him. "Oh really?" I lifted on eyebrow. "Then tell me Flynn, why the hell would you get naked with me on your living room floor, and then in the next moment throw me out? I thought I was your fucking boyfriend. Or was my mouth on your dick not proof enough?" I was livid.

Flynn blanched. At least he looked sorry, but I was still not going to forgive him if he threw me out. "I'm sorry," he whispered again.

"Really? I don't think you are. If you're choosing Zach over me on Christmas after I just blew you, then you can forget calling me tomorrow. Or

the day after that. I think I'll be busy from now until doomsday if this is the kind of treatment you give your boyfriends. It's shitty, Flynn, really fucking shitty."

"I know. I want to explain, but I'm not sure it's my place to tell you stuff. Just please, I'm sorry." He backed up and stepped through the doorway.

"I'm warning you Flynn. You can't treat me like this."

"I'm sorry," he said one final time, and then shut the front door in my face.

I stood there staring at the doorknob thinking any minute it would turn and the door would open. "What the fuck?" I mumbled, but no one was there to hear me.

Chapter 33

May 25, 2014: When God Intervenes

I wiped my eyes again and avoided Zach's heavy gaze.

"No wonder you hate me," he said softly.

"Yeah, well, it doesn't matter now, does it? You didn't come here to listen to my sob-story."

"No, I came here to tell you Flynn loves you, and I think you need to go to him."

Flynn loves me? Why'd he have to say that again?

"If Flynn loves me, then why is he sleeping with you?" I still had some acid left to expel.

Zach dipped his head and looked away. "I'm sorry." He sounded guilty and sad. "I never wanted it to be this way. I thought Flynn was it, ya know? We've always been so close that I thought then logical next step was... well, knowing him in the biblical sense. He wanted it too, Keith, but in New York we discovered it wasn't that simple. We'd grown into different people from when we were kids."

I felt my anger draining away with his soothing tone. Zach expressed his feeling so differently than I did. My feelings were normally explosive, and maybe corrosive, but his were sort of beautiful. I was seeing why Flynn cared for him, but I wouldn't admit it. My pride was holding firm.

"I've been in love with Flynn forever." Zach said. "In New York, he told me he thought he'd been in love with me too, only there was a 'but' after his confession. He explained his feeling was that people say—or parents, grownups, or whomever, referring to kids—that they don't understand love and therefore can't fall in love; well, he thought it was true. He said he'd been holding onto this idea of loving his best friend, and me loving him in return, ever since he realized he was gay. The kiss we shared when he was fourteen was like a rubber band that had him springing back to me in every situation, even if he didn't realize it.

"Flynn clung to the hope that he and I would finish our kiss for so long that he didn't realize he'd become consumed by it. Consumed by a kiss. See, I'd always been there for him. I was symbolically his older brother ever since Nate died. We've done everything together and I couldn't imagine a time when that wouldn't continue to be true. Flynn is a part of me. I know that's not what you want to hear."

"No, I don't. I also disagree with you. I knew from day one how much I loved Flynn. When he took my hand in art class, I knew without a doubt there would never be another man in my life."

"Then why did you break up with him so many times, and date Carter Langley?"

Leave it to Zach, the guy I hate, to use logic. "Fuck you, Zach. Every time I broke up with him it had something to do with you. Even dating Carter, on some level, was your fault. I knew I'd never love Carter. I couldn't even kiss him without feeling guilty about it."

"That's the same with me and Flynn," he pointed out. "He knew sleeping with me was wrong. He told me. He said he only wanted you, so we came home; and then all that shit happened with my parents and stuff. Yes, we're sleeping together, but only because the couch is too small. We sleep. That's it."

"Why didn't you move in with your sister?"

"Because Mr. Brewer asked me to stay with them. I think he's worried about me. He even said I could change my name to Brewer if I wanted to."

I wasn't forgiving him yet. "Are you sure that's it?" I asked flatly.

"Yes," he said, immediately followed by another apology. "And there may have been some snuggling because I like to cuddle, but Flynn never touched me intimately after we left New York. I swear. Well, except the kissing."

"Kissing?" I exclaimed loud enough for my dad to hear. I glanced over and he was definitely looking in our direction. I asked again, quieter than the first time. "Kissing? Why the hell would there be kissing?"

"Because now that we've been close like that, I guess it's hard to curb the habit."

"Curb it! Please. Or I might find it difficult restraining my fist from punching your face."

I thought Zach would take me seriously, but he snorted. Then he chuckled and smiled really wide. "I will."

"Why are you laughing?" I growled.

"Because. You wouldn't act this jealous if you weren't considering taking him back."

I jumped up and crossed my arms over my chest, stewing in my anger. Zach was right, and I hated him for it. I quickly changed the subject. "Isn't there something else you wanted? You said you wanted to talk to my dad?"

"Yeah. But only if we're done here."

"Oh, I'm done!" I stormed out of the gazebo and rejoined my dad, plopping down into the chair opposite him and re-crossing my arms.

"Did the chat go well?" my dad asked. I glared and he smiled. Oh, he infuriated me! Grace must have read me like a book because she remained silent. So did Kelly.

Zach sat down and picked up where he left off, no hesitation. "Mr. Leppo, I've been thinking a lot about God and my faith, and what I'm supposed to do now that my parents up and left me. I came here hoping you might have some answers. My therapist helped me see that hating isn't worth it when I've survived so much worse than abandonment. I wanted to apologize to Keith," he glanced at me, "and ask forgiveness." Zach turned back to my dad. "And if you don't mind, I think I want to go visit your church, because striving to do better and be perfect isn't working out for me. I want to understand a different way."

My dad said, "Of course Zach. It's always a good choice to seek out God for yourself and not rest on someone else's words. Even pastors are mere men. We'd love you come to church with us. Wouldn't we Keith? Keith?" My dad waited with that ever-present patient stare of his.

It could not have been clearer to me that God was indeed speaking. Loudly!

I stood up and rumbled my frustration to the heavens. "Okay, God, I get it!" God was all about forgiveness, acceptance, and kindness; attributes I lacked at that moment. I looked my father in the eyes across the table. "I hate that you're always right, I hate that you see God in every situation, and I hate that somehow I'm the one at fault, even though Zach stole my boyfriend." I stormed over to the edge of the deck and kicked one of the rocks that lined our flowerbed. It rolled four feet and stopped. "Ahhh! Fuck!" I yelled.

"Keith Aloysius Leppo!" my mom bellowed from door leading from the kitchen to the deck. "I don't care if you're twenty or sixty, you will not use that kind of language in my house. Is that understood, young man?"

I shrank down and mumbled, "Yes, Mom." Hearing her use my middle name reminded me there were still times when I acted like an immature adolescent instead of a man, and my mom was there to remind me to grow up.

"I couldn't hear you."

"Yes, Mother. I'm sorry." I addressed my father next, "I'm sorry, Dad. I've been out of sorts for a while. I guess... I don't know... I'm angry at myself for being this way. I just haven't figured out how to change yet." I shrugged and folded my arms over my chest. If one of them made fun of me, I'd probably scream again.

"Whoa, Keith, did Flynn write this poem?"

I turned toward my sister as she walked out onto the deck holding a piece of paper—my piece of paper. I checked my pocket, as I accused, "How did you get that?"

"I found it on the floor in the living room. It's good, and so romantic."

I snatched it away. "It's mine. You shouldn't read it!"

"Well, you shouldn't leave it on the floor, butt munch." Katie had a way with words, and I hoped she would take her words right on up the stairs and off my back.

I read over the poem again. Zach said they weren't together. Zach said Flynn loved me. Zach said I should go see him.

Could I? After everything....

"Shit!" I exclaimed as I ran into the house. I glanced at my mom. "Sorry," I pleaded as I kept moving, grabbing my keys off the coffee table.

I heard Zach holler, "Listen to the tape, Keith!"

"We're coming with you," the girls called after me.

I raced to my car, as Kelly and Grace jumped into theirs, leaving Zach with my dad. I needed Flynn back, because the air I breathed was like pure carbon dioxide without him.

Admitting I'm wrong has never been easy. Even though I'd figured it out with the ant analogy, I still hadn't managed to suck it up and go to see him. I had been waiting on Flynn. I was dead-set on him coming to me, not the other way around. Zach had humbled himself when he showed up at my house, so why couldn't I do the same? Answer: I could.

I drove like a madman through the streets of Westminster, hoping a cop wouldn't pull me over. As soon as I hit a red light, I fumbled with the voice recorder.

"What if Flynn recorded a farewell speech instead of something good?" I asked aloud before hitting play. "Breathe. Just breathe," I reminded myself. I could be stressing over nothing. Plus, I needed to pay attention to the tape and drive. Stressing more wasn't helping.

I hit play just as the light turned green.

"Hey." Flynn's voice forced a whimpered sigh from my throat. *"I wanted to talk to you in person, but I ended up in the hospital again. I guess I overdid it. I wanted to say I'm sorry... for everything. My memory's a little spotty, and I still can't remember anything from the day of the wedding, but I do know that I hurt you. I never meant to. I have no excuse other than stupidity, because all my fears about coming out to Zach were pointless. When he came out to me and said he was bisexual...,"* I widened my eyes. Bisexual? Really? I thought he was gay. Why didn't he tell me? *"I realized how much time I'd wasted with you. He and I shared similar secrets and if we'd just been honest with each other from the beginning, then the last couple of years could have been totally different. But would I change them? No."*

Flynn sniffled on the tape.

"Shit, I was trying not to cry. Anyway.... Going to New York helped me see my life differently. Zach and I found each other again in those couple of days. If we'd been honest years ago, then the closeness we shared in New York would have always been there. I have no doubt we'd have been together all this time. But the thing is—if I'd been with Zach—I would have never fallen in love with you. And I am you know, in love with you."

Exactly what Zach had told me.

"I think some part of me always wanted to know what would have happened if Zach and I went beyond that kiss. I wish we would've gone farther back then, and maybe gotten off with a hand job or something, so I could have dismissed it as lust. But we didn't, so my head got stuck in a loop

of what-ifs, like that episode of Buffy where she had to get the live mummy hand from the basement of the Magic Box."

I snickered. Flynn knew I loved Buffy.

"In New York, I feel like we gained closure." I heard muffled sounds on the recording, like a hand was over the speaker. *"My dad said I've talked enough and I need some sleep. Please come see me. I miss you so much. I guess I'll ask Kelly to bring you the poem I wrote and this voice recording. Keith...."* Flynn sniffled again and it broke my heart. I stopped the tape so I could remove my glasses, wipe my eyes, and calm down.

"Another red light," I grumbled. "Of course they're all red when I want to get to Flynn as quickly as possible." Flynn's luck was rubbing off on me. I wiped my eyes and put my glasses back on. I could do this. I was only two lights away; I'd be holding him soon.

"Keith, I love you." My breath hitched. I hit rewind so I could hear the words again. *"...come see me. I miss you so much. I guess I'll ask Kelly to bring you the poem I wrote and this voice recording. Keith... Keith, I love you. If I had any sense at all I would have kicked Carter Langley in the head and told him to get lost,"* he knew about Carter, *"that you were mine, but I didn't. I saw you get in his car at Christmas and I didn't even try to win you back. I was a coward and I thought you'd gotten over me. But Zach told me... he told me you stepped aside for him. Keith, that's the most selfless thing anyone has ever done for me. You gave me up for me to try and find happiness with Zach. Please, when you get this, come back to me."*

The recording ended. It didn't answer all my questions, but it gave me a good idea that Zach had been truthful. Flynn loved me and he wanted me back. There'd always been a pull between us that I could not deny, but was I really ready to overlook my issues? Flynn and I had always been a sort of living demonstration of Newton's universal law of gravitation, and wanting him wasn't a question. I wanted to know where Zach fit in. Was ours a simple linear equation? Or more of a complex variation of the Fourier inversion theorem?

"Or maybe I overanalyze our relationship by using too much scientific jargon to make sense," I fussed at myself.

One thing was true, though, Zach told me they'd had sex. Could I deal with that?

"No!" My stomach seized, I clenched my fists; I wanted to scream, punch something, and puke all at once. I leaned forward and brought my fist down on my dashboard twice, brain spinning, blood surging. I felt betrayed, yet I had no one to blame except myself. My eyes burned with traitorous tears that fought hard for freedom.

His touch was the one I wanted more than any other, yet he had touched Zach. Those same luscious fingers, which knew all the right ways to touch me and make me whimper and beg, had also touched Zach. Did they map out Zach's skin? Did they caress him with the same attentiveness?

The very thought of Zach touching Flynn, kissing Flynn, being inside of Flynn, made me sick. I wanted to punch him again and kick the shit out of his stupid, broken ass. I didn't care what kind of crap he'd been through. He'd been with Flynn and I was out of my mind with jealousy.

"Why is every fucking light red?" I screamed.

I heard screeching tires to my left and looked over just as a white pickup truck was struck from behind. A green car hit the truck so hard it lifted the back end off the ground and moved it several feet. Then the car flipped in the air and landed upside down, skidding across the intersection in my direction.

"Oh shit!"

I reached for my seatbelt.

***

May 26, 2014

I heard beeping. Steady, annoying, incessant beeping. I wanted to sleep, but that beeping! I opened my eyes. Or rather, I tried, but my eyelids felt like lead shutters. With great effort, I pried them open. I was staring at a drop ceiling: white, sectioned, with a curved track snaking around to partition something off with a curtain. A curtain. Even without my glasses I could see there was a curtain drawn around the foot of my bed, except my bed didn't have a curtain and my ceiling wasn't constructed from fiberboard material from The Home Depot.

Where the heck am I?

I turned my head, which took more effort than opening my eyes, and saw hospital monitors. Monitors with another curtain behind them, probably separating the room, and my mom; sitting in a chair by the wall, reading a pamphlet.

"M...." My first attempt to call her over probably sounded like nothing but air. I had no strength. My mind was foggy and my body felt like I'd been submerged in molasses. I flexed my fingers. *At least they're working.* I tried speaking again and this time it came out as a recognizable word, not merely a sound. "Mom?"

She looked up right away, which told me she could hear me; this wasn't a dream.

She jumped to my side. "Oh honey, you're awake," she said, before leaning down to kiss my head. "Everyone will be so relieved."

"What... happened? Why am I... so groggy?" It took effort to form a long sentence, but I wasn't without determination. "And who took my glasses?"

"You were in a car accident," she explained.

"What? When? I don't...."

She caressed the side of my face. "Yesterday afternoon. You were on your way to see Flynn. The girls saw the whole thing. Are you sure you want to hear all this now? You're only just waking up from surgery."

That was alarming. "Surgery? Yes, please, tell me. Where's Flynn?"

"He went with your dad to get coffee. They should be back any minute, but I'll text them." She got her phone out, texted, and then explained how I'd ended up in the hospital. "The girls told us a car struck your driver's side door while you were waiting at the red light. Grace said it's a miracle you're alive, since the front end of the car was practically in the driver's seat." She paused and wiped tears from her eyes. "Oh Keith. When Kelly called, I thought I'd lost you." She collapsed over me, curling her arms around my neck and snuggling her face into my hair.

"But... I'm okay, right? I didn't lose a...." I stopped myself. I hadn't thought about flexing my toes. What if my legs had been amputated? What if I was paralyzed? What if every bone in my body had been broken and that's why I felt as if I'd been sedated with elephant tranquilizers?

Before she could respond, I wiggled the toes of my right foot. I could feel them. Five distinct toes wriggled around inside my sock. Other foot. "Oh jeez!" I winced. Yes, I could feel my toes, but between my toes and my brain was a leg full of muscles that didn't appreciate random usage to assess toe movement or anything else.

"Are you okay?" my mom asked, concerned, lifting her head and peering at me with wide eyes. My mom was always concerned about something.

"Yeah, Mom. I moved my toes and my entire leg protested. What happened? Obviously it's still attached, but it hurts like hell."

She refrained from commenting about me saying "hell," thank goodness. "I'll call the nurse," she said. "She told us to let her know if you were in any pain."

"Pain. Yes. Lots!"

After the nurse arrived, and had injected something into my IV, she told us the doctor would be in shortly to check on me.

My mom resumed her description of the accident, but as she spoke, I felt my body getting lighter. The pain was definitely alleviated. Mom said, "Well, as close as I remember it being described to me: somehow you dove into the passenger's seat, even though your seatbelt was still fastened, and hit your head on the passenger door upon impact. They found your glasses on the floor of the passenger's side. The driver's side of the car was pushed in and the steering wheel pinned your left leg to the seat. They had to cut you out, honey."

"What did I need surgery for?" I asked, my muscles relaxing as the drugs took effect.

"Your leg bone was snapped in half below the knee. They said your tibia was sticking out." She descended on me again with hugs and kisses. I didn't mind. The drugs had me floating. "Oh Keith. I'm so glad you're still here."

I loved and appreciated my mom's attention, though normally it was a bit much. "Mom. I'm fine. I'll heal, right?"

She stood upright again and nodded, smoothing my hair back, which was something I hated because it always made my curls stick up. "Yes. It will take a while, but the doctor said he thought you'd make a full recovery."

My dad walked in with Flynn following him. It took two seconds for Flynn to weave around my dad and fling himself over my chest.

"Well, I guess that answers the 'who gets the next hug' question," my dad said lightheartedly.

Flynn's warmth encircled me. I could feel his soft hair against my face. He smelled like chlorine, which made me smile, because he always smelled like chlorine. People probably thought he used it as cologne, but those who knew him understood it was from how much time he spent in his pool. Shampoo couldn't even get the smell out, because it saturated his skin and hair.

"I missed you," I whispered.

Flynn made a noise and moved back so he could look at me. His eyes were red, but it could have been from swimming as easily as from crying.

"Honey, let's give them a few minutes," my mom said. Out of the corner of my eye I saw my parents leave.

It was just the two of us, and that stupid, beeping machine.

"I don't know where to start," Flynn's voice broke.

"Let me," I said, hating the grogginess, though my mind felt clearer than it had a few minutes ago. My right arm felt less weighted down, so maybe the anesthesia was wearing off, but I still felt as though I was floating in a whirlpool after the drug she'd just given me. I told him, "I love you."

Flynn smiled a crooked smile and a tear ran down the side of his face. "I love you too," he squeaked, sounding even more emotional.

I continued, "I can't remember everything right now. I don't remember the accident, and I can't think of everything Zach told me, but I remember I had to see you. I needed you. I needed you to know I loved you and how much I wanted us to be together."

Flynn sighed and relief showed on his adorable face. "I want that, too. Oh, God, Keith, I want that too. I'm so sorry for everything I've done. So many years we could have—"

I interrupted, "Stop. Don't rehash it right now. I can't think clearly." I lifted my thirty-pound arm and brushed the side of his face with my stiff fingers. He audibly choked on a sob as I continued ghosting over his skin and hair. It was softer than I remembered. "I like the pink hair, by the way."

Flynn chuckled through his tears. "Thanks. It's fuchsia," he corrected with a wink. "I got tired of the blue, so when the wedding came up I thought it was time for a change."

"Pink or fuchsia, I think it makes you even more adorable. And don't think I didn't notice you're wearing *my* gray plaid shirt." My mind was swirly but lucid.

"I like having your smell all over me."

I fingered the tips of the pink hair behind his left ear, and grinned. He remembered what I'd said the day I stole his shirt the first time we'd been naked together. Flynn was just as sentimental as me, and it got my blood pumping. If I wasn't in a hospital bed, and zinging on painkillers, I knew for sure I'd be flipping him over and diving in for a taste of his neck.

Flynn leaned back down and nestled his face into my neck, whispering, "I'm also wearing your shirt because it helps me dream about you."

I could smell the chlorine scent of his hair, and feel his nose rubbing me under my chin. He brought his arm up across my chest and caressed my neck, ear, and hair as we snuggled. Although I doubted he was comfortable, since the side of the bed was still up. I remembered what it felt like jammed into my chest when our positions were reversed not much more than a month ago.

I remembered waiting for him to awaken. I remembered feeling helpless and empty at the thought I might lose him. He'd been in a coma for days. I'd worried he might never wake up.

"Flynn, how long was I out? I mean, was I in a coma like you? My mom told me I hit my head."

Flynn remained as close as he could get and spoke under my chin. "Not real long after the first time you woke up."

"Huh?" I was confused.

Flynn explained, "You woke up when the doctor said the anesthesia would wear off, except you were really aggressive the first time so they gave you a sedative. You were in surgery for hours, but you woke up when they thought you might. You suffered a mild concussion, but not a big deal."

"I don't remember being awake before, let alone aggressive."

"The doctor said it was normal for young men to wake up from surgery like a bull in a China shop. I didn't like it. You moaned incoherently and thrashed about. I was glad they calmed you down with drugs. It made your mother cry."

"I'm sorry I scared you."

"It's okay." Flynn snuggled his face closer, maybe to escape the bad memory.

"Mom said the accident was yesterday. What time is it?"

"I'm not moving to look at my phone, but my best guess would be three in the morning."

"Is that why it seems so dark?"

"Yup."

Our alone time was interrupted by the doctor who came in to check on me. He said I had broken my leg in the accident. *Blah, blah, balh*.... The doctor said a bunch of other things about recovery and PT, but my brain shut off when I noticed Flynn standing in the corner of the room watching me. *Flynn.* My gut clenched, my breathing quickened and my tongue became a rubbery glob of goo that the orthodontist puts in your mouth when they need to make an impression for a retainer. *Flynn.* It took every bit of strength I had not scream at the freakin' doctor to get the hell out of Dodge so I could make out with my boyfriend. My boyfriend. He agreed with me when I said I wanted us to be together.

I had to be patient while the doctor rambled. For once, I was glad to have my parents present so they could listen to all the details, because my mind had checked out after the first couple minutes. *Flynn.* He was gorgeous. His innocent charm had captured my attention back in art class. He had no idea how beautiful he was.

"Thank you Dr. Green. If we think of any questions, my wife or I will call you." My dad shook the doctor's hand and he left the room.

My parents told me they'd come back later after some sleep. Mom said my brother would be in at 8:00 a.m. to sit with me for a couple hours, followed by my sister Katie. Of course, Grace and Kelly would be in, and Mr. Brewer planned to stop by as well. I wasn't sure how long I'd be in the hospital, but I knew I would rarely be alone.

Flynn was the last to leave. "I don't want to go," he said. "I feel like I just got you back." He caressed my cheek and gazed into my eyes.

"We can talk more tomorrow. Or today. Whatever. I'm not dead. I'm not breaking up with you ever again."

"Promise?" He looked dubious. "You said you couldn't remember everything."

"I remember enough," I told him. "I know I hate Zach enough to fill his bed with cockroaches and smear peanut butter under his car door handles."

I thought he'd laugh or chuckle a tiny bit at my jest, but the joke fell flat. "That's gross. You're not serious, right? I mean... Zach told me he went to see you yesterday. I know about the conversation and he apologized for

354 | Wade Kelly

not giving you my recording and the poem. He also said he mentioned living at my house. He did tell you that, right?"

Why did Flynn sound worried? "Um, yeah. He said he was living there after his parents left."

Flynn pulled back a few inches. I wasn't sure what that meant. What was he about to say that needed more distance? "Zach's been sleeping in my bed, Keith. The couch is too small, even if he was used to sleeping on a twin bed. He's been in my room for weeks."

My natural instinct would have said, "Argue about it, Keith. Tell him exactly what you feel!" But this time, it was as if something else whispered in my head. Maybe it was the Holy Spirit, whom I often ignored, who told me I'd been spared for a reason. If the accident was as bad as my mom's tears indicated, and I didn't die as I could have, then maybe God was giving me a second chance to practice forgiveness. I'd spent way too many years reacting to jealously.

"Come here. Don't pull away." When he did, I fingered his hair as I explained. "I'm not happy with you sleeping with Zach, but I'm working on getting over it. If you tell me there isn't anything going on, I'll believe you. Zach isn't my favorite person, but I understand why you've tried to protect him all these years. He's a good guy, and he didn't deserve the things his parents did to him."

I tear rolled down his cheek. "Thank you."

"If there are a two things I can learn from all this, the first would be that jealousy gets me nowhere. I remember feeling angry and extremely jealous in the car. I may not remember the accident itself, but I remember feeling those two things very strongly and they aren't healthy. Second, I didn't die. I think that's a sign that I should think about why. I always say I'm a Christian, but I often don't act like one. I'm not very loving and forgiving, as much as I'm controlling and possessive. I'm fine with preaching the truth to everyone else, but rarely do I turn the spotlight on my own life. If God allowed me to live, then I need to learn from it. I love you, Flynn." I felt tears slip from the corners of my eyes as I gazed into his beautiful face. "I want to show you every day how special you are to me, and I want to feel thankful that God gave me another chance. We can talk more about this when I get home, okay? For now, I want to kiss you."

Flynn smiled and leaned in, pressing his lips to mine. If ever heaven was within my reach, it was now.

Chapter 34

August 16, 2014: The Air I Breathe

The next couple months were interesting for me. One's desire to always be in control seriously takes a hit when you need everyone else to do things for you. I was in a cast forever, and sleeping on the couch in the living room until I had enough balance to make my way up the steps on crutches. Not the best goal to rush, but one I was determined to achieve. My bed was so much nicer than that stupid couch that smelled like my brother's stinky feet.

In my room, though, no one could hear when I needed help. I had to text my mom and wait for her to respond and come up to see me. The seclusion, however, was a definite bonus when Flynn visited, as we had the privacy to kiss and snuggle without people walking by, which had happened when I'd been on the living room couch. Hence my desire to take my broken leg upstairs.

We avoided serious conversation for a long time, opting to watch movies and pretend there weren't issues to work on, because I think we both knew talking in my living room meant anyone could overhear. Once I'd made it up the steps, we had time to shut the door and let our walls down. I think we'd been the most honest in those few discussions than ever before in the years we'd known each other.

Flynn said, "The stars aligned when I met you," and I knew he meant it.

His relationship with Zach was something I didn't really understand. They had a sixth sense about each other that creeped me out from time to time. I'd seen a YouTube video once about twins communicating without speech. If I hadn't known better, I would have assumed they were twins based on their seemingly telepathic communication. Plus, they'd been extremely affectionate in my presence, which I did not care for. It was difficult letting go of my jealousy when they seemed so comfortable touching, laughing, and reading each other's minds.

They celebrated their birthday in July at my house, which I appreciated on some level, but witnessing their bond was almost too much for my newly turned leaf of "forgiveness and acceptance" to handle. Lucky for me, Grace and Kelly were there to assure me they'd seen nothing between them to suggest a relationship beyond friendship. Except for some random kisses, which I protested against often enough myself.

After I got my cast off in August, I figured it was one step closer to regaining a normal life. Flynn came to visit me that weekend.

"Hey," he greeted me as he strolled into my bedroom leaving the door wide open.

"Hey, I was just thinking about you. How did the job go?" Flynn told me he'd spent all week designing a flower garden in the back of Mr. Blevins' yard.

"Good." He sat on the bed and rubbed my thigh. "I'm tired, though. I don't sleep much. I can't stop thinking about you. I don't see you enough."

"I don't disagree."

He grinned, kicked his shoes off, and climbed over me to crawl up the bed beside me. I wrapped my arm around his back as he pressed himself against my chest. "I wish I didn't have to work. All I want is to lie in bed with you all day, every day, and make love for hours."

My dick pulsed involuntarily. We hadn't made love for a very long time.

Since I'd been home, we never found enough time alone. He suggested closing the door, but I'd felt so isolated with the door closed while I had the cast on and couldn't jump up easily, that I'd gotten used to keeping it open.

I'd been walking on my leg less than a week, going to physical therapy, and I hoped it wouldn't be long until I could drive again. I suggested, "Maybe one day we can get our own place and make love in every room of the house."

Flynn chuckled. "Yeah." He slipped his hand under the hem of my shirt and swirled his fingers around my navel. It tickled, but it also sent shivers down to my groin, to which I could not bring myself to protest.

Despite his roving hand, which made its way up to my nipples, pinching them, as he knew I loved, I managed to ask, "How's Zach? Did his parents' house get sold? I know you mentioned a few weeks ago there was a sign out front about a contract pending."

"Oh, I guess I forgot to tell you. My dad bought it. He and Krista said our house is too small. He's having the inside remodeled, but we should move in after the wedding if not before."

"Wow. That's convenient. Moving will be easy. When's the date again?"

"October eighteenth." Flynn's fingers gently fingered the hairs of my chest. Not necessarily erotic, but I felt myself getting hard anyway.

"I suppose Zach will be moving in with you all?" I was jealous, but the anger I used to feel was lessening. Progress was slow, but it was there.

"Probably. He got his old job back, though. The tree company gave him another chance, so he'll be making good money. I bet he'll move out once he has enough saved. I can't imagine Carlos would want to visit if he told him he lived with his best friend and his parents."

"Who's Carlos?"

"The guy we met in New York. He's Zach's new boyfriend. So far they've only spoken over the phone, but I have a feeling it was dirty talk. I caught him with his hand down his pants once, and after that Zach talked to Carlos in the downstairs washroom with the door shut. It's funny."

"What about Gwendolyn? And Amelia? I haven't heard you talk about them for a while." The touch of his fingers almost made me forget everything else, and if I wasn't careful I was going to break my own rule about fooling around with the door open.

I felt Flynn nudge his groin against my leg as he spoke, and the sensation drove me crazy. "Gwendolyn's still in the picture. They're trying to make the relationship work, but he's also still attracted to me. I think meeting Carlos helped, because he's sorting out his attraction to men in general, not just to me. He's also talking to Gwen about it, and how they might work his bisexuality into their relationship dynamic. I don't really get it, but it's up to them who's in their bed."

"What about you? Would you want to be with Zach again?" I don't know why I asked, but something in my head needed to hear the answer.

"Only if it was a threesome with you."

I hesitated in shock. "Not the answer I wanted."

Flynn lifted his head and grinned. "I'm joking. Threesomes came up in New York because Zach thinks Gwendolyn might be into it, but I told him I didn't think you'd be interested."

"You thought right! The only threesome I want involves me, Zach, and my fist punching him in the face."

Flynn moved his hand and made slow circles across my stomach and chest. "Ease up, sweets, I told him I wouldn't without you. I'm not going to cheat on you. I told him if you and I are together, then everyone else is off limits."

I swallowed the lump in my throat. It was the first time Flynn used my term of endearment for him that had me feeling mushy inside instead of angry. "I admit I'm still having trust issues. I can't pretend I'm not insanely jealous every time I see the two of you together."

"I know." Flynn slid closer, smug little grin on his face. He maneuvered his way slowly across my waist, straddling me, rubbing his groin over mine as he brought his lips down on my mouth. The gravitational pull was stronger than ever. He tilted his hips into me and rocked as he kissed me so completely it was like learning how to use my tongue all over again.

He broke our kiss to remove his shirt, tossing it to the floor. *Oh fuck me, he's adorable. Plus, he was wearing the arrowhead I gave him.* "Flynn, where'd you get that necklace? I thought I lost it."

He undulated his hips again. "Taryn."

"The ninja nurse at the hospital?"

"Yeah. You had it on when you went into surgery. She gave it to me."

Flynn was writhing on top of me. He bent his head and went for my neck.

"You realize the door is open."

Flynn rocked again, creating lovely friction between our meshed groins as he gave me a hickey. "Want me to stop?"

I relented. "I could never deny how badly I want you." He slid his hands up my chest, pushing my shirt up. Flynn licked my nipples, one after the other, as he ground his body against mine. I licked my lips in anticipation of what I knew tasted so good.

Flynn pressed himself tightly against me and locked his mouth on mine, sliding one hand behind my head.

I took the opportunity to caress his back and squeeze his ass with both hands. I lifted my hips and he rutted against me.

Flynn kissed the life out of me as he grabbed both my arms and moved them above my head where he pinned them with one hand. "Keep them there," he whispered. His move was more a sign of control than dominance, I suspected, since he wasn't strong enough to hold both my arms in that position if I protested. I allowed him his way, enjoying the weight of his body on me.

Flynn's roaming hand found its way up underneath the hem of my shirt again as he kissed his way down to my neck. I felt a wave of heat trail over my skin everywhere his fingers and lips moved. "I've missed your skin," he whispered, "and your happy trail." He sighed contentedly as he made slow circles with his palm over my lower belly. He rubbed his cheek over mine, sighing again, "I love how your facial hair tickles my lips." Flynn playfully lipped my mustache. I'd have giggled if I weren't so turned on. He licked my Adam's apple and sucked the skin below it until I felt a sting. "I want to taste you, Keith. All of you," he breathed heavily.

He had me panting, burning, and willing to do anything to give him what he wanted.

I lifted my hips once more and rasped, "Flynn."

I heard a throat clearing from the doorway.

We both snapped our attention in that direction and found Mr. Brewer standing there with his eyebrow raised. "At least you're in Keith's bed this time. That's better than finding you on my couch." He shook his head.

Flynn smiled wide and pecked my lips again. "Sorry, Dad," he said.

Flynn started crawling off of me, but he father insisted, "Don't stop on my account. You're both twenty years old now. What you do in your bed is your business, although I recommend shutting the door. His siblings are downstairs. "

Flynn chuckled. He flopped down next to me, watching his father as he rubbed my stomach. "Deal."

Mr. Brewer smiled at me. "It's nice to see the two of you together, Keith. My boy missed you."

"Thanks." I looked back at Flynn and told Mr. Brewer, "I missed him too."

Flynn winked at me.

"I came up to tell you Mrs. Leppo said dinner will be served in twenty minutes. Krista and I are setting up the badminton net if you care to play Flynn. Keith, your mom said no go, even if your cast *is* off."

I huffed. "That sucks. I hate watching."

"I can play with my shirt off if that makes watching better for you. I could run the hose over my hair and let the water drip down my chest."

I groaned, "That would be so cruel."

Mr. Brewer chuckled. "How about I stall for another fifteen minutes and give you two some time to alleviate the sexual tension."

Flynn gaped at his father. "I cannot believe you just said that."

Mr. Brewer chuckled again as he closed the door, and I reflected on how easily we'd slipped back into the same relationship. Mr. Brewer had always done things to embarrass Flynn and make me laugh. It was as though we'd never been apart.

Flynn took his dad seriously and urged me to remove my shirt. When I did, he resumed rubbing my stomach. Fingers caressing, breath mingling, Flynn made me forget all the reasons I was ever jealous of Zach. He leaned in and kissed up my chest, nipped my neck, nibbled his was over to my ear, and whispered, "How would I describe my love, in sentences or pictures...."

His poem. My insides quivered. I had it framed and hung it over my desk.

"When nothing tangible can denote my heart's span of tinctures?" His fingers worked my zipper. Flynn kept whispering as he kissed and caressed my skin. "It flourishes of its own accord and surpasses every theme...," Flynn paused as he slipped my pants down my legs, shed his own shorts, and crawled back over my body, seducing me with poetry. "And when I feel I know its depths, love redefines my dream."

I felt his cock, stiff and ready, sliding next to mine with a barrier of cotton in between. He hadn't removed our underwear, but I suspected it was to build my anticipation and make me beg. Oh, I would beg all right... *soon.* Repositioning my hands above my head, he continued his poetical seduction. "Not found in smiles or softest touch, nor eye, nor lips, nor laughter," he murmured, licking a line straight up my chest.

"Flynn," I mewled. He had me aching and melting with every kiss, every touch, and every word. But it was that last line that made my heart explode.

He leaned back, gazed deeply into my eyes, and declared softly, "No, love is not a solid thing I choose to have or leave." I felt a tear slip from the corner of my eye as his affirmation washed over me. "It's in that space around your soul," he kissed me, "your breath, the air I breathe."

Epilogue

October 18, 2014: My Knight

He loves me. I could see it in his eyes, even at this distance, as he made his way around the venue floor to talk to several guests. The wedding venue, in Mount Vernon, Maryland, was like a castle, or an Episcopal church, with gothic windows and curve-topped doors. The reception was held in the ballroom, which boasted fifteen-foot ceilings and original chandeliers circa 1879. The place was like a trip back in time, and I, Keith Leppo, had the complete attention of the most handsome knight in all the realm.

I'd thought that Gwendolyn's idea of a "dream wedding" sounded stupid at first. Who had ever heard of a Victorian wedding before? Of course, when I voiced my discontent, she promptly showed me pictures on the Internet and I had apologized for my stupidity. I guess people really did have Victorian weddings. I didn't like the pantaloons that Flynn had worn at Zach's wedding, so I guess my mind couldn't conceive a non-traditional wedding being even remotely cool until Zach's aunt Krista suggested a medieval wedding.

This wedding was wicked awesome.

The first incredibly awesome part—no trees decided to fall on my man. Second—we got to dress up like Knights of the Round Table and carry weapons. True, the tunics resembled dresses on some of the guests, but the black leather vest Flynn wore, with the chainmail collar, made me burn with desire. I wanted to cross swords with him the entire day.

The part I didn't like was sitting with the guests while Flynn and Zach stood up front with the wedding party. Mr. Brewer made a point to tell me it was nothing personal and he wasn't picking Zach over me out of favoritism; he wanted his "sons" to stand with him. Since Zach's family had disappeared, Zach had lived with them and been taken in as an "adopted" son. While my jealousy rose often, if was hard to maintain a grudge when

Zach seemed so happy. He joked more and smiled a lot. I could actually see why Flynn had been drawn to him his whole life. The guy was infectious. In fact, I found myself smiling often while watching him interact with Mr. Brewer.

Damn!

Hard to hate a guy when he actually contained enough personality to turn anyone's frown upside down. *I can't believe he made me rhyme in my head.*

But that was Zach. He really was a great guy. Plus, I liked him. *Crap!*

So I watched the guests as my man made his way around to talk to people. I sipped apple cider and people-watched until Flynn was done thanking guests for attending. For a guy with few relatives, his father had tons friends from work. I was glad.

I felt hands clasp my shoulders from behind my chair and I flopped my head back to look at Flynn. I'd know his touch anywhere.

He leaned down and kissed me like MJ kissed Spiderman, only his hands slid down my chest and back up, cupping my face as he kissed me several times. I'd never imagined Flynn would be so openly affectionate in public, and I adored him for it. He rubbed his nose over mine and then took a seat. "So, my dad wants to talk to me in private. When I get back, I want to take you out on that dance floor. We haven't danced together since prom."

"Sounds good," I said.

Before Flynn walked away, Zach plopped down in the chair next to his and downed an entire glass of water. I may not have stood in the wedding party, but the new Mrs. Brewer was kind enough to seat me with Flynn at the head table.

"Hey," he said, setting the empty glass back down. "You having fun?"

He was looking at me, so I assumed he meant for me to answer. "Yup. You?"

"Best wedding I've ever been to!" he replied with gusto and a glowing smile. He was dressed like a knight also, but didn't look as sexy as Flynn. Zach was okay-looking.

"It's all because of our house guest," Flynn added.

"Is that your long distance boyfriend?" I asked, because I hadn't met him before.

"Yup. His name's Carlos Rodriguez," Zach said. "He works at the hotel we stayed at in New York. He's really hot, isn't he?"

Hot or not, I wasn't about to answer a question like that. Flynn was my hot guy; all other hot guys could wiggle their leather-clad asses anywhere they wanted as long as Flynn's remained exclusively mine. "What about Gwendolyn?" I changed the subject. I hadn't seen her since April, so I was beginning to wonder.

Flynn kissed me one more time and then pointed his finger at Zach, leaning close, he said, "You remember what I said?"

Zach rolled his eyes. "Yes, mother. I promise to use condoms."

I snorted and covered my smirk with my hand as Flynn smiled and finished his stern warning. "I'm not joking. All this freedom has you doing crazy things. I don't want you screwing up your life with the first guy you meet." Flynn was smiling, but Zach and I both knew he was dead serious.

Zach stood up and looked Flynn in the eyes. "Thanks Flynn. No worries, really; your dad took care of situation with a little… gift."

Zach said it sarcastically, I could tell. I had to ask, "Was it the kind of gift that comes in a brown paper bag?" I had a feeling one of Mr. Brewer's humorously embarrassing gifts had now been bestowed on Zach.

Zach gave me a look. "Yeah. How'd you know?"

I chuckled. "Let's just say Mr. Brewer likes to keep his boys safe."

Flynn laughed and Zach sat back down looking as if he'd missed the joke.

I added, "Did you get massage oil?"

"No," Zach said.

"Then I win." I beamed, feeling favored over Zach for the first time.

"I'll be right back," Flynn said. I received another kiss, and then he walked over to his dad. Mr. Brewer was dressed like King Author. *Hard not to love that costume.*

"So… Gwendolyn?" I asked again, refocusing our conversation.

"We're working on a long distance relationship until she can break away from her father. But so far, he's realizing my father was insane, he manipulated Mr. Pierce for his money and investments." Zach picked up another glass of water and sucked it down. He was sweating profusely from all the dancing he and Carlos had been doing. Also, I surmised, due to the layers of leather and chainmail armor. He looked the part, but his attire had to be an oven. Flynn said his was.

He continued, "Gwen's also visiting her sister often in the mental institution. The doctors say she suffers from bipolar affective disorder. When she was here, it was in the beginning stages and progressed quickly. Since the cause can be genetic or environmental, her family is sticking together for a while to help in whatever way they can. As far as our relationship goes," Zach smiled, "we're good. I'm more relaxed because I don't have the pressure of a looming wedding, and we've been talking on the phone a couple times a week to get to know one another. I still think she's amazing."

"And Carlos?"

I swear I heard Zach growl as he glanced over at the guy. "Oh Keith, the things that guy can do with his tongue. Oh fuck."

I held up my hand. "More than I needed to know."

Flynn returned as Zach stood up. "Hey, you okay?" Zach asked him, touching his arm all too intimately.

"Yeah. I'm fine." Flynn's bewildered expression made me question the truthfulness of his quick answer.

"Okay. I'll talk to ya later." Zach kissed him before he walked away.

"Hey!" I protested. "You did it again!"

Zach jumped back over to me and got down on his knee by my chair. "I am so sorry. I swear I didn't mean it."

"Just like you didn't mean it the other twelve times. Oh yeah, I'm counting." I was tough with Zach, but the frequency of random kisses really had diminished. I knew if I kept putting my foot down, they'd eventually stop. Well, I hoped they would.

"I'm trying to stop. Really. I promise." Zach crossed his fingers over his heart.

"Stop groveling and go play with your hot guy's tongue."

Zach patted my arm and grinned. "Ooh, you certainly know how to get rid of me."

"Go!"

Flynn sat down and placed an envelope on the table while staring off into the distance.

"What's up? You look dazed and confused." Not that I was referencing the '90s movie, or the song by Led Zeppelin. Flynn was seconds away from drool running out of his gaping lips.

"My dad," he replied.

"Your dad... what?"

He handed me the envelope and I opened it. It was a deed of some sort. Flynn's name was at the top. It had their home address on it. "What is this? It looks like it has to do with your house."

He nodded. "Dad's giving me the house."

"What?"

"After he bought the Mitchells' house, I thought he was going to sell ours. Their house is bigger and with a new wife I knew he wanted a fresh start. I never dreamed he'd give me ours."

I glanced over the paper again. "As in... *your own house?*" I repeated.

"Yes. Dad gave me the house. He said it was traditional to give the best man a present and that this one seemed the most practical. After the honeymoon, Dad's moving next door to live with Krista, and I get our current house all to myself."

"Holy shit!" I put the deed down and grabbed his hand. "You own a house?"

Flynn smiled. "I own a house."

"Oh my gosh! That's incredible."

"I know. So... you want to move in with me?"

"Yes!" I agreed emphatically. "I'm not letting you live with Zach all alone. It's bad enough he's still there."

"Then... are you all right sharing the house with him?"

I had reservations, but I couldn't deny that my feelings toward Zach changed that day in the cemetery. Something about the way he cowered when I punched him altered my perception. As the months progressed, I sort of felt the same protectiveness that Flynn felt for him, but I wasn't about to voice it. "Our mutual hatred is dwindling. As long as we get the bigger bedroom and he stays in your old room, I'm fine with it. Plus, I get to pick out our new bed."

Flynn's smile grew wider than I'd ever seen it. "You do love Zach. Admit it."

"I admit nothing."

Flynn leaned forward and kissed me, several times actually. He slid his hand behind my neck and held me fast as his lips and tongue took possession of my mouth. The image of dueling lances flashed inside my mind. *Mmm. Later, I'll unlace his vest, remove his armor, and mount that lance.*

He kissed down my neck and then over to my ear. I gasped, "Flynn... Oh, Flynn." He knew just how to get me going.

He held my face in both hands and smiled into my eyes. "I love you."

Flynn stood up when the minstrels started up another song. I'd been paying attention to it all afternoon because I couldn't remember a time when lutes and dulcimers ever sounded so lively. Or maybe it was this wedding in particular that brought out the liveliness, no matter the instruments. Either way I enjoyed it.

Flynn bowed formally to me, which made me blush, extended his hand and asked, "May I have this dance, fair sir?"

I clasped his hand, and he kissed my knuckles before leading me to the center of the dance floor where all eyes were on us. *The center, not over in the shadows.* His father smiled approvingly, and Flynn took me into his arms. "Go slow, okay sweets?" I warned. "My bone is in one piece, but I'm not the most coordinated yet."

"I gotcha," he assured me, holding me tight.

For the first time, we were just us: two people who fell in love and didn't have to hide it. Our path had gotten muddled, and our affection misplaced along the way, but we'd made it.

Cheek to cheek, Flynn whispered in my ear, "Do you think it will always feel this wonderful?"

I knew what he meant. "Yes."

Flynn nuzzled my ear with his nose. "Will you dance with me at *our* wedding?"

Chills raced down my spine. I whispered back, "Yes. And every day, for the rest of my life."

About The Author

Wade Kelly lives and writes in conservative, small-town America on the east coast where it's not easy to live free and open in one's beliefs. Wade writes passionately about controversial issues and strives to make a difference by making people think. Wade does not have a background in writing or philosophy, but still draws from personal experience to ponder contentious subjects on paper. There is a lot of pain in the world and people need hope. When not writing, she is thinking about writing, and more than likely scribbling ideas on sticky notes in the car while playing "taxi driver" for her three children. She likes snakes, can't spell, and has a tendency to make people cry.

Visit Wade Kelly at http://www.writerwadekelly.com
https://twitter.com/WriterWadeKelly
Subscribe to Wade's Blog to keep up to date on current news at: http://writerwadekelly.blogspot.com/
Contact Wade at writerwadekelly@gmail.com

Trademark Acknowledgments

The author acknowledges the trademarked status and trademark owners of the following trademarks mentioned in this work of fiction:

Airplane: Paramount Pictures
Alanis Morissette, *Ironic*: Alanis Morissette, Glen Ballard
All Time Low, *Therapy*: ALEXANDER WILLIAM GASKARTH, DAVID JONATHAN BENDETH, JACK BASSAM BARAKAT, ZACHARY STEVEN MERRICK, ROBERT RYAN DAWSON
America's Got Talent: NBC Universal
Arby's: Arby's IP Holder Trust.
Baltimore Ravens: NFL Enterprises LLC.
Batman: DC Comics, A Warner Bros. Entertainment Company
Bobcat: Bobcat Company
Boy Scout: Boy Scouts of America
Bud Lite: ANHEUSER-BUSCH,
Buffalo Wild Wings: Buffalo Wild Wings, Inc.
Buffy the Vampire Slayer: Twentieth Century Fox Film Corporation, The WB Television Network
Candy Land: Hasbro
Cheetos: Frito-Lay North America, Inc.
Cinderella: Walt Disney Productions
Conan the Barbarian: Universal Pictures
Converse: Converse, Inc.
Facebook: Facebook, Inc.
Fantasy Island: Columbia Pictures Television, Spelling-Goldberg Productions
GameStop: GameStop
Gone with the Wind: Selznick International Pictures, Metro-Goldwyn-Mayer
Google: Google Inc.
Gummy Bears: HARIBO of America, Inc.
Highland Park Scotch Whisky: Highland Park
iPod: Apple Inc.
Jack Daniel's: Jack Daniel's
Lord Of The Rings: Warner Bros. Entertainment Inc.
Mack Truck: Mack Trucks
Motrin: McNEIL-PPC, Inc.
Mythbusters: Discovery Communications, LLC.
Nintendo DS: Nintendo of America Inc.
Pepsi: PepsiCo
Phineas and Ferb: Disney Channel
Pictionary: Hasbro
Safari: Apple Inc.
Saturday Night Fever: Paramount Pictures
Solo: Dart Container Corporation
Speedo: Speedo International
Spiderman: Columbia Pictures Corporation, Marvel Enterprises
Starbucks: Starbucks Corporation
Super Glue: Super Glue Corp.
Target: Target Brands, Inc.
The Home Depot: Homer TLC, Inc.
The Matrix: Warner Bros., Village Roadshow Pictures, Groucho II Film Partnership, Silver Pictures
The Vampire Diaries: Alloy Entertainment, Bonanza Productions, Warner Bros. Television, CBS Television Studios, CW Television Network, Outerbanks Entertainment
The Walking Dead: AMC Studios
Twilight Zone: Cayuga Productions, Columbia Broadcasting System
U2, *Sunday Bloody Sunday*: U2
Valium: F. Hoffmann-La Roche Ltd
Wikipedia: Wikimedia Foundation, Inc.
Xbox: Microsoft
YouTube: Google Inc.

www.ingramcontent.com/pod-product-compliance
Lightning Source LLC
Chambersburg PA
CBHW071205250626
47159CB00001B/205